FLAMEſ OF REBELLION

ALSO BY JAY ALLAN

Far Stars
Shadow of Empire
Enemy in the Dark
Funeral Games

Crimson Worlds
Marines
The Cost of Victory
A Little Rebellion
The First Imperium
The Line Must Hold
To Hell's Heart
The Shadow Legions
Even Legends Die
The Fall
War Stories (Crimson Worlds Prequels)
MERCS (Crimson Worlds Successors I)

Portal Wars
Gehenna Dawn
The Ten Thousand

Pendragon Chronicles
The Dragon's Banner

FLAMES
OF REBELLION

JAY ALLAN

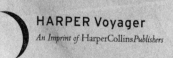
HARPER Voyager
An Imprint of HarperCollins*Publishers*

FLAMES OF REBELLION. Copyright © 2017 by Jay Allan Books. All rights reserved. Printed in the United States of America. No part of this book may be used or reproduced in any manner whatsoever without written permission except in the case of brief quotations embodied in critical articles and reviews. For information, address HarperCollins Publishers, 195 Broadway, New York, NY 10007.

HarperCollins books may be purchased for educational, business, or sales promotional use. For information, please email the Special Markets Department at SPsales@harpercollins.com.

Harper Voyager and design are trademarks of HarperCollins Publishers LLC.

FIRST EDITION

Designed by Paula Russell Szafranski

Map copyright © MMXVII Springer Cartographics LLC

Library of Congress Cataloging-in-Publication Data has been applied for.

ISBN 978-0-06-256680-5

17 18 19 20 21 LSC 10 9 8 7 6 5 4 3 2 1

CONTENTS

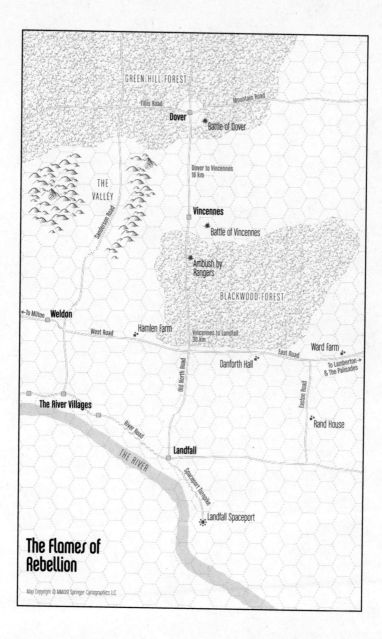

GREEN HILL FOREST

Tillis Road

Mountain Road

Dover

✳ Battle of Dover

THE VALLEY

Dover to Vincennes
16 km

Sanderson Road

Vincennes

✳ Battle of Vincennes

✳ Ambush by
Rangers

BLACKWOOD FOREST

←To Milton **Weldon**

West Road **Hamlen Farm**

Vincennes to Landfall
30 km

Ward Farm

East Road

To Lamberton →
& The Palisades

Danforth Hall

Old North Road

Easton Road

The River Villages

River Road

Rand House

THE RIVER

Landfall

Spaceport Turnpike

✳ Landfall Spaceport

The Flames of
Rebellion

Map Copyright © MMXVII Springer Cartographics LLC

FLAMES OF REBELLION

PROLOGUE

Top Secret—Eyes Only
Intelligence Report
Federal Colony Alpha-2
(Informally designated "Haven" by its inhabitants)
Epsilon Eridani II
Summary of Findings

Alpha-2 is the second major colony established by Federal America. It is currently the most populated extraterrestrial world, not only among Federal America's colonies, but those of any Earth power. Its GCP is nearly twice that of any other colony planet.

Initial colonization began sixty-one years ago with three separate corporate-sponsored expeditions. The colony, privately managed for its first twenty years of existence, was subsequently nationalized along with the entirety of the corporate ownership at the end of the Great Civil War. Colonization has continued since that time under federal settlement directives, including various incentives to encourage resettlement of undesirable terrestrial societal groups.

While a federal governor was assigned shortly after the takeover, the initial colonial constitution was allowed to remain largely in effect until two years ago, when it was terminated as part of a federal effort to minimize resistance to the takeovers of formerly private colonies. Over the past twenty-six months, the federal senate has passed a series of Acts (fourteen, in fact) pertaining to the operation of the colony and the rights and obligations of the colonists.

The senate actions were initiated largely in response to growing unrest and acts of civil disorder. However, all indications show they have failed to curtail such activities and, in fact, have only served to stir additional resistance and resulted in a marked increase in seditious incidents (more on this below).

ASSESSMENT OF PLANETARY WEALTH AND STRATEGIC VALUE

The mining operations established by the initial corporate sponsors have operated under the control of the Federal Resource Bureau since nationalization. The mines themselves have been staffed primarily by convicts offered reduced terms or commutation of death sentences in exchange for service on Alpha-2 and subsequent residency there after release.

Alpha-2 is a world rich in vital resources and a major source of revenue and precious minerals for Federal America, constituting 29 percent of the nation's total mineral wealth, and over 51 percent of the vital ores obtained from extraterrestrial sources. This makes the planet Federal America's most valuable colony by a considerable margin, and estimates place the percentage of federal GNP derived directly and indirectly from Alpha-2 at 11.3 percent. As such, the colony is deemed vital to the interests of Federal America, and the maintenance of order there to be a primary national interest.

ANALYSIS OF SUBVERSIVE ACTIVITY

As noted, Alpha-2 has exhibited increasing amounts of seditious activity over the past ten years, with a sharp acceleration in the incidence of unrest occurring over the most recent thirty months. Production and revenue have begun to be affected, and the first outright reductions in both categories have manifested in the most recent year. Frontier Command increased the security garrisons by 80 percent one year ago. This action has proven to be inadequate to arrest the accelerating decline in conditions, however.

There has been a subsequent correlation with the growing civil disobedience and the substantial increase in smuggling activity over the past twenty-four Earth months. We believe that the unauthorized goods include large amounts of illegal weaponry, obtained on both the black market and from rival Earth powers. These have, in turn, been delivered to proto-rebel cells that have proliferated around the major population centers.

Efforts to infiltrate and expose rebel groups have been largely unsuccessful, and losses among field operatives assigned to undercover operations have been high.

RECOMMENDATIONS

Prompt remediation of the situation on Alpha-2 is considered of extreme importance if open rebellion is to be prevented. Law and order must be imposed on the populace with considerable force, and seditious individuals must be identified and arrested. We must establish greater federal control on economy activity and the ongoing surveillance program must be strengthened. Specific recommendations include:

1. The immediate suspension of the planetary constitution and the implementation of limited martial law until further notice, to include customary measures such as curfews and the limitation of public assemblies.

2. The immediate appointment of a federal observer with full power to supersede the authority of the planetary governor in all matters involving security and the suppression of revolt.

3. An immediate 200 percent increase in the number of federal troops deployed to Alpha-2, and a transfer of authority from Frontier Command to the federal observer.

4. The institution of a complete planetary blockade and the implementation of substantially harsher penalties for smuggling activities, especially those involving weapons and ordnance. A planetwide supplementary tax on Alpha-2 is proposed to fund the cost of deploying naval squadrons to the system.

5. The immediate implementation of increased intelligence activity, including unrestricted search and surveillance authority by the federal observer and any designated subordinates. The rights against search and seizure previously carried over from the original planetary constitution to be terminated immediately.

6. The federal observer should be given the authority to institute summary judgments and forgo or overrule trials in cases deemed to address security matters.

7. The implementation of a program of censorship, affecting all media outlets, communication systems, and information transit hubs planetwide. Federal observer to be given power to institute a full government takeover of all affected systems at his/her sole discretion.

SUMMARY OF CONCLUSIONS

Alpha-2 is crucial colony, and its production and revenues are of considerable importance to Federal America. Additionally, as the single largest and most prominent settled planet, events on Alpha-2 are likely to influence inhabitants on other federal colonies, possibly promoting the spread of seditious and treasonous activity far beyond the Epsilon Eridani system. Clearly, there is significant danger in allowing the instability on Alpha-2 to continue or to spread.

Additionally, there is considerable concern that both the Eurasian Union and the Pacific Hegemony would provide clandestine support to any nascent rebel movement (if they aren't already), and in the event of measurable success by revolutionary forces, even an open alliance—one that could easily lead to war on Earth.

It is therefore essential to prevent any rebellion before it occurs and to restore Alpha-2 to compliance with federal regulations and standards, *by whatever means necessary.*

CHAPTER 1

"Captain, I'm picking up a high energy reading. It's about ninety thousand kilometers ahead, and—"

"Scanners off. Engines full stop." Sasha Nerov cut off her first officer, snapping out the order in a tone that left no doubt about its urgency. Nerov sat in the less than plush command chair at the center of *Vagabond*'s cramped control room, her face twisted into a worried grimace. "Shut down the reactor." She turned and stared at her first officer, her ice blue eyes locked on his in a withering gaze. "Now! Switch to battery power for life support and vital systems."

Griff Daniels nodded. "Yes, Captain," he replied nervously as he turned back to his workstation. He leaned forward over the intraship comm and repeated the captain's commands, nodding quietly to himself as the ship's engineer acknowledged the instructions. Almost immediately, the near-constant hum of *Vagabond*'s reactor ceased, leaving an eerie quiet.

Nerov watched her second in command for a few seconds before turning back toward the main viewscreen in front of her. It was a state-of-the-art, high-resolution display, looking a bit out of place surrounded by the dark steel girders and aging conduits. *Vagabond* was an old ship, dating back to the earliest days of interstellar travel, but Nerov had poured a king's ransom of smuggling profits into updating her vessel's key systems, creating a chaotic combination of old and new.

A few more runs as profitable as the last one, and the old girl will be as good as new.

Most of her peers squandered their smuggling gains with an abandon that would have shamed seventeenth century pirates ransacking the brothels and taverns of the Spanish Main, but not Sasha Nerov. Her tastes in recreation tended toward quieter pursuits, and her profits went mostly into her ship—and into well-hidden stashes. Her rainy-day fund.

Right now she was very worried about storm clouds.

Vagabond wasn't a match for a frontline warship in combat, of course, and it was far from a comfortable vessel for those who lived aboard, but its ECM and scanning suites were top of the line. And its engines were a match even for a federal craft. So while *Vagabond* couldn't fight a federal frigate with any hope of victory, she had at least some chance—albeit a small one—of running away from one.

But it was better to just not get caught, and that's why Nerov had shut down the engines.

"Passive scanners on full," she said, her eyes fixed on the blank screen. "Tie in the AI and see what it can do with the incoming data." She knew they were too far out to get much from the passive sensors, but running the active suite was essentially lighting a flare to anyone out there.

If they haven't picked us up already . . .

Nerov sat straight up in her chair, giving her crew the image of the fearless captain she knew they needed. But inside her stomach was clenched in a knot. She didn't have anything concrete, but she knew that was a federal frigate out there. She could feel it. And that was bad news. Especially since her cargo hold was full of weapons . . . and especially since those guns and ammunition were illegal and bound for the antigovernment forces on Haven.

"Passive scanners activated, Captain. We have limited readings at this range, but the AI is chewing on it."

Nerov opened her mouth, but she closed it again without speaking. She wanted to give the order to bolt, to engage the engines at full and run like hell. But she knew that was at best a gamble, and probably a worse one than staying put. *Vagabond* had maybe a fifty-fifty chance of getting away from a frigate, but that mostly depended on factors out of her control, things like how sharp a captain and crew she was facing. And she had to admit, as much as the federal navy was her adversary, it was a capable outfit, and most of its officers were combat veterans. No, she wouldn't run. Not yet. Her best bet right now was lying low, making like a hole in space and hoping to go unnoticed.

That, and praying.

"Captain . . ." Daniels turned toward Nerov. The bridge lights were dimmed, part of the energy reduction program to extend the ship's battery life, but she saw the concern on his face through the dark shadows. "It definitely looks like a federal ship," he continued. "A frigate, I'd bet. It's firing at another vessel . . ."

Nerov nodded, but she didn't reply. She'd been hearing rumors for months now that the federal navy intended to institute a blockade of Haven.

I guess I can upgrade that from rumor status.

She sighed softly. She'd known for a long time that things were bad on the troubled colony world—hell, you generally didn't need to smuggle weapons onto a world that was stable. But the unrest had been growing for years now, and there were secret groups all over the planet, plotting and scheming. Preparing for rebellion. And the latest increase in federal levies stationed there had only poured gas on a smoldering fire.

But a blockade? She had an idea of what it cost to station a naval squadron in the system, and if the federals had committed that kind of funding, they were serious about tightening their control. That meant this was a major escalation by the federals, one guaranteed to push the Havenites to the brink of open war. That wasn't just a guess on her part either—she was acquainted with enough of the independence leaders to know they would not take this lying down.

It didn't change the fact that she had bills to pay, though.

"Well, it looks like our jobs just got harder, boys." She glanced around at the three members of her bridge crew as she spoke, trying to sound as calm as she could for their benefit. Her people were experienced, so at least they had that going for them. But this was a very different situation than they'd been dealing with for the last two years. Before today, they had been cleaning up, shipping weapons to the rebels on Haven and making obscene profits doing it.

The situation had been nearly perfect. The Eurasian Union and Federal America's other rivals, anxious for any opportunity to shove a thorn in their adversary's side, had been more than willing to sell her cutting edge ordnance for a pittance. And she'd had little trouble slipping past the federal customs patrols to deliver those cargoes to her rebel clients, who paid exorbitant prices for her smuggled goods. She'd almost felt guilty about charging so much.

Almost.

It had been a milk run, the easiest money she and her people had ever made. But she suspected things had just become far more problematic. Slipping past a revenue cutter or two was child's play for a smuggler as capable as Nerov, but fencing with federal navy frigates was a different game, a far more dangerous one. And she didn't relish the thought of losing *Vagabond* and spending the next ten years in a federal penal colony for smuggling.

That is, if they weren't just blown out of space.

"Captain . . ."

The instant she heard Daniels, she knew something was wrong.

"I think the other ship is *Wasp* . . ."

Nerov felt a chill run down her spine. *Wasp* was another smuggler, and her captain was Sergei Brinker, Nerov's old first officer, gone out on his own six months before.

Sergei . . .

She turned back toward Daniels. "I want that confirmed, Griff."

"I'm as sure as I can be, Captain. At least without an active scanner pulse."

"Very well." Nerov spoke softly, a touch of emotion slipping through her cold veneer. "Maintain status."

Daniels hesitated. "Ah . . . yes, Captain," he finally said. Then he added, "*Wasp* doesn't have a chance, does it? Not unless . . ."

"Unless what? Unless we go barging in there and fire on a federal frigate?" Her voice had more edge than she'd intended. She just hated the idea of watching someone she knew, someone she cared about, get arrested by the federals. But her first responsibility was to her own ship and crew. And *Wasp* and *Vagabond* together were still no match for a federal frigate, at least not without an element of surprise they wouldn't have.

Nerov was glaring at her exec, but he didn't respond. Not that she expected him to—what could he possibly say? He just nodded slowly and turned back to his workstation.

Nerov fidgeted nervously in her chair. She knew Daniels hadn't deserved to be the target of her angst. It's just that she was worried about Brinker and his people. *Wasp*'s captain was a free spirit, a man who despised rules and authority. She couldn't imagine what ten years in a federal prison camp would do to him. Every fiber in her being was pushing her to intervene, to throw *Vagabond* into the ≠encounter and fight it out. But she couldn't. She *wouldn't*. Her crew came first, and she couldn't toss away their lives on a fool's errand. No, she couldn't help *Wasp*. All she could do was watch and hope the smuggler managed to escape. Somehow.

Come on, Sergei. Make a run for it. You can make it . . .

But she didn't really believe it.

"**Maintain pursuit, Lieutenant.** All batteries lock on target." Captain Gregory Jacobs spoke coldly, precisely. He stared out over *Condor*'s bridge, watching his veteran crew working with the precision he had taught them. *Condor* was a celebrated vessel, one of the navy's best. She had served with distinction in the last war, and her crew had received over a dozen citations for bravery and exemplary conduct in the face of the enemy.

And now we're police, chasing smugglers around one of our own colonies . . .

It was a bitter pill to swallow, an assignment Jacobs found distasteful and beneath the dignity of this ship. But orders were orders, and Jacobs and his people were creatures of duty. They didn't have to like their new posting, but they would obey commands to the last, every one of them.

And Jacobs himself would throw anyone who didn't out of the airlock.

"Yes, Captain. The vessel is attempting to flee, but we are maintaining contact." Lieutenant Merrill snapped out his report with precision, and with only the slightest twinge of the sullen dissatisfaction that had clung to most of the crew's words since they'd arrived in the Epsilon Eridani system. Merrill was a long service veteran, and he'd served under Jacobs since before the war. He was as rigidly career navy as his captain, meaning he would perform without question, and yet was able to let his tone convey all the displeasure he could without being insubordinate. "Weapons are charged and ready, Captain . . . and locked on."

Jacobs took a deep breath, pushing aside the hesitation creeping into his mind. His people were professional military, sworn to fight Federal America's foreign enemies. He didn't like firing on a civilian vessel, even one suspected of engaging in illegal activity. But he'd ordered the ship to disengage its engines and submit to inspection of its cargo holds. Three times. And his commands had been met with total silence. He had no choice.

"All batteries open fire. Target their engines." Jacobs knew the range was too great for precision shooting, but he said it anyway. It made him feel better.

"Yes, Captain." A few seconds later Jacobs heard the familiar hum of *Condor*'s laser cannons firing.

"Stay sharp," Jacobs said. "They may turn and try to fight." He knew that was unlikely. The freighter—and at this point he had no doubt it was a smuggler's vessel—was undoubtedly armed, but even so, it was no match for *Condor*. Still, desperation could make even a wild gamble seem sensible . . . and he hadn't brought his ship through a dozen battles and six years of war by being careless.

"Yes, Captain. All scanners are on full. They're still trying to get away. No indication they intend to turn and give battle."

"Stay with her, Lieutenant. And maintain fire." *Condor* was still at long range, which meant a hit would require a considerable amount of luck. Still, the frigate had four main batteries, and as long as they didn't lose their target, they would almost certainly score a certain number of hits. Given time, it was simple mathematics.

"Yes, Captain." An instant later: "Sir, the target is increasing the range. Readings suggest they've got their reactor at 110 percent, with all power going to the engines."

"Increase thrust to flank, Lieutenant."

"Increasing to flank, sir. All batteries maintaining fire."

"Very well, Lieutenant." Jacobs took a deep breath. Even with *Condor*'s force dampeners working on maximum, the g-forces would be uncomfortable at full thrust.

He stared straight ahead, trying to maintain his focus. But his mind drifted, and he found himself hoping the target wasn't carrying a shipment of illegal weapons. He had orders to carry out in that eventuality, too, a directive that weighed heavily on his warrior's honor. But Gregory Jacobs knew only one way. And that was to follow his orders, regardless of how he felt about them. Or how much they turned his stomach.

"Let's keep it together, people." Sergei Brinker knew his ship was in trouble, that his people were fast running out of options. But letting his crew lose heart wouldn't improve things. And Brinker wasn't ready to give up. However hopeless things looked.

And they looked pretty hopeless since a pair of laser hits had knocked out *Wasp*'s engines.

"Yes, Captain, but . . ."

"No buts, Chuck. Let's get everybody armed. They've got us dead in space, and that means they'll be boarding anytime now. We've got to hold them off, long enough at least for Rich and his crew to get the engines back online. Then we can make a run for it."

It was sheer bravado on his part. Rich Tomlinson was a gifted engineer, one Brinker knew he was lucky to have. But he was just as aware that the federal frigate's laser blasts had turned *Wasp*'s engines into a pile of half-melted junk. It would be a miracle if Tomlinson could get so much as a puff of thrust from the savaged wreck, and that meant finding enough power to get away from the federal ship was a pipe dream. Still, Brinker wasn't the type to give up, not until he was completely out of options. He knew he was close to that, but not quite there.

Not yet.

"Yes, Cap." Chuck Poole had been the first to sign on to *Wasp*'s crew, and he was completely loyal to Brinker. But loyalty and stupidity weren't the same thing, and he clearly saw the writing on the wall. Still, he opened the weapons locker. He reached inside and grabbed an assault rifle, passing it to Brinker. Then he grabbed another half dozen or so and turned, handing them out to the five men and two women standing in *Wasp*'s cramped corridor.

"Okay, let's get in position." Brinker reached out and took an ammunition pouch from Poole as he spoke, pulling out a cartridge and slamming it in place. "They'll most likely dock somewhere along the aft hold, where the hull is thinnest. So, that's where we'll wait for them." *Wasp* had a crew of fourteen, but four of those were working on the engines, and Lynch was still on the bridge, ready to blast away at full if the repair crew somehow managed to restore full thrust. That left nine of them to protect the ship, to beat back the federal shock troops who would soon be pouring through the ship's breached hull. And even a small frigate carried four squads of fully armed assault troops. Thirty-two soldiers plus a lieutenant in command.

Against nine of us.

He trotted down the corridor, ducking every few steps to avoid a conduit or low-hanging support. *Wasp* hadn't been built for comfort, that much was obvious. A small trading vessel, she'd had an unremarkable career hauling ores . . . at least before Brinker upgraded the engines and scanner suite and launched her on a new career as a smuggler's vessel. The upgrades increased the ship's speed and ECM capabilities considerably, but they didn't make her any bigger. And what space she had was dedicated to holding cargo, not to spacious hallways and comfortable lodgings for her crew.

Comfort was definitely the last thing on his mind right now.

Brinker glanced behind him as he turned a corner. His people were scared shitless, he knew that much. But they were all still with him. He could feel the defiance they had managed to work up, and he knew they'd put up a fight. He also knew, though, they were outgunned and, while he was ready to fight to the death himself— anything was preferable to a decade or more in a federal prison—he wasn't prepared to throw away the lives of his crew. If the federals got a foothold on *Wasp*, the battle would be lost. The only hope was keeping the boarders pinned down, unable to press forward deeper into the ship. Maybe he could trap them somewhere, take them hostage and negotiate with the federals. It was a desperate plan, but it was all he had.

And with a couple squads of fully armed shock troops that isn't going to happen.

He'd already decided. If the enemy got substantial forces aboard, he would surrender before he'd allow his people to be gunned down in a hopeless fight. The thought of a long prison sentence for smuggling horrified him, more even than death, but he told himself ten years wasn't forever. Most of his people were under thirty-five. They could serve their time and still have productive lives when they got out. Even if opportunities for ex-convicts were rare in Federal America.

It beats being dead.

He heard a loud noise, a clang followed by a long creaking sound. He stopped and turned abruptly. "Down there," he said, trying to sound calm as he pointed along the corridor. "Everybody grab some cover." Again, though, with the cramped interior of *Wasp*, that was easier said than done. A few of his people opened doors and slipped inside the compartments, leaning out just enough to point their rifles down the corridor. The rest crouched behind structural supports or whatever other equipment was jutting out into the hallway. It was far from a strong defensive position, but any cover was better than nothing.

"And remember, we're looking to pin them down, not kill anybody." Gunning down federal shock troops was a good way to upgrade a ten-year sentence for smuggling to a trip to the scaffold. Assuming the rest of the federals didn't just gun all his people down in revenge, that is.

The noise grew louder and steadier, and then a section of the hull glowed orange for a few seconds before it was blasted into the corridor. There was a pause, probably only a few seconds, though it felt like an eternity to Brinker as he waited for enemy troops to drop down into the corridor. But nothing happened.

A few seconds later he heard a loud crack, followed by another . . . and another. An explosion rocked the corridor. Then a second one. *Stun grenades*, he thought as he fell to the ground, his rifle slipping from his hand and clanging against the metal of the deck.

We didn't even hold them for ten seconds . . .

Then everything went dark.

Brinker stood just inside *Wasp*'s small wardroom, now hastily converted to a makeshift brig. Eleven of his people were penned in the tiny space with him, far more than the four or five it was designed to hold. Still, Brinker couldn't help but wish two more were crammed in the tight quarters. Nills and Cortez. He'd been disoriented when he first woke up, and it took him several minutes to clear his head and figure out which of his people were missing. He'd hoped the two men had just been wounded, that they were someplace being treated for their injuries. But that thought had been short-lived. Several of the others had seen what happened.

Cortez had ducked behind a bulkhead, largely escaping the effect of the stun grenades. He managed to get off half a dozen rounds, and hit one of the federals in the arm. At that point, the invaders returned fire, and he took a dozen shots to the head and body. He was dead before he hit the ground.

Nills had recovered while the federals were still dragging the crew members to the wardroom. He made a grab for one of their weapons, but he wasn't fast enough. There were several versions of the story making the rounds, ranging from the federal shooting him in self-defense to a cold-blooded execution. Brinker knew things like that morphed with each retelling, but all that mattered to him now was the one consistent vein in each story: Layne Nills was dead.

Brinker put his hand on his head. The aftereffects of the stun grenades weren't pleasant, and the headache he had almost defied description. But the pain of losing two crew members was worse, all the more because he blamed himself.

I should have surrendered. I knew we had no chance. But I had to put up a fight . . . a fight we couldn't win. Damn, I'm so stupid. I convinced myself we could hold out, at least for a while. But against federals? Fucking delusional. They swatted us away like so many flies. And now Nills and Cortez are dead.

He moved toward the door—and found that to be a challenge. He'd twisted his knee when he fell, and there was a sharp pain in his leg with every step he took. He tried his best to ignore it. He was determined to speak with the federal commander. He'd gotten two of his people killed, but now he was going to do what he could for the rest of his crew. Maybe, just maybe, he could convince the feds the crew was innocent, that they had all believed *Wasp* was carrying a legitimate cargo. Deep down he knew it was hopeless—the federals wouldn't care, and by the laws of Federal America, simply being a member of the crew constituted guilt—but he was grasping for anything right now.

Hell, doing something *was better than just waiting for their fate.* Maybe that explained his idiotic decision to try to put up a stand—

Suddenly, the door slid open, and two federal shock troopers came in, one of them with what Brinker recognized as a noncom's stripes on his arm. They stared at *Wasp*'s crew for a second, and then the corporal said, "Let's go, one at a time. Form up in single file in the corridor." He turned and looked toward Brinker. "You first," the soldier said, pointing at *Wasp*'s captain.

Brinker stared back for a few seconds. "Where are we going?"

The private moved forward and grabbed Brinker's arm, ignoring the question. "Let's go," he said again, pulling hard and shoving toward the door.

The captain fought back the urge to struggle. His pride had already cost his people too much, and now he was resolved to cooperate. "Okay," he said, biting down on his anger. "I'm coming."

The soldier loosened his grip slightly, but he still pushed Brinker forward. They moved through the door and down the corridor. *Wasp*'s captain turned his head and took a look behind as his people were hustled out of the wardroom and into a rough line behind him before the corporal barked, "Face forward!"

The soldiers led them from *Wasp*'s crew facilities down to the cargo hold, pushing them through the large bay doors once they arrived. One by one, they were lined up against the wall while another group of soldiers, as well as two men in naval uniforms, stood around staring at a row of open shipping crates.

Crates full of assault rifles and grenades.

"Yes, Captain," one of them said, speaking into a small handheld communicator. "We've got at least a thousand guns here, plus ammunition, grenades. Pretty sophisticated stuff. Definitely a gunrunner heading for Alpha-2, sir."

Brinker felt a cold feeling as reality closed in on him. Smuggling guns carried a mandatory ten-year sentence. Minimum. And his people had resisted, fired on federal soldiers. They hadn't killed any of them, but that still meant more time, maybe even twenty years total.

He'd been thinking about it all in general terms for the past hour or so, but now it really began to hit home. Federal penal camps were notoriously harsh, with rigid work schedules and brutal discipline. Worse, he was self-aware enough to know he didn't do well with authority. It would be a challenge for him to hold his defiance in check, to keep his head down and do his time. Because if he didn't, at the very least he'd see years added to his time. And at the worst . . .

"Yes, sir . . ." The naval officer's voice was stilted, uncomfortable. "I know, Captain. I understand there is no choice." Then a pause. "Yes, sir. At once, sir."

The officer turned toward a noncom clad in black body armor, gesturing toward the prisoners.

"Sir." The sergeant looked like a grim veteran, but he, too, seemed uncomfortable, and Brinker wondered what was going on. The sergeant paused, just for a few seconds. Then he turned and snapped out a series of orders to the soldiers standing next to him. They formed into a line facing *Wasp*'s crew.

Brinker watched as the naval officer moved forward, and he felt a wave of nausea as cold realization gripped him. *No, it can't be. Not without even a show trial . . .*

"Attention, crew of the freighter *Wasp*." The officer's voice was strong, but somehow brittle, too, despite his best attempts to hide it. Not that Brinker gave a shit about the federal's discomfort. But he could only stand there as the officer continued. "You are guilty of smuggling weapons to traitorous forces on the federal colony of Alpha-2. Pursuant to Special Order 374-A5, I hereby pronounce a sentence of summary execution, to be carried out immediately." He sucked in a deep breath as soon as he finished. Then he turned toward the detachment and croaked, "Proceed, Sergeant."

Brinker stared back in stunned shock. He'd been trying to accept the prison sentence he'd expected, but now these soldiers were going to shoot him . . . and all his people. Right here. Right now. He felt a wave of panic, but fought it down, knowing he somehow had to stand firm. There was nowhere to go, no way to escape. Still, he had to try something. *For my crew* . . .

"Lieutenant," he said, staring at the naval officer with as much firmness as he could muster. "My crew knew nothing of the weapons. The cargo was my doing, not theirs." Brinker knew he was dead, but if there was a chance—any chance—to save his people he had to try.

The soldier in command of the detachment looked at Brinker, but he didn't respond. He turned and glanced toward the lieutenant, who responded to the look with, "You have your orders, Sergeant." The lieutenant continued to ignore Brinker, his eyes fixed on the noncom, avoiding eye contact with any of the condemned men and women.

"Yes, sir." The soldier turned and stared down the line his squad had formed. "Ready," he said, his tone forced. The soldiers pulled their weapons up, holding them out in front of their bodies.

"Aim." The sergeant turned and stared back at the lieutenant, his eyes focused on his superior's, as if begging for a reprieve. But the naval officer simply stared back and nodded grimly.

"No, please . . . please!"

Brinker's head snapped around, looking to see which of his people had made the futile plea. But he never found out.

"Fire," the sergeant said, his voice choked with emotion. And his men obeyed, opening up on full auto. The volley was ragged. Some of the soldiers had hesitated, and one or two had failed to fire at all. But when the guns fell silent a few seconds later, the wall and floor of *Wasp*'s cargo hold were awash with blood.

And every member of her crew was dead.

Sasha Nerov sat in her chair, silently staring at the viewscreen in shock, just like everyone on *Vagabond*'s bridge. She'd ordered the readings checked three times, but they still told the same story. *Wasp* was gone, blasted to atoms by the federal ship's laser cannons.

"Maybe they took the crew back to the frigate . . ." It was Griff Daniels, but it didn't even sound like he believed what he was saying.

"No," Nerov said softly. "If the federals had arrested them, they would have needed the ship and cargo for trial." She was struggling to keep her voice calm, steady. "No . . . they killed them. They killed them all."

She felt a pang of guilt for not going to *Wasp*'s aid. Her rational mind tried to fight it, to tell herself it wasn't her fault. She knew the only thing that would have changed if she'd charged in was that *Vagabond* would now also be a cloud of plasma, her crew as dead as *Wasp*'s. She had done her job, kept her people alive. But all she could see was Sergei Brinker's face, looking back at her with that wide, slightly mischievous smile of his.

She pushed back the sadness, forced herself to focus. *Wasp* was gone, nothing could change that. *Vagabond* was her concern, and she knew her ship was still in danger. She wanted to get away from here, to crank the engines up to full power and put thousands of kilometers between her and the debris cloud that had been *Wasp*. But she knew she couldn't do that. Not now. Not without putting her people at greater risk.

"We stay right here with all systems shut down until that frigate is long gone. Understood?"

"Yes, Captain." Daniels turned and stared down at his workstation, his eyes avoiding Nerov's. "Understood."

Nerov sat quietly for a few minutes. She had a reputation for coldness, but now she could feel the wave of emotion coming on.

She stood up and walked toward the single hatch leading off the bridge. She knew it wasn't a time for her to leave her post, but she had no intention of allowing her crew to see her lose it. "I'll be in my quarters. Let me know if anything changes."

She slipped through the hatch and walked down the corridor, wiping away the tears that began to stream down her face, quickly entering her room and closing the door. She'd always known smuggling was a dangerous business, but understanding that and watching friends die were two different things . . .

"*Dammit!*"

She'd had her outburst, but now she slammed her discipline down in place, pushing Brinker and his crew out of her mind. She had responsibilities to a live crew: *hers*. And two things were foremost in her mind.

First, she'd been away from Haven for almost six months. Clearly things had escalated in that time. What was happening down there that could prompt such a draconian policy from the federal forces?

Second, smuggling weapons to the Haven rebels had just become a lot more dangerous.

And third, she had absolutely no idea what she was going to do about it.

CHAPTER 2

"Hey, Grant, let's go, man." Tomas Lopez spoke angrily, his face twisted into a scowl. He held a heavy bar of steel in one hand, and the other was raised above his head, curled into a defiant fist. He stared at Jamie Grant for a few seconds, as though he expected his fellow prisoner to leap up and rush to his side. But Jamie just stood next to the exposed rock wall and looked back.

"C'mon, Grant!" Lopez repeated. "It's time. We're shuttin' down this whole damned mine this time. Ain't nuthin' gonna stop us. They won't have no choice. They'll have to listen to us when the ore stops flowin'!" Lopez stood about two meters away from his workmate, his grimy coveralls almost black from the ore dust that hung in the very air of the mine. There was rage in his face, and it seemed to radiate all around him.

There was activity everywhere in the massive cavern, and more angry yells. Dozens of mine workers, hundreds perhaps, were streaming away from their workplaces. They almost acted as one, grabbing tools, metal bars, anything that looked remotely like a weapon. They were shouting, a riotous cacophony of rebel slogans along with more generic cries and screams. The sound reverberated off the low ceilings of the tunnel, and Jamie could barely hear his friend's words over the din.

"Not me, Tomas." Jamie's voice was grim, somber. He looked around the mine, feeling a wave of surprise at how many seemed to be joining the instigators. There had been work stoppages before, and a few outright riots, but this looked like something bigger, more dangerous. He felt the urge, just as his comrades did, to strike back against the federals, against the system that had stolen so much of his life. Against the guards who too often took sadistic delight in their work. But he couldn't. He wouldn't. There was something more important to him, and he struggled to stay focused on that.

"I'm staying right here," he said finally. He wanted to go; every fiber in his body was twitching to join the riot. But he fought back against the urge. "I've been here twelve years, Tomas. Twelve fucking years. I shoulda been outta this stinking shithole two years already. I can't afford more trouble."

Jamie had seen his share of disciplinary actions for sure. He'd been fifteen years old the day he was arrested for the third time. He'd gotten off twice before that with a flogging and a reduction in public assistance, but he'd only stolen food those times. The last time he'd taken money . . . and he'd used it to buy a hit of Blast. It hadn't been for him, but for his mother. But that hadn't made any difference.

Alicia Grant was a good-natured woman who'd become addicted to the drug when she'd been issued a month's supply to deal with her grief after Jamie's father was killed. Harold Grant had been shot when the federal police cracked down on a street rising. He'd lived for almost two hours, lying bleeding on the pavement, but by the time the authorities got around to the wounded rioters, it was too late.

Jamie's mother was registered as an addict, and she received government-issued dosages, but South Boston was a rough neighborhood, and her last delivery had been stolen . . . or sold on the black market. She did her best to stretch out what she had left, but she ran out with more than two weeks to go until her next allotment.

Blast was a nasty drug, one notoriously difficult to quit, so much so that the government just gave addicts maintenance doses instead of even attempting rehab. Jamie watched his mother suffer horribly from the withdrawal symptoms, sobbing through the night in constant pain. What he did was done out of desperation. But the magistrate hadn't cared. Indeed, he had hardly listened to the boy's pleas and impassioned explanation. His voice had been cold as he sentenced the fifteen-year-old on the spot, barely keeping the boredom from his tone as he did it. He gave Jamie a simple choice: the mandatory life sentence for a third offense . . . or exile to the colonies, and a ten-year term in the mines.

There hadn't been much to consider, and Jamie agreed on the spot, accepting exile and a decade's service digging precious ores from the depths of some alien world. At least he had a chance of surviving ten years in one of the mines — 30 to 40 percent, one of the court proctors had told him, depending on where he was sent. That was far from reassuring, but a hell of a lot better than going immediately to the scaffold.

He'd said his goodbyes to his mother right in the courtroom, forever, he knew. There was no chance Federal America was going to provide transit home for a con, even if he survived so many years in the mines. Twelve hours after his trial ended he was on a ship blasting out of Earth orbit, curled up along the wall and taking turns sobbing and vomiting from spacesickness.

Twelve years . . . my God, I've been here twelve years . . . He had just said it to Lopez, but it suddenly hit him very hard.

"C'mon, Grant." Lopez's words pulled Jamie from his thoughts. "You gotta come. We gotta stand together. All of us." His voice was strained, frustration coming out at Jamie's refusals.

"No," Jamie said, his tone stronger, more resolute. "I've gotten myself in enough trouble, Tomas. I can't give them another reason to add years on to my term."

Jamie Grant had come to Haven full of rage and defiance. And for years he'd stood up to the guards, taken their beatings, and stared icily into the face of the warden and the governor when they'd added years to his sentence. He had survived, as much to spite those who'd sent him to the mines to die as out of any real desire to live. But then he met Damian.

Damian Ward was a veteran, a retired soldier who had accepted a land grant on Haven as his mustering-out bonus and settled there after the war. Damian was an influential citizen, an officer who'd been decorated more than once for valor in combat.

The governor had given Ward a special authorization to hire out a work crew from the prison complex to assist him in getting his farm into full production. Jamie had been assigned, solely by chance, along with a dozen others. He hadn't complained—it was almost a respite, being sent from the dark, dusty hell of the mine to work outside for a few months. Sure, the work was just as backbreaking, but at least it meant something *different*. He'd provoked some of his beatings solely to *feel* anything, to remind himself that he was an actual being and not just a cog in the prison's machine. So the chance to break the monotony was more than welcome.

Meeting Damian was almost a bonus at that point.

But somehow, against all odds, he and Damian had become friends. And for the first time in his life, Jamie Grant found himself with someone in his corner, a true ally. And also for the first time, he had real hope that the future could hold something better than the poverty and deprivation he'd known all his life.

As long as he kept his head down and stayed out of trouble until his sentence was over, that is.

And he'd done just that, for three years now. He was scheduled for release in two and a half months, and he wasn't about to do anything to interfere with that. Certainly not get involved in a doomed riot. No matter how much he hated the federals.

"What the fuck, Grant?" Tomas was angry now, and his raised voice was drawing attention from the others. "What are you, some kind of fed sympathizer? Ain't you one of us no more?"

"Go fuck yourself, Tomas." Jamie gave his comrade a hard shove, his anger just as real as Lopez's now. "I've done more years in this fucking pit than most of you. And I've had more time tacked on to my sentence, too. So don't give me this fed-lover bullshit." It was hard enough to stand aside, to bite down on his rage and try to stay out of trouble. He didn't need an asshole like Tomas Lopez giving him shit.

Especially since there was no point to the rising anyway. No chance of victory.

Jamie knew exactly what was going to happen. Best case, the riot was easily contained, and the miners would be back at work within a matter of hours, battered and still coughing up the last of the stun gas from their lungs. Perhaps they'd be minus a couple of their number, a few of them shot down whether they resisted or as a lesson to the others. And they'd all have an extra six months added to their time on top of the other punitive measures the feds loved so much—ration reductions, extra work periods, and a few beatings for good measure.

Worst case, the uprising actually succeeded enough to scare the governor. If that happened, Jamie knew, a lot of his fellow workers wouldn't return at all. The reward for their brief success would be a company of security forces encircling the mine and starving them out. Or, if the governor got really nervous, storming the mine and retaking it. Jamie had watched federal forces clear riots before, and it wasn't something he wanted to see again.

Lopez stared back at Jamie for a second. Then he dropped the metal rod he was carrying and lunged forward, taking a wild swing at his fellow prisoner. It might have surprised him, but Jamie had been in the federal prison for twelve years, and he knew how to take care of himself. It was almost too easy. He stepped quickly to the side, giving Lopez a sharp punch to the gut, one that dropped him where he was standing.

"I don't want to fight you, Tomas," he said quietly, staring at the doubled-over figure at his feet. "Do whatever you want, asshole. Get yourself shot—or locked up in here for an extra year or two. Or kill a guard and get yourself snuffed.

"Just stay the fuck away from me."

Jamie turned back to the rock face and leaned down to pick up his drill, keeping an eye on Lopez as he did.

"You're a fuckin' piece of shit, Grant," Lopez said as he pulled himself up, still gasping for breath as he did. "Fed-lover." He glared at Jamie, but he didn't make another move.

Jamie felt the rage trying to bubble over inside him, but he clamped down on it. Still, he could see at least a half dozen of the other miners beginning to gather, to walk in his direction. His brief fight with Lopez had drawn attention he didn't want.

"Grant, what's your problem?" It was Ron Gavros, another of the prisoners, one of the few still remaining who'd been there when Jamie had arrived twelve years before. Gavros was one of the instigators of the uprising. He walked over and stopped a little over a meter from Jamie. "I know damned well you hate the stinking feds. You gonna let your friends stand on the front line while you sit here like the little bitch slave they made you?"

Grant sighed and turned around to face the new arrival. "Look, Ron, I don't want any trouble, okay? I'm less than three months from getting out of here." He knew as the words came out of his mouth it was the wrong thing to say. Gavros was a lifer, with no hope of release. No hope save for Haven to fall into the fires of revolution and somehow wrest itself free of Federal America.

"So you get out and the hell with the rest of us?" Gavros snapped back. He glanced back at the gathering crowd and then took another step toward Jamie. "Is that what you are now, Grant? A stinking turncoat? A sellout who doesn't give a shit about his friends?"

Grant set the drill down on the ground next to him. He'd been sure he could handle Lopez easily enough, and most of the others, too, at least one-on-one. But Gavros was big . . . and tough. He'd been forged in this hell even longer than Jamie had, and he'd arrived bigger and nastier to begin with. A fight with him would be deadly serious business. Not to mention the crowd would all be on Gavros's side.

"Ron, you've been here a long time. You know what's going to happen as well as I do. This uprising isn't going to accomplish a damned thing other than get a bunch of you killed." Grant took a breath and stared right at his fellow prisoner. He could see his words weren't accomplishing anything, either with Gavros or with the others gathered around. "Look," he said finally, "I'm not in your way. Do what you want. Just leave me out of it, all right? You going to waste all your time down here bitching at me while the feds rush in reinforcements? You want to fight with me or the feds?"

"You suck, Grant." Gavros stared at Jamie for a few more seconds, his eyes glittering with rage. But there was something else there, too, a distraction. Jamie saw that his last comment had scored some points.

"Fuck this fed-lover," Gavros said, turning toward the miners gathered around. "We'll deal with him later. It's time to take this to the stinking feds." He stepped toward the middle of the crowd and raised his hand above his head. "To the surface. Now!"

The crowd roared and followed Gavros as he moved toward the elevators and the ladders. Jamie stood and watched as the cavern emptied, and silence slowly replaced the wild shouting of the crowd. The miners had already taken prisoner the three guards from this level, and Jamie knew that was trouble. There was a good chance those guards were going to die, and probably not pleasantly. And that meant a lot of prisoners would be scragged . . . a lot more than three. Jamie had seen enough federal guards to know how they reacted when their own were hurt or killed. Guilt wouldn't matter much when that happened. Just being in the line of fire would be enough.

Now the mob was heading toward the upper sections to rally the prisoners there, and overwhelm the rest of the security forces on duty. It was a tragedy on its way to becoming a complete catastrophe.

He shook his head sadly. Despite all Lopez and Gavros had said in their anger, his sympathies *were* with his fellow prisoners. Some of them deserved to be here, he knew, but others had merely been victims of Federal America's unjust courts and the poverty and corruption that had driven them to whatever crimes they had committed.

None of that mattered, though. Whatever his sympathies, Jamie didn't have time for any of this. He hated the federals, but getting himself killed, or consigned here for another year or two, wouldn't accomplish a thing. And he had good reasons to keep his head down and get out, more than just Damian and the promise of a job on the farm and a place to live.

Katia . . .

He'd met Katia Rand at Damian's farm, when he'd been there as part of the work crew. From the moment she'd walked into his field of view, he hadn't been able to take his eyes off her. She'd been there with her father, working on the farm's electrical systems, and the two of them had hit it off immediately. They spent every fleeting moment together, in secret at first and then with Damian's assistance. By the time Jamie returned to the mine with the rest of the work detail, he had a new purpose. To finish his sentence and to accept Damian's offer of a job. And to marry Katia Rand.

So screw you, Gavros, and your pipe dream.

Because what he had told Gavros was true—their cause was hopeless. The prisoners had no chance of victory, not unless the rest of Haven rose up in rebellion. And for all the unrest sweeping the planet, Jamie knew things hadn't reached that point. It wasn't difficult for prisoners with no freedom and no hope to reach the desperation point. But for all Federal America's oppression and corruption, most Havenites had homes and jobs and families. They might bristle and protest over increased taxes and burdensome regulations, but it would take more to push things to the breaking point, some outrage that would galvanize the people and thrust them into open revolution.

And the conditions of convicted criminals certainly weren't going to be the straw that broke the camel's back.

He didn't know *what* might push Haven over the edge, or if he would rise up to that call when it did. What he knew was a dazzling smile and a brilliant pair of eyes . . .

He looked down at the drill, but he didn't pick it up again. He couldn't do anything by himself, at least nothing productive. So he let out a loud sigh and sat down on a large rock outcropping.

All he could do was wait.

And hope.

CHAPTER 3

"The uprising at the mine is serious, Governor. Production is at a complete halt, and the rioters have taken at least eight guards prisoner." Alexandra Thornton had marched briskly into the governor's office without preamble or announcement. She was the commander of his security forces, and the two had known each other for years. They shared a close working relationship and a greater than average amount of trust, and the two operated with quite a bit less formality than Governor Wells demanded of the others on his staff.

She stood before him now, and he could see as she continued her report that she was deeply concerned. "They control the entire facility, sir, including the buildings and storehouses aboveground."

Everett Wells looked up from the small tablet he'd been reading. The words on the screen told him much the same thing Thornton just had, but he preferred discussing things with her to fighting through the dry reports his staff had prepared. Besides, she'd been out to the mine and inspected things firsthand, and that gave her a perspective the pages of analysis on the tablet didn't have.

Thornton stood in front of the desk, at attention despite the governor's lack of a military rank. She was a soldier, through and through, and usually an image of military perfection as well. But now Wells noticed her less than freshly pressed grays and the two small platinum clusters that marked her major's rank, usually polished to a bright sheen but now a bit smudged. There was more than a little dirt caked on her uniform and boots, and one small spot Wells suspected was half-dried blood.

Things must really be bad, he thought as his eyes panned down Thornton's rumpled form. If there was one thing about Alexandra Thornton that made an impression, besides her competence and reliability, it was fastidiousness. The fact that she hadn't stopped in her quarters to change before coming to see him told him all he needed to know about the urgency of the situation.

"The entire complex is occupied?" Wells already knew the answer, and the fatigue in his voice made that obvious.

"Yes, Governor. The guards managed to hold at the outer perimeter fence, and my people have reinforced them there. But everything inside is occupied." She paused for an instant, reluctantly taking a seat after Wells gestured toward one of the chairs in front of his desk for the third time. "We don't think anyone has been killed or seriously injured," she continued, "well, not yet. But they have taken at least nine guards hostage." She paused. "They are obviously in great danger."

Her tone changed briefly when she mentioned the hostages. The prison guards weren't part of her colonial security force, and they reported directly to the federal authorities who ran the prison complex. Wells knew his military commander disapproved of many of the abuses that took place in the prison mine, just as he himself did. He'd had more than one go-around with Warden Vinson, but his authority as governor did not extend to the federal prison complexes on Alpha-2, and he and Vinson had a . . . strained . . . relationship.

"Who is in command on-site?" Wells asked.

"Captain Rennes, sir." Thornton paused. "I felt he would exercise the proper restraint."

"I agree completely, Major. Captain Rennes is a good choice. Please advise him that *he* is in command on the scene, and if Warden Vinson attempts to interfere, Rennes is to direct him to me."

Being in charge of Alpha-2 colony meant—notwithstanding muddled jurisdictions where federal facilities were involved—his authority was the last word in any emergency. At least, that's how he planned on interpreting it. He was pretty confident that hundreds of prisoners on the verge of breaking out constituted an emergency.

It certainly helped having the backing of Thornton and her soldiers in case there was a disagreement about the exact definition.

"Yes, sir." She hesitated, but then said, "I more or less told him that already." Another pause, longer this time. "I knew that's what you would want, Governor."

Wells just nodded. Thornton had overstepped her authority perhaps, but she was right, too. She did know what he would want, and she'd seen it done.

Wells didn't condone the general disobedience among the populace that had plagued his term as governor, and certainly not the violent uprising at the mine. His loyalties to the state were strong, and his sense of duty profound. But he was a moderate man, reluctant to use excessive force or to impose heavy restrictions on the population, preferring to try to negotiate with disaffected groups, to solve problems with words and not force. Nevertheless, in spite of his best efforts, he'd presided over four years of steadily increasing unrest. All his attempts to reason with the people seemed to fall on deaf ears, and things had continued to escalate, dangerously so over the past year. He'd come to Alpha-2 a rising star in Federal America's bureaucracy, but the deteriorating situation on his watch had brought his career to a precarious precipice.

He understood to a point how the residents—Havenites, they called themselves—felt, and he bristled at the callousness of the decrees that had continued to come in from the federal senate. The government was acting in response to the increasing disorder, but its actions were only feeding the growing rebellion and making his job almost impossible.

But he also believed Federal America was the lawful government of Alpha-2, and he disagreed vehemently with those who felt they were justified in disobeying the laws or resisting the dictates of the legitimate authorities. He saw revolution as treason, and he held that the people of Alpha-2 were bound to resolve their issues through normal government channels and not through civil disobedience.

And certainly not by open rebellion, which is exactly what more and more people were expecting.

Major Thornton and much of his staff shared the same views, but his moderation had only served to bring criticism and anger from both sides—from the Havenites, who, despite his restraint, still considered his policies too harsh, and from the federal authorities on Earth, who viewed his leadership as weak and indecisive.

Let any of them sit in this chair and see if they could do better.

"I'd like you to get back out to the scene, Major." He paused for a few seconds. "It's not that I don't trust Captain Rennes, but I'd prefer to see this end as quickly as possible. I think your judgment on scene will be helpful. Normally, I'd try to be patient, but . . ." Wells's voice trailed off.

"But the federal observer is due to arrive in two weeks." Thornton's tone suggested she didn't think any better of the assignment of a federal overseer to Alpha-2 than Wells did. But neither of them had been given a choice.

Observer, he thought. *What a measured title. Some master politician came up with that. She's a military governor, that's what she is. So the question is: How much authority will she have? And how much will I have left?*

He'd have to worry about that when the time came. For now, he could only reply to Thornton. "Yes, Major. She is. And if there is any way to defuse this situation before she gets here, I think we'll all be happier." He looked down at the desk for a few seconds and added, "And the prisoners most of all, I suspect. From what I hear, Asha Stanton is not to be trifled with."

Thornton nodded, but didn't respond to the comment about the observer. *Because she's smart enough to keep her personal opinions to herself,* Wells thought. Instead, she said, "I will do the best I can, sir. But if we can't talk them out, we'll have to storm the facility and take it by force. And that's going to be messy, especially if it has to be over in the next few days." Thornton's eyes found the governor's. "I'll need your approval for that, too, sir. So, you might want to consider exactly what you want us to do if negotiations are unsuccessful."

Wells sighed. "I will do that, Major." He stood up slowly, pushing his chair behind him as he did. "And I think now you should get back out there and do your best to keep me from having to make that decision."

Thornton sprang to her feet when Wells rose, and she snapped to attention. "Yes, Governor. I will do my best, sir."

"That's all any of us can do, Major. Dismissed."

He watched her leave and then he sat down again and reached his arm around, rubbing the knots in the back of his neck. He'd taken an analgesic earlier, but the headache and the pain in his neck had proven stubborn. He knew his ills were side effects of the growing stress from his job—and the lack of sleep that went along with it—but it didn't look like things were going to get better anytime soon, so he reached down to one of the compartments under his desk and pulled out the bottle, dropping another two pills into his hand.

He felt a brief rush of hope, a thought that the situation at the mine might be resolved without bloodshed. But that passed quickly. Thornton was a good officer, trustworthy and efficient. Those traits were admirable, yet they did nothing to actually change what was going on at the prison. With the way things stood, Wells had a feeling in his gut, one he'd had for days now.

Things were about to get a lot worse.

"I'm sorry to interrupt you, sir, but there's trouble at the mine. I thought you'd want to know immediately." Ben Withers was peering through the open door into the farmhouse's study. Withers was tall and muscular, and in the three years since he'd followed his platoon commander into retirement on Haven, he hadn't lost a bit of his combat conditioning nor added a gram of fat to his lean frame.

Damian Ward looked up from his work. "What kind of trouble, Ben?" Ward had tried for months after they'd arrived on Haven to get the now civilian Withers to stop calling him "sir," but to no avail. He finally gave up, and now he hardly even noticed it anymore.

Something in Withers's voice made him perk up this time, though.

"An uprising, sir. The inmate-workers have gained control of the facility. They've taken some of the guards hostage."

Ward's expression darkened. "They have the entire complex?"

"Yes, sir. At least, that's what I was told. The security forces still hold the outer wall, so the rioters are contained, for the moment. It's currently a standoff right now."

Ward slapped his hand down on his desk. "I hope Jamie's not involved in this idiocy," he said. "The kid can be a damned fool, and I wouldn't put it past him. But he's been so good recently. No, I can't believe he would jeopardize everything, not this close to getting out."

He realized he had said that all out loud, but he couldn't help it. Damian had found somewhat of a kindred spirit in the young Jamie Grant. He'd liked the kid immediately, and he saw in the troubled young man what he might have become if he hadn't ended up in the armed forces. His rank—received as a field promotion after distinguishing himself in battle—was a rare achievement for someone from his low social stratum and it had led him to this farm and the promise of a life of some prosperity, both in terms of being a respected resident of Haven, as well as generating a moderate level of wealth. All of which was a protracted way of saying he'd come a long way from the fetid slums of Federal America's old capital city of Washington, and that he knew he could have easily ended up in Jamie Grant's shoes.

And if I were in those shoes, I might easily find myself caught up in this nonsense in the prison.

"I'm sure Jamie is not involved, sir." Withers's expression suggested he wasn't at all sure.

Damian shook his head. "It may not matter. Even if he tries to stay out of it, if the whole place is in rebellion he's a part of it. Whether it's the inmates forcing him to participate or, when the authorities retake the place, the feds being unable to differentiate between those who rose up and those who didn't, he's *there*. So does it really matter what he chooses to do?" *Assuming Jamie doesn't just get killed in the crossfire*, he thought but didn't say.

He glanced up at Withers, noting the man's uncomfortable expression. He put his hand up. "I'm just thinking out loud, Ben. Not expecting you to have the answer."

Withers nodded, though he still looked troubled.

Damian sat quietly, deep in thought. He understood the discontent of the prisoners in the mine. Conditions there were an outrage, and he suspected many of the prisoners had received less than just and honest trials, Jamie Grant not the least among them. But they couldn't really think they would succeed, could they? Governor Wells wasn't a bad sort, not really—indeed, he and Damian had become friends of a sort. But sooner or later, he'd have to send in his security forces. And a bunch of prisoners with steel bars and knives weren't going to beat back trained troops with assault rifles and concussion grenades.

He felt for the prisoners, and the inevitable conclusion to the tragedy they had set in motion. But mostly his thoughts were on his friend. He'd sponsored Jamie, committed to give him a job upon his release. He had even posted a security bond to allow his friend to stay in one of the farm buildings between shifts in the mine, instead of in the grim and filthy prison residence wing. And now all he could see in his mind was Jamie rounded up with the others and sentenced to years more in that hellhole. Or summarily executed.

Damian knew he had helped to give Jamie hope, to focus the kid on the life he could have. And Katia had done the same. But Damian also knew it would break Jamie to hear the warden or the governor sentence him to years more at hard labor, to have his off-site sleeping privileges revoked and his work period increased from twelve hours a day to a more punitive fourteen or sixteen. To be denied visitors and lose his tenuous link with the outside . . .

He's not going to survive this. Either as the man he's become, or at all.

"Get the transport, Ben," he said suddenly. "I'm going into town to see the governor." There were advantages to being a war hero, and that had its own currency. Damian was a minor celebrity on Haven—*remember to call it Alpha-2 when you're talking to the governor*, he thought—and he knew his relationship with Wells would ensure access. Whether the governor would listen—or do anything— was another matter entirely. But he would cross that bridge when he came to it.

"The price is going up, gentlemen. Double what it was, and that's just for the next shipment. I can't guarantee what will happen after that, or if there'll even be any more runs." Sasha Nerov spoke softly, her eyes panning suspiciously around the room as she did, despite her certainty that she and the two men facing her were alone.

"Double? That's insane. You're already being paid twenty times the price of these weapons on Earth." Cal Jacen was a tall man whose patrician features looked out of place on a colony like Haven. He had been a law professor on Earth, until his outspoken—some said radical—views compelled him to leave his comfortable life behind and immigrate to the colonies under circumstances that were still shrouded in mystery.

Regardless, she wasn't going to have this former lecturer lecture her.

"Then go buy them on Earth and haul them here yourself. It's not like I'm dying to have another run at the federal blockade." Nerov didn't try to moderate the sharpness of her voice. She still couldn't get the image of *Wasp*'s destruction—of Sergei Brinker's death—out of her mind. She didn't blame Jacen or the rest of the revolutionaries on Haven for what had happened—Brinker had chosen his life as a smuggler, just as she had—but she wasn't about to haggle either, let alone put up with any of Cal Jacen's shit. Not when it was *her* people that had to sneak loads of guns past a squadron of federal frigates. And if Jacen gave her any more trouble—one more word she didn't like—she was ready to turn around and walk out the door. She already had enough money stashed away to last her a good long time, and sitting out the rest of Haven's unfolding drama on a beach somewhere far away seemed like a pretty good alternative to facing summary execution at the hands of the federal navy.

In fact, Nerov wasn't sure why she was even considering another run. No—that wasn't true. What she wasn't sure of was whether or not she wanted to admit to herself that she was more than a cold-blooded mercenary—that she sympathized strongly with the rebels and wanted to aid their cause, no matter the risk. Her support had its limits—it didn't prevent her from charging exorbitant fees for her weapons, for example. But it kept her from abandoning the rebels and pushed her to take the much greater risk running guns now carried with it. And every thought of Brinker and his crew murdered by the federals only inflamed her anger, and made her more of a rebel inside.

Still, just one *more word . . .*

Jacen actually opened his mouth, looking as if he was about to throw an angry retort back at her and give Nerov all the excuse she needed, but the man standing next to him spoke first. "Double, it is, Captain Nerov. And I assure you, we are most grateful to you and your crew for your willingness to continue your shipments in spite of the . . . enhanced . . . federal presence."

Nerov turned and looked at the older man at Jacen's side. She nodded her acceptance. "Thank you, Mr. Danforth. My crew needs a few days of rest, and *Vagabond* needs some minor maintenance, but we will be lifting off in four days, five at most."

"That should work out well, I think. It will allow me to prepare your advance payment." He paused for a few seconds. "Shall we meet back here in two days? Same time?"

Nerov nodded, pushing back against the frown that was trying to slip onto her face. Danforth had always had the deposit for the next run along with her payment for the delivered weapons. This was the first time he'd shown any difficulty in producing the funds. But she also realized how difficult it must be to put together that much platinum on Haven, especially without drawing too much attention. Danforth was one of the planet's richest men, which she suspected only made his clandestine activities that much more difficult to conceal. But he'd always kept his word in his dealings with her. And a smuggler couldn't exactly accept payment by electronic transfer.

"That will be fine, Mr. Danforth," she replied softly. "Back here in two days." Her eyes darted to the side for an instant, toward Cal Jacen. She was willing to trust John Danforth, at least as much as she trusted anyone, but Jacen was a different story. He was more abrasive than Danforth, and his revolutionary zeal seemed to have a sinister feel that the older man's lacked. She'd always dealt with both of them together, and her opinion of Jacen had never changed. Fortunately, her actual business was with Danforth, and so that was how she looked at it.

"Again, you have my thanks, Captain. We need these guns desperately, and I know very well the risks you take in bringing them here." He took a deep breath. "How soon do you think you can return with the next shipment?"

Nerov thought for a moment before answering. It wasn't just the trip to Earth and back. Running a direct route would be like broadcasting her smuggling activities. *Vagabond* was bringing a shipment of high-value ores back on its return trip from Haven. It would look strange, after all, if a freighter showed up with no cargo. And when she left, her departure documents would show she was taking manufactured goods and electronics to some planet out on the frontier, preferably one belonging to another power, one that wasn't seething with discontent and drawing the prying eyes of every customs inspector and government spook in Federal America. There was just too much heat on vessels departing Earth for Haven. It was much safer to travel to a different destination, and then come back to Haven from someplace with less security. But it turned a four-week trip into one lasting months.

She said as much.

"Our round trip this time was a little over five months. I think we can do that again." She paused. "Unless we need to hide in the outer system waiting for a chance to slip past the blockade."

Danforth looked back, an uncomfortable expression on his face. He turned and exchanged glances with Jacen before returning his gaze to her. "Is there any chance you can shave some time off that?"

Nerov started shaking her head, but then she stopped and said, "Maybe we can cut off a month. *Maybe.*"

"Is there any chance you can be back here in six weeks, eight outside?"

She stared back, but she didn't respond right away. *Things are worse than I thought. He expects everything to hit the fan soon . . .*

"I know that is very tight timing, Captain," Danforth added, "but if you were able to make delivery in eight weeks, we could pay you triple instead of double." He hesitated. "Of course, you'd have to give me a bit more time to put that much platinum together."

Triple? He is desperate.

"I can't promise anything," she replied cautiously. "But for triple I will try." She knew any attempt to meet that timetable was reckless and foolhardy. *But triple . . .*

You always have been greedy. It will be the death of you.

But we all have to die someday. Just ask Sergei.

"Very well, Captain." He stepped forward and extended his hand. "I will see you back here in two days. Same time."

She nodded and took his hand. "Two days," she repeated.

CHAPTER 4

Jamie sat quietly against the cold rock wall of the cavern, staring down as he poked at the loose gravel with his foot. It had been almost eighteen hours since the uprising began, and he was surrounded by an eerie silence. He was on the twentieth level, and he suspected everyone else had moved up toward the surface.

Twenty levels, he thought. *There were only eight when I got here.*

He took a deep breath, filling his lungs with the mine's fetid air. He had his daily water ration, and he'd been drinking it slowly, cautiously, unsure of how long it had to last him. There was no food, at least not on this level. He was hungry, and he thought about trying to find something to eat, but he stayed put. He didn't want to get caught anywhere near the rebelling prisoners. He was going to stay right where he was, at his assigned work area, until the disturbance was over.

He was tired, too, but he didn't dare sleep. As far as he could tell, he was the only person left on the level, but he wasn't about to take any chances. Sure, he'd stared down Lopez and Gavros, but he didn't fool himself that the danger had passed. He'd made enemies among his fellow prisoners, and the resentment would only worsen when the authorities clamped down and rioters began dying.

Fuck.

He shook his head. He was worried enough about escaping blame for the uprising, but it was now dawning on him that even if he did, he still had almost three months to survive in the mines. Around people who hated him. Damian had secured him a partial work release, allowing him to spend several days a week at the farm, as long as he met his production quotas in the mine. But the rest of the time was down here, and two and a half months was a long time, more than enough for him to get a shiv shoved into his back or to end up in a mine "accident."

Not that he deserved their anger. He'd literally done nothing to upset their plans. But measured reason wasn't what he associated with the crowd at Alacomara, and when the uprising was crushed and the survivors were back at work—with years tacked on to their sentences, brutal injuries from vengeful guards, and comrades dead—he knew they would blame him. It didn't make much sense, but he'd been in the mines long enough to know how prisoners thought about things. They would crave a scapegoat to blame for their failure, and with the guard rotations massively increased, they would have to turn that anger away from the feds. Turn it toward one of their own, someone they could get to. Toward *him*.

Fuck.

"Governor, please. I am asking for your help in this matter. I will do whatever I must to satisfy any concerns you have." Damian sat in the plush guest chair, facing Governor Wells across the massive desk. He was unaccustomed to pleading to bureaucrats for assistance, but he was also unaccustomed to having friends. Most of his life had been to give orders or receive orders, but civilian life had brought an unexpected consequence: Jamie Grant wasn't his subordinate.

He was his friend.

And after three years of working to secure Grant's release, committing to provide a job, posting a surety bond, throwing his influence as a decorated veteran into the effort, he wasn't about to see that friendship burned to ash in a prison riot. Still, he knew this was going to be difficult.

"Lieutenant Ward, I wish I could help you, but I'm afraid my hands are tied. If Mr. Grant was foolish enough to get himself involved in this uprising, there is nothing I can do." He paused. "I am trying to find a way to end this without a river of blood flowing . . . and I am far from certain I will be successful. I'm afraid I have little time to worry about one prisoner, especially one with a disciplinary record as poor as Jamie Grant's."

Damian sat unmoving, ignoring Wells's body language suggesting their meeting was over. "Governor, I understand you are extremely busy, especially right now. But I am not here asking you to overlook Jamie's involvement in the uprising. I am sure he has stayed out of this. But when the standoff ends—*however it ends*—you know as well as I do that in the confusion, it will be hard to tell who was involved and who wasn't. Jamie will get caught up with the others, even if he didn't raise a hand to aid the rioters."

Wells sighed softly. He frowned and opened his mouth to reply, but just as quickly closed it. His expression changed, softened, and then he said, "Lieutenant, I believe I would throw anyone else out of my office right now." He hesitated, and sighed again. "But I think we can help each other. Although, frankly, I don't see the potential in Mr. Grant that you do. While one could sympathize with the situation that led him here, he has been far from an exemplary prisoner in the years since."

Damian was about to respond when Wells held up his hand. "Please, Lieutenant, allow me to finish. Whatever my feelings, it is clear that you see something in him." Wells looked across the desk at Damian. "And you are a man I must take seriously. So I will offer you a bargain of sorts."

Bargain?

"What do you have in mind, Governor?"

Wells stood up and walked over toward a small table against the wall, picking up a small bottle. "May I offer you a drink, Lieutenant? Kentucky bourbon, imported from Earth. A luxury I allow myself from time to time."

Damian wasn't much of a drinker, and almost never more than a beer or a glass of wine. But he wanted to see where this was going.

"Yes, Governor, thank you. Just a little, please." He held up his hand with two fingers spaced a couple centimeters apart.

Wells turned over two small glasses, setting them down and filling both considerably past the level Damian had requested. He moved back toward the desk, handing one of the drinks to his guest.

"I'm afraid I need a bit more to get through my day lately." His tone suggested he was joking, but Damian had a feeling the jest was closer to the truth than Wells wanted to admit. He took the glass and held it up, tapping it against the governor's. Then he put it to his lips, downing it in one gulp. He didn't particularly care for it, but it was a lot smoother than he'd expected, and he could tell it was high quality. He couldn't imagine what it cost, especially with the expense of importing it to Haven.

He put the glass down on the desk, noting that Wells had taken his own considerably larger drink in one swig as well. He almost asked again what the governor had in mind, but he decided to wait and let Wells get to it at his own pace. Patience wasn't a virtue Damian had developed in combat, but he suspected it would serve him now.

"Lieutenant . . . first, please call me Everett. I think we can ignore the formalities, don't you? I have come to consider you a friend."

"Very well, Everett. And I am Damian. And I appreciate that, because I have come to consider you a friend as well." That was an overstatement, he realized. He did like the governor, or at least sympathized with the man, but he wouldn't go any further than that. *But we swallow our pride and get the mission done.* With a chuckle he hoped didn't sound forced, he said, "I can't get my assistant to stop calling me lieutenant, though I'm a civilian almost four years now."

"Damian . . ." Wells stared across the desk and paused. "As I said, I will do everything I can to save your friend."

Here it comes . . .

Wells took a breath. "And in return, I'd like you to help me . . . to help me keep the peace."

Damian just stared back for a few seconds. Then he said, "I'd like to see things calm down myself, but I'm not sure what I can do to help. I'm afraid I keep to myself most of the time. I don't have very much influence."

"You underestimate yourself, Damian. You are one of Alpha-2's more celebrated residents, a decorated officer and a successful farmer. I think your words alone, urging calm, would have significant impact."

Damian took a deep breath and held it for a few seconds. He tended not to think of himself in such terms, but he knew Wells was right. The fact was, any perceived lack of influence was purposeful on his part. He'd made every effort to keep to himself since he'd arrived nearly four years earlier. He'd seen too much war. War at its worst and most brutal. War that had seemed high-minded, that had been the result of the words of "influential" men and women.

Now he longed for nothing save peace and solitude.

Which made the idea of speaking to crowds, of calling leading citizens to his home for private conferences, repugnant. *I've already turned my swords into plowshares. I've done my part to grow peace.*

But he knew he had to agree.

For Jamie, certainly, but also because Wells was right. Haven was on the verge of terrible catastrophe, and if there was any chance to avert it, he had to try. Even if it seemed like an impossible task.

His fellow Havenites were strong-willed and stubborn, *and* few of them had seen the true horror of combat. The last war had largely bypassed the planet, with most of the fighting farther out on the frontier. But Damian had no trouble visualizing what revolution would mean for his adopted home. He pictured the neatly arrayed buildings of the capital in flames, the charred wreckage smoking for days after the fires subsided. The dead lying everywhere, bloated, rotting bodies twisted into grotesque poses. Men, women, children, unburied and unrecognizable.

In closed rooms, revolution was painted as a grand and romantic picture. In the streets, the revolution would be painted with the blood of soldiers and innocents alike.

If it truly came to war, it would be all-consuming. A few skirmishes would not win Haven freedom. Alpha-2 was too valuable to Federal America, and the politicians who ran things would know any weakness shown to rebels here would only encourage unrest elsewhere. They were already refusing to loosen their grip—if anything, they were doing the opposite—and if the rebels became violent, there would be no compromise.

They would respond with deadly force.

The problem is, these would-be rebels see the colonial security forces, and they think that is all they would face. They think they can prevail. For some reason, they don't realize the federals will send troops here. Real troops . . . like those I served with. And the Havenites have never faced anything like that before.

There weren't many still alive who had.

More than anything, that's what focused his decision. Four years later, and he still had nightmares. He didn't want anyone to have to experience them, too—let alone him having to live them again. He took a deep breath before saying, "Very well, Everett. I agree that we must do all we can to avert the tragedy of open rebellion. We may come to that point of view from somewhat different perspectives, but I think we can both agree the humanitarian toll of such a conflict would be unthinkable." Damian stared at Wells, trying to read the governor's reaction.

He believed peace was the best thing for his adopted home world, but he also knew the degree of anger the people felt. It wouldn't be easy to speak out, and he would risk making himself a target of the worst extremists. But once more he came to the inevitable conclusion: he didn't have a choice. Not if he wanted to save Jamie . . . and the life of peace he'd fought so hard to attain. Wells looked at him with a question in his eyes.

"Right. Spare Jamie from any retribution for the uprising, release him early, allow him to serve his last couple of months on work detail on my farm . . . and I will do as you ask. I will speak out, urge calm. I will do all that I can to encourage the people of Haven that war is not the answer."

Wells was silent for a moment, sitting there staring across the desk. Slowly, he nodded. "Very well, Damian. We have a deal." He stood up and extended his hand across the desk.

Damian rose as well, reaching out to take Wells's hand, but the governor pulled it back. "As long as Jamie Grant is not actively involved in the uprising. If he is, I'm afraid my hands are tied." He stared at Damian, moving his hand forward again.

Damian paused. He wanted to argue, to demand an unconditional guarantee as the cost of his cooperation, especially since he had no way to verify Jamie's involvement. But he knew Wells was offering all he could.

A lot rested on Jamie. Damian wanted to believe the young man had been smart enough to stay out of trouble—and he did believe it, at least to an extent. But there were doubts, too—how could there not be? Jamie was impetuous, bitter at his fate at the hands of Federal America.

And twelve years in prison wasn't exactly the greatest environment to experience personal growth.

It doesn't matter. This is all I can get.

He extended his hand. "I understand." The two shook on it. After a brief pause, Damian added, "I know you are busy, so I will go now. You will let me know?"

"As soon as I have any information on Mr. Grant, I will send it to you immediately."

Damian nodded. Then he turned and walked toward the door.

So that's what a deal with the devil feels like. He knew he wasn't being fair to Wells, but there wasn't really anything fair about this kind of conversation. *I hope to God you can hold up your end of the bargain, Jamie.*

He stepped out into the hallway, closing the door and almost bumping into a young woman about to enter the office.

"Excuse me," he said, pausing for a few seconds until he realized he was staring. He couldn't help it. She was striking, tall with long dark brown hair, and he found himself terribly distracted, his soldier's control failing him for once.

"Not at all," she said softly. "I'm afraid I wasn't looking where I was going. I tend to barge in on my father whenever the mood strikes me. Not a particularly responsible way for the governor's daughter to behave, I suppose."

"His daughter?" Damian's memory stirred. Yes, Wells had a daughter. Violetta, he thought he recalled.

She nodded. "Yes, his daughter. Violetta Wells. And you are Damian Ward, aren't you?"

"Yes," he answered, somewhat surprised. "Do we know each other?"

"Not exactly. I saw you interviewed on the vid. Your hair was quite a bit shorter, but I recognized you anyway. I have to admit, I watch it every time it is on. I am quite the fan, Lieutenant."

"Ah," he said, sighing softly. *One of those.* "Will those interviews never fade away?" He'd refused all media requests when he had first arrived on Haven, fresh from Earth, where he'd received his decorations from the hand of the Speaker himself. But John Danforth in particular had been persistent and refused to take no for an answer. His constant pressure had finally worn down Damian, who reluctantly agreed to sit down for a pair of roundtables, mostly talking about his experiences during the war . . . probably his least favorite topic.

He'd hoped that would satisfy the public interest in a decorated veteran settling on Haven, and he'd be left alone. And that had partially been the case. The demands for appearances did diminish as his reluctance became widely known, but Danforth had proven as relentless in recycling and rebroadcasting the interviews as he'd been in obtaining them. They'd become somewhat of a late-night staple on the Danforth network.

And apparently she watches them often.

"No," Violetta said. "You shouldn't think that way. You were very good. I've wanted to meet you since the first time I watched." Her eyes darted back and forth quickly, and she leaned forward and whispered, "You were much better on air than my father is, more relaxed. I've told him a hundred times he always looks nervous when he's being interviewed or giving a speech, but he doesn't listen. Maybe you can give him some pointers."

"Your father has a lot more stress on him than I did. It's rather easy to be a retired soldier receiving undeserved acclamation, more difficult by far to shoulder the burdens of the governor." A thought hit him, and he couldn't help but feel his admiration for Governor Wells grow. Violetta was beautiful and charming, and she could have gone a long way toward softening her father's public image. Yet Damian had never seen her before, not once. A lot of political types wouldn't hesitate to use their families to further their agendas, but it was clear Everett Wells was not one of them.

"Yes, he is under a lot of pressure, but aren't we all these days?"

"*Indeed, we are . . .*" He quickly fished around for the correct prefix for a governor's daughter. "Lady Wells . . . I won't detain you further. It was a pleasure to meet you."

"Violetta."

"Excuse me?"

"My name, Lieutenant. Please call me Violetta. 'Lady Wells' makes me feel so old."

"You are certainly not that, Violetta," he said. "Please just call me Damian. It's been a while since I wore my lieutenant's bars." He extended his hand and said, "I hope to see you again, Violetta."

"Indeed, Damian. I look forward to it." Then she turned and walked into her father's office, the door closing behind her.

"Yeah, baby! This is what I'm talkin' about." Lopez took the gun from the man and gripped it with both hands.

"You need to be careful with that, Lopez. Do you have any idea how hard it was to get these weapons in here?" Zig Welch shook his head as he looked at the excited prisoner. "No, of course you don't," he muttered to himself. Louder he said, "You don't have much ammunition, and there isn't going to be any more, so make every shot count when the fighting starts."

"Oh yeah, I'll make it count."

Welch tried to catch his sigh, but most of it slipped out anyway. Not that Lopez would notice—the man was too into the object in his hands. It didn't matter that Zig had taken a crazy risk sneaking the weapons into the mine. What mattered was that these prisoners now had guns, and that meant his highest priority was making sure imbeciles like Lopez didn't go completely crazy and waste their ammo pointlessly—or worse, start killing *each other*.

"I'll make sure he does." The voice was deep, coarse. Gavros stepped out of the shadows, walking up behind Lopez. His face was covered in sweat and grime, and there was a long, jagged scar running from his hair all the way down to his neck. "Thanks again for the guns, Mr. . . . ." He paused. "I never caught your name."

"No," Welch said calmly, "you didn't." He stared back at the prisoner, hiding his revulsion. He knew many of the inmates were victims of Federal America's harsh justice system, but Gavros was a real criminal by anyone's standards, and a bad one at that. The man had a lot of blood on his hands, and the only reason he had escaped the electrocution chamber was due to a shortage of prison labor on colonies like Haven and not any legitimate grounds for commutation.

But he's exactly the tool we need . . .

The Society of the Red Flag had put considerable resources into this plan. A small fortune had gone into bribes to slip the weapons into the mine—and the guns themselves had been expensive, too. The Guardians of Liberty were buying every weapon smuggled to Haven, their acquisitions fueled mostly by John Danforth's considerable personal wealth. The more radical Society had been forced to get by on scraps . . . plus whatever they'd managed to steal from the Guardians' storehouses.

Gavros stared back at the operative for a few seconds, but then he lost interest and returned his gaze to the assault rifle in his hands.

"Listen carefully. You will wait until the government forces attack. Is that understood?" Welch stared at the murderer. Gavros had become the de facto leader of the uprising through a time honored method: everybody else was scared of him. Welch could understand that—he felt the same cold uneasiness. He kept his composure, though—the only thing that mattered was making sure the plan worked. And getting out alive.

"I'm getting sick of sitting here waiting," Gavros growled. "I say we take 'em all out at the fence and get the fuck out of here."

"No," Welch said, trying hard to conceal his own impatience. "If you want more weapons later, more ammo—if you are expecting money and support once you get out—you will do as you are told."

Welch could see the anger in Gavros's face, but the prisoner didn't lash out. Gavros was a psychopath, but he wasn't stupid. And that was pretty much all he and the Society could hope for at this point.

"All right, we'll wait. For now." Gavros's voice was sullen, and Welch could see he had made his point. He nodded. Then he turned and walked away.

He had to leave. *Right away.* He'd bought his way in, paid off one of the noncoms to slip him through the lines surrounding the mine, but he had to be out before daybreak. That gave him twenty minutes. He stared down at the small chronometer on his wrist. At most. He quickened his pace.

He thought about Gavros. The man had a certain intelligence, sure, but a lot of that was more street smarts than actually cunning. Because if the prisoner had thought about it, he might have actually questioned why Welch was helping him in the first place.

Hell, the imbecile was expecting more help, without even wondering why he got what he did.

Which was the whole point. While Gavros thought Welch was here to help them escape, the Society had a very different endgame in mind—and all Gavros had to do to serve it was die . . . along with as many of his fellow prisoners as possible. Because when the people of Haven saw the images of federal security troops unleashing deadly force, they would be outraged. It was common knowledge that most of the inmates working the mines had been sentenced on trumped-up charges and shipped to Haven to fill the work quotas.

They may not all be innocents, but they're about to play that role on the vids.

"They have weapons, Major. More than can be accounted for by what they could have seized from the captured guards." Lieutenant Dawn Keller stood next to Thornton on the dirt floor of the makeshift command post. "I can't explain it."

Thornton looked at her subordinate for a few seconds before her eyes dropped back to the large tablet on the table below them both. The layout of the mine was displayed, the surface showing, with a series of numbers to the side for the lower levels.

"They've got control of the admin sections now. Could they have raided the armory?"

Keller shook her head. "No, Major." She turned and looked toward a cluster of the prison guards off to the side, making no attempt to disguise her contempt. "Warden Vinson assured me the autodestruct system was triggered and that all weapons on-site were destroyed." Despite her words, her tone suggested she wouldn't have believed Vinson if he'd told her the sky was blue. But then she added, with more certainty, "I checked the data logs myself, and the prison AI confirms that all charges were detonated. It is extremely unlikely the prisoners were able to obtain weapons there."

Thornton just stood there, glancing out at the activity along the perimeter fencing and then back to the tablet. She reached down, toggled the map through the levels of the mine, though her thoughts were not on what she was seeing.

She didn't think much of the prison guards, viewing them as a bunch of bullies in federal uniforms. She knew her own colonial troops had been little better when she'd taken command, but Thornton was a veteran of the real army, and she'd seen plenty of action in the last war. When she arrived on-planet, she quickly whipped the slovenly group of pseudo-soldiers she'd found into a respectable force. They were nothing like the regulars she'd served with in combat. But she'd made them as good as they could be, and learned to accept their limitations. And one thing she knew: they were far better trained and disciplined than the prison guards.

"I want to know what weapons those rioters have, Lieutenant, and I want to know now."

"Yes, Major. We're trying to gain control over the internal surveillance systems. We suspect the prisoners have destroyed a lot of the cameras, but they won't know where the clandestine units are hidden. We should have some data shortly."

"See that we do," Thornton snapped. "Because the governor's orders are clear. He wants this situation resolved immediately. If we're going to have to go in, I want to know exactly what we are facing."

"Yes, Major."

CHAPTER 5

The cell was dark and cramped, a cube just over a meter in each direction. Officially designated Punitive Facility A2, it was called the "Pit," by both the guards and inmates. No one seemed to remember who had first coined the name. Not that it mattered, really. Not to the federals who ran the place, and certainly not to Jonas Holcomb, who held the unofficial record for time spent there.

Holcomb sat twisted in the corner, breathing as deeply as he could, his body bent into the position he'd found to be least painful in his many hours in the Pit. His legs ached, and the pain in his back was like fire, but he'd been through it all before, and each torturous session only hardened his resolve and defiance. He knew they could hurt him only so much. They needed him back, or at least they wanted him badly, and that had spared him the worst forms of . . . persuasion . . . employed in the prison.

Holcomb didn't look like a hard-core criminal. Indeed, he wasn't a criminal at all, at least not by normal standards. He was a political prisoner, like everyone else in the Pit. The prison at the mines was a work camp; it existed primarily to extract ore. But Cargraves was different. Its purpose was detention, pure and simple. And punishment.

Federal America did not tolerate much in the way of dissent, and nothing at all that it considered truly subversive. In the months immediately following the end of the Great Civil War forty years before, the execution chambers ran night and day, as the victors crushed the last opposition, rooting out sympathizers—or anyone even *suspected* of sympathy toward the defeated antigovernment forces.

Holcomb's parents had died in that purge, just two more bodies among the nearly one hundred million that had lost their lives. He owed his own survival to timing. His parents had been highly ranked, and they had been questioned—no, *questioned* was the wrong word; *tortured* was closer to the mark—for a long time, until every scrap of knowledge they possessed that might help the federals root out and destroy any of their former allies was pulled from their bodies and minds. By the time that process had ended, the energy of the immediate postwar retributions had waned somewhat. Holcomb's parents still went to the scaffold, his father pushed there in a power chair, his legs too withered from repeated torture to carry him to his own execution.

But Jonas was spared as part of a campaign to show "the war was over." He was made a ward of the state and raised in an orphanage, destined for a life of menial work . . . until his extraordinary intelligence became evident. He was educated and employed by the government, and he'd become one of the top designers of military-grade weapons systems in Federal America.

He remembered the years of resentment toward his parents, his shame and hatred at their "treason." But now he knew that was all propaganda. The "history" of the civil war was largely a government-written fiction, he suspected, with the young indoctrinated from an early age to accept the official versions of events . . . and the old who remembered that time too terrified to dispute any of it.

So for the longest time, he'd considered himself the son of two criminals, mass murderers, and he had hated them. His position, his prosperity, all stemmed from Federal America, and that washed away any doubts he had about his government. For all his keen intellect, he had believed that nonsense for years. But then he woke up, and told himself, *No more*.

And now I'm in the Pit.

But he wasn't alone—no, even that mercy had been denied him. "Jonas, friend, I am here for our daily discussion. I do so enjoy our time together." The voice—cloying, mocking—belonged to Davis Reid. As Holcomb's interrogator, he was the man who, more than anyone else, sent him to the Pit, who determined what he ate—or, more likely, when he went hungry. Who sat and watched as the guards administered cautious beatings, careful to inflict pain without doing any serious damage. That wasn't out of any ethical constraints—Holcomb was pretty sure there was no such thing at Cargraves. For the most part, the prisoners in the Pit had been sent there to rot away, to disappear, to die in the shadows. Holcomb was different, though.

Holcomb was there for attitude adjustment.

"Reid, I've told you a hundred times, I will not design any more weapons. I am finished."

The federal interrogator knelt down, bringing his face to the same level as Holcomb's. "You are a stubborn man, Jonas, that much is certainly true. And an unappreciative one at that. Who owes more to Federal America than you? The son of traitors, spared, educated, given a chance to live a life of wealth and privilege. You lived for years on the stipends the government paid you, did you not? You had an apartment in Washington, a beach house in Virginia. All because Federal America cared for your every need. And how did you repay that kindness?"

"Kindness?" Holcomb's voice was a coarse rasp. "They provided me with that life so I would build weapons for them, make them more efficient killers. And to my shame, for years I did just that. Until I realized how my creations were used." Holcomb twisted his body, struggling to hold back a grunt as he moved in the confined space. "No, Reid. Never again. No matter how long you put me in here, how many beatings you give me . . . how long I remain a prisoner."

Reid sighed. "Surely you realize there are more . . . aggressive means of extracting cooperation. You have been spared these."

If Holcomb could have mustered up the muscle strength to shrug, he would have. "Go ahead . . . do your worst. Cripple me, kill me . . . but you won't get what you want from me." His words were bravado. He had some idea of what went on in the lower chambers, and he didn't fool himself into believing he could endure every torment they might throw at him. He was stubborn, but when he pushed his captors far enough, they *would* break him.

"Cripple you? Kill you? My dear Dr. Holcomb, how misguided you are. I have no wish to harm you. Quite to the contrary, it is my intention to return you to your life of comfort. I just need your cooperation."

"Never."

"That is such a strong word, Doctor. Let us agree to disagree for the moment." Reid paused and looked into the Pit, shaking his head. "But for now, let us take you out of this dreadful place, shall we?"

He stood up and looked down the hall. "Corporal, please remove Dr. Holcomb from the punitive facility, and bring him to the infirmary, Section Z."

He turned back and locked his eyes on Holcomb's. "Since you have been so obdurate, I believe we must try alternate methods. You are a sick man, Jonas, and you need treatment. You need help to see things . . . correctly. I will provide that help."

Holcomb's stomach twisted into a knot. He knew they did all kinds of drug therapy and brainwashing in the Pit, but he'd always been spared from it. The feds didn't want to mess with his brain. They wanted him back at 100 percent, working for them.

He had steeled himself against the pain, the discomfort they'd inflicted, refusing utterly to return to his former station. Indeed, he'd impressed himself with his efforts, with how the scared, bookish man who'd been dragged here three years before had remained rock solid for so long. He was different now than he'd been then, in ways he didn't yet fully understand. Something new was driving him, more than the simple outrage that had spurred him to cease his research . . . and to refuse all demands that he resume his old work.

It was deep inside him, hot, like the fires of hell itself. Anger, rage. He'd disapproved of Federal America before, but now, after they had sent him here with the intentions of scaring and beating him into submission, those feelings had morphed into something terrible.

He heard the sound of the hatch sliding open. It was a noise that usually triggered a sense of relief that his time in the Pit was over, at least for a while. But for the first time in a very long time, he didn't know what to expect. They hadn't used drugs on him. Yet. Perhaps now, though, that barrier had been dropped. He always knew there would come a time when the authorities would give up, when they would employ more extreme measures, regardless of the risk.

Had that time come?

He felt the hands grabbing him, pulling him out of the confined space, yanking him up. His legs dropped down slowly, his feet touching the floor. He was weak, feeling the effects of a day and a half twisted and hunched over, without food or water. He wobbled, but the guards held him up. There was pain in his legs, but also in his arms where the two federals held him firmly. And in his back, feeling the effects of the Pit, the agony was so intense he could feel the water welling up in his eyes as he gritted his teeth and endured.

"Let's go, Doctor."

It wasn't Reid's smarmy tone now. It was one of the guards. He felt the hands holding him, pushing forward, urging him on.

But on to what?

"I want better imagery. Retask the satellite and get me some good overhead shots." John Danforth was sitting at his desk, barking at the cluster of nervous-looking employees standing in his office.

"Mr. Danforth, the governor has just issued an executive order prohibiting any but officially sanctioned coverage. That means no video, no photos—nothing. At least, nothing we don't get from the government media office."

"That's bullshit," Danforth yelled. His face was red, puffy, his frustration building with each passing second. The Danforth family had been one of the first to land on Haven, and John was the third generation to run the family's media empire.

And I'll be the last if I don't watch my ass . . .

He wanted to slam his fist down on the desk, to shout out to his people to ignore the governor's ban and to move their satellite with or without permission. But he caught himself. The authorities were already suspicious about his political leanings, and they were right to be. On the surface, Danforth ran one of the most respectable businesses on Haven, the closest thing the fledgling colony had to a true media and communications behemoth. And that was probably enough to make any government nervous. But he had a private side, too, a secret one. For in the shadows, Danforth was a revolutionary who believed only secession from Federal America could provide Haven the future it deserved. As the head of the Guardians of Liberty, he pulled the strings on a rebellious network and had spent a huge chunk of his fortune buying illegal weapons for their efforts.

As much as it galled him to accept the governor's censorship, it was more important to keep scrutiny off his activities. At least until the day Haven was truly free.

"All right," he said, staring up into the uncertain faces looking back at him. "Do what you can, all of you." He turned toward his personal assistant. "Suze, get me the governor's office. I'll see what I can do."

"Yes, sir." His assistant nodded and turned to leave the room. The others stood there, looking uncertain about what to do.

"Go," Danforth said, gesturing with his hands for them to leave. "Earn your salaries. Get as close to the mine as the feds will let you. Question everybody you can find. Maybe somebody will let something slip, and we'll get an idea of what's really going on." Danforth tried his best to sound like a dedicated journalist, and to an extent he was, though his only real interest was exposing anything that could embarrass and discredit Federal America and weaken its hold on Haven.

"Go!" he roared again when his people moved too slowly for his taste. "The one who gets me something here keeps his job." He watched them all quickly file out, and then he put his head down in his hands. The headache was bad, but it was more than that. Something was happening, more than just a riot at the mine complex. There had been disturbances before, but none this large . . . and none that had gone on for so long.

Half the federal security troops on Haven are out there . . . and they won't let anybody near. But they haven't ended it yet, which makes no sense. There might be a lot of prisoners, but it isn't like they could actually win, not fighting against assault rifles with sticks and stones.

What the hell is going on?

The door opened again. He looked up slowly, pulling his face from his hands to see Suze walk back in. She'd been Danforth's aide for years, and the two worked seamlessly together. Sometimes he swore she could read his mind. But he still wished she'd learn how to knock before barging in.

"What is it, Suze?"

"The governor's office says no one is available to discuss the situation at this time, but they will respond as soon as possible."

"That's bullshit." Danforth shook his head. Everett Wells wasn't exactly an easy source of information, but he was usually available to Danforth on the phone, at least to repeat the official bullshit with added authority.

What the hell is going on?

"Something else, Suze?" He noticed she was still standing inside the door, hovering.

"Yes, sir . . ." She took a few steps inside and lowered her voice. "Mr. Haggerty is here."

Danforth nodded. "Oh . . . very well. Show him in." He looked around the room, more by habit than anything else. His office was private; he made sure of that by having it swept for surveillance devices twice a day. Still, he didn't like meeting Haggerty at his office, but he didn't have any choice—he was short of time.

"Mr. Danforth?" The man standing by the door was massive, tall and broad shouldered. He had long stringy hair hanging down well past his shoulders, brown once but now mostly gray. He looked more like a drifter or some kind of wilderness explorer than someone who would be meeting the head of the planet's top communications concern. But he had his own special abilities, and right now Danforth needed those.

"Yes, Zach, thanks for coming on such short notice." A pause. "Can you help me out on this one?"

The man had a troubled expression on his face. "That is a lot of platinum, Mr. Danforth. You need it immediately?"

"Immediately, Zach. It's very important." He suspected Haggerty knew what he was doing with the precious metal, and he'd never have worked with the black marketeer if he hadn't been certain of the man's rebel sympathies. Still, the fewer people who knew—or even suspected—that Danforth was stockpiling weapons, the better.

Haggerty took a deep breath and exhaled hard. "For anyone else, I'd say no way . . . but for you, I will try. It will be riskier than usual, though. Secrecy is my trade, you know. But if I am going to round up that much so quickly, I'll have to take more chances than I usually do.

"Which means I'll have to double my commission."

Danforth expected that. He got up and walked around his desk. "Thank you, Zach. I wouldn't ask you to work so quickly if it wasn't important. And double the usual fee . . . agreed."

Danforth had considered canceling the whole operation, but he needed more guns. Sasha Nerov's price was exorbitant, but she was also the most reliable of the smugglers he'd worked with, and one of the few willing to challenge the growing federal blockade. He suspected, too, that somewhere under her hard, mercenary exterior, she was a true rebel sympathizer. Most of the other gunrunners were profiteers and had already quit, scared off by the rumors that a smuggler's vessel had been intercepted and the crew murdered by the federal authorities.

Nerov had the guts to go, though, and the skill as a pilot to make it past the blockade. But sympathies or no, she still expected to get paid. And that meant two hundred kilos of platinum. By tomorrow night.

"Okay, Mr. Danforth. If I'm going to get your two hundred kilos by tomorrow, I'd better get started."

Danforth walked up and shook Haggerty's hand. "Again, Zach, you have my profound gratitude."

"I will contact you by midday tomorrow with a meeting place for delivery—only you, Mr. Danforth, as usual."

"I will come alone, Zach. Just let me know where and when."

"I'm sorry, Captain Nerov, but all ore deliveries are on hold pending a resolution of the disturbance at the mine." The port manager was calm and professional, but there wasn't a hint of sympathy for Nerov's situation.

"No," Nerov said, staring at the man behind the desk. "That won't do. I have a schedule to keep, a very important one. We cannot be delayed here." She was tense, anxious to get her ship ready to launch. Waiting around could only increase the risk.

And the rebels need those guns . . .

She hadn't admitted to herself how much she cared about the revolutionaries, clinging stubbornly to her belief that she was motivated by profit only. But deep down, even she realized that was bullshit. She couldn't help but respect men like John Danforth, born into privilege but willing to risk it all for a chance at freedom. As a smuggler, used to making her own rules, she didn't even try to kid herself that she could live the censored and regulation-choked existence of Federal America's citizens Earthside.

Especially not surrounded by petty bureaucrats like this asshole.

"I am sorry, Captain, but there is nothing I can do. We were already short on inventory before the disturbance, and I'm afraid the warehouse is empty. Even if the governor ordered it, we couldn't provide you with ore. Not until the mine resumes operation."

Sasha wanted to argue, to insist again that she couldn't wait. But she realized it was pointless . . . and as much as she didn't want to remain in port longer than necessary, drawing too much attention to herself would be worse.

Sasha knew her business. There wasn't a weapon left in *Vagabond*'s hold, not so much as a single bullet or cartridge. She'd wiped her ship's security logs, replacing the days of records with carefully prepared fakes, images that showed machine parts in her hold and not crate after crate of military-grade ordnance. But it was still unhealthy for a smuggler to hang around too long in port. *Vagabond* could pass as a freighter, but anyone taking a hard look at her ship's systems would see she was massively overpowered for a standard cargo hauler. And the weapons suite would be another warning sign—not outright illegal, but enough to draw scrutiny if anyone paid sufficient attention to notice. So while there was no proof of her smuggling activities, and even less that she'd been running guns, she was experienced enough to know proof wasn't really necessary, not in Federal America. Not if the suspicion was strong enough.

Think . . .

"I expect to receive a priority allocation as soon as the standoff at the mine is over," she said. "This delay is enormously costly, and my ship must be loaded and ready to launch as quickly as possible."

"I will do all I can to accommodate yours needs, Captain Nerov. I'm sure you are aware yours isn't the only freighter waiting for cargo." The noncommittal tone of the port manager was morphing into one of mild annoyance at her insistence.

Something about the way he said "freighter" set alarm bells ringing in her head.

Did he just pause when he said freighter? Is he suspicious?

Or was it just his way of pushing her back, of putting an end to her complaining with veiled threats of scrutiny no captain would want, not even a legitimate freight carrier? There wasn't the port manager ever made who couldn't find enough violations to ground any ship. Was that it? Or was it something else, more dangerous?

Whatever it was, she had to back off . . . and hope for the best.

"Thank you for your efforts," she said, trying to sound as pleasant as the anger and stress dueling inside her allowed. She turned and walked away, through the hallway of the port office and out into the midafternoon sun. She tried to put the concerns out of her mind, but she couldn't help but worry that she'd pushed things too hard. She prided herself on being rational and careful . . . but taking her frustration out on a bureaucrat who could drop a shitstorm on her with a few words to a superior didn't qualify as either.

She pulled the small comm unit from her pocket and glanced at the clock display. It was almost time to go meet Danforth and Jacen and collect her first payment for the voyage. She wasn't sure what to do. Should she take it now, even though she had no idea when she'd be able to leave? Or should she just return to Earth without any cargo?

No, that won't work. No legitimate freighter could pay the bills carrying loads one way.

She couldn't think of a better way of screaming "smuggler" than arriving in home port with no cargo.

She walked down the street, back to her lodging. She just had time to change her clothes and get to the rendezvous point. Although she wasn't sure if it even made sense to take the payment now, considering she couldn't leave. Not to mention if she did take the money, she didn't know where she'd hide it. Putting it on the ship, especially now, was out of the question. But she had no way to reach Danforth to postpone the meeting, not without raising even more suspicion. A freighter captain barging into Danforth's office would draw as much attention as arriving back on Earth with an empty hold.

She shook her head.

Dammit.

CHAPTER 6

"We still have no idea how the prisoners got the weapons, Governor, but we've managed to activate portions of the surveillance system, and we've confirmed they are indeed heavily armed." Thornton paused, her eyes fixed on the live feed from the mine displayed on her tablet. "This is going to be a lot messier than we thought. It's going to cost, sir, no matter what we do. But I don't see any alternative. It will take weeks to starve them out. Someone outside is obviously helping the prisoners, and that's an unknown that will cast a shadow over everything we do, wondering what will happen next. Especially if we wait."

"You sound like a woman who has a plan, Alexandra. So why don't you just let me know what it is?"

Apparently Thornton had awakened the governor. She felt a twinge of guilt. Wells probably hadn't slept more than a few hours in the past three days, and she'd managed to zero in on one of the few times he'd dozed off. It didn't occur to her that she hadn't slept at all during those three days herself, but that was her military training showing again. She was in battle—of a sort at least—and there would be time for sleep later. In the meanwhile her adrenaline—and the half dozen stims she'd popped over the last two days—would have to keep her going.

And then maybe we can all get some sleep.

But if that was going to happen, she'd have to end this riot. And as Wells had guessed, she thought she knew how to do it. "Yes, Governor. I request permission to storm the facility. I'd like to go in just before dawn. The prisoners will be the least alert and prepared then. In addition, we still have limited control over the internal systems, enough to cut off some of their power and lighting."

"How bad will it be?" She tended to doubt most politicians cared much about the butcher's bill, but Wells was different than most of his kind, and she believed his concern was sincere.

Unfortunately, she had no idea what to tell him. There was just too much she couldn't know, too many uncertainties hanging over the operation.

"I don't know, Governor," was her honest answer. The fact was, she'd spent a lot of her own time pondering this very subject, and that was the best she'd been able to come up with. "I'd expect at least a dozen casualties . . . and probably two or three times that." A pause. "Perhaps even more. Those mines aren't exactly the easiest target to attack, and our surveillance is incomplete at best."

"And the prisoners?"

"It will be bad, sir. If they surrender immediately, most of them will survive. If they fight . . ."

"Yes, Major? If they fight?"

"Then we could be looking at close to 100 percent casualties, Governor. I can't send my people in there with half-assed rules of engagement. If they go in, it's got to be with orders to target all armed militants . . . and shoot to kill."

After a moment of silence, Wells said, "Very well, Major. You are authorized to proceed at your own discretion." Wells didn't sound happy, but there was a firmness to his voice nevertheless. "Just make sure your people only shoot armed rioters. We have no idea if all the prisoners are involved or just a group."

"That may be difficult, Governor. My troops could end up in an intense firefight. Once they start taking losses—"

"When they start taking losses they will realize they are professional soldiers, and they will act as such. They are authorized to

defend themselves, to use deadly force against any and all armed
threats. But if they start blowing away unarmed personnel who are
not resisting, I promise you they will face charges. Understood?"

"Yes, sir. Understood." *Do you understand, though?* It was easy for
the governor to sit behind a desk and talk about a battle in a theoretical sense. But for a solder on the front line, dodging incoming fire
and watching friends die? It was easy to say spare unarmed personnel
before the shooting starts, a lot harder to enforce it, especially when
a "noncombatant" could pull a hidden weapon out at any time and
kill the soldier who'd held his fire.

Wells added, "I know this will be hard on your people, Alex, and
I'm counting on you to keep control of the situation. Just do your best
to take anyone who surrenders prisoner. We don't need to feed the
rebels' stories about soldiers shooting down miners with their hands
up." There was a short silence, then: "There is no one I trust more."

"Yes, Governor," she responded, surprised once again at Wells's
insight. Sure, the governor had never been a soldier, but he was the
kind of politician a warrior could honorably serve.

"Good luck, Alex. And take care of yourself." The genuine concern was obvious in his voice.

"I will, sir. Thornton out."

That went quick.

She'd expected to have a fight on her hands to convince him. But
the more she thought about it, the better she understood. There was
no other choice, not even for a man like the governor, who tried to
avoid violence whenever possible. This situation was dangerous, and
more so for the unanswered questions, specifically the one concern-
ing the unidentified source of support for the rioters. If her people
somehow allowed armed prisoners to slip by them, to escape, the
civilian toll could be disastrous.

No, they couldn't wait. And she knew Everett Wells realized it as
much as she did.

Jamie climbed down the ladder, focusing on each step and keeping his
grip as he grabbed one rung after another. He was exhausted, his eyes
heavy like lead as he fought to keep them open. He'd found enough

water, and even some food—though sitting out for three days did nothing to improve the already half-rancid prison rations. Still, they provided nutrients, and it was amazing what starvation could do to make anything seem like a delicacy. Even reconstituted beans.

Sleep was the real problem. For more than three days he had struggled to stay awake. He'd been mostly alone on the twentieth level, but he still didn't dare take the chance of shutting his eyes for a second. Yes, he'd been in the mine for a long time, and he had a reputation, one that had generally discouraged anyone from taking him on directly. And when a couple groups had come down to the level, mostly scavenging for food and water, he'd been able to face off against them and stand his ground, and they'd left him alone, no more than a few insults hurled his way. But he didn't doubt one of the rioters, worked up and on edge as they were now, would have slit his throat if he'd been asleep.

It was definitely starting to take a toll.

He'd stayed within a few meters of his assigned workspace, but now he was heading down, to the lowest levels of the mine. He had to find a place to get some rest, and he figured the bottom was the best bet. The twenty-second level was still being excavated, mostly by robot-controlled machines. There would be no food, water, hand tools—nothing that would draw any of the other prisoners down there. And that made it a good place to hide for a while. To sleep.

He could feel his arms shaking as he struggled to hold himself on the ladder. His legs felt like dead hunks of meat as he slowly lowered himself.

He looked down . . . just another few meters and he'd be at the bottom. He felt a wave of excitement, and he quickened his pace . . . too much. His foot slipped off the ladder, and he tightened the grip with his hands. But he was too exhausted. His grip held, for a second, and then he fell off the ladder, tumbling to the rough rock floor below.

He only dropped about two meters, but it was enough to send a blast of pain up his leg as he hit the ground. And then the air forced from his lungs as the rest of his body slammed into the rocky floor.

There was pain everywhere: his side, his arm, even his head. But he knew right away it was his leg that was truly hurt. He was covered with scrapes and bruises, but the pain in his leg was different.

He stayed where he was for a few minutes, hoping to catch his breath. Then he moved his leg.

He gasped for air.

Pain. Tearing through his body. He tried to hold back the shout but it came anyway. He let himself fall back, felt the worst of the pain gradually subside.

Okay, don't do that again.

He turned slowly, twisting as far as he could before he felt the agony coming on again. He was up on one arm, bent up at the waist. He looked down at his leg . . . and he understood the pain. There was a large bruise running from his ankle almost up to his thigh, already a dark purple, almost black. There was a cut, too, deep and throbbing with pain.

He turned, slowly this time. It still hurt, but he controlled it, stopping when he had to. He reached out, put his hand under the stricken leg. He knew this was going to be excruciating, but he had to move himself so he could try to work on the leg.

He took a deep breath and then he bit down hard, shoving his hip to the side, doing his best to hold up the injured leg as he did. The pain was the worst he'd experienced, almost unbearable, but he held on, forced himself to endure until he was sitting up.

He was covered in sweat, and he realized his face was soaked not just from perspiration but from tears. The pain lessened when he stopped moving, though. At least that was something. And now he had a perfect view of the leg.

It wasn't a pretty sight.

His eyes focused on the tear in the skin, the blood pouring out, oozing down his leg. He felt himself retch as he looked, and he clamped down, holding most of it back. He spit out a little foam, but he took a breath and calmed himself. He'd seen men die before, witnessed terrible injuries in the mine, men far more torn up than he was. He could handle this.

He took another deep breath, sucking in as much air as he could. It was stale, almost certainly oxygen-deficient. Production hadn't begun yet this far down, and even the marginal ventilation systems the prison-mine employed hadn't been installed yet.

One problem at a time.

He looked down at his leg, and he knew what he had to do. The first thing at least. And the thought made him sick to his stomach again.

He leaned forward, reaching down, gently touching the stricken limb. He couldn't be helpless, not now. And that meant he'd need to work up some sort of bandage to stop the bleeding, and a splint, something that would let him hobble around.

He tore off a section of cloth from his coverall, wrapping it around the gaping wound. Then the hard part—he pulled, hard, tight.

He screamed in agony, so consumed by pain he didn't even worry about calling attention to himself. He'd grown up in Boston's worst slum, gotten into fights in the street, and then spent twelve years amid the frequent violence of the mine. But this was the hardest thing he'd ever faced.

His gut heaved again, emptying completely this time, and he fell back, gasping desperately for breath. But somehow, he'd held on, endured the pain just long enough to stretch out the wounded leg and take stock of his injury. He looked down at the blood-covered limb, and he knew he'd never be able to stand, much less walk, unless he could support it with something.

He glanced up at the ladder, eyes focused, but there was nothing. No movement . . . and no sound either. He knew how loudly he had screamed, but now he dared to believe no one had been close enough to hear.

He took stock of his surroundings then, looking for something, anything, he could use to brace his leg. Pickings were slim, but eventually his eyes locked on a wood crate, half smashed open against the wall of the cavern. It was better than he'd hoped to find.

It was also at least ten meters away.

Fuck . . .

He sat for a few minutes, steeling himself for the effort.

Working himself up, he suddenly put his hands behind him and lifted his body, pulling himself back, toward the crate.

The pain was sharp, brutal . . . but it was tolerable. Barely. He paused, gasping in air, giving himself a moment to recover before he repeated what he had done.

Again. Effort, pain. Then rest. He turned his head, looking toward the wall. He'd guessed he had nine and a half meters to go. Two lunges had taken him perhaps a third of a meter. That meant maybe thirty more to go.

No, no use counting. Just keep going.

He sucked in a deep breath and lunged, wincing as the pain came again and he flopped back to the ground. It was going to take forever to get there.

Not like I have anything else to do . . .

"I shouldn't take that, Mr. Danforth. I'm sorry, but I'm going to have to delay my departure. And I wouldn't feel right accepting payment until I'm ready to go." Nerov stared at the open case, having trouble disguising her smuggler's greed. The box was small, and it contained an assortment of platinum items, some ten-kilo bars, as well as a pile of one-kilogram ones. There were even a few bags she suspected held ten-gram bits. It was clear Danforth hadn't had the easiest time assembling the needed quantity, and she felt a twinge of guilt that she had to foul up the works after he'd gone to so much effort.

"What do you mean you're not ready to go?" It was Jacen, not Danforth, who answered first, and his argumentative tone drove back her guilt and replaced it with anger. She didn't like Jacen, and if it hadn't been for Danforth, she'd have told the obnoxious bastard to go fuck himself a long time ago.

"I can't get my consignment of ore for the return trip, not until the standoff at the mine is over."

"Your *ore*? After what we're paying you, you want to wait here so you can add a transit fee for a few tons of ore to your take?"

"Don't talk to me like you can possibly understand what I do or the risks I take."

Jacen looked apoplectic, and it was all Nerov could do to maintain her calm for Danforth's sake if nothing else. The older man had been as reliable a contact as she could have hoped for, true to his word on every occasion she could recall. And she considered herself a professional. But if Jacen opened his mouth one more time she was liable to close it for good. Her hand moved, slowly, almost imperceptibly, toward the pistol tucked into the back of her belt.

As if he could read her mind, Danforth spoke up. "Cal, please. Captain Nerov has never let us down. Her willingness to brave the federal blockade puts her in a small group of people we can rely upon." He turned and looked over at Nerov. "And if I am not mistaken, it would be problematic for a smuggler posing as a freighter to return to port with no cargo. It would risk drawing unwanted attention, would it not?"

"Yes, Mr. Danforth, it would. Under normal circumstances, I might risk it, but with the present conditions, it is quite out of the question. Federal authorities are clearly on high alert . . . and my people face a death sentence if they are caught with weapons on board. I simply can't risk it. Not until I get my consignment."

Again Jacen opened his mouth as if he was going to respond, but Danforth held his hand up, silencing his companion once more. The foul-tempered lawyer had a scowl on his face, and he looked like he'd tasted something sour, but he kept his mouth shut.

"We understand, Captain," Danforth said. "So you are still willing to go when you get your ore?"

"Yes, Mr. Danforth. I committed to you, and I will follow through. Unless things change drastically."

"Then take the platinum, Captain. Frankly, it will be easier for you to hide it than for me. Besides, if we can't trust each other, this dangerous business of ours becomes downright suicidal, wouldn't you agree?"

She paused, wondering for an instant if there was some kind of veiled threat in Danforth's words, in his use of a word like *suicidal*. As paranoid as she'd become in the last few days, though, she decided he was just being straightforward. The magnate may be deep in revolutionary politics, but he'd always struck her as a reasonable and honest man. And they *had* worked together for a long time. He had made her a rich woman. And she had always delivered. But the thought still nagged.

Mistrust was a trait that kept a smuggler alive.

"Very well, Mr. Danforth. I find your confidence gratifying." The platinum was a burden now, at least until she managed to get the ship ready to launch. But Danforth had made a gesture, trusting her, and she didn't see how she could turn it down.

Besides, it was worth it just for the expression on Jacen's face. The rebel was a loudmouth, argumentative and inclined to talk over anyone else present. But he also clearly needed Danforth. The whole rebel movement needed Danforth. Whether they stared Federal America's government down and obtained the freedoms and guarantees they were demanding in the form of a revised constitution—or if the open rebellion everyone had been fearing for the past few years actually broke out—Danforth's money was critical.

Nerov stood for a moment, looking at the two men. She only made an effort to tolerate Jacen because of the older man. If it had been just the two of them, Nerov would have put a bullet in the bastard's head long ago. But she'd never understood why Danforth seemed to trust Jacen. They shared an agenda certainly, at least to a point. For while Danforth wanted to secure freedom for his home world, the liberty the people of Federal America on Earth had long ago lost, he was at least somewhat open to seeking that goal through negotiation. Only in failing that did he seem ready to support outright revolution. Overall, though, there was moderation in him, and she knew he considered the humanitarian cost of his goals.

Jacen was different—half cold fish, half incendiary bomb-thrower. She'd never discussed politics with him, but it was apparent he was far more radical than Danforth . . . and much less concerned with how many people died in the pursuit of his agenda. She knew rebellion would be a nightmare for Haven, but she shuddered to think of it with someone like Jacen in charge.

I hope Danforth keeps an eye on him. There isn't much I don't think he'd do to get his way . . .

She pushed the thoughts aside. Danforth was an intelligent man, and if he was okay with Jacen, then she wouldn't question his judgment. And as long as Jacen needed the media mogul, that should be enough to keep him under control.

"We'd better be going, gentlemen," she said. "Nothing good can come from increasing the risk of being found here." She moved toward the box of platinum, closing it slowly and pulling the small grav sled. The box and its contents weighed over two hundred kilos, but she had no trouble pulling it along behind her.

"Goodbye, Mr. Danforth," she said, nodding and offering her client a quick smile as she moved toward the door. "Mr. Jacen," she added, trying to keep her voice even, but suspecting some of her disdain leaked out.

"Stay safe, Captain Nerov," Danforth said, moving to slide the door open for her. "With any luck, the crisis at the mine will be over soon, and you will be able to get your ore."

"Let's hope." She paused for a few seconds, and then she walked out of the small farmhouse and into the night.

She was troubled, worries about Jacen still nagging at her. She trusted Danforth, as much as she trusted anyone, but she felt an urge to wait outside and simply end the radical revolutionary after Danforth left. She put the thought aside, but she couldn't shake the idea that she'd save everyone a lot of pain and trouble if she just killed the bastard now.

CHAPTER 7

"All units report ready, Major." Will Rennes stood next to Thornton, clad in light body armor. It was light, at least in comparison to the gear the two of them had worn in the war. Rennes was another veteran, a former corporal who had retired alongside Thornton and followed her into a new profession commanding colonial security forces.

"Very well, Captain. We move in exactly ten minutes."

Rennes nodded. "Yes, Major." He moved his hand, halfway to a salute, and then he paused. Thornton understood his confusion. You didn't salute on the battlefield. Never. It was a gift to snipers, an easy way for them to spot officers. Targets. But service on Alpha-2 was different, less intense, even with the unrest sweeping the planet. And saluting was standard practice. Nevertheless, this standoff felt a lot more like a real battlefield than anything she'd experienced on Alpha-2.

Rennes stood unmoving for a few seconds. "This reminds me of Beta-9."

Thornton turned back toward her exec. "Let's hope not, Captain. That was a hard day." Beta-9 was a moon surrounding a gas giant in the Algol system. Over a thousand federal soldiers had assaulted the colony there, seeking to liberate it from Eurasian control. The final battle was fought in a large refining and manufacturing facility.

She had to admit, however, that Rennes was right. The mine, at least the aboveground portion, resembled the Beta-9 complex. She hoped the similarities ended there, because there had been four hundred Eurasian commandoes dug into the Beta-9 complex, and the assault forces saw half their number killed or wounded before the battle was done.

Her people now weren't a match for the soldiers who fought on Beta-9, but she was also sure they would get the job done. She was equally certain they would suffer heavy losses, and she wondered how that would affect the survivors. Would it harden them, begin to turn them into veterans—"real" soldiers? Or would it unnerve them, fatally demoralize them just as the planet was sliding closer to open rebellion?

Because, while the prisoners were untrained, poorly organized, they were also well-armed . . . and defending. A *lot of my people are going to die, and if it breaks the survivors' spirits, then a lot more people could die as well.* She made a note to herself—a promise, really— that she would take vengeance for every man and woman she lost in the operation when she found whomever had supplied the miners with weapons. She was a creature of duty, but that day she would set her hat and her major's clusters aside. It would be personal.

The present had her attention now, though, and it was hard not to be a little worried about how her troopers would react to real combat conditions. Thornton had acquired as many military veterans as she'd been able to manage, but it still wasn't a lot, maybe a dozen total. Most of her troopers were recruits from Earth, half police and half soldiers. They were more accustomed to situations where they outmanned and outgunned their opposition, but this assault felt a little too much like real war to her. And she knew just what war was like.

Her eyes dropped to the small tablet in her hand, checking the position of each assault group. They were back from the perimeter fence, and that meant another hundred meters to travel once they stepped off. But it also provided some cover, keeping the prisoners in the dark about exactly what they faced. When she gave the word, her people would advance from all sides . . . and they would go in and finish things.

She looked at the upper corner of the tablet, to the countdown clock.

Six minutes, thirty seconds.

Twenty-nine.

Twenty-eight . . .

"Wake the fuck up. What do you think this is, a vacation?" Gavros kicked Lopez hard in the ribs. The stricken prisoner howled, and he jumped up, looking like he was ready for a fight. Until he saw it was Gavros.

"Oh, uh, sorry, Ron," he stammered. "I'm just fucking tired, man. We're surrounded—there's no way we're gettin' out of here, is there?" The arrogance Lopez had shown Jamie was long gone. "Maybe we should see if we can negotiate somethin'. 'Cause otherwise—"

"Shut your mouth, Lopez, or I'll shut it for you. We ain't surrendering, you got that? We're armed as well as those jackboots out there, or close to it. If they're so ready to come in here, where the hell are they?"

"They don't have to come. They can just starve us out. We're almost out of food already."

Gavros glared at his shaken companion. "Get that shit out of your head, now." His voice dripped with menace. "If they come, we'll send them runnin' back with their tails between their legs. And then we'll bust outta here while they're still on the run, get to the woods and disappear."

Lopez swallowed hard. He could see now. Gavros had lost it. He was insane, believing his own foolishness. He cursed himself for being blind earlier, for getting himself into this mess.

The thing was, he'd bought into the excitement when the uprising started. He didn't know what had set things off, or how weapons had gotten into the mine, but now he was realizing it was all a trap. There was no way they were getting out of here. And if they scragged a bunch of guards and colonial troopers in the fight, they were finished. That wasn't an extra year tacked onto a sentence; it wasn't an increase in workload or decrease in rations. It was a death sentence. Assuming the soldiers didn't just shoot them all down while they were retaking the facility.

He had to admit: he was scared.

He wanted to drop his gun, run out with his hands up, and beg for his life. But he knew Gavros would kill him if he took a step toward the exit. And it wasn't just Gavros. All the ringleaders were watching.

He took a deep breath, trying to keep his nerves in check. He wished he'd listened to Jamie Grant. Grant wasn't a bad guy, and he was smart.

Smart enough to stay out of this kind of trouble.

"You hear me, Lopez? Stay the fuck awake, and keep your eyes open. They could make a move at any—"

Suddenly, the lights flickered and went out, and the cavern went completely dark. A few seconds later, the battery-powered units came on. There weren't many of them, and the mine was a grim dusk at best. But it wasn't the light that bothered Lopez. It was what it meant.

The soldiers were coming.

He was wide awake now.

The transport zipped through the streets of Landfall, moving through an industrial area filled with warehouses and small factories. It was well out of the way to get to the federal building, but Wells had told his driver to avoid any problems. Protests were common on Alpha-2, and especially in Landfall. But things had gotten worse over the past couple months, and even more so since the standoff at the mine had begun. Now there were protests that ran around the clock, with colonists camping out on the streets, which meant his driver was taking a circuitous route to steer clear of them.

And even then, there's no guarantees. They're not going to get any better. Not when word spreads that I just ordered a thousand troops to storm the mine. Not when images start leaking showing the bodies . . .

Still, Wells was surprised at the crowds, especially since it was just after dawn. God knows he was exhausted. At least he had an excuse, though: there was no chance of getting back to sleep after he'd given Thornton the go-ahead to attack. He'd figured he might as well get some work done while he waited for news. He had sat in his study for perhaps an hour before he decided he'd be better off in his office, where he could deal with the fallout as it hit.

"Governor, there are crowds all around the federal building. It looks bad. Should we turn around and go back to the house?"

Wells sighed softly. He'd never been in the military, but he wasn't a coward. He had his job, too, and running from mobs in the street wasn't going to get it done.

"No, Sam. I'm not about to let a bunch of protestors dictate where I do or don't go. Just try to bring us in from whatever direction is easiest."

"Yes, sir."

For all his bravado, Wells's stomach was unsettled, the acid backing up his throat, burning like fire. He'd tried to eat some breakfast, just a little dry toast and coffee, but he couldn't get any of it down. This situation was getting more and more out of hand, and he had no idea what he could do to stop the disaster he saw coming.

For some reason, Jamie Grant popped into his mind. He'd agreed to try and save Grant because he wanted Damian Ward's help in trying to maintain the calm. But in truth, though Grant had been a pain in the ass more than once during his term in the mines, Wells felt the kid had paid enough for what he had done. If he'd managed to keep his calm and not act out as much as he had, he'd have been out two years already.

That's easy to say, a bureaucrat's answer. But what would you do if you found yourself ripped from everything—everyone—you knew for life, sentenced to years of backbreaking labor for a minor crime?

Then a worse thought hit him, and he forgot all about Jamie.

How would you feel if it was Violetta?

He'd acted as if he'd done Damian a favor, but in truth he felt good about giving the Grant kid a chance.

I just hope he isn't involved in any of this . . .

He looked out the window of the transport. They were close now, and he could see the streets lined with protestors. They seemed peaceful at least, though reports suggested that wasn't the case everywhere. He just hoped there was no real violence, not while most of the security forces were deployed to the mine raid. The streets were being patrolled by a skeleton crew, and that meant the remaining troopers could be feeling alone and outnumbered . . . and maybe be a lot quicker to employ deadly force.

And that could push this whole thing over the edge.

Wells knew he had every cause to curse Alpha-2 and its rebels. He'd been a rising star in Federal America's government, one who had managed to advance without getting too closely aligned to any of the cliques or subparties that feuded with each other so often. He'd managed to maintain at least marginal respect from all sides, a testament to his idealism, if a passing one. He'd taken the post as Alpha-2's governor because it was a sizable promotion, and because it seemed like a logical step on his advancement toward senator. But he'd since presided over an almost constantly worsening situation, one he knew he'd inherited and not caused. But his rivals back home had made good use of it to discredit him, and now he was blamed in many quarters for being too soft on the rebels.

There had been whispers at first, nothing more. But now he knew they were shouting it from the rooftops.

Wells is too soft!

Wells is a rebel sympathizer!

Wells has failed!

It was depressing, all the more because he had pushed his own morals aside, sent his soldiers to break up rallies, and imposed prison sentences on subversives. He'd even increased his surveillance activities, almost to the point that citizens on Alpha-2 were as spied on as those on Earth. He'd had to fight back against his self-hatred as he struggled to forestall the tide of rebellion. But for all his efforts, he was still hated by the colonists . . . and he was despised as a weakling by politicians on Earth, some of whom were anxious to make an example of Alpha-2, to see the streets run red with blood.

"Governor . . ."

He shook himself out of his self-pity and looked into the forward cab of the transport. "Yes, Sam. What is it?"

"Major Thornton sent a signal, sir. She is leading her forces in now."

Wells felt another twinge in his stomach. He'd almost forbidden Thornton from leading the attack in person. She hadn't mentioned anything about that, but he knew her well enough to suspect. He also knew people had to do what they had to do. A man or woman had to be able to look in the mirror without despair. Which is why he had held back his order.

"Very well . . . take us in the rear garage. It's closest, and you should be able to get past the crowds."

"Yes, sir."

Wells stared out the window of the transport at the crowds.

What will you do if the mine becomes a bloodbath?

He took a deep breath and closed his eyes for a second. He'd be in his office in five minutes.

Worry about the raid now, about your people in danger. There will be plenty of time to deal with the fallout after it's done.

And there will certainly be fallout.

"We managed to knock out the reactor, Major. All power to the mine is cut."

Thornton smiled as she listened to the report. The prisoners had cut some of the communications lines, and they'd trashed a lot of the computer systems. But they hadn't been thorough enough, and her people had managed to gain control of the remnants of the AI system. And now they'd been able to cut off the power.

"Well done, Lieutenant." She flipped the switch on her comm to Rennes's channel. "All right, Will, time to go. We can't be sure the reactor's restart routines have been bypassed. They could get power back anytime."

"We're ready, Major." A pause. "Major, I really wish you would stay—"

"We've discussed that already, Captain. I'm going in with the assault teams, and that's the last we're going to talk about it."

"Yes, Major."

Thornton knew her exec was right, of course. She had absolutely no business exposing herself to this kind of danger, not when she was in command of the security forces planetwide. But she knew her half-soldiers were going to have a hard time of it, and she felt she had to be there. She just had to.

She flipped the comm unit's controls again, this time to the main frequency. "All assault teams . . . advance."

She was behind a large tree, a hidden spot with a good vantage point of the facility. She swung around, out into the open grassland. The perimeter fence was about two hundred meters ahead, not far, but enough ground to cover if someone was shooting at you. Which they weren't, at least not yet.

She knew the prisoners had pickets on the surface. Her satellite intel had given her a pretty good idea of their positions. There weren't many of them.

Not enough actually. I'm glad they don't have anybody there who knows infantry tactics.

Still, it would only take one to spot her people coming.

She was moving quickly, but not running. Her body was hunched forward, presenting as low a profile as possible in the predawn darkness. It was all second nature to her now, combat reflexes. But she could see that at least half her troops were lumbering straight ahead, despite the fact that they'd been ordered three times to get down. Were they trying to present the easiest target possible?

She reached up over her head, pulled down her infrared goggles. The rebels had guns, but she doubted they had the rest of the gear her people did. It was a gamble, of course, but one she'd take even if they did—it's one thing to have equipment, another to know how to use it. Her people at least had put in the time with the infrared, and that meant the last hour of night was a huge tactical advantage for her forces . . . as the darkness in the mine would be.

If they don't get the reactor back online . . .

She shook her head slightly even as she moved steadily toward the fence. The prisoners still hadn't even noticed her people.

If those were Eurasian snipers over there, I'd have twenty dead by now, she thought as memories from the war flooded back to her.

She reached the fence, and she turned her head, looking back at the squad of troopers right behind her. She gestured toward the heavy chain-link barrier, and two men with heavy clippers moved up and started cutting through. It was slow and low tech, but a plasma torch would be visible for hundreds of meters. Since her people still had stealth on their side, they could afford the slight delay.

It didn't make it any easier on her, though. She leaned down, checking her assault rifle, as much by habit as any real need. She knew it had only been a few seconds, but she chafed at the time that was passing. She was a veteran, but it had been four years since she'd been in battle, and that made her agitated. No one ever really got used to combat. She'd been scared every time . . . and the men and women she'd served with had been, too. The fearless warrior was insane. Or a myth.

Finally, one of the soldiers ripped away a chunk of the heavy fencing, leaving a hole big enough for a single man or woman to get through. She waved her arms, gesturing for the troopers to step aside. She was going first.

She leaned forward, slipping through the opening as carefully as she could in her body armor. She tossed her rifle ahead of her, and put her hands down, pulling one leg at a time through. Then she saw a flash.

The sound followed almost immediately. A gunshot. Then another. Screaming, more gunfire. The fire wasn't coming her way, not yet.

But one thing was certain: the prisoners definitely knew her people were coming.

CHAPTER 8

Private Kendrick Johnson was mad, as thoroughly, insanely pissed as he had ever been. And his rage had a single focus.

The prisoners.

He'd been scared when his unit first stepped off to storm the facility, and that had ramped up to sheer terror when the prisoners on the surface started firing. He'd have sworn he felt a bullet whiz past his face, and he'd barely kept control of his bladder. But then he just followed the training, as most of his comrades did. And it worked. Maybe thirty seconds later, every prisoner on the surface was down, most of them hit with multiple shots. Only one of the soldiers was shot, and it was just a hit to the leg. Johnson's confidence had soared, driving back the fear.

Until he got into the mine itself. Into hell.

The fighting there had been brutal, deadly. He and his comrades had fought for every centimeter. And they had paid. In blood.

The prisoners had suffered heavy losses, too, far heavier, in fact, than the soldiers. But Johnson didn't care. Not now. He'd gone in calling out for the prisoners to surrender before he fired. But that was twenty minutes—and half a dozen dead friends—ago. Now he was just gunning them down, including two or three who'd thrown down their weapons and put their hands in the air before he'd blown them away.

It amazed him how quickly his fear had turned into all-consuming rage.

"Hey, Billings, what the hell level is this?" He snapped off the question into his comm, but Billings was only a few meters away, and he shouted back his answer. "Eighteen, Kenny. They say there are only twenty-two, so we've got to be close to done here. These guys are all running now; it's just a question of cleaning up, and then we'll be headed back to barracks."

Johnson glanced over at Billings. "Hey, man, don't be worried about barracks yet—stay focused on these bastards until they're all scragged." The two had been friends a long time, ever since they'd entered training together. Billings had always been the less serious of the two, and Johnson didn't want his friend to get careless.

"Yeah, yeah, old lady. Don't worry about me. Worry about the fuckers who run this mine, 'cause by the time we're done they ain't gonna have nobody left to work the place."

Johnson was about to reply when the comm crackled again. "Fourth Platoon, advance to level nineteen." It was Rennes. Johnson was struck by the steadiness of the captain's voice.

How can he sound so calm in the middle of all this?

"Acknowledged, sir," Sergeant Ridge said.

"And, Sergeant—and listen to this, Fourth Platoon, all of you— you are only to engage those who move against you or present a credible threat of attack. All surrenders are to be accepted. Understood?"

"Yes, sir," Ridge replied with what sounded to Johnson like a minimum of sincerity. Some of the noncoms and officers were trying to restrain their troops, but Johnson had watched Ridge put a bullet in the forehead of a kid who couldn't have been more than eighteen . . . and didn't have a weapon in sight.

Johnson liked Captain Rennes, and he knew the officer had served in the war with Major Thornton. He respected Rennes, and he thought the captain was fair, not a bad sort at all for an officer.

But Will Rennes can go fuck himself about these prisoners. They're all scum, and they're all going down.

He popped the spent cartridge out of his rifle and slammed another one in place. Then he turned toward Billings and nodded. "Let's go, Clyde. Let's finish off these bastards. We're almost done. Just a few more to kill." The hatred was practically coming off him in waves.

He turned back and moved toward the ladder leading down to the next level.

Just three more to go.

Thornton swung around, holding her pistol out in front of her. She'd wandered out too far, away from her escort. She knew she shouldn't be here alone, but despite the rank her positon on Alpha-2 carried with it, at heart she was still a foot soldier.

She was alert, her mind sharp, focused, as it had always been in battle. Her fears about the assault had been realized. Her people had suffered more than three dozen casualties, and for a few minutes, the fight had been as intense as any she could remember from the war. Her forces had been compelled to claw their way through a narrow approach, into a hail of concentrated enemy fire. And the guns the prisoners were firing were every bit as effective as those her people carried. They were familiar to her, state-of-the-art Eurasian assault rifles, just like the ones she'd encountered during the war.

Not for the first time, she thought. *If I ever find out who supplied these prisoners with weapons . . .*

She felt her tension recede just a bit. The hallway was empty. Her people had mostly cleared the level. Indeed, despite her initial urges, she'd mostly stayed back from the front edge of battle, humoring her subordinates . . . at least somewhat.

The last time Thornton had been in a fight like this, she'd worn a sergeant's stripes, and her place *was* on the battle line. In front of the line. She had led a force recon team, a dozen specialists whose place had been as often as not behind the enemy lines. Her reflexes pushed her to advance, to get right in the middle of the fight, but she knew her responsibilities were different now. She would only be one gun in the battle, but if she went down, the disorganization could kill dozens of her people.

Still, she needed to be *here*, because trying to command this clus-terfuck from outside the mine would have been a worse nightmare.

But her forces were slowly taking control of the mine, and she was sure her meticulous direction had aided her people—or at least cut down on the losses.

She moved slowly down the roughly bored tunnel, her eyes flit-ting back and forth. Her forces had swept through the level, but there hadn't been time for an intensive search, not while the fight was still raging down below. She'd moved reserve forces in behind the assault units, and they were sweeping the area now. They had already made one pass, but she was cautious anyway. She knew how carelessness got soldiers killed; she'd seen it herself many times. The prisoners might be on the verge of defeat, but all it would take was one desper-ate, hidden refugee to put her down.

"Major, I've got a platoon pushing down to the last three lev-els." Rennes's voice was loud in her earpiece. "Estimate the facility should be secure within twenty minutes."

"Very well, Captain. Proceed." She almost told him to remind his troops to be careful. The last wounded enemy hiding in a dark corner could shoot a soldier dead. But she knew Will Rennes well enough to understand he didn't need the reminder.

If anything, he'd be giving it to me.

She'd almost asked him for an update on the casualty count, too, but she decided she didn't want to know.

There would be time for that later.

And there would be casualties—and not simply the dead. The many soldiers in her command who had never experienced a battle would be forever changed by what they had gone through over the past two hours. A few would be destroyed by it, broken by the terror, by the unimaginable pressure of a protracted firefight. But most of them would be better for it. They were blooded now, and the next time they faced a fight they would be far more effective in battle.

But that wasn't necessarily a good thing—there was a downside, too. The men and women would be harder, more intractable. Most of them had allowed themselves to hate their adversaries trying to kill them, just as she had hated the Eurasians. And now that they had learned to hate an enemy, would they turn that upon the rebels? The protestors in the street?

There had already been anger among her people, at the speeches that denounced them all as mindless government thugs. Most of her soldiers were from Earth, where speakers saying anything of the sort would be hauled away in minutes.

And likely sent someplace just like these mines. At least if they were repeat offenders.

The changes wouldn't be overt. But there would be more resentment and less patience for the protestors, and even the rest of the citizenry. It was mathematical. Not every encounter would be noticeably different, but overall more of them would end badly. Arrests would increase, incidents of at least some level of brutality. It would all feed the relentless cycle of civil disobedience provoking an enforcement response. Leading to more disobedience . . . and more enforcement—with the emphasis on "force."

And that will lead to open rebellion. War. Exactly what Governor Wells has been trying to avoid.

She looked down the hallway and sighed. There were four bodies, all prisoners. She had hoped the rebels would lose heart when her people stormed the mine, but many of them had fought with a desperation that had surprised her.

And too many of the ones that didn't were gunned down by my people . . .

The standoff was almost over, and that meant the fallout had hardly begun. The rebel leaders would do all they could to use this tragedy and turn it into a rallying cry. Never mind these men were prisoners. Never mind that they had illegal weapons, and had taken hostages. Shut down production and hurt Alpha-2's economy. None of that would matter to the rebels. What mattered was convincing just one more person, one more group, that the federals were evil and freedom was the only answer. And if they were successful, Alpha-2 would learn what war truly was. Slogans were easy. Marches and protests, too. But burned buildings, dead fighters—and civilians—that was something else entirely. Something few thought seriously about before they grabbed their flags and signs and poured into the streets, before they clamored for violence as a solution.

She shook her head sadly. She was surrounded by death, deep in a hellscape filled with darkness and blood, and yet all she could think was, *I'm glad I'm not Governor Wells now . . .*

"Fuck," Johnson roared, staring down at his side. There was a chunk taken out of his body armor, and a trickle of blood dripping down. The wound was nothing. He was so amped up, it didn't even hurt all that much. But if he hadn't had his armor, the rebel might have finished him for good.

He pulled his finger tight, firing again on full auto. He'd taken the bastard down already; the shot that hit him had been the prisoner's last. But riddling the body with bullets was somehow pleasing, as if he could hurt the offending rebel more by mutilating his body.

Johnson was wired, running on adrenaline and stims, and he felt the drive to finish things, an urgency to find the last of the rebels, and kill them all before Rennes or some other officer came along and made him take prisoners.

He wasn't a bad-natured guy, not usually, though he was sick and tired of the abuse he and his comrades took every day. He knew it wasn't all the people of Alpha-2; indeed, he had seen the reports showing that nearly half the colony's population was solidly loyal to Federal America . . . and that the true radicals were actually a minority. But it didn't feel that way walking down the street on patrol, almost *feeling* the hatred of the crowds. And now he'd seen prisoners—criminals—killing men and women who had been his friends. And with each one that fell, his moderation receded, and the anger grew.

"You all right there, Kenny?" It was Sergeant Ridge. Johnson's squad leader had his own injury, a cut to the forearm he'd gotten half an hour before when a prisoner caught him from behind. He'd tied a filthy strip of cloth torn from a uniform around it, but the blood had soaked through anyway, and now it had partially dried and caked all

around the makeshift bandage, making the wound look more grue-
some than it was.

Johnson held back a little smile. The rebel who had inflicted that
wound was dead, too.

"I'm fine, Sarge. The armor caught most of it."

"These bastards put up one hell of a fight." Ridge looked around,
and he put his hand over his comm unit's microphone and lowered
his voice. "I want to clean out these bottom levels fast, Kenny." He
had a scowl on his face. "The major and the captain have a lot of
shit on them from the top to take prisoners, but you and I know what
needs to happen down here."

Johnson stared back. "Yes, sir, I believe we do."

"I hear we've got forty casualties, and half of them are dead.
These fuckers don't get to kill twenty of our people and walk away,
you understand me?"

"Yes, Sergeant. You bet I do."

Ridge looked over his shoulder again, then back to Johnson. "I
knew you would, Kenny. I'm just afraid what will happen if we don't
handle this. The governor's too damned soft on these people. These
fuckers should all be looking at summary execution anyway, but if
the governor decides to make a gesture, show leniency . . . fuck that.
I'm not going to be down here only to find out our people are dead
and these bastards get off with longer sentences and heavier work-
loads."

Johnson's expression hardened. "No way, Sarge. We won't let that
happen. No way."

"All right, Private Johnson. Then let's finish this, shall we?"

"Absolutely, Sarge." Johnson gripped his rifle tightly. "Absolutely."

Jamie sat on the ground, hunched over, doing his best to stay out of
sight. He could hear the sounds of battle above. It had been loud for
a while, a full-blown firefight, he suspected, but now the shots were
fewer, more occasional.

He could feel his heart racing, the beats pounding in his ears.

He'd been hiding for days, nothing but fear to ward off the intense boredom. He'd managed to scrounge up enough water, and perhaps half enough food, but the waiting had been interminable. He'd even gotten his leg braced and patched up enough to let him hobble around. He felt like he'd been down there for months, but now, as he listened to those bursts of gunfire, all he wanted was more time to wait.

He climbed slowly to his feet. He was tired, sore, and his leg hurt like fire . . . but he managed to stand with the help of a length of wood he'd turned into a makeshift cane. He had to surrender; that is, if anybody gave him a chance. Not that it would matter—if soldiers had been killed, the rioting miners would most likely face execution anyway. Rioting was one thing, but even Governor Wells would have to condemn men and women who had killed his soldiers. But he'd rather take that chance than be butchered in this godforsaken mine.

He took a few steps toward the ladder, slow, gritting his teeth against the pain. Going up didn't seem possible. He couldn't put any weight on the stricken leg, and he was far too exhausted to pull himself up with his arms. But if he stood right in front of the ladder—or, better yet, sat down there with his hands behind his head—he had the best chance. It was no guarantee, but it was all he could think to do.

Then he froze. There was a sound, coming down the ladder. It was loud, someone hurrying, heavy boots slamming into the metal rungs. He knelt down and clasped his hands behind his head. "I am not a rioter," he said loudly, clearly. "I surrender. I have been down here for three days. I have not taken part in the fighting." He stared at the ground, drawing shallow breaths and trying to control the fear and pain, to stop the shaking that threatened to take his body.

"You really are a turncoat piece of shit, Grant." The voice was angry, caustic. And it was familiar.

Gavros.

Jamie's head snapped up, but too late. All he saw was a shadow, and then the boot took him in the side of his head and sent him falling onto his back.

He landed hard, and he felt the wind knocked out of his lungs.

The pain in his leg as it slammed to the ground hit him like a blinding light. His mind was racing, disoriented, struggling to gain control of his body, to react to the situation. Unlike last time, Gavros had a huge edge over him. And the man had to be desperate now.

Jamie was in a fight to the death, and he was halfway to losing it.

That made him desperate, too, though. His reflexes kicked in; he spun to the side, rolling painfully across the hard stone floor, barely avoiding Gavros's boot as it stomped hard right next to his head.

He sucked in a deep breath and put all his strength into one strong lunge at his adversary's feet, but just as he did, Gavros's fist slammed into his back. He could feel the impact, and he'd have sworn he heard one of his ribs cracking just before he fell forward and his face hit the ground.

He could feel the blood filling his mouth, and he spat hard, even as he stumbled around, trying to turn over onto his back, to face his enemy. He reached out, trying to grab Gavros's leg again, but his vision was blurry and the big man jumped back, evading the blow.

He tried to pull back himself then, to get away from Gavros's immediate reach. As he did, the hazy image of the prisoner cleared up a little. Gavros was coming after him again, and Jamie realized he didn't see a gun in his hand.

Must have burned through all his ammo. The only reason I'm still alive. But that gives me a chance . . .

My ass, it does. He doesn't need a gun to finish me off.

Out of options, he reached behind him, grasped the makeshift cane, and swung it around with everything he had left behind it. Gavros saw it, but he was coming in too fast, and it was too late to avoid the blow entirely. He spun around, just as the cane took him in the back of the legs.

Gavros let out a yell as he stumbled forward, reeling from the hit. But Jamie howled as well, and clutched his leg as his momentum pushed him around, twisting the savaged limb.

Jamie fought against the pain, tried to stay focused, but Gavros recovered much quicker. The other prisoner pulled a knife he'd had shoved into his belt behind his back. His eyes were locked on Jamie's as he moved slowly forward.

"Time to go to hell, Grant . . . with all the other traitors." He took another step, but Jamie wasn't about to let him pick his moment. Digging into the last of his strength, he lunged forward, reaching up and grabbing the arm with the knife with both hands. He pushed hard, trying to dislodge the weapon, but the pain was just too much, and he could feel his strength draining away. He couldn't exert enough power to force the blade from Gavros's hand.

Then he felt the impact—Gavros's other hand slamming into his kidneys.

The breath blasted out of his lungs, and he dropped to his back, staring up helplessly.

Gavros kicked him hard, the man's boot taking Jamie right in the side of his abdomen. He struggled for a few seconds, tried to marshal the strength to sit up, but it was no use. He lay where he was, staring up as the enraged prisoner moved toward him, knife in hand.

Jamie screamed at himself within, a last cry to marshal his strength, to try and pull himself together, to resist one more time. But it was over. There was too much pain, too much fatigue. He was looking at his death standing over him. His strength was gone, even his fear. There was only one feeling left in his destroyed body: sadness.

I'm sorry, Katia . . . I tried.

CHAPTER 9

"Now, Jonas . . . just lie back. Relax, stop fighting the drug and the pain will stop." Reid was standing along the wall, about a meter from where Holcomb lay on the hospital cot, restraints fastened across his arms, chest, and legs. "Resisting only makes it hurt more . . . and if you fight for too long you can cause some rather nasty side effects, most of which, I'm afraid, are permanent."

Holcomb was still, his body almost frozen, but in his head he was fighting the greatest battle of his life. He could feel the drug working on him, draining away his inhibitions. The thoughts were there, speaking to him. *Go back to your life. Give up this foolish fight.*

No! his thoughts roared back to . . . himself, he realized. Reid was there, he knew, standing nearby, speaking. But the words that truly pounded at his resolve weren't those of his jailor. No, they were his own. His weakness. His wish to leave this terrible place. To sleep in his bed again, walk the Virginia Beach coast as he had so many times . . . the cool sea breeze, the warm sun on his skin . . .

This is all my doing. I don't need to be here. I can go home anytime I want. Federal America is merciful. They will give me my life back, even after all this. All I have to do is return to my work, to do my fair share in return for all I have received.

He moaned loudly, his response to himself coming out as a muffled cry. "No . . . no . . . never again . . ."

"Listen to yourself, Jonas." Reid spoke softly, sounding almost compassionate, even vaguely hypnotic. "You are listening to nothing except your own thoughts, your deepest desires. Heed what they say to you. This can all end, Jonas. Now. We don't want to hurt you. We just want you back. You are one of us. Come home . . ."

Yes . . . just agree. Say you will go back, that you will use the education the government gave you for the national good. Your weapons protect the people, they provide national security.

"No," he said, his voice a soft, ragged whisper. "The weapons were misused, turned on the people . . ."

He could feel the drug, twisting his thoughts. He struggled, tried to hang on to his true beliefs . . . but somehow he knew what Reid had said was the truth. The thoughts *were* all his. He didn't want to make more weapons, see them ill-used. But he wanted to go home. He wanted to go home so badly . . .

He twisted and pulled against the restraints, babbling incoherently, arguing with himself. His face, his entire body, was covered with sweat. He could taste something metallic. Blood, he realized. He'd bitten his lip.

Home, he thought again. Sleeping in a soft bed, breakfast on the terrace overlooking the ocean. He'd lived a privileged existence. Was he really right to resist Federal America, his country that had given him all he'd ever had? How ungrateful was he?

He felt himself weakening as Reid's words drifted into his mind. "Come back to us, Jonas. Take your life back. You will be forgiven your mental breakdown. You will be welcome back to the life you led before . . ."

He wanted to scream out, "Yes," to embrace what he was offered. His resistance was weakening. If he refused he knew he would go back to his cell, to the cold that cut through him every night, making sleep almost impossible. To the Pit . . .

But there was strength still, somewhere deep within, and he felt it pouring out, taking charge.

"No," he said, his voice firmer. "Never." He could feel his hands balling up into fists. "No," he repeated, louder. "No!"

He could see Reid standing against the wall, hear his tormentor's sigh. "Take him back to his cell," the federal said, the frustration clear in his tone. Then, softer: "I'll have to give him a higher dose . . . but I need approval before I risk it. Besides, he needs to rest first. If we administered it now, it would kill him."

Holcomb listened to it all, but the meaning was hazy, unclear. There was just one part he heard. *"Take him back to his cell."*

He took a deep breath, and a weak smile slipped onto his face. *Take him back to his cell.*

He had not given in. They had not broken him. Yet.

Gavros stood looking down at Jamie, a jagged smile on his lips. He held the knife tightly in his hand as he moved forward. "Time to die, traitor."

Suddenly, Gavros's head spun around, his body following an instant later, shifting to the side of the ladder. Jamie watched, groggy, struggling to maintain consciousness. He was confused at first, but then he heard. And understood.

Someone else was coming down the ladder.

Gavros slid around, ducking off to the side as a pair of legs dropped into view. Jamie could see the brown uniform pants. He wasn't sure what was happening, but right then he'd have taken anything.

He could also see Gavros lying in wait, though, and his hope once more warred with uncertainty. He wanted to shout out a warning, to alert the soldier. But he hated the federals as much as any prisoner who had joined the rebellion. If he stayed quiet, though, Gavros would kill the man . . . and then turn that knife back on him. And if he saved one of the soldiers, he had a much better chance of successfully surrendering.

And yet . . .

The idea of aiding the soldiers, of betraying a prisoner to them, even a psychopath like Gavros, made him sick. Gavros was his enemy, but the fight between the two of them was their own, and they were more the same than different, both opponents of the federals. The soldiers were his true enemy, the armed henchmen of those who had stolen his life.

For an instant, perhaps half a second, he paused, wondering if he wouldn't prefer death to truly earning the turncoat title the others had given him. Then he decided he wanted to live, whatever it took.

It might have been half a second, but that turned out to be too long.

Gavros lunged at the soldier, grabbing the man's legs and pulling him from the ladder. The trooper fell hard to the ground, landing with a dull thud.

Jamie lay on the ground with his mouth open, but no words came. He could hear sounds from the upper level, the soldier's comrades, no doubt. They were shouting down, calling to the trooper. A second later there was another sound, more feet on the metal rungs.

Gavros lunged after the fallen soldier, pulling him up and grabbing his hair, yanking his head back and moving his blade to the man's throat.

The soldier coming down the ladder dropped to the ground, spinning around, assault rifle in hand. He froze when he saw his comrade's position.

"Drop the knife," the federal said.

"Back up," Gavros spat back. "Drop the gun and move against the wall, or I'll slit his throat." He saw another set of boots climbing down, and he shouted, "Get back up there. I've got your man down here, and I'll kill him."

The captive soldier stared back, clearly terrified. His comrade looked at him, their eyes connecting. The other soldier looked up and yelled, "Hauser, do what he says. He's got Johnson with a knife to his throat." He took a step back, but he held on to his gun, holding it still, being careful not to make any threatening gestures.

Jamie was watching, holding still himself, barely breathing. Gavros's last-ditch ploy was only going to make the soldiers angrier. And if he killed the trooper, there was no question the others would unload. They would shoot Gavros, and most likely Jamie, too. And anyone else still hiding in the bowels of the mine. Unless . . .

He turned his head, slowly, almost imperceptibly. He needed a weapon, something.

There was nothing.

Damn.

He'd have to attack with his bare hands. It was a crazy risk, he was sure of that. If Gavros heard him he would almost certainly cut the soldier's throat . . . and the other one would open fire, killing them both. *But what other choice do I have? Besides, I'm dead if I do nothing anyway.*

"Drop the gun . . . now." Gavros's voice was an angry growl, and his knife hand moved closer to the captive soldier, the point just breaking the skin, sending a droplet of blood down the man's neck.

"Stay cool," the other soldier said, still holding his weapon. But he did loosen his grip, letting the barrel drop down toward the ground. "We can work this out."

"We ain't working shit out. Not unless you drop that gun. *Now.*"

Jamie took a long, slow breath. He knew he'd only have one chance, a second or two . . . maybe. And if he failed, he would almost certainly be dead in a less than a minute.

He tensed his body. He started to twist, moving slowly, closer to Gavros, all the while struggling to stay quiet. The pain in his leg was severe, but he bit down, suppressing any sound. He looked over at the other soldier, trying his best to communicate wordlessly that he was trying to help.

This is going to hurt.

Go!

He lunged forward, leaping up and grabbing Gavros's leg, pulling with all the strength he could manage. The pain in his leg shot up through his entire body in waves of unbearable agony. He screamed, and he fell to the ground, lying facedown, gasping for air.

But his attack had startled its target as he'd planned, and Gavros stumbled backward, his blade slipping away from the enemy soldier. Gavros wobbled for an instant, and then he started to fall. But before he did, the soldier against the wall opened fire, taking him in the chest with at least half a dozen shots. The stricken prisoner stumbled back about a meter and fell to the ground, dead.

The soldier he'd held captive took a step away from where he'd been, his hand moving toward the cut on his neck. He was shaking, with both fear and rage, Jamie suspected. He reached down and scooped his own rifle off the floor, and then he turned and fired at

least ten shots into Gavros's body. "Fucker," he yelled as he mutilated the corpse. Then he stopped shooting, turning slowly.

Jamie saw the man's eyes, and he knew what he planned to do.
He could see the rifle moving around toward him, and he opened
his mouth to shout out his surrender, one last attempt to survive. But
before he could say anything he heard the other soldier's voice.

"Kenny, no! He saved your life, man."

Jamie could see the terrifying indecision in the soldier's eyes, the
man's desire to kill him wrestling with the knowledge his comrade
had just given him. For a few seconds, a period of time that seemed
to stretch into eternity, Jamie wasn't sure what the soldier would do,
and for the second time that day—for the second time in less than
five minutes—he resigned his fate to another man's hands. Then
he saw the twitch, the slight relaxation in the man's body. The rifle
dropped down a few centimeters.

"I wasn't involved in the uprising," Jamie said, forcing himself to
speak calmly despite the near panic he felt in every centimeter of his
body. "I surrender."

The soldier stared down, wordlessly, for a few seconds. Then he
said, "Get up." The tone was harsh, angry. But the cold-blooded rage
was gone.

Jamie tried to struggle to his feet, gritting his teeth and trying to
ignore the pain wracking his body. But he'd shaken his splint loose,
and he couldn't manage more than to sit up.

The soldier sighed, as if Jamie's injury existed solely to inconve-
nience him. He pulled the comm unit from his shoulder and spoke
into it. "This is Johnson . . . I've got a prisoner down here who needs
medical assistance." His voice was annoyed.

Jamie just sat quietly, taking quick shallow breaths, trying to endure the pain. He was beginning to believe he'd made it through. If
they believed him, he might even escape punishment.

And if they didn't, he'd probably die on the scaffold with any of
the other prisoners who had survived the assault.

He was too tired to worry about that anymore and, the adrenaline
drained from his body, he finally passed out.

"**Fuck you, you asshole.** I told you a million times to cut the shit, watch out for yourself. Why the hell couldn't you listen?" Johnson was sitting on the cold rock floor staring down at the body of his friend.

He and Clyde Billings had gotten each other through training. They'd been inseparable, closer than brothers. And now that brother was dead, shot through the heart by a rebel, by a criminal probably spared a death sentence for his crimes and shipped to Alpha-2.

He looked at the corpse, lined up next to twenty-five others, laid out in two long rows. Twenty dead men and six women, all his comrades, all killed by the murderous prisoners.

No, he thought, *not just prisoners.*

Rebels.

He could feel the anger coursing through him. No, not anger. Hatred. For those who had done this. For those who had supported them. For every whining, protesting rebel on this godforsaken planet.

"Damn you," he said, putting his hand out, touching his friend's arm. It was cold, stiff, and he felt another wave of emotion. Clyde Billings hadn't been the smartest guy or the best at anything. But Johnson could remember times he'd had the barracks in hysterics with his offbeat sense of humor.

Whatever you want to say about Clyde Billings, you had to admit he was truly alive. *And now he's dead.*

Johnson's eyes were watery, but he wouldn't allow a tear to escape. There was no place for that. He would not indulge weakness. But he *would* take his revenge. And he knew he wasn't alone. The governor was a weakling. That had been whispered before, but now those voices would be louder. The officers were bound to support the governor, to enforce his wishes, whatever they themselves might think. But the rank and file were different; Johnson knew many of them felt as he did. They were tired of being yelled at by protestors, harassed by rebellious colonists. And now they had seen more than two dozen of their comrades killed in action.

He knew, on some level, that the convicts in the mine weren't representative of the population at large. But even if someone hadn't instigated the uprising from outside, they *had* somehow smuggled weapons to the miners. The same weapons that had created this line of his friends on the floor. If his comrades had been facing prisoners armed with makeshift clubs and knives, the fight would have been over in minutes, and the casualties would have been a fraction of what they'd been. But someone had given military weapons to the rebels. And that guilt stained the population of Alpha-2, the protestors in the street, the ringleaders who met in secret, who conspired in the night. They would pay.

They would all fucking pay.

Johnson took one last look at Billings's face, eyes closed, a strangely peaceful look for a man who had died so violently.

"Goodbye, buddy," he said, barely containing the sadness he felt. "I'll write to your folks. I'll tell them . . . I'll tell them something to make them feel better."

Though I have no idea what that will be.

He stood up slowly, taking a deep breath. He turned and took a few steps, and then he stopped and turned back one more time toward Billings's body.

"And we will make them pay, old friend," he whispered. "Your comrades will never forget."

"I will be speaking live tonight." Wells was sitting at his desk looking across toward Thornton. He knew she'd just gotten back from the mine, but somehow she'd found time to ditch her combat gear and change into her service uniform. "It is important to get ahead of this, to do whatever we can to quell the backlash."

Thornton nodded. "Yes, sir." Her words were clipped.

"Alex, I know this is difficult." *What an understatement.* Thornton had lost twenty-six of her people . . . and another two dozen were in the hospital, a couple of them in rough shape and in serious danger of becoming number twenty-seven.

"I am fine, Governor." She stared back, unmoving, looking like the perfect military automaton. Which he knew she wasn't. He knew she wasn't "fine" either.

"I mourn those lost as much as you do." He paused, thinking he should have phrased that differently. He'd never been military, but he knew the soldiers well enough to have an idea how they viewed things. And he was sure they felt no one cared as much as they did about those lost in battle. "I mean, I know how upsetting it is for you."

"Honestly, Governor, I am fine." She sat silently for a few seconds, then she added, "I saw worse during the war. Much worse."

"I know, Alex. But it's okay to say whatever you're feeling. At least when it's just the two of us."

"It's not your fault, sir. There was no choice." Her face hardened. "But with your permission, I intend to find out who smuggled those guns into the mine. Our losses would have been a fraction of what they were without those weapons."

"You have my permission, Alex, but try to keep it quiet. We don't want to give the rebel leaders any more ammunition to inflame the public. If your people go out kicking down doors and hauling in crowds for questioning, we're just playing into their hands."

"I understand." She said the words, but Wells could tell she disagreed with him, too.

"I hope you do. We *will* find out who was behind this. You have my word. But if we react too forcefully and spark open rebellion, your people will lose more than twenty-six of their number." He took a deep breath. "I know everybody thinks I'm too soft in how I respond, but I think I understand just what a war on this planet would do. As terrible as the last international conflict may have been, at least you knew your enemy. Knew where they were, and *who* could be shot at and who couldn't. This will be guerilla war, every alley, every patrol route outside the city a potential trap, a place where a group of your troopers can be ambushed."

Wells shook his head slowly. "And every time we respond, we will kill as many innocents, men and women who've done nothing. And with each such death, the revolt will grow, the hatred." He locked his eyes on Thornton's. "You are a veteran, Alex, so you understand the experience of war. But I am a historian. My father died in the civil war. It is easy to divide into opposing camps, to shout rhetoric back and forth. But few understand the nature of the tragedy they are creating until it is upon them."

He sat silently for a moment before he continued. "I have done all

I could to prevent this rebellion from becoming a reality . . . because in my mind I can see it already: the destruction, the hatred unleashed. The dead. Not twenty-six soldiers—or even a hundred miners—but thousands. Troopers, rebels, civilians. The cruelty of such catastrophes, the naked brutality, will cover the planet. If we slide into that nightmare, Major, you will find your soldiers mutilated and dumped on the streets. Kidnapped and tortured. Burned bodies, unrecognizable."

Thornton sat silently, listening.

"You will respond, of course, as much in kind as your professionalism allows. You will seek out those responsible, and of course I will give you death warrants for colonists guilty of murdering soldiers. But that will not be enough for the troops. As much as they respect your command, they will take matters into their own hands. You will find civilians, too, lying in the smoking ruins of their homes. Men, woman—even children—tortured, murdered. The soldiers will be silent . . . no one will seem to know anything about the incidents. And it will grow from there, each atrocity provoking an escalation from the other side. And with each dead civilian, the revolution will grow. To stop it we will have to destroy Alpha-2, or come perilously close to that." He looked up at Thornton. "Is that what you wish, Alex? To be the military commander of a virtual genocide?"

She sat quietly for a few seconds before answering. "No," she finally said, "of course not. But what do we do?" she asked, frustrated. "Someone smuggled weapons into that mine, Governor. Today twenty-six soldiers and over a hundred prisoners died. What will it be next time? Twice that? Ten times?" She looked down at his desk for a moment before snapping her eyes back up to meet his. "How do we stop what you fear from happening? Surely not by allowing those who engineered this tragedy to escape? To repeat their actions on an even greater scale?"

"No—"

"Then *what*, sir? We have tried to penetrate the rebel networks, but we have had little success. The agents we still have deployed are on the periphery at best, with no knowledge of the actual ringleaders. If we do not up the pressure, if we don't increase the intensity of our operations and intelligence-gathering, how do we prevent the next disaster?"

She was right. For all the impassioned rhetoric he'd just laid on her, he was all too aware that nothing he had tried had even remotely prevented the situation from escalating. He had held back, been lenient, allowed protests as long as they didn't become too violent. But none of that had worked. He knew harsher crackdowns would only fuel the disruption . . . but his efforts to date had failed just as utterly. Twenty-six troopers dead. Hundreds of prisoners as well. Protests on the streets. Illegal guns flowing onto the planet. Things were spiraling out of control and, truth be told, he didn't know what to do about it.

Thornton stared across the desk, a sympathetic look on her face. Wells returned the gaze. He could see she was upset . . . but she didn't realize how fortunate she was. Because whether he authorized her to crack down hard or commanded her to back off and let the guilty go free, she would have the solace that she was following orders. *His* orders. *His* answers to the impossible question put before them. He wondered if she could truly understand the burden on him right now. Whatever actions had been taken, whatever happened in the coming months, it was all on him. And if revolution broke out despite his best efforts, his hands would be awash in blood.

"There is one more thing, Governor . . ."

He knew what she was going to say, but he was silent, staring across the desk as she spoke.

"The federal observer will be here in a matter of days. We—you—are going to have to have some answers ready." She paused. "And I suspect a passive response will not sit well."

"No, Major," Wells said softly, "I don't suppose it will." Wells didn't know what orders the observer carried or what authority she would have. But he could guess she wasn't coming to propose a peaceful sit-down with the rebel leaders.

The comm unit buzzed.

"Yes?" he said, a hint of impatience in his tone.

"Governor, Lieutenant Ward is here."

"Very well, send him in." His eyes flitted up toward Thornton. "I'm sorry, Major, but I need to take this meeting."

"Of course, sir." A pause, then: "Damian Ward?"

"Yes, Major. The lieutenant and I have come to an understanding. He is going to use his influence to help us keep things under control. You know Lieutenant Ward, Major?"

"We've crossed paths, sir. On the frontier during the war."

The door slid open, and a second later Damian walked in. "Hello, Governor. I got here as quickly as I could. The streets are . . ." He turned and looked at Thornton. "Alex," he said. "I knew you were posted here. I'm surprised we haven't run into each other before." He looked a little uncomfortable, but quickly gained his composure. "I should have looked you up sooner. I meant to . . . but . . ."

"But time has a way of passing quickly, doesn't it?" Thornton voice was odd as well. "I'd heard you had a farm here. I meant to visit you as well, but I wasn't sure . . . and then, with all the disturbances, I was just so busy . . ."

"It's okay, Alex. I'm just glad we finally saw each other." He walked up to her, looking for a moment like he might put his arms around her. But he just extended his hand. "You look well."

Thornton reached out and took Damian's hand. "You do, too. Civilian life seems to suit you."

Clearly there was some kind of past between the two, something beyond simply having "crossed paths," as Thornton had put it. He wondered for a moment if that would help or hinder his plans to use Damian to help him calm the population. Would the two of them work together as old friends? Or was there some festering resentment there, the lingering feelings of a jilted lover?

"Damian, I don't mean to cut the reunion short, but we're pressed for time."

"Of course. Alex . . . we should get together. Talk about old times."

"I'd like that, Damian." Thornton paused for a second. Then she looked over at the governor. "With your permission, sir."

Wells nodded, and Alex took one last look at Damian, and then she turned and walked out the door.

Wells was tempted to ask Damian about the encounter, but he decided against it. It was none of his business. He gestured toward the chair Thornton had vacated. "Please have a seat. As you saw, the streets are full of protestors, and things are in a dangerous state. I need to address the planet . . . and I'd like you to do it with me. Let's discuss some ideas."

CHAPTER 10

Brevet-Corporal Johnson stood along the barricades, staring out at the crowd. The people were loud, restless, but they were staying within the blocked-off area. It wasn't a riot, not yet at least, but he could feel the anger.

Yeah, I got anger for all of you . . . enough to blow every one of you into bloody chunks of meat . . .

Johnson was exhausted. He'd expected a trip back to the barracks, and a long rest after the fight in the mine, but instead he and his new team had been rushed to Landfall City to bolster the overwhelmed security forces patrolling the streets. The shit had really hit the fan as word spread of the hundred-plus prisoners killed when the troops retook the mine.

He didn't give a shit about dead prisoners, and he wasn't sure why the people did either. They were *criminals.* And if they hadn't been before, as some people claimed, they certainly were when those bastards had shot at him and the other soldiers. When they had killed his friends. He was only sorry that more than half the rebels had been taken alive. For as much as he would enjoy watching their executions, he didn't have a guess when that would be. Once more Governor Wells was showing himself for the coward he was. If *he'd* been governor, the prisoners who surrendered would have already been lined up against a wall—

"Kenny, er, Corporal, they're starting to get restless along the southern end of this group. They're still staying back, but if they don't like what the governor says . . ."

Johnson turned toward the voice. It was Cole, the senior private on his team. He fought back a small laugh. His people were still struggling with his promotion-in-progress, uncertain what to call him. Major Thornton had handed him his stripes, changed his assignment on the spot, and sent him to help patrol the streets. But he hadn't had time to get his uniform updated . . . and he knew none of it was official anyway until Governor Wells signed off on it.

Still, his promotion to corporal might not be official yet, but Major Thornton had already placed him in command of a five-person team, half a squad. So, somewhere between private and corporal, he tried to act like the commander of four other soldiers.

"I'll call it in, see if we can get some backup." He looked around, out at the crowds, with a sour look on his face. "If I had my way, we'd send them home in a heartbeat. At a dead run. A couple machine-gun blasts and these troublemakers would piss themselves."

He turned back toward Cole. "But I don't have my way, so do the best you can. And remember, our orders of engagement allow us to return fire, so if any piece of shit in that mob has a weapon and shoots at you, your orders are to take him out on the spot, however much force you need to use. Understood?" The rules of engagement he'd been given also required extreme care be exercised to prevent any collateral damage when engaging hostiles, but Johnson didn't mention that.

"Yes, Corporal." Cole turned and jogged back toward his assigned position.

Johnson looked up at the federal complex. The building was by far the largest in Landfall, twelve levels and surrounded by a high wall. He could see the sentries along the top, staring out over the crowds like soldiers on the battlement of some medieval castle. He felt a touch of jealousy for the troops deployed inside while he and his people were out with the crowds.

There were technicians working as well, completing the setup of a large screen on the side of the building. The governor would be giving an address in less than half an hour. It would be broadcast on every network on the planet, but Governor Wells had ordered screens set up throughout Landfall as well, so that the protestors and anyone else in the streets could see and hear what he had to say.

Johnson wasn't sure he thought it was a good idea, but he was dead certain no one had asked his opinion. Still, he could see there were twice as many guards as usual on the walls of the federal complex, so it was clear he wasn't the only one with concerns about how the crowds would react.

Part of him hoped the mob would be enraged by what Wells said, that they would try to storm the complex. It would be dangerous for him and for his troops, of course, but the thought of hundreds of vicious, ungrateful troublemakers going down under the automatic fire of the guards appealed to the part of him that craved revenge, the part that was still thinking about Clyde Billings and the twenty-five other soldiers killed in that mine. Twenty-eight actually. Two more had died in the hospital the last he'd heard.

He looked around, scanning the area, searching for the spots where he would deploy his troops when the broadcast began. If the guards on the walls opened fire, the mob would panic, stampede. And he had no intention of allowing the four troopers he'd commanded for less than an hour to get caught in that.

No . . . no way. If anybody else dies today it will be these rebels . . .

"Citizens of Federal Colony Alpha-2, I come to you today to speak of a terrible tragedy, one I tried in every way available to me to avert." Everett Wells wore a spotless black suit, and he stood behind a nondescript podium. He'd had the seal removed, the flags of both Federal America and Alpha-2 moved offscreen. He knew he had only one chance to keep the peace, and that meant he had to reach the colonists on a personal level, not as the symbol of Federal America.

"Sadly, that has not come to pass. All attempts to negotiate with the armed prisoners failed, and I was left with a difficult choice. Order the colonial security forces to retake the facility or risk allowing dangerous armed convicts to escape. It is no secret there has been planetwide unrest and that we face challenges to maintain the peace we all cherish. But it is essential that every citizen understands that the prisoners in the mine are all convicted criminals, many of them guilty of terrible, violent offenses. They are not people in the street. They are not nonviolent protestors, nor even citizens who have ignored curfews, damaged property.

"As governor, I simply could not risk allowing any of these dangerous men and women to escape, especially heavily armed as they were. The chance of innocents being hurt—or killed—was simply too great. So, with extreme reluctance, I issued the order for the security forces to retake the facility. I did this on my own authority after exhausting all other options."

He paused, staring into the camera. He was maintaining an air of authoritative calm. He had discussed it with his advisors, and they suspected most of those listening would consider any stronger hints of anguish to be a bit of theater intended to enhance his persuasion. But the occasional hesitation, the mild faltering in his voice . . . it was all real. Wells knew how perilously close Alpha-2 was to disaster, and he also realized if he didn't get through to enough people now, that catastrophe could begin in minutes. And he was genuinely shaken, upset for the soldiers he'd lost, but also for at least some of the prisoners. Those who'd been intimidated into accepting exile and a work period in the mines. Now dead, alongside the murderers and violent criminals.

"I can say that I am sorry for the loss of life resulting from that decision. I can tell you all I believed the troops could retake the mine with far lower losses on both sides. All that is true. But none of it matters now. The dead are dead, and what happens next, whether tragedy escalates—or whether we take this event and learn from it—is up to us. We have this one opportunity, perhaps a last chance, to pull back from the brink, to work together to prevent anything like this from happening again. And I, for my part, am prepared to take the first step."

He paused, taking a deep breath. "There will be no punitive actions against the general populace following this terrible event. No new restrictions, no expanded curfews."

He hesitated again. He'd decided what he was going to do, a last-ditch effort to defuse the situation. It might work with the people, but it would give him another problem, this one with his own personnel. He hadn't even told Major Thornton what he was planning. He'd intended to, but he knew she wouldn't like it, and he couldn't afford her trying to dissuade him from this course of action. The fact was, he respected her too much, that there was a good chance she might have done just that.

He continued.

"Further, there will be no punitive actions against the prisoners who surrendered, even those who were apprehended with weapons in their possession. They will serve the rest of their existing terms, and then they will be released." He felt his stomach tighten, imagining the blowback he would get from his own people. "This was a difficult decision, one made more so by the tremendous loss of life, among the soldiers who fought to quell this rebellion . . . and the prisoners as well. I ask that you all consider this, and accept it as a true expression of my desire to maintain the peace."

He could imagine the soldiers stationed around the city, all over the planet, the wave of anger they would feel. They would see this as a betrayal and would speak out against him among themselves. But he saw things differently—it was part of the burden of his position. He considered how many of them would die if the planet erupted into full-scale rebellion. He *was* thinking about the soldiers, about how to save hundreds of them . . . thousands. He'd rather have them hate him, though, than the people they were supposed to protect.

"Now I would like to bring out a man most of you have heard of. Damian Ward is a winner of the Federal Medal of Honor, a true hero of the last war, and a retired warrior all citizens of Alpha-2 are proud to count as one of their own. Damian Ward."

Wells moved slowly to the side, making room at the podium. Damian walked out, wearing his uniform as Wells had requested. It had been a few years since he'd worn it, a period devoid of the physical intensity of war and military training, and he'd had to squeeze himself into it, especially the pants. But he managed it, and now he looked the part.

Wells knew his own internal security forces were symbols of federal power, and that they were widely resented—if not outright hated—by many of the citizens. But he also realized that the actual military forces, those that had fought against the union and the hegemony, who had died defending many colonial worlds, were still popular. He'd always thought it strange that people on the verge of rising up in revolt could maintain an odd sort of patriotism.

And if I can use that to avert tragedy, that is exactly what I will do.

He stood silently and watched as Damian stepped up to the podium.

"Fucker."

Johnson cursed softly as he stared up at the giant screen. He was so angry he could feel his body shaking. He'd been worried Wells might delay punishing the miners who had rebelled, or that he might spare them the trip to the scaffold they had earned.

Criminals who murdered twenty-eight loyal soldiers . . .

But he had never in his wildest nightmares thought the governor would refuse to punish them at all. He'd shaken his head when he heard it, convinced for a moment he'd misunderstood. But then he looked out over the crowd, saw the response. Silence. Approval. Even scattered applause. And as he watched, his rage grew.

You fucking turncoat . . .

He turned his head back toward the screen. The governor was barely visible now, off to the side. Damian Ward was speaking. Johnson knew well who Ward was, though he'd never met the man. He had mixed feelings. Respect for the war hero certainly, tempered by resentment, bitterness at how the frontline soldiers were lauded as heroes while he and his comrades in the internal security battalions were considered second class, and hated by the people. But more than that, he hated that this man was standing next to that bag of shit who called himself governor.

His hands gripped his rifle tightly, his finger on the trigger, ready to fire. He'd checked the cartridge at least three times, confirming he was fully loaded, that the clip was firmly seated in the weapon, but he did it again, just to keep his mind engaged. He'd been ready for a fight, anxious even. He'd imagined the crowd going berserk during the address, surging over the barricades, toward the federal complex in a wave of mass hysteria . . .

But it didn't happen. Wells had come on the screen, and within a few seconds he had yielded entirely. He had decreed the murderers from the mine would go unpunished, that no one would be held responsible for what had happened. And the governor's pandering, his moral cowardice, had defused the mob's anger.

He stood, watching as the silent crowd looked up at the screen. There were no more chants, no shouts of anger. Just silence. Even the signs, the red flags of rebellion, were mostly lowered.

No, Johnson thought. *These people can't get away with this. My friends didn't die only to be betrayed by a man in a fancy suit sitting in a fancy office.*

These people will fucking pay.

"Thank you, Governor Wells."

Damian stared into the camera, looking stiff, he supposed. He didn't like this, not at all. Neither the message he was about to give, nor the fact that he was about to give a speech at all. Public speaking had never been his thing, and he could practically feel the millions of eyes on him. But he had given his word, and Wells had held up his end of the bargain. Besides, he wasn't a rabid revolutionary, not even close. He had his problems with how Federal America managed Haven, and especially about the newest restrictions and curtailments of freedoms the senate had implemented, but he had fought for the federal flag, bled for it. And he wasn't ready to stand against it.

I've faced down enemies with guns. I can look down the barrel of a camera . . .

"I want to add my voice to the governor's. We do not agree on everything, certainly. But as one who has seen the face of war, endured the nightmare of armed conflict, I want to say it must always be a choice of last resort."

Getting those first words out, he had managed to steady himself, and his voice became stronger and more authoritative as he continued.

"I have seen colonies like ours virtually destroyed by war. I have seen the dead in the streets, ashes where houses once stood, where families had lived their lives.

"Rebellion, revolution—whatever we choose to call it—make no mistake: if it comes, it will come on the wings of war. Those dead bodies could be here, on Haven," he said, deliberately using the colloquial name. "And if not you, it will be your neighbors, your friends. Your *children*. Those ashes could be our own homes, the businesses you've built in our neat, pleasant cities. We can't allow this to happen. We can't allow for such darkness to come to our world. We must resolve our differences peacefully, and only when every attempt has failed, only when the outrages become too much to endure, to consider that last terrible step. Thank you."

Wells wasn't going to like that last bit.

Tough.

He was supposed to tell them revolution was never an option. But though he meant all he had said about avoiding violence any way possible, he knew if he was pushed hard enough, he, too, would take up the rifle. And while he would support the governor, at least to a point, he would not lie to his friends and neighbors . . . and the rest of his fellow Havenites.

"Thank you, Lieutenant Ward." Wells stepped back toward the center of the podium. "Before I conclude I would like to take a moment to introduce you to a second individual." He turned and motioned toward the side of the stage.

A tall man walked on, clad in tattered clothes, his blond hair long and filthy, hanging around his face is a twisted clump of knots.

"This is James Grant, one of the prisoners from the mine."

Damian stood to the side, his eyes on Jamie. He knew his friend had strong rebel sympathies. But Jamie had proven he could control his impulses during the uprising, and Damian believed he could now.

"Mr. Grant not only did not participate in the armed insurrection, he actually saved one of the soldiers sent to restore order by attacking the rioter about to kill him."

Damian winced. He knew Jamie would be ashamed of what he had done, not proud. He wished Wells had told him what he'd intended to say so he could have warned him off.

C'mon, Jamie. Just smile and say something noncommittal. Don't argue now, not this close to freedom . . .

But he couldn't read the young man. Jamie just stood at attention, rigid, as if everything he had was going into remaining calm.

"And now, I will show my own good faith. It is with great pleasure that I hereby commute Mr. Grant's sentence to time served. At the conclusion of this speech, he will leave this facility a free man, and begin a new life." Wells turned to face Jamie, gesturing toward the podium.

Jamie hesitated, just for a second or two. Then he walked slowly toward the microphone, favoring his still-sore leg. "Thank you, Governor," he said, hoarse and uncertain. He stood in place for a few seconds, and then he turned and walked to the side of the stage.

Wells was startled. The governor had clearly expected Jamie to speak for longer—Damian certainly had—but Wells recovered quickly and slid behind the podium.

"In closing, I urge patience, and I promise an honest effort to reach out, to listen to the various voices of Haven, and come to an understanding that solves the disagreements that plague us. Good night."

He held in place, staring at the camera until a technician told him he was off the air. Then he turned toward one of his aides. "Status? The crowds?" Damian heard the tension in his words. He had listened, and it was clear to him Wells didn't have the slightest idea how to solve Haven's growing problems. Empty political rhetoric wasn't something that tended to sway his own opinions, but he was different from most people.

The aide stared down at her display, holding her hand over her earpiece, obviously listening to some incoming information. A few seconds later she smiled. "It's good, Governor. No reports of any violence, and in several locations the crowds are beginning to disperse."

Wells nodded, and he let out a heavy sigh. Then he turned toward Damian. "Thank you, Lieutenant. Your help is greatly appreciated." He glanced over at Jamie, his expression changing, betraying some annoyance with the former prisoner's conduct. Then his eyes shot back to Damian. "Why don't you take your friend home now."

Damian nodded. "I will. I think we are all exhausted. Thank you, Governor." He flashed a glance toward Jamie, one that communicated one thing clearly: not another word. Then he walked across the room, grabbing Jamie gently by the arm and hurrying toward the elevator.

"I really thought the fight at the mine would be enough." Cal Jacen sat at a small wooden table, looking out at half a dozen of his comrades. Jacen was a member of Danforth's Guardians of Liberty, but his true views were far more radical than those of the communications magnate. It was here, with his associates of the Society of the Red Flag that he was able to speak freely about his goals, and the actions he took to secure them.

Danforth knew about the existence of the Red Flag, of course, but Jacen had taken measures to ensure his own involvement—and the size and reach of the group—was a closely held secret. Danforth was a rebel; there was no question of that. He was ready to use violence to secure the freedoms he wanted for Haven.

That wasn't enough for Jacen and his cohorts.

The guilty had to *pay* for all they had done—the federals, of course, but also the disloyal among the colonial population. Those whose allegiance was to Federal America . . . and even those who refused to embrace all that was necessary to make revolution a success.

The streets would run red with blood to wash away the sins of the masters, of the apathetic, of the greedy. Haven would become what only the revolution would allow: a paradise, a worker's dream . . . and any who resisted would be destroyed.

His companions were silent now. He knew they had all believed as he did, and they were still trying to understand what had gone wrong, why the people hadn't flooded into the street immediately in response to how the riot was put down. Why they weren't, even as the group sat here, attacking the federal soldiers, burning down everything in their paths.

There had been protests, of course, and some violent incidents, but all in all, things were no closer than they had been to a final break. To revolution.

Jacen thought he knew why. "I believe we miscalculated in our choice of targets. We know the prison at the mines is a symbol of injustice, of the tyranny of Federal America. And *we* know that many of those imprisoned there are guilty of minor offenses . . . or nothing at all. But *the people* are unaware. When they see a convict, they see danger, a threat to them and to their families. Their first reaction is to assume guilt, not to question what kind of corrupt court condemned another man or woman to servitude."

"The governor is a problem, too, Cal." Zig Welch sat across from Jacen, at the far end of the table. "His speech was well-received. And the presence of Damian Ward with him was a surprise. I've always heard Ward wasn't political, that he mostly kept to himself. I was surprised to see him supporting the federals."

"I wouldn't go so far as to say he supports them, Zig," said Pietro Sandoval from his seat next to Jacen. "He's just coming out against violence." Unlike most of those present, who were lawyers, Sandoval was ex-military. He was as angry as any of them, as committed to whatever radical actions it took to redress the injustices that plagued Haven. But he'd seen war and death up close, and sometimes he worried that his comrades were a little too anxious to see fighting and death in the streets.

"But that's the problem, Pietro—we *need* violence. You can't cut out the cancer eating away at our society without a knife." Jacen stared at his comrade as he spoke. "I know you sympathize with Lieutenant Ward, and I understand. You both served in the same unjust war. But there can be no confusion here. Zig is correct. Ward's presence hurt us. He is very popular with the people, all the more so because he so rarely seeks any attention."

"We must move against him." Welch's voice was cold, firm.

"*Kill* him?" Sandoval was shocked. And angry.

"No," Jacen interjected, speaking before his allies could get deeper into an argument. "Killing him would be too dangerous. If we were blamed, even if people suspected our involvement, the backlash would be disastrous. And the veterans would turn on us dangerously." He paused, staring across the table at Welch. *Idiot.* He had no doubt his fiery colleague had indeed been entirely serious that they should kill Ward. But there were too many retired military personnel on Haven, and Damian Ward was enormously popular with them.

Besides, there was a better way.

"So what do we do, then?" Welch demanded. "Allow him to run around with the governor, discouraging the very call to action we have labored to create?"

Jacen shook his head, resisting the urge to roll his eyes. "No, Zig. Damian Ward needs to learn the cost of his collaboration."

"You mean attack him?"

"Isn't that dangerous, Cal?" Sandoval asked. "He is a war hero. If we are implicated . . ."

"No, of course we can't kill Damian. Not yet at least. But there are ways to inflict pain without assassinating the man. He has a farm, buildings, equipment. People who work for him. A *reputation*. These are all vulnerabilities, weaknesses."

The room was silent. Moving against a figure like Damian Ward was dangerous, a step beyond anything they had done before.

"We can no longer rely on single operations like the prison uprising," Jacen continued. "We've been trying to sting the government; our actions must now be blows they—and the people—can't ignore."

Jacen stood up and slammed his hand down on the table. "The governor's response has prevented the kinds of clashes we had hoped to provoke. Somehow his weakness proved to be our undoing. Our plans depended on dead protestors, on the rage that would follow federal soldiers firing on the crowds, in Landfall and the other cities. But they have not done so, though I suspect many of the troopers themselves would have if allowed. Would do so even against orders if they are pushed hard enough."

He took a deep breath and continued. "Indeed, there are already rumors that some of the soldiers exceeded the scope of their orders in the raid, that prisoners trying to surrender were gunned down." He looked around the table. "The governor's people deny this, of course, but I suspect there is truth to it. Which means that for all the orders the governor may give, there's certainly not ironclad discipline among his soldiers."

"You are proposing actions against the troopers, then? Attacks designed to provoke them to retaliate."

"Yes, Zig. That is exactly what I am proposing. A few killings will overwhelm the governor's ability to control the soldiers. If we push them hard enough, they *will* strike back, and without specific targets, they will do so indiscriminately. We will have the victims we need to light the fires of revolution."

"We will have to choose our targets carefully," Zig noted. "The killings will have to be perfectly executed, and they must be brutal. We have to enrage the soldiers, push them to committing the worst possible acts of retribution."

"Agreed. And I believe I know just how to proceed. I won't go into the specifics—you're all better off not knowing everything—but I have the green light, yes?"

He could see his companions nodding their heads, and he heard a soft chorus of yeses. All save one.

"No." It was Pietro Sandoval.

Jacen felt a flush of anger, but he held it in check, turning toward his comrade with as neutral an expression as he could muster. "No? What, then, do you propose, Pietro?"

"I don't know, but not this. We cannot slander a man like Damian Ward. He should be our ally, not our enemy. And I cannot condone the murder of soldiers in cold blood. In battle, fighting for what we believe in? Yes. But not like assassins in the dead of night."

Jacen heard several of his comrades rustling around the table, and he caught Zig out of the corner of his eye about to say something. But he held up his hand. "Gentlemen, I believe we should adjourn this meeting and convene again tomorrow night. We can consider alternative plans in the interim. Perhaps we can address some of Pietro's concerns and still develop a plan of action that serves our purposes."

"Thank you, Cal." Pietro nodded. "I am sure we can. We don't have to become monsters to serve the revolution."

"No, you are right. Perhaps you could stay for a few minutes, discuss some other options with me. You may have saved us from acting in haste, reeling from the events in the mine."

"Certainly, Cal."

Jacen turned toward the others. "I will see the rest of you here tomorrow." He sat quietly as the others nodded and rose, moving toward the door. All except Zig Welch. He stood behind his chair and stared across the table.

Jacen looked over, flashed a glance his way. Finally, realization came to his expression, and he nodded once before walking out of the room.

Jacen waited until the door closed, and then he said, "Do you have any suggestions, Pietro? We must do something, and sooner rather than later. The more we wait, the more the cause suffers."

"Like I said, I don't know, Cal. I am as anxious as you to secure Haven's independence, but there are some things we simply can't do. Perhaps we should—"

"I'm sorry to interrupt, but I need a drink. Today was a long day. I think I have half a bottle of brandy stashed in here. Can I offer you some?"

Pietro nodded. "Good idea. I think I could use a strong drink now myself."

Jacen stood up and walked over toward a small chest on the ground next to the far wall. He knelt down and pulled out a bottle and two small metal cups.

"So, you were saying, Pietro?" he said as he brought the brandy back to the table.

"Well . . . as you know, I was never strongly in favor of the mine uprising. Perhaps we can come up with less drastic—"

Jacen set the bottle and the two cups down on the table. One of the cups was too close to the edge, and it tipped over and fell to the floor.

"Ugh," Jacen said. "I'm tired, and it's making me clumsy."

"No worries, Cal." Pietro leaned forward, reaching down to grab the cup. "As I was saying—"

Pietro's words halted abruptly, leaving only a gurgling sound. Jacen was standing behind him, his hand still gripping the knife he'd shoved through the back of his victim's neck. He pulled it out hard, and gave Pietro a shove to the side, watching as he fell hard onto his back.

"I'm sorry, Pietro, I really am." He stood and watched as the dying man spasmed, clutching at his stricken neck.

He stood there another minute, perhaps two, waiting. Then he heard a sound behind him.

"Is he dead?" It was Welch.

"Yes, Zig. He's dead." There was no joy in Jacen's voice. Neither was there any sadness, though. He did what had to be done, and now it was on to other tasks. "See if you can find a cloth or tarp we can use to move him. We'll bury him in the woods."

Welch nodded, and ducked back out the door.

Jacen just stood there, calm, staring down at the body at his feet. He had known Pietro Sandoval for four years. They had worked closely together, been two of the founding members of the Society. But now he felt nothing. No guilt, remorse, pity for his friend. Just a cold resolve. Pietro had been weak, and there was no place for that in the Society. Not now.

The revolution was all that mattered.

CHAPTER 11

"Thank you, Damian. You know . . . it's crazy. I've never had a friend like you, one I could depend on. I'm not even sure I've ever had a *friend*. Not really. I'm never going to be able to repay you for what you've done for me." Jamie Grant sat on a chair next to the fireplace, still trying to process what had happened in his life the last few days. He was freshly showered and wearing clean clothes, and his injured leg was wrapped neatly with a clean bandage. It was something most people took for granted, but he reveled in the simple luxury of it all.

No more twelve-hour shifts in the dark caverns, choking on ore dust. No more abusive guards. No more wondering if a fellow prisoner was going to kill him over a perceived slight. He was here, and he would stay. He kept going over it again and again in his mind, and while he knew it was all true, somehow it still didn't seem quite real.

He looked up at Damian, unsure what else to say. His friend just smiled, though. "You're welcome. But I didn't really do all that much—you're just as responsible for your freedom as I am. I'll admit—I was worried, Jamie. Worried you would be swept into the chaos. You have had so much anger inside you—and rightfully so. And for so long, you had let that anger and resentment guide you. But you held firm in the darkest hour. I can't imagine it was easy."

Jamie looked down at the ground, letting out a harsh laugh. "It *wasn't* easy. I wanted to join them, Damian. I wanted it so badly it almost drove me mad to stay out of it."

"I know. But instead you focused on what is truly important. You should be proud of your strength and discipline."

"Proud? I feel like a turncoat," Jamie said. "Gavros was a piece of shit, but he was fighting the security troopers. That mine was full of men who fought against our enemy. Against *my* enemy. And I switched sides because I wanted to live. You see strength, but I just looked in the mirror after my shower, and all I can remember is a coward staring back at me."

"That's bullshit, Jamie, and you know it. Gavros wasn't a symbol of the oppressed prisoners. He wasn't fighting for justice. He wasn't like you, shipped here for a minor crime. Wells showed me his file. He was a murderer, a cold-blooded killer. If he'd gotten out of there he would have victimized innocent people. And I know you are feeling guilt over what happened to him—that's because you're a decent human being, and you should *never* get used to seeing death. But you didn't kill him, and—" he held up his hand as Jamie was about to protest "—your actions didn't get him killed. His did. He was threatening a guard. He was threatening *you*. You told me yourself that if you didn't move against him, he was going to kill you. Gavros isn't a hero. And he didn't die a martyr.

"He died because he was a man who needed killing."

"I know, but—"

"There are no buts. You did the right thing, my friend. You had to survive, and that's what you did. Trust me, Jamie, I know what it's like to carry a burden like this, the weight of guilt on your back. Let it go . . . or it will crush you."

Jamie looked up at Damian, forcing a half-smile to his lips. "I guess you're right." He wasn't convinced, at least not completely. But he trusted Damian, and was aware if there was a man on Haven who might understand what he was going through, it was his friend. "I still can't believe I'm out."

"You're out. You rest for a while, take some time to adjust, and when you feel you're ready, you can start helping me make this the most productive farm on Haven."

"You have no idea how good that sounds." Jamie weak grin erupted into a full-blown smile.

"Jamie? Jamie? Is he here?" The words came from around the corner, out in the house's main entry. Jamie immediately recognized the sweet voice and leapt to his feet just as Katia Rand ran into the room, tears streaming down her cheeks. Ben Withers followed along behind her. "I'm sorry, Lieutenant, but she wouldn't wait while I announced her."

"That's quite all right, Ben," Damian said. "Katia has waited for this moment for a long time." But the words meant nothing to Jamie at this point. He barely noticed Withers slipping out of the room. The only thing that mattered was the woman in his arms.

"Katia," Jamie said softly as he tightened his arms around her. "I am so glad you are here."

"I couldn't believe it when I saw you on the vid. I had to rewind and watch again three times when the governor said he was commuting your sentence. Is it true? Are you really free? And your leg, my God, what happened to you?"

"It's true. And my leg is better. Still a little sore, but definitely on the mend."

Sort of true, he thought. Technically he had been paroled and was still subject to weekly meetings and monthly evaluations.

Technically the governor could revoke his freedom with a signature.

But if that man thinks I'd risk this, he's crazy, he thought, squeezing her tighter.

She let out an involuntarily squeak at his hug, and her smile seemed to get even brighter. "Wonderful! It has been so long, and another couple of months seemed like an eternity."

"It's been *too* long. But I'm here now, and I'm not going anywhere. I'm going to be working with Damian on the farm. I'll have an income, a home. And as soon as I get settled, I'm going to marry you, Katia Rand."

Jamie smiled as he looked at her, the shadow of his previous doubts gone, at least for the moment. Theirs hadn't been a traditional relationship, certainly, but he'd fallen in love almost the moment he'd set eyes on Katia, and their mutual devotion had survived for three years while he completed his sentence in the mines.

"Yes, you will, James Grant. We have waited long enough."

"Too long." Damian echoed Jamie, walked up toward the two of them. "And there is no need to wait any longer. Jamie, I'm going to work you hard, but I think I can come up with a few rewards to inspire you. There's a section along the perimeter. It's a little rocky, and it needs some work to get it into production. But I'd wager with enough effort we could get it done." He paused and smiled. "We might even find the time and resources to get a little house built out there, one that might work for two people . . . maybe even a third eventually."

"Damian," Katia shrieked, turning and throwing her arms around him. "Thank you so much!"

Jamie stood silently for a moment. Then he said, "Damian, I don't know what to say. You are the best friend I could have hoped for. I'd have died in that mine if I hadn't met you three years ago. And now you are giving me the chance at a life, a real life. I was right. There is no way I can thank you enough."

"Then don't waste time trying. Work your ass off for me making this farm a success . . . and use the chance at a life well. Make something of it. If you do that, I will consider us even." He held out his hand and smiled.

"Thank you, Damian." Jamie reached out and took his friend's hand. "I will. You have my word."

"Lieutenant . . ." It was Withers. He'd just come back into the room, and even in his ecstatic state, Jamie could tell something was wrong.

"What is it?" Damian asked as he turned to face his aide.

"One of the barns is on fire, Lieutenant."

Damian turned back toward his friends. "Katia, stay here. Jamie, come with me." He rushed through the door, out toward the house's main entrance.

Jamie nodded, and he flashed a quick glance back at Katia. Then he followed his friend, limping but still managing to keep up.

Into fire . . .

The soldier walked down the street. It was a routine patrol, the same one he'd walked every night for the last three months. He and his partner were lucky. Their sector was a quiet area, one that saw little protest activity. Some of the other patrol teams had gotten into sticky situations, sometimes getting into altercations with colonists. He was grateful he'd been spared that, not just because that kind of thing could get dangerous, but because the red tape involved with arresting protestors was a serious pain in the ass.

On Alpha-2, the bureaucratic BS was even worse. That was mostly the governor's fault. He had insisted on meticulous records being kept when bringing charges against the colonists. The soldier had understood that at first, but the more he'd seen his comrades dealing with the reports and depositions and trials, the more he thought things should be streamlined. Due process was one thing, but so was practicality. When a patrolling trooper arrested someone, they had good reason, and they didn't deserve to be questioned endlessly about it. Unfortunately, no one asked him his opinion and there was nothing he could do about it, so he was just glad his beat didn't involve him in that mess very often.

"Quiet tonight," his partner said, looking around as they continued down the street. Their assigned area was rarely a trouble spot, but now it was almost eerily silent.

"Yeah, the governor's speech really calmed things down. It's amazing what you can accomplish by selling us out and giving these colonists everything they want." The soldier hadn't lost any close friends in the fight at the mine, but he knew all the names of the dead . . . and his mind cycled through the times he'd crossed paths with each of them: in the mess, the barracks, in the streets.

"Be cool, man," the other soldier said, his voice barely above a whisper. "I agree with you, but shootin' off your mouth ain't gonna get you nothin' but trouble."

"Maybe so, but it still ain't right."

He continued walking, his partner about a meter to the side. It was late . . . another half hour and they'd be off-duty. The thought of grabbing a meal and hitting his bunk was pretty appealing. He'd drawn a double-patrol—there'd been a lot of those lately—and he was dead tired.

He turned and looked off to the right, down the empty, quiet street. The he heard something. Or *felt* it. Either way, he spun around toward his partner . . . but no one was there. He twisted around, sliding his rifle from his shoulder, acting on pure instinct. His partner, down on the street surface, looking up at him with a shocked expression . . .

And a huge circle of blood on his midsection, growing larger with each second.

He saw a shadow behind him, and he rushed to bring the weapon to bear, but before he could turn he felt a blow to his side, something hard, a rod or a club.

He dropped to one knee, gritting his teeth against the pain. He almost panicked, but he caught himself. The attack was a surprise, but now he knew he was fighting for his life.

He ducked forward, using the momentum to turn and lunge back to his feet, to try and find his attacker. He shouted as loudly as he could for help—not sure if any of the other patrols were close enough to hear.

He fired his weapon blindly as he moved around, spraying automatic fire into the darkness. Then he sensed something behind him, and he swung his arms backward, slamming the butt of his rifle into something. Someone.

He heard the yell, felt the movement as whoever was there stumbled back, away from the blow. He turned as quickly as he could, fumbling to get his finger back on the trigger . . . but he never made it. There was a flash of movement from the other side. Another assailant. Then pain in his back. Not a punch this time.

A knife.

He froze, holding himself up for a few seconds. The panic he'd fought off came back, and it took control.

Run . . . I have to run . . .

But there was no time. He was weak; he could feel the blood pouring from the wound, the rifle slipping from his hands. Then pressure, and arm around him, grabbing his head, pulling back.

"Die, federal scum."

Then he saw the hand move, felt cold on his neck, then warm. Not pain, not really. Just a slight awareness. Then wetness, of blood pouring out from his slit throat.

And darkness taking him.

Damian stared at the sign, his rage growing with every passing second. His eyes were fixed, and though he tried he couldn't force himself to look away. He just read the words, again and again.

TRAITOR.

FED-LOVER.

At first, he'd thought the fire was an accident, an errant spark igniting the bales of hay stacked in the barn. But then they'd found the canisters of flammable liquid, discarded carelessly around the perimeter of the building. Arson, he realized, thinking whoever had done this was careless, stupid.

Then he saw the sign, and he knew. No, not careless. They wanted him to know it was deliberate. And they'd left him the sign so he had no doubt why they had targeted him.

Even if it's a fucking lie.

Still, it wasn't the first time he'd been called those things. He'd seen it on his trips into town, hushed whispers, people pointing toward him as he walked by. His only concern was for his home, and for its people. But some of them didn't see it that way. They just saw him standing next to the governor.

He looked down at the charred body lying just outside the burned building. It was too badly disfigured to tell who it was, but there wasn't much doubt. Marv Irving was one of his hands, and he'd been working in the barn alone . . . and now he wasn't responding to any of Smithers's calls.

"Anybody see who did this, Ben?" For years, Damian had been the model of a friendly farmer. A bit standoffish perhaps—he'd even been classified an introvert on one of his psych profiles—but never cold. Always a good neighbor. But that's when his biggest concern was bugs. Frost. A broken farm machine.

Now, after being attacked . . .

The Damian Ward who was a war hero was coming up from deep inside.

And that wasn't the sort of person you invited over for a barbeque.

A calm had come over him. Passionate anger was for civilians. Cold, calculation—that was Damian's mind-set now.

He did *not* take well to being attacked.

And that is exactly what had just happened. Arson would have been enough to flip the switch—maybe. But murder? Of his friend? He didn't give a shit whether the people who did this had known Irving was there, or if it was just an added tragedy. When he found those responsible, he vowed he would see them mount the scaffold.

Or I will kill them myself.

"No, sir," Withers replied, seething. Withers was a veteran who had served alongside Damian throughout the war, and his expression left little doubt it was the grizzled noncom standing there and not the assistant to a gentleman farmer.

Damian looked around, his eyes pausing on the surrounding buildings. The barns were all metal prefab units. Even the burned out one was still standing, though Damian suspected the heat had compromised the strength of the metal, making the structure a total loss. There were two cameras on one of the other barns, but there had been none on this one, nor on the one adjacent.

And that means we have almost nothing to go on.

He cursed his decision to skimp on the security system. It hadn't seemed necessary when he'd first started building up the farm complex. Haven didn't have a lot of crime, and what disturbances the planet experienced were almost all political . . . and never directed at him.

Damian hadn't been a wealthy man when he'd arrived on Haven. His mustering-out bonus and the cash donatives that had come with his medals were all he had, and that meant early expenses on the farm were ruled by necessity and productivity. Even now, when he had things running at a healthy profit, there were always more needs than resources.

He turned abruptly. "I want cameras on all these barns, Ben. Immediately. Take the money from the reserve fund."

"Yes, Lieutenant. I will see to it."

Jamie stood a few meters away, his eyes as fixed on the sign as Damian's had been. "This is because of what you did for me, isn't it?" His voice was soft. "That stupid speech. I'm sorry, Damian."

"You have nothing to be sorry about, so stop that foolishness right now. You did nothing wrong. *I* did nothing wrong. Whoever did this is a criminal, nothing more. No doubt they consider themselves rebels, justified in such actions. But they are just cowards and murderers. So I will find them.

"And then I will kill them."

Cal Jacen sat and listened. The leaders of the Society were gathered to hear the fruits of the most recent campaigns to destabilize Haven.

The others had been a bit surprised, even shocked, at the scope of what he had ordered. What he had seen done. But after he laid it out for them, they were all nodding in approval.

In two nights, seven soldiers had been murdered, in several cases tortured, their bodies left in the streets as open symbols of defiance.

There had been fires, too, and ransacked property, mostly in Landfall. They all knew the key to planetwide rebellion was the capital. If the residents of Landfall rose up, Jacen had no doubt the rest of Haven would follow.

There had also been specific warnings to those individuals who might stand in the way of revolution. Damian Ward had been sent such a message, a taste of the consequences of siding with the governor. Jacen felt his message couldn't have been clearer: there would be more where that came from, too.

There was no mark of the Society at any of the scenes—indeed, he had gone to great lengths to ensure nothing could be traced back to his organization, or even to the Guardians of Liberty or any of the other groups. These acts had been carried out in the name of the people of Haven. With no specific target, the governor would have no choice but to strike back at the planetary population at large. And when that happened . . .

"I believe the day we have awaited is near." Zig Welch looked across the table at Jacen. "I must commend your zeal, Cal. I had doubts we could do so much so quickly, especially after the disappointment of the operation at the mine."

"Thank you, comrade. It is crucial that we all do whatever must be done. It is time. First, the cleansing revolution, to drive the federals from Haven."

There was a rough series of nods around the table.

"Here, here!" Zig said. "Now we wait for the fruits of our efforts . . ."

"No." Jacen stared across the table at Zig. "We are too close for that. There can be no slacking off. We will continue to press the attacks, pressure the governor to strike back even harder. And when the entire planet is ready to explode, we issue the final blow, one that will force Danforth, the Guardians, and every freedom-craving Havenite into the streets, weapons in hand. And *then* we'll have the fruits of our efforts: revolution."

"Revolution," the others repeated in a ragged chorus.

"I submit we must consider one other thing now." The others seemed to lean forward, drawn in by Jacen's words. He felt the energy in the room, and reveled in it. "The federals *will* be defeated, overwhelmed by the army of the people. But they are not the only enemy. There are Havenites, too, loyal to federal tyranny. Traitors to their own people. We must have lists, names, addresses. We must rid ourselves of this cancer, the threat that could eat away at us from within. And then the new order will reign supreme . . . and the purge of all those who would stand in the way shall cleanse our republic."

"Yes!" Zig said. "When the federals are gone, we shall turn the fury of revolution on them . . . and paint the way to the future with the blood of traitors."

"Yes," Jacen said, slamming his fist on the table. "Let nothing stop us."

CHAPTER 12

"Well, now, isn't this . . . rustic." Asha Stanton walked down the steps from the shuttle, stopping as she reached the bottom and looking behind her at the vessel that had brought her down from orbit.

Quaint little craft.

It was just past planetary noon, and Epsilon Eridani was high in the sky. She held her hand over her eyes to block the brightness as she turned to face her companion. "It's not quite like Federal Spaceport in Washington, is it, Colonel?"

"No, Your Excellency, it most certainly is not."

Colonel Robert Semmes stood next to Stanton, clad in full dress uniform. It seemed a bit over the top, even to Stanton, but she'd come to realize Semmes was an odd sort in more than one way during the voyage. For one thing, Semmes had a stiff demeanor. For another, he spoke like an aristocrat, which in essence he was. Being the son of Senator Alistair Semmes, the head of the senatorial subcommittee on colonial affairs, Robert's assignment as Stanton's military aide had been no random circumstance. He had two older brothers to follow in the patriarch's footsteps as a political power broker, so Robert had been destined for a military career from an early age. But service in the real army had proven to be a bit too dangerous for a senator's son, third in line or not, so Semmes had been commissioned into the internal security forces immediately after graduation.

Alpha-2 was a crucial colony, and Stanton suspected that as soon as Semmes returned from successfully commanding the forces that crushed the unrest sweeping the planet, his father would arrange for his son to obtain his general's stars . . . and a plum position commanding internal security someplace like Washington or New York.

Makes sense. Alpha-2 is important enough to get attention, but defeating these rebels will also be easy enough. We'll take some losses, but I imagine Semmes can manage to keep himself out of the line of fire. He gets to play at commander, build up plausibility for his potential promotion . . . all without having to face a truly dangerous enemy.

Stanton couldn't be too critical. Her reasons for accepting the assignment were similar. She had her own political ambitions, no less than one day acquiring a seat in the senate. She came from money, and from a family that had been slowly expanding its political influence for three generations, ever since her grandfather had struck it rich selling weapons to the government during the Great Civil War. But unlike Semmes, she wasn't truly *anointed*. And despite her wealth and the work she'd done to get to where she was, the senate was a lofty goal for someone not from an old-line political family. It had been a long time since there had been any elections in Federal America that were more than a sham, and her path to the senate was more about her ability to win over enough government functionaries and not the population at large.

She stared around the spaceport. It was small, a fraction of the size of Federal, and it lacked the amenities as well. Disembarking down a ladder onto the tarmac seemed like something out of a movie, not the way someone of her stature traveled.

Unless one ventures to the frontier . . .

Still, for all Granddad's money, and the senatorial orders she carried granting her near-vice-regal authority, she didn't have the political power behind her Semmes did. If she was going to wear a senator's regalia one day she needed to be a star. And quelling the trouble on Alpha-2 would certainly be a point on that star.

There was a small carpet laid out about ten meters from the shuttle, with a few soldiers and a small group of officials waiting.

My, what a regal reception.

"Well, Colonel, shall we get this over with?" She began walking without waiting for an answer. She stopped just on the edge of the carpet, her eyes moving over the group.

"Observer Stanton, please allow me to be the first to welcome you to Alpha-2."

Her eyes locked on the speaker, a man she would have guessed was in his early fifties if she hadn't known he was fifty-eight. She'd studied the file on Governor Wells. Indeed, she had read it through completely. Twice. She believed in being prepared . . . and there had been precious little else for her to do on the voyage.

"Governor, it is a great pleasure to meet you at last. I have been an admirer from afar for many years." There *was* truth to the platitude. Everett Wells had masterfully advanced through the civil service, considered somewhat of a "whiz kid" in his early years for his creative solutions to problems. But his carefully constructed career was in shambles now—all courtesy of the backwater rock she now stood on. Stanton had taken it as a warning. Wells had been too soft on the colonists, and now he was the butt of jokes back on Earth. She would not make the same mistake.

She would *not* be a punchline.

Wells inclined his head at her polite words before saying, "May I introduce you to Major Thornton, the commander of my colonial forces?"

"Major, I have heard wonderful things about you as well. You served in the Third Regiment at Beta-9, did you not?" Stanton hadn't known Alexandra Thornton existed until she'd reviewed the dossiers of Alpha-2's key personnel. But she was a politician at heart, and she knew how to work people who could be useful to her.

Thornton stood at attention. "Yes, Your Excellency. Under Barrington." Her crisp answer caught Stanton's attention, and she took a quick look back and forth between the major and Wells.

Tension? All my intel suggested they work very closely together. What's changed?

And how can I use it?

Even as her mind shifted into overdrive, she introduced her military aide. "Governor, Major . . . may I present Colonel Robert Semmes?"

Semmes just nodded, not even trying to hide his boredom.

"Welcome, Colonel," Wells said.

Thornton snapped off a salute. "Colonel," she said sharply.

"Major," Semmes said without emotion or preamble, "I would like to meet with you this afternoon to discuss the deployments and the transition of command."

"Transition of command?" It was Wells, not Thornton, who asked first.

"Ah, yes, Governor," Stanton said. "I'm afraid I have several resolutions from the senate regarding operations here. Including one placing Colonel Semmes in overall command of all colonial forces—your people, and the two battalions of reinforcements we brought with us."

Thornton was silent, her face noncommittal. Wells was far less reserved.

"Reinforcements?" he asked. "I was not advised of any additional military forces."

You better believe you weren't advised. "Indeed, Governor. I must apologize for that myself. I'm afraid I was too concerned about the information leaking before we arrived, so I forestalled any communications prior to my arrival. We will be significantly increasing enforcement operations, and I rather thought the additional troops would have more impact if they were somewhat of a surprise to the . . . problematic . . . elements of the population." She moved her hand, trying to block more of the blazing sunshine. "Might we continue this discussion later, Governor? I would be eternally grateful if we could get out of this sun. I've been on that ship for quite some time, and would appreciate seeing my quarters and cleaning up. We could meet for dinner later if that is convenient, and I can update you then."

"Of course, Your Excellency. My apologies. I'm afraid I've become quite accustomed to the noon heat after three years." He gestured toward a waiting transport. "And dinner would be ideal. Shall we say eight this evening?" He then added, "Please remember our day is just under twenty-six Earth hours, so we have a little over sixty-five minutes per hour, not sixty."

"Thank you, Governor. I believe my AI has made the suitable adjustments, but I will double-check." She walked up toward the transport, waiting as an attendant opened the door. She stepped inside the vehicle and turned, leaning her head out of the portal as Semmes followed her through.

"Dinner, then, Governor. I look forward to it." She suspected Wells had intended to ride back with her, but she'd endured about as many pointless pleasantries as she could handle, at least before she had a chance to rest and change clothes. Dinner would be bad enough. Wells was not likely to react well to the decrees she carried . . . nor the fact that her mandate essentially transferred all his powers to her.

She didn't have anything against Wells. Indeed, she felt sorry for how he had destroyed his brilliant career. But she had no intention of making the same mistakes he had . . . or staying on this primitive rock one day longer than she had to. She was here to see all rebellious elements of Alpha-2's population rooted out and law and order returned.

That is just what she intended to do.

"You will be my executive officer, Major. As soon as we settle in the reinforcements I brought with me, we will be substantially ramping up anti-insurgency efforts. Your people have been rather passive in conducting operations. We will be changing that immediately."

Thornton looked directly at Semmes, standing at attention as her new commander lectured her on the proper way to crush insurgents and rebels. She didn't like the colonel, and her stomach was telling her he'd brought nothing but trouble with him. But she'd been a soldier long enough to respect the chain of command, even when her position at its top was ripped from her without warning.

And replaced with a man who had never seen a day of combat in his life.

She was thankful for the iron discipline she'd learned in the war.

Without it, she might have punched the smug look right off this man's face. Instead, she said, "The governor's strategy was quite moderate, Colonel. Our rules of engagement were fairly restrictive. And the planetary constitution contains vestigial rights from the original colonial charter. I'm afraid our abilities to arrest suspects have been quite limited."

"Not anymore." There was something in his voice, something that gave her a chill.

Eagerness?

Sadism?

"Excuse me, sir, but 'not anymore' what? The rules of engagement? Our strat—"

"Any of it. Moderate policies, restrictive rules of engagement, vestigial rights."

"But, sir, the constitution . . ."

"Will be revoked, Major. Observer Stanton carries orders from the senate canceling the planetary constitution and authorizing her to declare martial law. I expect that she will act upon that within the next few days." He paused, staring hard into her eyes. "We are finished playing with these people, Major. They are subject to the rule of Federal America, and while Governor Wells has been given plenty of time to test his theories of enlightened governance, he has nothing to show for it but failure."

"His recent speech appeared to reduce tensions . . ." But she let her words trail off. She had resented Wells for what he had promised the people, for his failure to punish the prisoners who had killed her soldiers. And now she found herself defending his policies. She was confused, uncertain what she truly thought.

"Don't mistake me, Major. I am not here—the observer is not here—to buy momentary solutions. They clearly have not worked. We are here to crush this rebellion before it starts by finding and exterminating disloyalty wherever it hides among the people. We will tear it out root and branch, Major, and when we are done, Alpha-2 will once again take its place as a productive and docile colony of Federal America." He stared at her, his eyes blazing like fire. "Or, God help me, we will leave this planet a graveyard."

"Yes, sir." Thornton held her superior's stare, marshaling everything she had to remain professional. But inside, there was one thought, one that made her stomach flip: *My God . . . he is insane.*

Wellr rtood in the media center, staring down at his feet as the crews prepared for the observer's first broadcast. Just days before, he had been there to make his own address, one that had seemed to reduce the tensions in the city and throughout Alpha-2. He'd actually believed things might have turned the corner, that a peaceful solution was possible, as he'd insisted these past three years. But that moment of hope had been short-lived. Seven soldiers had been ambushed and murdered in four separate incidents since then, a totally unexpected turn of events. He knew it was only a matter of time now before the patrols on the streets retaliated, regardless of what orders they received.

And now he had Asha Stanton to deal with. The observer was polite enough, if a bit arrogant. He could deal with a personality issue, but she had also come with a stack of decrees, senatorial orders that gave her virtual total authority over him, and others that imposed new restrictions on the population, outrages almost certain to provoke open rebellion. He supposed he should be grateful he still retained the title, though he didn't fool himself there was any real meaning to that, nor that he would have much of his career left when he finally returned to Earth.

At least I still have my title.

He almost laughed out loud at that absurd thought, and the thing that stopped him was that he could see the tragedy beginning to happen all around him. And he couldn't help but realize that much of the blame probably lay with him. He had used up so much time on a peaceful solution, and only now was he understanding there was little he could do to stop the escalation of violence. He'd tried to explain the danger to Stanton, but she lacked his appreciation of the mettle of the colonists. They would be intimidated, she'd told him confidently, by a show of force stronger than any they had seen before. Her forces would round up the troublemakers, the leaders, and the rest would meekly slip back into line. It would be ugly, violent perhaps, but it would also be short and definitive. Or so Asha Stanton had predicted.

Wells knew the people of Alpha-2 better than that. They weren't like the masses on Earth, accustomed to strict regulations and little freedom. Those who had immigrated out into space were predominantly drawn from the most troublesome groups on Earth. Indeed, that had been deliberate, an attempt to rid the urban populations of those most likely to cause unrest. That policy had come home to roost here, and the citizens of Alpha-2 were not so easily cowed as those back home. But Stanton didn't seem to recognize the difference.

She's forgotten her history. She wasn't born during the Great Civil War. She doesn't know why that fight was so brutal—because humans are willing to die for things they believe in.

The people of Alpha-2 are no different in that regard.

He looked over to her. She was so young. Not that much older than Violetta, if he thought about it. And while he wouldn't call her naïve, he had to believe she was in for quite the shock.

Stanton saw him looking and gave Wells a polite nod. "Governor, if you are ready, won't you join me at the podium? I think it will be helpful if we present a united front, don't you agree?"

He just nodded. It didn't call for a more elaborate answer. Stanton didn't really care what he thought, and her words had formed an invitation rather than an order as a courtesy only. The two of them knew who was really running Alpha-2 now.

He walked up to the podium and stood next to Stanton. She was wearing a civilian business suit, stylish and clearly expensive. Her longish reddish-blond hair was tied up neatly behind her head, in a manner that was just becoming popular when Wells had left Earth to take up his post on Alpha-2.

Probably the height of fashion now. On Earth at least. No one here will even notice.

Stanton turned toward one of the technicians and nodded. A few seconds later the man said, "You are on in three . . . two . . . one . . ."

"Citizens of colony Alpha-2, greetings. My name is Asha Stanton. I am the newly appointed federal observer assigned to assist Governor Wells in addressing the various problems facing this colony."

He had to give her credit: she definitely had a presence in front of the cameras. He could almost see why someone might be drawn to her. She just exuded professional competence.

Let's see how far that gets you here.

"As you all know, there have been rampant protests in the cities of this world. Work stoppages. Acts of sabotage. General unrest that has not only endangered the safety of law-abiding colonists, but has also impacted the economy severely, resulting in the first instances of contraction in both the economic activity of the colony and the revenue provided through taxation to support the enormous costs of supplying and protecting this system."

Her voice had only changed slightly, but Wells caught it: a slight tightening, a hint of sternness.

"That ends now. When dissidents and criminals are allowed to conduct their despicable acts with impunity, they make a mockery of civilized society. When provisions of the planetary constitution are misinterpreted to protect dangerous and hostile forms of speech and expression, they aid those who would destroy civilized society, not protect it.

"Effective immediately, the planetary constitution is hereby suspended and replaced by the standard legal code of Federal America. No longer will acts that are crimes on Earth be tolerated on Alpha-2.

"No longer will the streets be filled with protestors interfering with normal traffic and business affairs. Henceforth, all public gatherings are limited to a maximum of three participants. All public addresses without a permit issued by my office are prohibited. A curfew is now in place. All citizens without specific authorization are required to be in their homes by 8:00 P.M.

"These changes may seem harsh to many of you. They may provoke feelings of confusion or anger. But such resentment should be directed toward the rebellious elements of Alpha-2's population, toward the criminals who have made the streets unsafe. Who have killed seven loyal federal soldiers in the past three days alone.

"I will repeat: these are the deeds of *criminals*, of evil men and women who seek to cause a disaster that will shake this world to its core. I will not allow this to happen.

"Governor Wells and I call upon you now to reaffirm your allegiance to Federal America—to your nation—and, as its loyal citizens, to oppose all who would bring the scourge of revolution and war to this prosperous planet. Those who accept this sacred duty will stand with us, and with the soldiers who put themselves at risk every day to protect the peaceful citizens.

"But those who insist upon pursuing a course of destruction, who continue to try to lead their neighbors with sedition and treason, heed my warning now: your actions will no longer be tolerated. You *will* be held accountable for your misdeeds. We *will* come for you. We *will* stop your illegal insurrection, and we shall not rest until your evil is removed from the hills and valleys and cities of Alpha-2."

She paused a moment, glaring into the camera. Then she made a gesture with her hand, and the technician cut the broadcast.

She turned toward Wells, and he could only imagine what his face betrayed now that the camera was off. She was politic enough to just say, "You looked troubled, Everett. Don't be. You tried it your way for three years. It didn't work. Now it's time to give my way a chance. I'm going to miss one opera season while I'm deployed here dealing with all this. I don't intend to miss two."

She smiled and walked across the studio, toward the elevators. Wells just stood and watched. He knew she would be more aggressive than he had been, but he'd just watched her virtually challenge the people to rise up in rebellion. He'd worried she would inadvertently cause the revolution she'd come to prevent, but now he knew he'd misinterpreted her purpose.

She *wanted* to provoke the revolution he'd been desperately trying to avoid. And when it came, she planned to crush it once and for all, with as much force as it took.

He stood still for another moment. Then he hurried toward the restroom and emptied his stomach.

CHAPTER 13

"Things are getting out of hand, Damian. I've agreed with you from the beginning about staying out of it all, but that's getting harder and harder." Devlin Kerr sat in the great room of Damian's farmhouse, staring at his friend and host.

There were a half dozen of them clustered around the fire roaring in the massive stone hearth. Damian had felt the first hint of autumn, so he'd ordered it lit before the others arrived. But now he thought it was a bit too symbolic. Haven wasn't exactly in flames yet, but no one in the room doubted that's where things were heading.

"He's right, Damian," Luci Morgan said. "Half of my people are involved in some kind of rebel group or another. I've looked the other way, but if the federals are going to crack down, what do I do? Turn them all in? Or risk getting dragged into this mess?" Like Damian and Devlin, Luci was a retired officer. Like most of the others in the room as well. They'd all taken farms on Haven as their bonuses, and for the most part, they'd made successes out of their postmilitary lives.

Successes threatened by the current situation.

"That is why I asked you all here tonight. This affects more than just us. There are many retired veterans on Haven, men and women those of us in this room led in battle. And many others, too. They find themselves in the same situation as us. Our adopted home is sliding into a nightmare. The protestors, the rebels . . . they shout calls for war, without knowing the true nature of the hell they so badly seek to unleash."

Damian looked across the room. Everyone present was a veteran of the last war, most of them officers. All except Jamie. He was sitting across the room, silent. Damian knew his friend sympathized with the rebels. He suspected those sympathies were strong enough to tempt Grant into signing up for one of the militia units the Guardians of Liberty were hurriedly raising. He even understood. And if it hadn't been for his influence—and obviously Katia's—the young man might be with the revolutionaries right now.

He gave Jamie a small nod, a touch of pleading in his eyes. *Just a little patience, my friend.*

He was gratified when Jamie bit his lip, but then nodded in return.

Good. He continued. "I feel I can speak freely to all of you. I sympathize with many of the rebels' positions. Haven is my home now, if an adopted one, and I feel the call to be a true son of this world. I have bristled at the restrictions that have been imposed, in a seemingly endless barrage since I arrived here. And I am as outraged as any Havenite at the new decrees, the suspension of the planetary constitution, the curfews. I feel the same things our neighbors feel, that I suspect each of you feels."

He looked around the room once more. Most of those present were nodding, and all were staring, clearly looking to him for leadership. A mantle he still wasn't sure he wanted to wear. He basically said as much in his next breath.

"But there is another side to all this, for me at least, and for all of you as well, I suspect. I was born in Federal America, I joined her military, I fought under that flag, *for* that flag. I lost friends on the battlefields of Federal America's last war, and when that conflict was over, I was decorated, given a chance to build a new life. I say all this now because I want to be very clear: for all I sympathize with the rebels, I do not believe I can take arms against the nation I shed blood to protect. I cannot help this new world that I love so much destroy itself, to plunge blindly into war not truly understanding, as we here surely do, the true cost of that kind of conflict."

"You're reading my mind, Damian," Tucker Jones said. He had served for a time in the same company as Damian, though they were never particularly close. "But we have come to a difficult place. It is all well to speak of allegiances and loyalty. But it seems now that war is unavoidable. Do we really believe we will be able to stand apart from it? To remain neutral even as both sides demand our participation?"

"Tucker is right, Damian," Kerr said. "I want peace. But is that a choice we truly have, or is it just wishful thinking? Put another way: What will you do, Damian, if the rebel leadership comes to you seeking your aid? Or the governor? Would you refuse the revolutionaries, risk more attacks and vandalism? Or would you risk the wrath of the governor . . . and of this new federal observer?"

"Forget that—what if they call us back to duty?" Luci interjected. "What if we receive notice to report, to take the field to crush the rebellion? We are all on reserve status. By the papers we signed, the oaths we swore, they have every right to do so. Can you imagine donning your old uniform . . . and shooting your neighbors down if they refuse to yield?"

Damian's head was pounding. *No—I definitely don't want the mantle.* Yet, somehow, that's exactly the position he found himself in. Everyone was asking him questions that, try as he might, he didn't have any answers to. He said as much.

"I honestly don't know if there are answers to your questions. At least, none with any degree of certitude. I, for one, though, will do nothing. I will conduct the business of this farm. If I am left to my own affairs, I will not interfere with events that do not concern me. If those who work on my farm wish to leave and join revolutionary forces, I shall do nothing. If they want to join the colonial forces, I would not stop them either. I will neither aid nor hinder them . . . but I will not join them."

The room was quiet for a few seconds, nothing but the crackling of the logs in the fireplace breaking the silence. Finally, Kerr spoke. "I know you have not sought to be our leader. But we've placed that on your shoulders anyway. You are the one we will follow, Damian, though I suspect this fact is little but a burden to you. And I, for one, will stand with you, follow your decisions." He looked around the room. "I suspect everyone here will do the same. And the other veterans, the noncoms and privates . . . they will look to all of *us* for direction. Are we agreed? That we stand together with Damian. That we remain neutral, and resist all efforts of both sides to draw us into any conflict."

"Agreed," Tucker Jones said.

The others in the room followed suit almost immediately. All except Luci Morgan. She sat quietly for a second and then said, "I am with you all, of course. But I ask again: How will we respond if we are called back to service? A refusal is a violation of all we have sworn. It is also a crime. Do we ignore such a call, sit on our farms, and wait to see what the governor—or the observer—does in response? Do we encourage the other veterans to do the same, to risk all they have, their very freedom even, in pursuit of a neutrality that may not be possible?"

Damian looked at Morgan. He remembered her from the war. Though they hadn't served in the same unit, he knew her reputation as a gifted officer and a no-nonsense tactician. *And now she's cut right to the point, to the one action that would force us to choose a side.*

And once more, he had no satisfying answer for her.

"I don't know, Luci," he said. "We will just have to proceed as we can and wait and see what happens." He didn't like the uncertainty of the plan, and he doubted any of the others did either. But what were the alternatives?

"And if things change, we'll decide what to do then."

"I am with you . . . of course. But I suggest we all consider now how we will react to changes in the situation. Being ordered to active status is only one of the possibilities. What if an army—from either side—marches across our farms? What if they raid and plunder from us? What if one side employs a level of brutality beyond that we are willing to allow? Would we stand by if extreme rebel groups continue to ambush and murder colonial regulars? Would we sit and do nothing if the federal observer sets up death camps and begins a program of genocide against all those suspected of rebel sympathies? Don't fool yourselves—this *is* a war already. It's going to happen. Don't allow wishful thinking to replace cold judgment. And because it's war, these are all possibilities. We may not be given actual choices in the future. We may be forced into one side or the other. Indeed, that is almost a certainty in my estimation. So we can't just watch and see. We have to—at least—all consider this: What side would that be?"

And this is why I don't want to be the leader. But he wasn't one to ever shirk responsibility, and if he was their man, he'd do his duty to them.

"Luci is right. But I also worry about what it would mean for us to voice our opinions right now. I do disagree with her—there is still a chance this war might be averted. A small one, sure, but I won't dismiss hope so easily. So I suggest we modify my original proposal. We will remain neutral, at least as long as that is a possibility that remains open to us. In the meantime, though, I strongly urge you to decide what side you expect to be on if we're sucked in. Know that I won't accept recriminations based on what others decide. You are to search your own conscience, and if we're forced to make an action, we will convene one more time and decide on a new course of action. If we find ourselves opposed, I will be saddened by that, but no one who comes to this room for that meeting will be in danger from anyone here—I pledge my oath on that. After, we'll either stay united, or go our separate ways. Until then, though, we are all in agreement to stay out of it, yes?"

A somber chorus of agreement echoed throughout the room. He didn't know what would happen, or if they would be able to maintain neutrality, but the veterans of Haven were united with each other. For the time being at least. He wasn't sure what that meant, but he knew in his gut it was something.

His eyes darted over toward Jamie. His friend had remained respectfully silent, but Damian could see his inner torment writ large across his face. Jamie had been outraged at the observer's speech, and if Damian had to guess, he'd say the young man was struggling with himself, as he had in the mine, fighting the urge to take up arms, to strike back at Federal America's tyranny.

To atone for the perceived sin of selling out to save his own skin.

It wasn't true, of course, but no matter how many times Damian tried to point that out, it hadn't penetrated the shield of guilt and resentment surrounding his friend. He'd keep trying, though, because that's what he promised Jamie he'd do. He would counsel calm, and he knew Katia would do the same. All the same, though, if Jamie decided to go, he would not stand in the way. He had meant what he'd said to the room. He'd made his own decision, but he also knew, if he'd been in Jamie's position, if he had gone through what his friend had, he would be just as anxious to strike back.

"I waj told I could load my shipment as soon as the stalemate at the mine was over. It is almost two weeks later, and you are still telling me there is no ore." Sasha Nerov was trying to remain calm, but the tension burned in her gut like fire. Things had been bad enough before, but now with the federal observer in charge and the new soldiers patrolling the streets, the planet was a powder keg. Her run would be dangerous enough, and she wanted to get on her way before open war broke out.

"I am sorry, Captain Nerov. Mine production is delayed until further notice. The facility was badly damaged in the fighting, and there are inadequate staffing levels to resume full operations at present."

Maybe if you hadn't killed all the prisoners, you'd have a goddamn mining staff!

Nerov felt the frustration bubbling up inside her, but she swallowed it down. *Hard.* The last thing she needed was to draw attention to herself.

The clerk behind the desk looked down at a small screen for a few seconds, then back at Nerov.

"I'm afraid there is another problem as well, Captain. Pursuant to the orders of the federal observer, a hold has been placed on your vessel pending further investigation. You will be required to appear for an interview at which you will be compelled to present your records documenting your last three ports of call."

Nerov felt her stomach clench, and not out of anger this time. She'd been worried about an increased level of port security in the wake of the institution of the blockade. Now those fears took shape, morphed into reality.

Granted, she had all her documents in order, and her ship's records and security logs as well. They were all fake, of course. Good fakes, too. But there was no such thing as a perfect forgery. Enough scrutiny would turn something up that raised questions. And that would be the end. It wouldn't take more than suspicion to get her and her entire crew arrested as smugglers.

And it might not take more than suspicion to get us all hanged either . . .

Nerov was a quick thinker, though—you didn't survive long in this business if you weren't. So if *Vagabond* wasn't lifting off anytime soon anyway, she figured she'd rather be aggressive and push to get her review right away in order to deflect suspicion. "That is no problem. I will assemble the required documents immediately. When can I schedule the interview?"

"We can do it immediately, Captain Nerov. If you will just wait here, I will . . ."

And they called my bluff.

Shit.

Nerov felt a controlled panic taking hold. Her mind shifted, the clerk's words slipping away as she focused on the reality.

"I don't have the records *with* me. Perhaps we can—"

"That is not a problem, Captain Nerov. You can provide the records after the interview."

Her mind focused like a laser. She was about to be arrested. She knew she had to do something. She looked behind her. There were two guards in view, both on the other end of the open concourse, at the security station. And the man behind the desk was staring down at a screen, his hands hidden from her view, obviously moving over a keyboard.

The clerk is calling for soldiers. You have to make your move now . . .

She nodded to the clerk, as if agreeing. Then she turned and took off, running down toward the door. It wasn't an elegant plan, certainly, but she knew every second she waited was time for more troops to appear.

She was unarmed—she'd had to leave her pistol outside of the building, on the other side of the security checkpoint. So she wasn't going to fight her way out, not against any real numbers.

All she could do then was keep moving. She did so as quickly as she could, pushing several people out of her way as she headed for the exit. She had gotten halfway there before she heard the sound of the alarm. Her eyes darted toward the two guards at the entrance. The exit was to the side, perhaps five meters from the entry checkpoint. One of the guards was moving to intercept her.

She kept going, ignoring the soldier's yells for her to stop. She watched as he pulled up his weapon, and she realized he'd shoot her long before she got to him. There was no way she was going to escape just by running.

She slowed her pace, put her arms up in the air as she got closer to the guard. He had his rifle on her, and he was barking out angry commands, telling her to lie down on the floor.

She kept moving forward, though, slowing and keeping her hands up, but not stopping. He repeated the command, but he had waited too long. She was less than a meter in front of him. Close enough . . .

"I surrender."

She leaned forward, looking as though she was dropping to the floor as he'd commanded. Then she stopped abruptly and took a gulp of air before lunging up with her knee, slamming it into the soldier's gut.

The man howled in pain and fell back a step, doubled over. Nerov swung to the side, reaching out and grabbing the soldier's rifle, wresting it from his hand.

Her head spun around, toward the other soldier. He was responding to what she had done . . . but his surprise at her sudden move slowed him. Nerov brought her weapon around and fired. Then again.

And now he was slowed even more.

The guard fell, blood pouring from both his legs. Nerov was a crack shot—another vestige of her shadowy past—but she knew actually killing a guard could only make her position worse, so she'd disabled him instead.

She turned back toward the first soldier. He was pulling himself up, reaching toward the rifle in her hands to try to grab it. She pulled back hard, but he managed to grab hold, and the two struggled for control of the weapon. She knew he was stronger, that eventually he would wrest it from her. And time wasn't on her side—she could already see other security forces approaching. If she was going to escape, she had about five seconds . . .

She lunged forward, letting go of the weapon at the same time and slipping around the soldier, positioning herself to his side, almost behind him. She lashed out with her arm, connecting with the guard's neck. It was a move she knew well, one she'd learned long ago as part of her martial arts training. It wasn't a death move, but if it was done correctly, it would render the target unconscious. And she had done it perfectly.

The soldier collapsed, and she took off again before he even hit the ground. Her path was clearer now. The crowd had scattered in response to the disturbance, running away from the fight, toward the other end of the concourse.

Nerov pushed herself harder, racing through the doors and out into the midday sunshine. She moved to the side, to a trash receptacle just outside the entrance. She kicked it over, dumping its contents on the walkway and fishing through them for a second.

She reached down and grabbed the weapon she'd stashed there before entering the spaceport. It was a small pistol, military grade, relatively easy to hide yet powerful, with considerable hitting power. She wrapped her hand around it, feeling the grip she'd worn smooth over years of use.

She looked behind her, and then around. She'd fight if she had to, but she knew running was her only real chance. So that's exactly what she did. Sasha raced along the walkway, out into the crowds on the street, slipping the pistol inside her jacket.

Once in the open, she changed to a quick walk. She moved to the intersection ahead and turned onto the cross street. There were cameras everywhere, she knew, but it would take some time for her pursuers to access the network. She simply had to be gone by then, out of sight.

Yes—real simple.

She kept moving, turning again onto a small side street, one populated mostly with trashy bars, serving the crews from the ships in the spaceport. She passed half a dozen of them and then slipped quickly inside a door under a sign that read LOUIS's.

The place was mostly deserted. It was late morning, early even for the most die-hard spacers to drink themselves into a stupor. She flashed a glance at an old man standing behind the bar.

"I'm in trouble, Louie. They're looking for me."

The man nodded, his expression noncommittal. "You're the last one I expected to have to hide, Sasha."

"Yeah, well, we all make mistakes."

You knew you should lie low, she thought, *wait and not push so hard. But you let your sympathies for the rebels control your judgment. All that platinum hadn't helped.*

Fool.

She moved behind the bar as the man pulled open a small trap-door. "You can't stay down there. It's too risky. You'll have to slip out through the sewers, Sash. The way things have been going, if they come in here, they'll search every millimeter of the place."

"I'm gone, Louie. I'll be out of here in thirty seconds." She stepped down into the opening, her legs moving around, finding the rungs of the rickety wooden ladder leading down to the storeroom. She lowered herself halfway down and paused, looking up. "Thanks, Louie."

"Anytime, Sash. I owe you more than one, that's for sure." He reached under the bar, grabbing something and handing it down to her.

She flipped on the flashlight he'd given her and continued down, her feet landing on the rough concrete floor just as the bartender closed the door above her.

She moved across the dimly lit area, slipping around stacks of crates. She reached the far wall, and she put her free hand out, feeling around for the lever. It was well-hidden, one of the best-constructed secret doors she had ever seen. She could hear her heart beating, and she knew it wouldn't be long before her pursuers tracked her down to the Spacer's District. As far as she knew, there weren't any working street cameras in the area—the smugglers and other rogues who frequented the bars and brothels destroyed them as quickly as the authorities could replace them. But the soldiers would search all the establishments on the block. If they caught her here, she knew Louie would go down with her. And however dark and shady her past, Sasha Nerov did not sell out her friends.

Click.

There it was. She pushed harder, and the device clicked again. Then a small panel on the wall slid open. A wave of stench came blasting out at her. Most of Landfall had modern utility systems, neatly laid out underground passages with enclosed sewer pipes alongside power conduits and communications lines. But the Spacer's District had grown up over the initial settlements, streets, and buildings built before Haven's settlers had access to large quantities of high-tech materials, and its infrastructure had as much in common with seventeenth century Paris as it did with a modern city.

She took one last breath of the stale but comparatively refreshing air of the cellar, and then she climbed through the passage, sealing it closed behind her.

It was pitch-black in the sewer, and she turned on the small light Louie had given her. It was bright enough to illuminate her way, but she knew it could just as easily give her away if anyone was down here looking for her. But she'd risk that—she had no desire to be stuck down here without light.

They won't get to the sewers for a while. I'll have time to get out of here.

But where do I go?

She knew she couldn't go back to her lodging. That was the first place they'd look.

Shit. Everything is there. Currency, weapons, most of my documentation . . .

She realized her documents were useless. Everything. ID, passport, captain's license. Sasha Nerov was a wanted outlaw now. Her survival depended on her ability to hide, to assume another identity, at least in public.

Which meant her stash bag. She had to get to it. Everything she needed was in there. Money, false identity documents, weapons. It was in a storage facility on the outskirts of town, hidden among a mundane assortment of farm and industrial equipment. She had one in pretty much every major port, and she said a quick prayer to the god of smugglers, Paranoia.

But there was something she had to do first: warn her people. The authorities would come looking for them soon enough. And they had no idea what was coming.

Trouble was, she didn't keep track of her crew's whereabouts when they were in port. She figured they were scattered around in every tavern and whorehouse in Landfall, half of them probably lying on the floor somewhere drunk.

Griff.

Griff Daniels took his job as first officer seriously. So even if he was having a good time, he'd have kept tabs on the crew and have a much better chance of reaching them quickly. It helped that she knew where to find him, too. Daniels had a regular woman on Haven, a widow with a small farm a few kilometers outside the city. He'd be there. She was sure of it.

I just hope I can reach him in time.

She stepped slowly across the open sewer, trying not to think too much about the putrid flow—or the exact makeup of the slimy gunk that coated almost every surface.

It's better than getting caught . . . getting shot.

But she wasn't sure how much better . . .

"How'd we draw this duty?" The soldier was looking toward his partner, his eyes bleary, half open. The pair had pulled the night shift at the entrance to the mine, and they'd been sitting there for six hours now, with no more activity than a bit of rustling in the woods when the breeze kicked up.

"On the one hand, I'm not complaining—it's probably the safest duty we could get." The other trooper looked around, over his shoulder toward the perimeter fence and the main gate. Things had been patched back together, but the scars of the battle were still visible everywhere. "Still, I don't like it any better than you. I had friends who died here. And I keep thinking back to the governor's speech . . ." His voice trailed off, and he froze, looking into the distance, beyond the gate, to the road that cut through the dense woods surrounding the facility.

"What is it, Rog?" The other man turned . . . and froze. There was light visible in the distance . . . and then sound. Someone was approaching. A *lot* of someones. "What the hell is that?"

Rogers didn't know, but for all his bluster about the colonists, he had no desire to face down a large group of them, especially if they were armed. And who else would be coming to the prison at this hour? He gripped his rifle, holding it out at the ready. "We better report this." He got up and started moving toward the small guardhouse, motioning for the other soldier to stay and keep an eye on the approaching group.

But even as he was about to call it in, the approaching force already at the gate, Rogers and his partner tensed. It was only after the leader stepped into the light that the two guards sighed with relief: he was wearing a federal uniform. Not the same one they wore, but the darker garb of the anti-insurgency forces the observer brought with her. The column was large, at least three hundred strong, marching in perfect order behind the officer.

The two guards moved up toward the main gate, standing behind the fence and watching as the soldiers marched up. About five meters from the gate, the column halted.

"Open the gate." The voice was loud, commanding. "I am Captain Arthur Crandall, federal anti-insurgency forces. Per the orders of the federal observer, the pardons issued by the governor for the prisoners of this establishment are hereby revoked. All rioters are hereby sentenced to death—summary executions to be carried out at once."

Rogers looked at his companion, a stunned look on his face. There was a rush of excitement, of vindication, but it only lasted for a few seconds. Then uncertainty took over. It was one thing to be angry, to feel as though the soldiers lost in the uprising had not received justice. But this didn't seem like justice either. No trials, no courtrooms, nothing.

Just hundreds of executions.

Murders?

"Open the gate." The officer repeated himself, his voice louder, more insistent. He moved forward from the column. "Now."

The guards looked at each other for a second longer. Then, without a word spoken, they moved to the side, pulling the gate open.

Rogers watched as the new arrivals marched inside the complex, moving toward the main entrance of the mines—and then inside, down to the levels where the prisoners waited for the doom they didn't know was coming.

The soldier looked out at the vengeance he had craved so desperately, but now he was unsure, his stomach twisted into knots.

CHAPTER 14

"Dammit." Damian Ward stared down at the body of the man—a boy, really—lying facedown on the muddy bank of the stream. The kid had a hole in the back of his head, and his hair was crusted with blood and brains.

Damian knelt, feeling the wetness of the soft ground on his knees as he did. He reached down, grabbing the kid, rolling him over. He knew his shot had been a fatal one, but he had to confirm it. Just to himself. One look at the cold, dead face reinforced his regret at his combat reflexes and deadly aim.

Not that he hadn't been justified. The kid had been caught planting a bomb on one of the irrigation pumping stations, an act of vandalism Damian hadn't had the slightest intention of tolerating. His people had chased the vandal—terrorist—across half the farm and all the way to the river on the edge of the property. Damian had called out three times for him to surrender, but he'd just kept running. Damian dropped him with one shot.

Then he saw how young his victim was.

He shook his head. The kid looked fifteen, maybe sixteen. Damian felt conflicting emotions. Guilt and regret at having shot the boy. But, more than that, rage at whoever had recruited a child to commit such a crime. As he had said before, he sympathized with the rebels, but things like this cooled any urge he felt to actively support rebellion.

"He's dead." Damian didn't turn, but he heard his people run up behind him. His eyes were fixed on the kid, but he wasn't seeing his victim. He was seeing Jamie, even himself. Both of them had been angry, rebellious teenagers, born into poverty and angry at the world. He knew either of them could have been recruited at such a young age, that if they had been born in different times and places either of them could have ended up lying in the mud of the riverbank.

Still, I never had to run away from a veteran soldier with a sharp-shooter's badge.

"Get him out of this muck. Take him to one of the barns. Clean the body and wrap it up. It's the least we can do." Which wasn't exactly true.

Because when I find whoever is responsible for all this . . .

"Ben, make sure this gets done. Then come back to the house. We need to figure out how to protect the farm against people who send children to fight their battles."

"Yes, sir."

Damian sighed and took a last look at the kid, dirty blond hair, blue eyes still staring at him lifelessly. He reached out, moving his hand over the boy's face and closing his eyes. Then he stood up, and turned back toward Withers.

"I'm going to contact the governor's office and arrange for someone to come for the body."

He closed his eyes for a few seconds, and then he turned and walked back toward the house.

The soldiers marched down the street, a hundred strong, wearing body armor and carrying assault rifles. The people in the street moved away, many turning down side roads to avoid the imposing display of force. But the troopers weren't paying attention to the civilians, not even the occasional cluster of four or five who were in violation of the federal observer's orders against public assemblages. They had their orders, and they were on the way to carry them out.

The column turned onto the main street of Landfall, marching into the center of the small city's business district. Haven's capital had grown around two primary nodes, development clustering around both the colony's governmental functions and its growing industrial center.

They moved steadily toward the largest building in the district, the ten-story headquarters of Danforth Communications—one of the largest private concerns in Landfall.

At least until today.

The soldiers stopped just outside the main entrance. A quarter of them fanned out, covering the area, chasing away any civilians curious—and brave—enough to gather around and watch. The rest of the force followed an officer inside.

The commander was a woman wearing the insignia of a captain. She stepped up to the reception desk and glared down at the man seated there. "I am Captain Yolanda Sanchez, Federal America security forces. In the name of the federal observer, the honorable Asha Stanton, this enterprise is hereby nationalized. All broadcast operations are to cease immediately, pending the installation of federal censors to approve or reject all content. All facilities are now the property of the federal colony of Alpha-2."

The man at the desk stared back with a stunned look on his face. Then he reached down toward a comm station. The officer nodded to a soldier standing next to him. The trooper slammed down his rifle butt on the unit, smashing it. The man pulled his hand back, barely in time. He looked up, eyes wide.

"You are to remain where you are," Sanchez said. "You are to talk to no one. Lieutenant Fargus, station your people here. No one is to leave until we have arrested everyone on the proscription list. You are authorized to use deadly force at your discretion. Understood?"

"Understood, Captain."

"Lieutenant Regis, you and your people are to come with me."

"Yes, Captain," Regis snapped back, gesturing for his soldiers to line up.

The captain moved toward the bank of elevators, stepping inside the first car to open. A dozen soldiers followed her in, but she motioned for Regis to stay. "Bring the rest of your people up as soon as you can, Lieutenant."

"Yes, Captain Sanchez."

The captain reached out, pressing the button for the top floor. The executive suite. There were sixty-two people at Danforth Communications on the proscription list, men and women suspected of rebel sympathies . . . or even outright support of subversive activities. But she was most concerned with the name at the top of the list.

John Danforth.

Asha Stanton sat at her desk—Governor Wells's desk, really—and looked down at the small screen of the comm unit. "You heard me correctly, Lieutenant. I want all communications jammed. Planetwide. Everything but the specified federal frequencies."

"Your Excellency, that will cause widespread disruptions. All major broadcasting networks will be affected, as will almost all legitimate business communications. Even personal traffic will be affected, portable phones and comm units. Everything. It will cause panic and enormous disruption. Business will crash to a halt."

"I am aware of that. Is there anything in the order I gave you that you do not understand? I do not recall asking for a breakdown of the effects of jamming all comms. If I gave any impression that I wanted your thoughts or opinions—or anything but your obedience—allow me to clear that up right now. You are ordered to initiate jamming of all planetary overair communications, save the specified channels, and you are to do so at once." She paused, glaring down at the man's image on the screen, drawing a bit of amusement from the look on his face. "Now, is that sufficiently clear, or do I have to relieve you with an officer who understands how orders work?"

"No, Your Excellency . . . I mean, yes. I mean, I understand. Your order will be obeyed at once." The officer paused. "Your Excellency . . . implementing your order will require enormous energy output. We may need assistance from some of the vessels on blockade duty to supplement our own reactor."

"Very well, Lieutenant. See to it. I will request Commodore Karras's cooperation." Stanton had complete authority on Alpha-2, but

Karras and his people were navy. She knew his forces had been directed to cooperate with her, but she really couldn't do more than make a request.

Just a touch shortsighted of the senate, if you ask me. But she'd make it work.

"Yes, Your Excellency. Thank you."

"Very well, Lieutenant." Stanton almost cut the line, but then she added, "And the next time I give you an order, I expect it to be obeyed without the need to discuss the merits first."

"Yes, Your Excellency." The officer was clearly shaken, but he was doing an admirable job holding himself together. *Good.* "Planetary jamming commencing in ten minutes. All except the designated frequencies."

Stanton flipped the comm unit off without saying anything else.

Wells was really soft on his people. I'm going to have to remind them their purpose is to do as they are told . . . not to think. And certainly not to offer opinions.

She didn't understand how Wells had excelled so much in his previous postings. The more she was down here, the more she saw the results of his three years of work, the more she saw his weakness. She saw a bleeding heart, one that showed an almost total reluctance to impose harsh measures on the population. But it was more than that. Wells wasn't just opposed to the violence; he had become completely unnerved by the *prospect* of it.

It's one thing to try to prevent violence. But to shy away from it? What kind of governor can afford such squeamishness? Besides, it was such a waste of time. Violence is so often the expedient solution to a problem.

As she was about to demonstrate.

Not that she particularly enjoyed using harsh methods—at least, not like Semmes did—but she wouldn't hesitate to employ whatever it took to crush the rebel elements on Alpha-2.

And get me off this miserable rock as soon as possible.

"All right, our orders are simple." Captain Leslie stood in front of the line of soldiers, all of them clad in full body armor and holding heavy assault rifles. "There are multiple protests out there, all of them in flagrant violation of the mandate against large assemblages. We are to break them up and arrest any protestors who do not immediately disperse."

Johnson stood in the line, he and his four troopers part of the large force formed up just inside the federal complex. The regular colonial soldiers had been paired off with companion units from the newly arrived anti-insurgency troops. Johnson and the other colonial regulars were positioned on the left of the overall formation.

His hands were wrapped around the new rifle. His people had been rearmed, their light weapons replaced by powerful military-grade rifles. The guns had a higher rate of fire, and they shot a heavier projectile. They were designed for one purpose: to kill. Johnson tried to maintain a noncommittal expression, but he couldn't hold the smile from his lips.

Finally, we are done letting these people walk all over us.

"The rules of engagement are as follows. Protestors who disperse upon command will be allowed to return to their homes, others will be arrested immediately and without further warning. You are authorized to fire on any civilians resisting arrest. You are also authorized to open fire if you feel threatened by the mob."

Johnson listened, but he barely heard the words. He could only see Billings's corpse lying on the floor of the mine . . .

"All right, people . . . let's go."

Leslie turned and walked toward the gate. "Open," he yelled, looking up at the troopers in the two small towers flanking the three-story gate.

He stood and waited as the two giant metal doors slid open, each side slipping into a slot in the wall. The sound of the crowd poured through, massively louder without the closed gate in the way. There were hundreds of civilians in the square in front of the complex, perhaps thousands. They were marching, shouting, carrying signs.

Johnson looked out at them. He knew, at least on some level, that the citizens of Landfall weren't the same ones who had killed his friends in the mine, but he didn't care anymore. The murderers had almost escaped punishment. He had no doubt Governor Wells would have pardoned them all to appease the city mob. At least the federal observer had intervened—and given the killers exactly what they deserved.

Now this bloody mob will be appeased in a different way.

Johnson stood for a few seconds and watched as the formation began to move, following Leslie out into the square. Then it was time for his people. He stepped forward and turned sharply to the left, moving in step toward the open gate. He could see the crowd reacting to the soldiers. The volume of their shouts rose, and they surged forward, moving toward the approaching formation.

"By the authority of the federal observer, I order all of you to disperse at once." Leslie spoke into a small comm unit, and his voice was broadcast from every outdoor speaker on the federal building. "There will be no second warning." His last words were ominous, and the crowd seemed to hesitate for a moment.

Johnson stood and watched, thinking for a moment that the civilians would back down. But then one of them pushed out of the crowd, raising his arms in the air and shouting to the rest of the mob. Johnson couldn't hear his words, but he could see the effect. Those around him stopped moving back, and they turned toward him. Then more of the mob moved out, inspired by the single figure in the front.

Others followed suit, all through the crowd, men and women moving out from the masses, shouting and pointing and pumping fists in the air. And around each one, more gathered, rally points in the mob, hundreds of civilians holding their ground, defying Leslie's orders.

"Form up in two lines." It was Leslie's voice, broadcast over the speakers, though the words were meant for his soldiers. Johnson moved into positon, looking to the side to see that his four troopers had complied. His people were on the extreme left of the federal line.

He stood in place, waiting to see what would happen next. The crowd was still there. Indeed, the agitators up front had worked them into a near-frenzy.

"All units, present arms."

Johnson pulled his rifle up, holding it out in front of him. When he'd been in the mine, he hadn't hesitated to lash out against the prisoners. But now that he might have his opportunity—the one he'd been waiting for so long—he was surprised how twisted his stomach was.

Jesus, people—just back the fuck down. Let us arrest you.

"Ready . . ." Leslie's voice was hard, cold.

He's going to give the order, Johnson thought, feeling not at all like he thought he would.

The mob was growing angrier, those on the front edge moving slowly toward the soldiers.

"Aim . . ." Leslie's voice was partially drowned out by the sound of a gunshot. Johnson leaned forward, looking down the line. One of the soldiers near the center was on the ground. Johnson couldn't see how badly wounded his comrade was, but any doubts he had were replaced by a resurgence of his anger.

Bastards.

"Fire," Leslie screamed, his own rage clear in his ragged tone.

Johnson hesitated, just for an instant, and then he pulled the trigger. The heavy gun had a lot more kick that his old weapon, and he let his finger slip off for a second, giving him an instant to reposition himself, to dig his feet in before he opened fire again.

He saw a nightmare unfold in front of him as dozens of citizens went down under the withering fire of two hundred heavy assault rifles. His rage drove him on, filling him with a grim satisfaction. Yet there was more there, something floating around in his mind, seemingly at odds with the need for vengeance.

Shame?

Pity?

He saw a woman go down under the relentless fire, and as she did, something fell from her arms. It took a second for it to sink in, but then Johnson realized it was a child. He felt the urge to call for his comrades to cease fire, to run across the field and see if the child was still alive. But he didn't. He just continued shooting, stopping only to reload when he had burned through his clip.

The mob was fleeing now. There were at least a hundred down on the square, and the rest were panicked, trampling their fellow protestors as they struggled to escape.

Order us to stop firing . . .

Johnson could feel the sweat pouring down his neck, his back. He wanted to stop shooting, to let the terrified civilians run. His thirst for revenge had been quenched, and now he angled his weapon upward, deliberately shooting over the heads of the terrified, fleeing protestors.

Please . . . please stop this.

"Maintain your fire." Leslie's voice was like ice, not a shred of pity for those dropping under the relentless fire.

Johnson almost dropped his weapon, desperate to turn and walk back to the barracks. But he didn't dare. He had his orders, a command he had craved since the day his unit had stormed the prison mine.

Now all he wanted was for it to stop.

But it didn't. The fire became a bit more ragged—he realized he wasn't the only trooper in the line disgusted by what he was doing—but it continued.

The square was covered in bodies, and the blood was literally flowing in rivulets, filling the cracks in the road surface. And still, the fire continued.

Finally, Leslie gave the command to cease fire, and the guns fell silent. Johnson stood where he was, his legs struggling to hold himself up. The mob was gone, the survivors out of range now, fleeing in every direction . . . and an eerie silence hung over the square, pierced only by the cries of the wounded . . . and the screaming in his own mind.

Nerov pressed herself against the wall, turning her head, looking in every direction. She was exhausted, her legs aching. But she knew she couldn't stop.

She could hear the sound off in the distance. It was far away, a faint rumble, hard to identify. But she'd been enough places, in enough bad situations, to know what it was. Massed gunfire. She had no idea what was happening, but she knew it had to be bad.

Has the rebellion begun?

She slipped down a tiny side street, trying to stay hidden. She'd made her way as far as she could in the sewers, but that route ended at the edge of the Spacer's District. She'd climbed out, making her way through the streets from there, trying to avoid as much contact as she could. Her clothes were nondescript, and she hoped she was far enough from the spaceport to elude any immediate pursuit, but she had no illusions about how she smelled. Blending in just wasn't an option, not until she got a shower and a change of clothes.

She was tempted to move toward the gunfire, to try to find out what was happening. Once again she found herself more concerned about the Havenites than her persona as a hard-edged mercenary could support. She wondered what disaster was taking place a couple kilometers from where she stood. A wave of sadness came over her, as she realized civilians were most likely dying. But she had no way to stop whatever was happening, and she wouldn't save anyone by getting herself captured or killed. Her first loyalty was to her own people. She had to get to Griff and warn him and the rest of her crew.

She turned away from the sound and moved through the outskirts of the city. There were fewer buildings there, and they were spaced farther apart. She'd come this way because the district was one filled mostly with warehouses, with very little foot traffic. She was tired, her legs heavy. But she kept moving, and the buildings began to thin out until she found herself in open countryside. Haven was a young colony, just sixty-one years old, and its cities tended to end abruptly, with no belts of suburban development between the urban area and the farmlands and countryside beyond.

She came to a large hill. Her exhausted legs burned like fire as she walked over the crest, and as she came down the other side, the city was gone, her view of it completely blocked by the looming hillside.

She tried to remember where the farm was. She'd been there once before, to collect Daniels and bring him back to the ship. Her first officer seemed uptight on first impression, like a ramrod-stiff naval officer. But there was a true pirate's persona beneath that staid exterior, and Daniels came close to the old cliché of having a woman in every port. This one was different, though, special to him. He spent almost every minute with her each time they were on Haven.

There's a dirt road up here somewhere . . .

She squinted and looked out across the countryside, trying to decide if anything seemed familiar. She was so tired she felt as though she might fall over, but she couldn't afford to stop. Or could she . . .

Maybe whatever is happening in Landfall will buy some time.

She felt an immediate wave of guilt for drawing relief from what was almost certainly a tragedy. But she just as quickly dismissed it. Her crew came first. They were her friends, her family . . . and the only people in the galaxy she even came close to trusting. And they were out there, completely unaware they were in grave danger.

She stopped and looked around again, turning three hundred and sixty degrees, feeling the frustration grow as she didn't see anything familiar. She wanted to give up, to go find someplace she could hide, look for a brook or pond where she could get some water. But there was no time. Every minute increased the chances of her people ending up in prison. Or on the scaffold.

She gazed up at the sky, figuring it was halfway between midday and sunset. She *had* to find Daniels before dark. If she didn't, she knew it was almost certain he and the rest of her people would be captured. She'd seen enough of anti-insurgency troopers to know they favored smashing down doors in the dead of night.

She reached the road—more of a dirt track—and stopped. There was something there . . . yes, this was the road she'd taken the last time she'd been there. She turned and continued out from the city, ducking into the brush along the edge of the road the two times she heard a vehicle approach.

Finally, she saw it. The small farmhouse. The moment she walked around a bend and set eyes on it she knew she was there. She hurried her pace, ignoring the fatigue. It was only when she was about halfway to the house that she suddenly froze. *What if the feds beat me to Griff?* They could be waiting for her. She hesitated, looking around. There were no signs of any kind of struggle—and she was fairly certain Daniels would have put up a fight. Moreover, there were no fresh tracks or signs of heavy transports on the ground.

She pushed the fears aside. There was no covered approach to the house, and she hadn't come all this way to turn back now and abandon Daniels and her crew. She walked straight up to the house, and she banged on the door. No answer. She pounded her fist again. And again. Louder. Still nothing.

Am I too late?

This time the fear almost took her. If the feds had been there, if they had taken Daniels away, they might have left someone here in case she turned up.

She looked all around, her hand slipping under her jacket and pulling out the pistol. Then she heard something—someone— walking around the side of the house. She crept up toward the corner, slowly, quietly. And then she spun around, weapon at the ready.

There were two figures there, a man and a woman. The man reacted quickly, shoving the woman to the side, putting himself between her and the threat. Then he focused on Nerov.

"Captain?" he said, confusion in his voice.

"Griff," she replied, her tone heavy with relief as she lowered her gun. "I'm glad I found you."

Daniels moved forward toward her, recognizing immediately that something was terribly wrong. The woman just stood still, quietly looking on.

"What are you doing here, Captain?"

"You have to leave, Griff. Now. And we need to get to the crew. They've all got to go into hiding." She paused, not wanting to even say the words.

"The feds have *Vagabond*, Griff. They know we're smugglers."

"Hurry, we've got to get out of here. Run down to the secure room, and download the core files. Then wipe the system." It had been less than ten minutes since Suze Lingon had sent the signal from the office, and Danforth was just lucky to have been home at the time. He knew his loyal aide had taken a terrible chance warning him. But he'd made the arrangements with her months before, a fail-safe if the government ever found out about his activities and made a move on him. He'd half thought it had been paranoia that led him to set up the whole thing.

Now he knew it wasn't.

"On my way, John." Tyler Danforth was John's cousin, and his ally as an agitator and proponent of Haven independence. He turned and left the room, not exactly at a run, but something faster than a walk.

It was unclear if Tyler was on the proscription list along with

John, but if he wasn't, there was little doubt he would be soon. The younger Danforth had a less public profile than his cousin, but he was every bit as involved in the growing rebel movement.

John Danforth was in his library, looking out over the carefully tended groves of apple trees that had been his grandfather's pride and joy, the first successful Haven cultivation of the old man's favorite Earth fruit. He remembered his grandfather declaring, perhaps with more pride than objectivity, that the Haven variety was tarter and juicier, superior to its Earthly cousins.

He paused as he stared out over the beautiful grounds of the family farm, the idyllic setting where he'd grown up. The hills, the trees, the small, winding streams.

And said goodbye to all of it.

Time to run, John. If you're not too late already.

He turned back to his desk, digging through the drawers, pawing through the data chips and tablets. He tossed most aside, occasionally stuffing one into a small duffel bag.

He'd thought about it, of course, what it would be like if open rebellion became a reality, but now it was different. Nothing, he now realized, could truly prepare one for this moment. The speeches were over, the machinations behind the scenes no longer necessary. The planning, the plotting. There were soldiers, no doubt on the way right now, and they planned to arrest him, to drag him back to face charges of treason and sedition. Accusations that could very well lead to the scaffold.

So this is courage, he thought. *This is what it feels like when convictions and rhetoric become reality.*

It was one thing to call for rebellion, to support it. Quite another, he now realized, to stare it in the face, while deciding what few possessions to take before running off to hide.

No doubt soldiers were already on their way, coming to search his house. Prepared to ransack it, looking for incriminating information . . . or anything that might lead them to him. He could see them in his mind, breaking down the door, running through the house, smashing things, bringing destruction to the place that had been his family's home for almost sixty years.

He leaned forward, pressing his thumb against the sensor pad on the locked bottom drawer. It popped open, and he reached inside. He grabbed a box of data units and a large sack full of small platinum bars. He also took a stack of plastic cards, each accessing a bank account under a different false name, and a handful of ID chips. He was one of the richest men on Haven, but if the feds hadn't frozen his accounts yet, they would within minutes. These few precautions, this small stash he'd kept in his drawer, it was all he had now.

"John, we've got to go . . . now!" It was Tyler, calling from out in the hall. "I can see a convoy on the road, no more than three kilometers out." One advantage to Danforth Hall was that it was set on a high hill, commanding the ground all around. Still, he didn't have much of a head start. The feds would cover the distance to the house in minutes.

John slammed the drawer shut, and slung the bag over his shoulder. "Okay, let's go." Then: "I wonder why Geoff didn't signal us." Geoff Nettles was one of his most trusted aides . . . and he was down the road, watching the main approach.

"I think there's something wrong with communications, John." Tyler followed as his cousin stepped through the door and out into the manicured yards between the house and the orchards. "I can't raise anybody on my comm unit."

"We'll worry about that later. For now we have to get to the woods. I've got a transport stashed down there." He moved quickly, his cousin on his heels, through an opening in the large brick wall enclosing the garden and out into the large grove of apple trees.

"What could be wrong with communications?" His response was a bit delayed. "Suze got cut off, too. One second she had been transmitting, and the next all I had was static." Danforth had figured his loyal aide had cut the line suddenly to avoid getting caught warning him. But now he wondered.

He pulled out his own portable comm. He'd had it off out of fear the feds would use it to track him, but now he flipped it on as he continued down the hill behind the orchard. Nothing but static.

"You're right, Ty. Even my comm is dead. What do you think that means?" He asked the question, but then he answered it himself before his cousin could. "They're jamming communications. They must be doing it from the orbital platform. God—that means they've taken control of the whole satellite network."

"But that would shut down everything. Network broadcasts, even the ability of the governor to address the planet."

"No—I'm sure they've still got dedicated frequencies for the government. It was built in when my grandfather was starting the business. There's no way they would prevent themselves from commanding their own forces."

The two moved through the woods as they spoke, climbing down the hillside toward a small road.

"And that means it's truly begun, Ty. The military is moving in. It's the only possibility. They wouldn't be expending so much energy just to mess with normal planetwide communications." He ran up to the transport, pressing his hand against a panel on the side. The doors slid open, and he climbed in, waving for Tyler to get around to the other side. Then he flipped on the vehicle's AI. "Hamlen's Farm, maximum possible speed," he barked.

"Hamlen's Farm," the unit responded. An instant later the doors slammed shut and the vehicle lurched forward hard and bounced around wildly as it raced down the narrow dirt road.

"We've got to get the word out, Ty," he continued. "We can't know what the feds know, or what they're up to . . . but if we don't assemble the Guardians, we risk losing the rebellion before it even begins."

"If we rally the Guardians openly, it's a declaration of war against the federals." Tyler turned toward his cousin.

"Yes, Ty. That is exactly what it is. But the feds have clearly already declared war on us—that's what the communication breakdown means. Besides, our only other choice is captivity . . . and possibly death. And that is no choice."

John Danforth paused, taking a deep breath before continuing. "We have spoken of this for several years now, given rousing speeches in secret basement meetings. Well, now those words, the slogans of rebellion and the cries for freedom . . . they have come home to roost. We called for rebellion, for war. And that is exactly what we are getting."

CHAPTER 15

"John, I can't tell you how relieved I am that you escaped." Cal Jacen walked out of the darkness and into the small farmhouse, scanning the room as he did. There were half a dozen men and two women there, all leading revolutionaries. They were the lucky ones, those who had managed to escape the federal purge the day before. At least half of their compatriots hadn't been so fortunate. They were in federal custody now . . . or dead if they had refused to surrender.

"Same to you, Cal. I figured if they were bold enough to come for me, you had to be on the list, too." With Jacen's background of dissent back on Earth, Danforth knew his ally *had* to be at the *top* of any suspects list the feds had compiled.

"I was fortunate enough to be out when they came for me. I got a warning, and I hid until nightfall. I didn't want to come out here until I was sure I wasn't being followed. And I figured if I waited until dark, their satellites couldn't track me either."

Danforth nodded, and he rubbed his eyes. It had been a brutally stressful day, and now it was after midnight. He was exhausted, but he knew sleep was nowhere in sight. Shaking his head to get the blood flowing, he said, "I just hope everyone else was as careful. Not that there's so many of us left—they have a lot of our people in custody." He paused. "We can't stay here long. Somebody will break, and then we'll have federal troopers pouring out of these woods."

Hamlen's Farm was one of the Guardians' hideouts, a meeting place intended for situations just like the current one. But too many people who knew its location hadn't made it out. Danforth knew the feds were skilled at extracting information from captives . . . and if half the reports filtering in from Landfall were true, Governor Wells's moderate policies were a thing of the past.

"There's more than that to worry about," Jacen said. "I have some intel from one of my spies inside the federal complex. It's not good, John. The feds know about Vincennes. They're sending a column of soldiers to seize it all."

Danforth felt as if he'd been punched in the gut. Vincennes was one of the Guardians' primary weapons storage areas. A federal move against the village meant that almost half the guns and ordnance they'd acquired—at great risk and expense—were in jeopardy. If the federals took Vincennes, the revolution was over before it began.

He looked around the room, at the grim faces of his compatriots. "That's it, then—that is where we make our first stand. Where we take the fight out into the open."

"Yes!" Fist clenched and thrust into the air, Jacen's excitement was obvious. "To arms—we will fight until no federal oppressors breathe Haven air."

The men and women in the room had been glum, tired, seeming more like hunted animals than fiery revolutionaries. But now they began to come alive once more. The reality of all they'd been planning was finally coming to fruition. And the terror of the previous day—of being on the run for their lives—was now a thing of the past. Now they were going to be running *toward* the feds . . . and their guns would be blazing. These were brave men and women— the defiance it required to go to secret meetings and make speeches in barns late at night was proof of that. And now that bravery would need to evolve, to turn into the courage to stand against enemy soldiers, to defy death on the battlefield. To fight the war they had so long sought, yet never truly understood.

Danforth felt it, too.

One by one, the others shouted, "Yes!" and followed Jacen's lead, thrusting their hands in the air.

John Danforth was the last. He stepped forward, standing between Jacen and his cousin. He raised his own arm up. "To victory."

"To victory!"

"But now we have work to do," Jacen said. "We have to get the word out, rally the Guardians. We must have our forces assembled at Vincennes by midday tomorrow, armed and ready for battle."

"We have been trying to contact as many of the Guardians as possible, Cal. I wanted to warn them in case any are on the feds' list. But the federals are jamming all our comms . . . and using the ground lines would be like lighting a signal flare about where we are."

"We knew this was coming, though. I've got men ready to spread the word—by transport, by speeder . . . even on foot, if need be. I'll send them out immediately."

"But will that be enough?"

Jacen thought about it. "Probably not. So let us ride as well. All of us. If we spread out, we should be able to get it done in time."

"Yes." Danforth put his hand on Jacen's shoulder. "Let us ride, all of us. Let us carry the warning and rouse the people. It is time . . . time to fight for their freedom."

"It is time," they all repeated.

He walked over to a map that was spread on a nearby table. Pointing at various locations, Danforth started divvying up the area around the capital. "Cal, you head west, toward Weldon and Milton." He turned. "Annie, you and Charles go north, and alert everyone in the valley. Jack, Tony . . . south, to the villages along the river. But be careful, you'll be close to Landfall." Finally, he turned toward his cousin. "And Ty and I will head east, to Lamberton and the Palisades."

He paused and looked around the room. "And never forget, this is the day we have worked for . . . our one chance to preserve Haven's liberty, to fight off the oppression of Federal America . . . to live our own lives, to create a better world, for our children and grandchildren. Do not stop, any of you, until you have completed your missions. I know you're tired—God knows I am. And I know you're afraid, at least on some level. We'd be stupid not to be. But our task is righteous. The Guardians are ready to fight. We'll have time to rest when the last feds are off Haven . . . or when we're dead!"

He was breathing hard now. "I have never been prouder in my life than I am now in all of you. Go! Rouse the Guardians—and all others who will rally to our cause—and light the fire of revolution!"

The small group broke out in a cheer, and each of them in turn stepped forward, gripping Danforth's hand or embracing the rebel leader.

Then they filtered out, one and two at a time. Some of them climbed into transports, others mounted small speeders. They headed off, each in a different direction, to spread the same message: *the federals are coming.*

"**Do you see** why I insisted you come?" Griff Daniels was speaking to a slightly built woman. Elisa Hendricks stood just over a meter and a half, and she didn't weigh a gram more than forty-five kilos. She was lying on the ground looking over the crest of a small hill at a house. *Her* house.

There were federal soldiers there, at least a dozen. They had arrived in two transports, and they had poured out of their vehicles, moving immediately toward the building. They didn't pause, didn't bother with the formality of knocking. They just smashed the door down and made their way inside, armed to the teeth.

"That farm is all I have," Elisa said, the despair clear in her tone. "Perhaps if I'd stayed . . ."

"No." Nerov turned and looked at her. "They're here for you as much as anyone else. It's the only thing that makes sense. They clearly know more than we think."

"What do you mean?" Elisa asked.

"Just that there are no official records of Griff having a relationship with you, no documentation of any kind. No one knows at all as far as I am aware of, save for me . . . and whoever else on the crew Griff told."

Daniels shook his head. "No one."

"So how did they know he was with me?"

"Exactly," Nerov said. "The federals have tremendous surveillance capability. They control the satellite network. There are cameras everywhere, too. And even though the governor had a passive strategy, it would be a mistake to say that just because he didn't use information, he didn't have it." She turned toward her first officer. "Indeed, they clearly had more on us than we thought, Griff. They flagged *Vagabond* almost immediately after the federal observer took charge."

He grimaced, turning to Elisa. "I'm so sorry. I should never have gotten involved with you. As a smuggler, I knew that there was always the potential the government would come after me."

Elisa just shook her head, though, and reached out to put her hand on Daniel's shoulder. "No, Griff. Don't say that. I knew what you were when we first met, and I went in with my eyes open. And I would have lost this farm by now without your help. I let you pay off my debts, and I'd be a liar if I said I didn't know where that money came from."

Nerov had turned back toward the house, giving Griff and Elisa what minuscule level of privacy she could. But a few seconds later she looked back toward them. "We better get out of here." She gestured toward the house. The soldiers were coming back out, some moving toward their vehicles, others setting out across the fields surrounding the house. "They're going to search the area. We need to be gone. Now."

She took a last look. Two of the soldiers were standing in front of the house. They walked back about twenty meters and then one of them held out a small device. An instant later there was an explosion, and plumes of flame burst through the house's windows.

Elisa let out a startled cry, watching as the troops burned her home. Griff had moved next to her, and he put his hand over her mouth to stifle her shout almost as soon as it was out. They were probably too far away to be heard, but there was no sense taking chances.

"We've got to get to the others." Nerov stood up, moving back into the woods. "It may be too late, but we have to try."

Daniels looked down at the ground for a few seconds, clearly thinking. "There's an inn a bunch of the crew stay at. And I know a brothel where a few of the boys spend most of their shore time." He looked up at Nerov, a concerned look on his face. "But they're both in Landfall, Captain."

"Then we head back to Landfall, Griff. There's no choice. I owe you all too much to not try." And as she watched Elisa's home burn to the ground, the thought of getting into the thick of things was starting to have more and more appeal to her.

Jacen sat at the controls of the small transport, driving it down the winding country road at a pace that could only be described as reckless. He'd already been to the village of Weldon, and he'd rallied the Guardians there, and half the other townsfolk as well. Weldon was hard-core rebel country, and before he left he'd seen most of the fighting-age men and women in the village formed up, ready to march . . . and the half dozen loyalists in the village imprisoned in a storage shed. He'd have preferred a more decisive solution for the traitors—Jacen had no pity for those who stood in the way of the revolution—but he knew it would be too much to expect the citizens of Weldon to shoot their neighbors in cold blood.

At least for now. Wait until there have been a few battles, when the lists of the dead are posted and the feds begin executing rebels en masse. Then the rage will come . . . and neighbor will fall upon neighbor, and cleanse away those without the vision to see the future.

He turned sharply onto a small road, not much more than a trail, really. The transport barely fit, and he could hear the branches and leaves scraping against the side of the vehicle. But the path was a familiar one, and Jacen continued on, stopping as soon as he came to a clearing. He looked ahead. There was another vehicle, similar to his own, parked, a man standing in front of it.

He opened the hatch and stepped out, walking across the small meadow. It was a secluded spot, completely surrounded by woods. It was just after 2:00 A.M., and neither moon was visible. The only light came from the two transports.

"It is here, my friend." There was excitement in Jacen's voice, satisfaction. He walked toward the other vehicle. "The day we have waited for, worked for. Revolution."

Zig Welch moved toward Jacen, extending his arm and shaking his ally's hand. "I heard about the violence in Landfall. They are saying over a hundred were killed. That will surely be the spark to ignite rebellion."

It dawned on Jacen that with the comms down, Zig hadn't heard. And for some reason, that made him even more excited. "Well over a hundred. And two hundred more injured. But that's of no moment."

"*What?*"

"We need not rely on the people anymore. Their deaths are terrible, but war is all but certain without them. In fact, it will begin this very day."

"*What?*" Zig repeated. "Tell me—what else has happened?"

Jacen smiled. "The federals know of the Guardians' weapons cache at Vincennes. They are sending a force—even now they are likely making preparations."

"Do the Guardians know?"

"They are alerted. Indeed, I am charged with rallying those in Weldon and Milton and the area all around." His smile turned vicious. "It's finally here, Zig."

"At last. What good fortune. We could hardly have planned it better."

Jacen stared back at his compatriot. "Fortune is for fools, my friend. The revolution is too important to trust to the vagaries of fate. Indeed, this is all part of the plan, come at last to fruition."

"You don't mean . . ."

Jacen smiled. "Of course . . . how do you think the feds got the information about Vincennes and the weapons hidden there?"

Welch stared back, confusion on his face giving way to shock. "You . . ."

"I told them. Of course I did. Or at least I helped them find the information."

"My God, Cal. I understand your intention to incite hostilities, but should you have risked something as vital as Vincennes?"

"There was no choice. It had to be something the Guardians *had* to defend. I wouldn't allow there to be a chance they would choose not to fight. With luck, the weapons will be saved, but even if they are lost, we will have what we desperately need. Revolution."

Welch stood silently for a moment. Then he said simply, "Revolution."

"I must go. I need to reach Milton as soon as possible. We must have as much strength as possible at Vincennes when the federals arrive."

Welch nodded.

"And you must go as well. Warn the brotherhood. They, too, must come to Vincennes. We need every man or woman, even children old enough to wield a gun."

"Consider it done, Cal." Welch nodded. "I will see you in the morning, comrade . . . on the first battlefield of the revolution."

Jacen nodded back. "The revolution," he repeated. Then he turned and walked back to the transport.

"**Awaken! Arise! Get** your weapons, and march now to Vincennes." Tyler Danforth stood in the middle of the small village's main road, shouting as loudly as he could manage.

Lamberton wasn't much to look at, but it was the center of a fertile farming sector. It was also a community almost totally united in its support for the rebel cause.

John Danforth walked down the street, banging on doors, adding his own voice to his cousin's. "Citizens of Lamberton, it's time! We march to face the federals, to unfurl the flag of freedom."

Danforth had to suppress a bit of bitter amusement at the primitive nature of his call to action. Mankind was a spacefaring race, yet he and his people were scurrying from town to town, shouting and beating on doors. *We might as well be using lanterns in church steeples.* But even if they wanted to risk physical connection, there were no landlines out in farming country.

All down the streets he could see lights coming on, and bleary-eyed men and women pouring out into the street, many with weapons already in hand.

"It is John and Tyler Danforth," John shouted to a group in front of him. "We bring the call for the Guardians of Liberty. You are needed. They have murdered hundreds in the streets of Landfall! They have been rounding up innocent citizens of Haven! Revolution is upon us, and even now the federals prepare to march on Vincennes. We need your help. Go to Vincennes, and stand with your brothers and sisters. It is time to fight for your homes, for freedom!"

The people lining the roads were mostly quiet at first, but then a ragged cheer began. Danforth could see the Guardians beginning to gather on the road in front of them, and as they did the cheer rode in intensity.

The Guardians wore work clothes and coveralls, and all manner of boots. They were farmers and tradesfolk, laborers and skilled professionals, but they formed up as one, and on each of their heads there was a black hat with a white cockade, the symbol of their resolve. They had long hidden their badge, but now it was displayed proudly on fifty heads . . . and more were coming. And on the outskirts of the village, children were already running off over the hills, sent out to spread the word to the surrounding farms.

Danforth stepped into the crowds, reaching out, shaking hands, and grabbing on to his comrades. "Will you go? Will you do as I ask and stand with me to face the federals?"

The roar was almost deafening, a single word that seemed to echo again and again off the surrounding hillsides. "Yes!"

Ty walked up to his cousin. "I almost pity the federals," he said, clearly moved by the response of the villagers.

John nodded, but he didn't say anything. As much as any one man, he was the living, breathing heart of the revolution. And he was proud of these people, of those who had joined the Guardians, and of the other villagers, clearly rallying to the cause, some of them standing with nothing more than tools and farming implements for weapons. They were good people, and in them he saw the greatness of Haven. The greatness that could be. But he also knew some of them would die before the day was out. That these cheers would be replaced by the cries and wails of family members learning their husbands and wives, sons and daughters, would never return. He believed with all his heart that freedom was worth fighting for, even dying for, but he also knew that didn't lessen the cost war extracted. If Haven could win its independence, there would be celebrations and wild, unrestrained joy. But there would also be sadness and tears, the somber remembrance of those who had died in the struggle.

And that starts today . . .

"Ty, go on to the Palisades without me. Tell the people there as we did here, and I will meet you at Vincennes before dawn."

Tyler turned and looked at his cousin. "Where are you going?"

"There is one more person I would see, who I would bring into our cause if I am able."

"Is one man really worth your time?"

"He is if his name is Damian Ward."

"Daddy . . . Daddy . . . please open the door . . ." Katia Rand was prone on the front porch, banging as hard as she could manage. The first rays of light were just poking their way over the eastern mountains. She'd been running, hiding, desperately trying to get home since the day before.

The door opened a crack, a man's face barely visible. "Who is the . . . ?" His words stopped abruptly, and he swung open the door. "Katia! Katia! I have been looking for you all night."

He stepped out of the door, fully dressed, his clothes disheveled, his boots caked with mud. "Where have you been?"

He knelt down next to his daughter, his eyes moving over her. She had a cut on her face, covered now with dried blood. Her shirt was torn, hanging in front of her like a rag, with only her hand holding it up. Her pants had half a dozen rips in them, and she had fastened what was left with a strip of fabric torn from her jacket and turned into a makeshift belt. He imagined a hundred nightmares, horrors that might have befallen her, but he forced them all away. She was here, she was alive . . . and that was all that mattered to him.

"I'm so sorry, Daddy." Her words were choked with sobs, and tears streamed down her face. "I know you told me to stay away, but I went to Landfall, to the protest."

Alexi exhaled hard, pushing back the anger, the frustration, at his daughter's foolishness. He knew she sympathized with the Guardians, with all the rebel groups, but he'd warned her of the dangers . . . and begged her to stay out of trouble. This wasn't the time for recrimination, however. "Katia . . . my Katia . . ." He put his hand on her face, wiped away her tears.

He closed his eyes and reached out, putting his arms around his daughter and pulling her close. He could see images, another face, not unlike Katia's. His wife, Anya. First as she was when they met, young, vibrant, smiling at him as she had that first day. Then lying on a filthy bed, covered in sweat despite half a dozen blankets, holding her shriveled arm up to him, like a thin, gauzy fabric hanging from the bone.

Anya Rand had died from a disease that could have been cured, would have been had Alexi not been barred from openly pursing his livelihood as an electrical engineer. Few people knew their way around computers and other high-tech gear like Alexi, but he was self-taught, lacking the expensive government-sanctioned credentials required in Federal America. He'd survived by working unofficially, for a fraction of what a government-certified engineer would have charged, but his medical priority rating was that of a laborer, far too low to obtain the expensive drugs and therapies Anya had needed. So he'd knelt by her side, loved her, cooled her face with a wet towel as he spoke softly to her . . . and he'd watched her waste away and die.

That tragedy had almost destroyed him. It would have, in fact, had it not been for Katia, and for the promise he'd made to his dying wife. He'd sworn to Anya he would look after their daughter, that he would somehow see that she had a better life than theirs. And that had driven him since. It had led him to Haven, and it had kept him from getting involved in the rebellion. And now it would drive him to arms, to stand with the revolutionaries . . .

"I tried to get home, but there were soldiers everywhere. They were chasing people, arresting them. Killing them. They shot people in the streets. It was awful." She broke down in tears again, sobbing uncontrollably.

Alexi tightened his grip on his daughter. "It's okay, my love.

You're home now." He could feel the wetness from her tears as she buried her face against his shoulder, her body shaking.

He thought again of that day, of the moment he'd realized that Anya was gone. He'd felt an emptiness he couldn't describe, and a relief, too, that her pain was over. It had almost broken him watching his wife, once so energetic—so alive—wasting away in agony. He'd been devastated, and only one thing drove the sadness back from the front of his mind. Hatred. He hated Federal America, the entrenched politicians who lived such luxurious lives while people like Anya were denied basic care. He detested the cronies of the politicians who controlled the economy, crushing people like him, keeping them down with regulations and endless mandates. They had killed Anya as far as he was concerned, no less than if they'd put a gun to her head and pulled the trigger. But he put his hatred aside, for perhaps the only reason he could have done so. To keep his promise to Anya.

And he had done just that, trading his services on a bulk freighter for passage to Haven, a place where a man with his skills could practice his trade unfettered. He had built a business, and given his daughter a life. But the hatred was only controlled, not extinguished, and he struggled to contain it as he held his terrified, brutalized daughter in his arms.

Alexi had heard about the massacre the day before and, when Katia had failed to come home, he had feared she had given in to her rebel sympathies and gone to the protest.

The vid networks were all down, but there were other ways for word to spread, and the search for his daughter had taken him to a dozen homes. Each person had told him a single fact or rumor, one bit of information of dubious reliability. But the persistency of his efforts gave him enough snippets to piece together a likely scenario of what had happened in Landfall. It terrified him.

There had been rumors, too, of what had taken place after the massacre, of federal troops roaming the streets, kicking down doors searching for protestors who had fled the carnage and escaped arrest. And other stories, too, of gangs of soldiers wandering the streets, terrorizing civilians. There had been more murders, he suspected, and rapes and beatings. The normally safe streets of Landfall had become the most dangerous place in the galaxy.

And Katia had been there.

What he hadn't been able to determine was what had happened to her. Had she been arrested? Or had something worse happened? The questions had haunted him all night. But now she was back, alive despite whatever nightmare she had endured. He was grateful that he hadn't lost the only thing that really mattered to him. But his relief only lasted a moment.

His eyes caught the movement, and his head snapped up. He could see someone approaching, a transport . . . no, two. Big ones, with room for troops up front, and what looked like large holding areas in the rear. *More troops? Or for prisoners?*

They were coming down the road, leaving a trail of dust billowing up behind their heavy bulk.

He stood, putting his arms under Katia's shoulders, pulling her up. "Go inside, Katia. *Now.*"

Katia hesitated, moving a hand across her face, wiping away tears. "What is it?"

"Just *go*," he said, his voice firmer. He pushed her gently toward the door, just as the transports pulled up in front of the house.

"Stay where you are," a voice boomed out of a speaker on the front vehicle. The hatch opened, and four federal soldiers climbed out. They wore riot gear and carried assault rifles.

A man stepped toward the house, flanked by two other troopers. The rear transport had opened as well, and soldiers were pouring out of it. They weren't normal colonial regulars. They wore the darker uniforms of the newly arrived internal security forces.

"What can I do for you?" Alexi asked. *Besides asking you all to go straight to hell.* His eyes scanned the area in front of him. The two soldiers behind the apparent leader had their weapons pointed at him.

"What is this? A cooperative colonist? I thought you were all piss and vinegar and revolutionary slogans?" The soldier turned toward the others and let out a caustic laugh.

"I am not a revolutionary." Alexi stood on the porch, almost shaking as he forced himself to be respectful. "My name is Alexi Rand, and I've been a citizen of Haven for a long time."

"Well, I'm Sergeant Cole and I know who you are. And if you're the loyal citizen of *Alpha-2*—a colony of *Federal America*—as you claim, the first thing you can do is hand over that traitor standing behind you. She was recorded on multiple cameras participating in seditious activities in direct defiance of the federal observer's order against unlawful assemblages. Her identity has been confirmed by AI scan of the footage. She is also charged with resisting arrest and assaulting federal enforcement personnel. Katia Rand, you are under arrest."

Alexi could feel Katia behind him, pressing into him, as if she could hide behind him. She was shaking uncontrollably and sobbing loudly. "Please, no . . ."

"Corporal," the sergeant shouted, turning toward a soldier who had just walked up from the rear transport. "Take the prisoner."

Alexi Rand moved fully between the soldier and Katia. "Wait . . . please."

The corporal moved up toward Rand. "Stand aside." His voice was a raspy growl.

"No, you can't. Plea—"

The corporal slammed his rifle butt into Alexi's midsection. The big man doubled over, dropping to his knees and gasping for breath.

"Take her to the detention area, Corporal."

"Yes, Sergeant."

She screamed and struggled, thrashing wildly to escape. The corporal stopped, and he punched her hard. She dropped down to her knees, her face a bloody mess, staring up with undisguised hatred. The corporal just grabbed her arm and pulled her forward, dragging her toward the road. He'd only taken a few steps, though, when he went down hard to the ground, Alexi Rand on top of him.

Alexi jumped back up, off the stricken soldier, his eyes moving all around, fixing on the other federals. He dove for the sergeant, but halfway there he felt as though a train slammed into him. He staggered and tried to continue, but he could feel his strength draining away. His hands moved toward his chest, and he felt the blood.

"Katia!" Alexi's cry was desperate, all anger and frustration. He stumbled forward, falling to his hands and knees. He tried to get back on his feet but then he felt a boot in his stomach, and he fell to the ground, facedown in the dirt.

"Go, Corporal." The sergeant waved toward the stricken noncom as he climbed back to his feet. "Take her, and we will handle things here." He looked to the side, to one of the soldiers standing behind him. "Let's search the house, Private. I'm wondering now if this *is* another rebel we have here." He stared down at Alexi, still trying to get to his feet. He walked over and kicked him again, sending his victim back to the ground.

The corporal dragged Katia across the road toward the transport. He pushed her inside and slammed the rear hatch shut, moving around toward the front of the vehicle and climbing in. Three other troopers followed him, and then the side doors slammed shut and the vehicle roared to life. A second later it began to move, turning around and heading down the forest road, and the last thing Alexi saw was the feds taking his daughter away from him . . . just like the feds had taken Anya.

CHAPTER 16

The soldiers formed up just before dawn, five hundred strong. They wore body armor over their camouflage uniforms, and they carried assault rifles and a wartime complement of reloads. They had even been issued grenades, and every platoon had two heavy weapons, mostly tripod-mounted autoguns. They were outfitted not for police duties, not for patrolling.

They were ready for *war*.

They marched in single file toward the waiting trucks, silent as they loaded up. For many, this would be their first real taste of combat. Their faces were a mix of veteran impassiveness, rookie fear, and—for some on both sides—eager anticipation.

They were moving quickly, trying to maintain secrecy around the operation. But they were heading to capture the rebels' primary supply dump of illegal weapons, and it seemed unlikely such a target would be entirely undefended.

Johnson took a deep breath, fighting back the nausea. He'd mostly passed on the predawn breakfast, eating half a piece of dry toast and deciding that was about all his stomach could handle. For weeks he had craved battle. All he had wanted was the chance to avenge his friends. But the carnage of the day before had hit him hard. He'd walked the square after the shooting ended. He'd had to tread carefully, slowly, to avoid slipping on the pools of blood. He saw men and women lying on the pavement, their bodies almost torn apart by the relentless automatic fire. He saw a man whose head had been split open like an egg, a sickly gray ooze dripping out on the street. He saw severed limbs lying on the ground. And he saw the baby that had fallen from her mother's arms, her still-open eyes looking lifelessly at the sky.

Now he was heading for another fight, more death . . . and all he wanted was to curl up and hide.

Especially as another thought struck him: *And this time you may be dealing with an enemy that is shooting back.*

He shuffled forward, his body following through, though his mind was elsewhere. Two days ago, he'd been livid. Yesterday, he had been disgusted.

Today, he was scared.

He reached up, grabbing the handhold on the end of the transport and hauling himself up and in. He moved to the side, sitting on the long metal bench, and watched as his four subordinates did the same.

Lieutenant Fritz was sitting on the other side of the transport, looking a lot more confident than Johnson felt. Fritz was the platoon commander, one of the many officers who'd come to Alpha-2 with the federal observer. Johnson didn't know much about the new forces, but he was sure Fritz had more experience than he did in gunning people down. He wondered if the officer had ever faced a foe fighting back on anything like even terms.

Because God knows I haven't. It didn't matter how much he exaggerated the fight in the mine—those prisoners had modern weapons, but they were also outnumbered, untrained, and disorganized. On the other hand, the rebel groups have been organizing in secret for years, and based on the mission briefing, it seemed they had access to military-grade weapons, too.

And probably knew how to actually use them.

"All right, let's go." He heard the voice outside, another officer walking down the line of transports. "Get mounted up and keep your mouths shut. We're pulling out in ten minutes."

"Damian, I'm sorry to disturb you without calling first, but with the comm lines jammed . . ." John Danforth stood outside the door of Damian's farmhouse. It was almost dawn, and the barest morning rays dimly lit the porch.

"That's fine, John. You know you are always welcome here. In fact, you'd better come in," Damian said, pulling Danforth into his house. He had known the communications mogul almost since the day he'd arrived on Haven, and he considered the man a friend . . . despite the underhanded way Danforth had made him a staple of late-night programming.

They moved quickly inside, and Danforth started by saying, "I'm sorry for my appearance, Damian. I'm afraid I have had quite a night."

"I have as well, John. Katia Rand is missing, and I've been out all night searching for her. I just got back, and I was about to go out again." Damian paused. "Jamie is going crazy. He really loves the girl."

"I'm sorry to hear that, Damian. I've never met Katia, but her father has done work for me at the network. I always regarded him as a good man."

"He is. And Katia is a wonderful girl." His voice darkened. "I'll admit I'm extremely worried about her. With all that is happening . . ."

"I know. If there's anything I can do, please let me know. Although . . ."

"What?"

"It's happening, Damian. The rebellion. The federals are on the move, and the Guardians are going to meet them."

Damian frowned. "I hope you're not here for congratulations, John. I did everything I could to prevent this tragedy. You have caused a nightmare, for yourselves—and for all of us. You haven't seen war up close, John, have you? I have."

"It was not a *choice*, Damian. The federals left us no alternative.

There were, what, a hundred people killed in front of the federal complex yesterday? How many more after that? More than sixty of my employees were arrested, marched off, without charges, without due process. Why do you think the Rand girl is missing?" He paused, realizing that he might have pushed too far.

"I don't know where she is, John, but that is my priority now, not helping Haven commit suicide. You wanted this war . . . you go fight it, you and all those who clamored for it. Just don't expect me to join in chanting your revolutionary slogans. You may pride yourself on all those you led to this, your Guardians and those who support them. But have you thought—*truly thought*—about how many of them will die today? Tomorrow? How many are boys who haven't shaved once? Girls still on the cusp of womanhood? Because I have. And I don't want the responsibility, John. I may not be able to stop this disaster, but I damned sure don't intend to help make it happen."

Danforth stood still, calm, allowing Damian to vent his anger. After a few silent ticks, though, he said, "Damian, I'm sorry, but—"

"But what? You want me to gather the veterans, to march the only real soldiers on this planet to stand with your farmers and carpenters and teenagers and fight the federals. The thing you all so easily seem to forget is that they—and I—fought for *that* flag you are so ready to make war upon. I had friends die in battle, wearing the uniform of Federal America. I have as many grievances as you do, as many concerns about the future of this world I have chosen as my home. But I am not ready to throw away every vestige of my earlier allegiance, to violate the oaths I took, like so many empty words. Moreover, I have friends still in the colonial forces, John, soldiers I fought with in the war who now live here and who call this world home as I do. Good men and women. Would you celebrate their deaths in battle, notch your rifle stocks for each of them you put in the grave? Men and women you celebrated a few years ago when they came here, fresh from victory against the union and the hegemony, even as you hounded me to do your interviews?"

"I'm—I am sorry, my friend." Danforth stood in the foyer, struggling to hold Damian's gaze. "I didn't mean to upset you. Yes, I was hoping you would help. And yes, you're right to say I might not have thought everything through. But this war is *here*. They *killed* peaceful protestors, Damian. Hundreds of them, as if they were pests that needed to be exterminated. They are breaking down doors. Snatching people off the street. Hunting us down. So while I respect what you say, know that I don't ask any of this lightly." A deep breath, then: "I do respect you, Damian. No matter what, at least I hope I can still call you my friend."

Damian sighed softly and stared back silently for a few seconds. "Of course, John. We may disagree on this, but I know you are a man of integrity. You do what you feel you must. As I do." He paused. "And what I must do now is go back out and find Katia Rand."

Danforth nodded silently, opening the door and stepping back out onto the porch.

"And, John . . ."

Danforth turned around, and the two men's eyes locked.

"I *will* wish the best for you, and for your followers. For all of us." Damian stared at Danforth for a few seconds, and then he closed the door.

"Anybody who doesn't have a modern weapon, come up to the barn behind me and get a rifle and ammunition." Tyler Danforth stood on top of a small tractor, looking out at the assembled mass of citizen-soldiers, rebels ready to fight for their freedom. He was proud, of the men and women milling around in front of him, and at his cousin and himself, for the work they had done to create such a force. It was one thing to repeat slogans, to cry for liberty in dark gathering places . . . and another entirely to march to war to achieve it. And the Guardians had answered the call; they had come, bringing sons and daughters and friends in tow.

"Even if you have a good weapon, if you don't have at least a hundred rounds of ammunition, come up and get a new gun." He watched as a crowd surged forward, dozens of men and women who'd come with nothing more than farm tools and knives. And hundreds more, who had shotguns and pistols, weapons suitable for hunting small game or for protecting a household from intruders perhaps, but hardly proper equipment for facing armed federal troops.

He watched as Guardians walked away from the barn carrying their assault rifles, mostly union Karkarovs, but also some of the new hegemony Diahmins. It was state-of-the-art stuff, a match for anything the federals would have. This was what he and John had worked so hard for, the day these weapons would be used to strike a blow for freedom. But he couldn't help but feel strange as he watched them pouring out from the cache. The Danforths weren't the only financial supporters of the Guardians, but they were the biggest by far. Tyler knew his cousin had poured an enormous amount of the family's wealth into smuggling these guns to Haven.

He'd objected at first, but John had won him around in the end. Wealth would be nothing without liberty, he had said. And Tyler had realized he was right. The Danforths were titans on Haven, but the oligarchs and government cronies on Earth who, more and more, were beginning to call the shots on Haven had a hundred times the wealth he and John controlled. The Danforths might live well under increased federal control of Haven, assuming they kept their mouths shut and didn't cause trouble, but they would be little better than slaves in a gilded cage.

There were hundreds milling about in the clearing, perhaps nearly a thousand. Guardians, and others, too—men and women who had never joined the Guardians of Liberty, but who were now rallying to the cry for rebellion.

No doubt yesterday's massacre has been an effective recruiting tool for us . . .

He turned back toward the barn. "If any of you are uncertain how to use those guns, we've got people all along the back side of the barn to help. Please, these are complex weapons. If you're not sure how to use them, get up there and ask."

Please . . . my family almost bankrupted itself getting them here, and it wasn't so you could stand around when the feds get here and not know how to fire . . .

He looked out toward the woods, and the small road cutting through the dense trees. It was almost certainly the way the federal soldiers would come, but Tyler's mind was elsewhere now.

Where are you, John?

Tyler Danforth knew he didn't have his cousin's charisma, nor John's basic leadership skills. He was a quiet man, unaccustomed to this kind of role. He was doing his best, but he would feel nothing but relief when John's transport came down that road. He stared for a few seconds more, watching as a group of fifty or more, another batch of Guardians, marched down the road and into the clearing. But still no sign of John.

"Again . . . anybody who doesn't have a modern weapon and at least a hundred rounds of ammunition, come to the barn behind me and get a gun."

And hope to hell John gets here before the feds . . .

Patrick Killian crouched down along the side of the road. His troops were stretched out along both sides, hidden and waiting for the federals.

Killian was a veteran of the army, like Damian Ward and Alexandra Thornton, a forward scout and a special forces operative who'd had an almost unmatched record in the service. At least until he'd come under the command of an officer so incompetent he'd have been bounced out of the service in a heartbeat . . . if his family hadn't been so well connected politically. In the end, almost fifty soldiers died because the officer froze in the middle of a major operation. None of that came as a surprise to Killian. What was a shock, though, was how he was scapegoated for the disaster and dishonorably discharged . . . while the officer received a field promotion and a decoration.

Patrick Killian came to Haven without any pension or mustering-out bonus. He had only two things. An extraordinarily diverse skill set . . . and a burning hatred of the federals. And now he was using both.

"You all remember what I taught you." He got up and walked through the dense woods, a few meters in from the road. "You'd fucking well better remember, my little babies, or the feds will have your guts dripping down your legs." Killian seemed to think that his soldiers wouldn't take anything seriously if he didn't swear at them while he was saying it.

Killian was one of the first members of the Guardians of Liberty, and as soon as John Danforth had heard about his training and experiences he'd tapped him to form his own unit. Killian's rangers didn't look much like a spit and polished elite military force. That's because they were as far from that as one could possibly imagine. Killian did that on purpose, though, having scoured Haven for every manner of ne'er-do-well and petty criminal who knew his way around in the wild. He'd won their loyalty, as often as not by beating the disobedience out of them, and he'd taught them everything he knew. Almost everything.

John Danforth had just left, heading back toward the main force at Vincennes, leaving Killian and his people five kilometers closer to Landfall.

The feds had fired the first shots when they slaughtered those people in Landfall. Those men and women had been unarmed, though, and so this was the first chance for the revolution to fire back. And Killian's rangers would have the honor of being the ones to pull the trigger, not the massed Guardians on the green at Vincennes.

Killian looked out at the road, and then he panned his head down the woods, looking toward Landfall. His people were deployed over more than a kilometer. They'd spent most of the night planting mines and laying traps, felling trees and building makeshift roadblocks. And now they were hidden all along the federals' line of march, fifty-three snipers and bushwhackers, and some of the dirtiest fighters ever to grab a rifle or a well-used blade.

Killian had his orders. He was to shoot up the federal column, inflict as many casualties—and cause as much disorder—as he could. And he was to buy time, time to get the forces at Vincennes organized.

He moved through the woods, past a dozen of his people, so well-hidden even he could barely see them. Ideally, he'd have positioned himself in the middle of his forces, but the lack of communications was cumbersome. He'd given his rangers detailed orders, and now he just had to trust their judgment. But he was damned sure going to position himself up front, where he could see the feds as they moved into his ambush.

He was careful in the woods, placing his feet carefully, making almost no sound as he hurried forward. Then he stopped and looked around, finding the forward elements of his unit positioned just where he had placed them. Everything was ready.

He stood for a minute perhaps, and then he heard it. The sound of transports coming down the road. He knew the federals had limited airpower on Haven. The troops at Vincennes might have to deal with a gunship or two—and he didn't underestimate the danger aircraft would represent to the defenders there—but the feds didn't have nearly enough capacity to execute an airmobile operation. And that meant the sound he heard was the main force, hundreds of heavily armed security troopers mounted up on their transports and heading for Vincennes.

He took a deep breath. It had been nearly six years since he'd seen battle. As he had been back then, he was scared, though he'd never admit it to anyone. But there was something else.

He felt like he was going home.

"I don't like this route, Major. We're vulnerable here, exposed." Captain Ian Frasier looked out from the top of the transport, his eyes panning along both sides of the column. There was nothing there but trees, endless masses of them in full bloom. The road was narrow, unpaved, and it wound torturously through the deep forest. It was early morning on a bright sunny day, but the road was covered in a gray gloom, illuminated only by a few rays of light penetrating the canopy of the trees.

"Vulnerable to what?" Major Randall Stein was a tall man. He looked military through and through, from his closely cropped brown hair to the cold focus of his eyes. "What could be out there, Captain? There is no military force opposing us, only a rabble of revolutionaries. It won't take us more than a few minutes to send them running . . . and in the pursuit we will end this rebellion once and for all."

"We should at least send out some scouts, flank guards. Just to be sure. Our visibility in here is—"

"Our orders are clear, Captain. To proceed to Vincennes and seize the weapons stored there . . . and to crush any armed force that stands in our way. We would have to halt the column to deploy scouts . . . and there is no way to move any vehicles in those woods. We would be slowed to a crawl."

"Yes, sir, but—"

"No buts, Captain. Your advice is noted. The column will proceed at full speed toward Vin—"

The sound was loud, almost deafening. Stein stared ahead, frozen in place. His view of the lead elements of the column was blocked by a curve in the road.

Frasier leapt onto the ladder, climbing quickly down the side of the vehicle.

"Captain Frasier, where are you going?"

"We're under attack, sir. We need to deploy forces now."

"We will do no such thing." Stein looked down at a small tablet he held in his hand. "I am getting the report now. It appears the lead vehicle struck some kind of improvised explosive."

"Sir, we have to—"

"We have to do nothing, Captain, except clear the damaged vehicle from the road and continue on to Vincennes. The fact that the enemy terrorists were able to plant one explosive is hardly justification for this column to deviate from its orders."

Frasier held back his frustration. He was one of Alexandra Thornton's officers, and a resident of Haven himself. Stein had come along with Colonel Semmes, and the best thing Frasier could say about the major was that he wasn't as bad as his commanding officer. Frasier was a fool, but he lacked Semmes's naked brutality.

"Major, I request permission to move to the front of the column to assess damage and see how quickly the wreckage can be cleared." There was no point arguing, and anything that got him forward and away from the pompous ass running this mission would be a blessing.

"Very well, Captain, but my orders stand. You are to clear the damaged vehicle and that is all. We do not have time to deploy forces to the woods to chase shadows."

"Yes, Major." He turned and moved forward, staring off into the woods as he did. He was far less confident than Stein that there was no one out there.

John Danforth raced toward Vincennes, pushing his vehicle as hard as he dared on the winding, rutted forest road. He was late, and he had to get there as quickly as possible.

He'd moved forward after his unsuccessful visit to Damian's farm, scouting out the route he expected the federals to take. He'd ordered Pat Killian to deploy his rangers along the projected line of march, but he wanted to check on the deployments himself before joining the others in Vincennes. Not that he didn't trust Killian. He just . . .

I just wanted to see it for myself, he admitted. Which, in hindsight, might have been a pretty stupid thing to do. His place was in Vincennes, not pretending he knew more about ambushes than a veteran like Killian.

He *had* been impressed, though. Killian had given him a rundown on what he had done—the mines, the roadblocks, his fifty-plus cutthroats hidden in the woods. It was more than Danforth had imagined, and he almost felt sorry for the federals.

They'd get through, of course; fifty men weren't going to stop an armored column with hundreds of trained soldiers. But by the time they got to Vincennes, the feds would be in decidedly worse shape than when they'd left Landfall.

Danforth had recruited Killian himself, and he'd taken the bitter ex-soldier into his inner circle. But the man still gave him a chill whenever they were together. He was glad, at least, that Killian was on his side. He had a brief image in his mind of the cold-blooded killer as a federal operative, slipping into his room, cutting his throat.

The transport turned hard, and the woods fell away on both sides. Which is when he saw it: Vincennes. The results of his labors, of all the risks he'd taken, the commitment that had lost him his grandfather's company, and sent sixty of his loyal employees into federal captivity.

My God . . . there must be a thousand of them . . .

He'd built the Guardians, visited the villages and farming hamlets, given speeches in the dead of night, to all who would listen to his fiery revolutionary oratory. And one by one the people had joined him, and with each the Guardians of Liberty grew.

Now they were gathered all together, and his pride knew no bounds.

A dozen men surged forward, surrounding the vehicle. He popped the hatch and stepped out, careful at first until he was sure they knew it was him. His citizen-soldiers were bound to be jumpy. Then he jogged forward, arms in the air, into the center of the mass of his Guardians.

"John!" The shout came from a distance, barely audible. But he would have recognized Tyler's voice anywhere.

"Well done," he said as he ran toward the voice. "Well done," he repeated, lunging forward and embracing his cousin.

"I am glad to see you, John. I was worried."

"I'm sorry, Ty. I went up to check Killian's positions before I came back."

"And Damian? The veterans?"

John just shook his head.

"That . . . that's too bad. I just hope they don't join the federals."

"No," John said, with as much conviction as he could muster. "Damian Ward would never support the oppressors; he would never fight against us."

I hope.

"But we are on our own now, cousin. And it is nearly time." He turned back toward the mass of rebels gathered together, and he raised his arms above his head.

A wild cheer rose up, and the crowd moved, morphed, encircling Danforth.

"Friends! Fellow Havenites! The time is upon us at last. Here we stand, faithful to our beliefs, dedicated to our home, to our families and our neighbors. We have been given a choice, one between freedom and servitude . . . and each man and woman here has given a resounding answer! Never shall we accept the chains Federal America seeks to bind us with. Never will we surrender the freedom that is ours by every measure of morality and justice that exists."

Danforth moved through the crowd, reaching out, shaking hands and patting the Guardians on their shoulders.

"Have no doubt, friends. The federals are on their way." He pointed toward the road from which he'd just come. "They will be here soon, and they have come to take what is ours, to drag us all away, to brutal captivity or worse. But I say never. Never! They will take me away when they haul my dead body off and not until then, for with my dying breath I will lash out at the tyrants . . . and at the brutal henchmen who serve them."

He thrust his hands up again, and the crowd went mad, screaming, yelling, chanting, "Guardians! Guardians!"

He held his hands up to quiet them, and slowly they stopped. He smiled. "Your enthusiasm is a credit to your commitment. But it is time. Go now, get into position. Listen to your leaders—they'll tell you where to go. And prepare yourselves. For the shots we fire here today will be heard across the galaxy . . . all the way to the halls of power back on Earth."

He moved through the cheering crowd, directing as many of his people as he could into good positions. "Turn over those trailers," he yelled to one group. "Bring that tractor around, and take cover behind it." It was a little disquieting that this hadn't been done already. Danforth was no soldier, but he knew the federals who came out of those woods would be heavily armed. Without cover, his Guardians would be gunned down in clumps.

"To the barn," he cried. "And up on the roof, on the far slope."

He stood and watched as his Guardians ran about, following his orders. He took a deep breath and tried to steady himself.

You have been preparing for this moment for a long time . . . but are you truly ready?

Jamie was walking through the woods, taking the shortcut from Damian's farm to the Rand place. He was exhausted, and every muscle in his body ached. But none of that was important. Only one thing mattered. Katia.

He and Damian been searching for her all night, but they hadn't found a clue. Finally, they had gone back to the farm, to check and see if any word had come in, and to grab some of the hands and broaden the search. Damian was organizing his people even now, and Jamie had decided to check in and see if Alexi Rand had heard anything.

He stopped suddenly. He'd heard something . . . voices. He crouched down, moving carefully. He didn't know if anything was wrong, but he had a bad feeling. Then he heard a gunshot.

His stomach clenched. He looked all around, searching for anything he could use as a weapon. He reached down and grabbed a large, thick branch, breaking off a few small spurs and creating a workable club. Then he continued slowly forward.

He could see the shadowy figures through the trees. There were at least half a dozen, possibly more. Half of them seemed to be moving away from the house, toward a large transport. He saw several climb on board and then he saw the truck begin to move, turning around and heading away from the house.

He paused at the edge of the woods, peering from behind a large tree. They were soldiers. Two that he could see. And someone else, lying on the ground facedown. He stared for a few seconds before he realized.

Alexi!

That was all it took. He lunged from the cover of the trees, charging for the nearest of the soldiers. The man heard him coming and turned to face him, but he was too slow. Jamie was on him, swinging his club with every gram of strength he could muster.

The heavy branch caught the soldier on the side of the face, and Jamie could hear the sickening crunch as it shattered the man's jaw . . . and fractured his skull. The trooper fell hard, a muffled grunt coming from his wrecked mouth as he dropped to the ground, already unconscious before he hit. But Jamie was already focused on the other man.

That soldier had pulled his assault rifle off his back, and he was moving it to bear. Jamie rushed forward, but he knew he was too late. The fed would get off at least one shot.

His mind raced, his eyes following the movement of the rifle. He was counting to himself, trying to sync with the soldier's movement.

Now, he thought as he ducked hard to the side, just as the sergeant opened fire, firing a burst where Jamie had been. The soldier adjusted his aim, but Jamie smashed into him before he could get off another shot.

The man fell backward from the impact, Jamie's momentum carrying him over as well. The two landed hard on the ground and the soldier was immediately reaching over, trying to grab the weapon he'd dropped. But Jamie was on him, grabbing his arm and pulling it aside, away from the gun. Then he slammed his other fist down into the trooper's side.

The fed grunted from the impact, but from the pain in Jamie's hand, it was obvious the man was wearing some sort of body armor. The soldier pushed back hard, throwing Jamie off him. Before he could get up, though, Jamie tackled him, and now the two grappled on the ground. This was no boxing match. There were no rules here. This was a fight to the death, in all its horror and ugliness. The two men punched, kicked, and grabbed each other. Fingers acted as claws, teeth gnashed.

The soldier reached around to his side, trying to grab the heavy survival knife from the sheath that hung from his belt. But Jamie's hand was there, holding the fed's wrist, twisting sharply. Jamie gritted his teeth and pulled as hard as he could, and the soldier screamed as his wrist snapped.

Now it was Jamie's hand moving toward the knife, using the man's pain to give him the time he needed to pull it free and jab it toward the soldier's side, where the flak jacket had much less protection. The sergeant rolled to his left, trying to escape the blow, so the blade just grazed him. It left a nasty cut, but spared him the gutting Jamie had intended.

Jamie scrambled after his opponent, grabbing the man and pushing him down on his back. Pinning the man down with his body weight, he brought the blade down toward the fed's neck. The terrified soldier reached up, trying to push back Jamie's arms. The two struggled, putting the last of their strength into the contest.

With a scream, Jamie leaned down, pushing with everything he had, staring down into the trooper's panicked eyes as he slowly shoved the blade into the man's neck. The federal tried to scream, but all he could do was gurgle blood. Jamie could feel the man's strength draining away as his blood poured out of the hideous wound, and suddenly Jamie fell forward, the soldier's arms no longer able to hold him up.

For all the violence of the slum where Jamie had grown up, and the fights and turf wars in the mine, he'd never killed before. He stared down, looking at the dead man under him, and he felt an instant of confusion, of hesitation.

I am a killer now . . .

But there was no time for introspection. He leapt up, wincing in pain from his own injuries, and he scrambled over toward Alexi. "Mr. Rand . . ." He looked down, panicked, thinking for an instant Katia's father was dead. But then Alexi turned his head and opened his eyes.

"Jamie," he said, his voice soft, weak. "Two more . . . in the house . . ."

Jamie hesitated for a second, and then he understood the warning. More soldiers . . . in the house.

He moved quickly, scrambling for the rifle the fed had dropped. He scooped it up, staring frantically at the trigger, the controls, trying to figure how to work the thing.

He heard something, noise from the house. He looked up just as the door swung open, and another soldier came running out. He whipped the assault rifle around, still not sure he knew how to fire it. He pressed his finger down hard, aiming for the doorway.

The kick took him by surprise, and it knocked him to the side, throwing his aim off. He struggled to pull himself back, to re-aim the gun, but then he saw. The soldier was down, lying in a pool of blood on the front porch. His first shot had been dead-on.

Two more . . .

Alexi's words echoed in Jamie's head. There was another soldier in the house . . . and this one couldn't have missed the sounds of the fire.

Jamie realized he was out in the open. He dove behind a pile of cut logs, seeking cover just as a burst of fire ripped through the air where he had stood an instant earlier.

He ducked below the stack of firewood, struggling to maintain his calm. Jamie wasn't a soldier, and this was his first experience of battle. His heart was pounding, and he could feel sweat pouring down his back. He peered over the top, looking at the house, trying to find the fed. There was nothing at first . . . then he saw the flash of movement, and he ducked back into cover just as his adversary opened fire.

He held himself ready, pushing back against the fear, listening, waiting. Then the firing stopped. He leapt up, bringing his rifle to bear on the window the soldier had shot from. He squeezed the trigger, cutting loose on full auto.

The bullets shattered the window, and decimated the wood all around it. He kept firing, moving the weapon slowly, blasting all around the target area.

He thought he heard a scream, and an instant later it was confirmed. The federal slumped forward, his still body hanging over the wrecked window. *Three men. I killed three of them.*

Jamie dropped the gun and ran back to Katia's father. "Alexi, let me see . . ." He pulled at the wounded man's shirt, moving the fabric as carefully as he could. There was a lot of blood, but he didn't think the bullet had hit anything vital.

But I've got to stop this bleeding . . .

He took off his shirt, wadding it up and pressing it against the wound.

"Jamie . . ."

"Just lie back. You're going to be okay."

"No . . . Katia . . ." Alexi struggled, trying to sit up.

"Lie back, don't move. You'll just make the bleed—"

"Katia . . . soldiers . . . took . . . her . . ."

Jamie felt a coldness in his stomach. "What are you saying? The transport?" He looked around frantically, as if the vehicle might still be in sight. He looked back at Alexi. "They took her? *Where?*"

"Don't know . . . back to Landfall . . . probably." Alexi gasped for air. "Save her . . . please . . ."

Shit . . .

"Alexi, stay where you are." He grabbed Alexi's hand, moved it to the bunched-up shirt. "Hold this as tight as you can against the wound. Damian is coming; he will be here soon. He'll help you."

He jumped up, looking around, seeing one of the federals' rifles on the ground near the first man he'd fought. He reached down and grabbed it, his eye catching the wounded soldier, lying on his back, whimpering. His ruined face was covered with blood, and he coughed and spat, trying to clear his airways.

Jamie moved over to him, reaching down, grabbing the ammunition belt strapped over the man's shoulder, and throwing it over his own. Then he raised his rifle, aiming it downward, pulling the trigger. He wasn't sure if he killed the man out of pity or rage—probably both.

He turned and ran toward the transport, punching at the outside controls, opening the hatch. He jumped inside, staring at the panel, staring at the various buttons. *Too many fucking buttons.* He'd driven a tractor on Damian's farm, but that was the extent of his experience. And this military transport was a hell of a lot more complicated.

He forced himself to concentrate. He leaned in close to read the tiny words on each button. Finally, he came to IGNITION, and he punched it. The engine roared to life. He grabbed the main control and pushed it forward, feeling the heavy transport lurch forward.

He turned it around and pushed the throttle further, taking off down the winding forest road. Katia was in trouble . . . and Jamie knew he had to get to her before the federals got her to Landfall. He'd kill the bastards with his bare hands if he had to. But he would save her.

Somehow . . .

CHAPTER 17

Killian was running through the forest, leaping over fallen trees and ducking under hulking branches. The federal column was pushing down the road, but every hundred meters or so, one of the mines his rangers had planted blew, taking a transport and another handful of soldiers with it. The first time, the federals had dismounted two dozen soldiers to move the wreck, but his people had taught them never to make that mistake again. They'd opened up from two sides, firing at carefully plotted angles to prevent hitting each other. And they'd taken down nearly twenty of the enemy before the soldiers managed to return the fire effectively. His people had retreated as he'd ordered, disappearing into the dense woods like so many ghosts.

After that, the feds didn't leave their vehicles; they just drove forward into the disabled trucks, pushing them out of the way. But the roadblocks Killian's people had set up were different. The rangers had built the heavy structures from large tree trunks, and they'd stacked up boulders behind. The feds had tried to drive through them, but there was too much weight to just push out of the way. They had to stop and send soldiers forward, enough to remove the barricades, plus more to engage the raiders in the woods.

Which meant more fucking targets.

Killian had a perpetual scowl on his face, but inside he was smiling. His people had cut up the federals badly, killing at least fifty, and delaying them for hours. Their column was a disordered mess, and many of their transports were damaged. Killian could only imagine the state of their morale, but he suspected it wasn't good.

And now for the last . . . and the best.

He came to a halt, looking around and whispering to the rangers he knew were hiding all around him. "It's time. Let's move."

The feds would reach the final roadblock any minute. They would stop the whole column, Killian knew, and they would send troops en masse—some to the clear the barricade and more to move out into the woods and engage any bushwhackers. But this time they wouldn't be facing two or three snipers. Killian had half his people deployed here, waiting. And half a dozen of them had armor-piercing rocket launchers. The weapons had been enormously expensive, and he knew Danforth had entrusted his people with almost half the Guardians' total supply. He was determined to prove the rangers were worthy of that kind of trust.

He moved through the heavy brush, about fifty meters toward the road. He held his hands out behind him, signaling for his people to halt, but he continued forward himself a few more meters before crouching down and putting a small pair of binoculars to his eyes.

The enemy was there, transports stopped and stacked up as far back as he could see. There were soldiers, too, standing around the massive roadblock . . . and others moving slowly into the woods. He waited, watching, getting a rough count on the troopers in the woods.

And he waited some more.

Then . . . an explosion. A big one. This last roadblock was more than a barricade, as the federals had just discovered. He peered through the binoculars again, risking the slight movement. The troops coming his way had stopped and turned, looking back toward their comrades in the road. At least fifteen of them were down, and the others were running around in disorder. It was time.

He stretched his arms out in both directions, his fists clenched. It was a signal. He felt the ripple in the woods, the soft sounds his rangers made as they swept forward through the brush.

The enemy soldiers who'd advanced into the forest were looking away, back toward the road. They didn't hear the approaching rangers, not until it was too late.

Killian lunged forward, reaching his arm around one of the soldiers, driving his knee forward and grabbing the man's hair as he ran his blade across the soldier's throat. He felt the man's hot blood pouring out over his hand, and he threw the body to the side.

Another trooper was turning around, but Killian caught him before he could bring his weapon to bear. He shoved the notched blade into the man's abdomen, twisting hard and slicing upward.

Killian grabbed the dying man and pulled him up, slashing the blade across his head, scalping him. He held up the bloody chunk of hair as he moved forward, and he shouted a bloodcurdling battle cry.

He pulled out his pistol and moved to the edge of the woods, firing at the soldiers gathered around in the open. Then he threw the bloody scalp into the road. The sooner the federals realized they were fighting a nightmare, the better.

He heard the whoosh of a rocket firing, followed by an explosion as it hit. He turned and looked down the road, seeing the plume of smoke.

With any luck, that transport is on fire and the murdering feds inside are burning, too.

He had no sympathy at all. As far as he was concerned, anyone who fought for the federals deserved the worst death he could give them.

He heard another rocket launch . . . and hit. Then another. He exulted, and the urge to turn this into a fight to the death was strong. But he held back. He knew he didn't have enough rangers to defeat the entire federal force. Besides, he'd promised John Danforth. And Danforth was one of the few men Killian truly respected.

"All right," he shouted, "let's get out of here, rangers! Our work is done!"

He looked around, making sure there were no threats close to him. Then he turned and slipped back into the dense woods, virtu-ally disappearing.

He could have been frustrated at leaving when his people could have killed more federals, but he was savvy enough to understand continuing the battle would be a bloody affair for the rangers, too. They'd had surprise and preparation in their favor so far, but if they kept fighting, the federal numbers would begin to tell. As it was now, his best guess was he'd lost five of his people.

Still, that was nothing when compared to the nearly one hundred enemy troopers they'd taken out.

A victory by any measure.

But it wasn't as if this battle was over, let alone the war. Not by a long shot.

He turned, heading north. He knew there was going to be one hell of a fight at Vincennes, and he had no intention of letting the rangers sit it out.

"Fuck." Frasier muttered to himself as he tied a bandage around his arm. He'd moved forward at the last roadblock, and he'd caught a round just before the enemy withdrew. The wound wasn't serious, but it hurt like hell.

"Captain, I have requested permission to abort the mission, but we have been ordered to proceed." Major Stein was looking at the column's exec as he pulled the headset off, his eyes wide with un-disguised confusion. Every trace of his earlier bravado was gone, his arrogance replaced by shock.

Never mind that none of this would have happened if you'd let me send out flankers when I suggested it.

Now wasn't the time to get into a fight with his superior, though. Now they had to keep moving. "We'll be fine, Major. They just took us by surprise, that's all. We've taken some losses, and they'd delayed us, but we've still got a significant battle-ready force. But we've got to get the troops back in order. They're a little shaken up, but with orders to focus on, they'll do the job."

Stein swallowed and—to his credit—nodded his head. "You are right, Captain. Send scouts out to both flanks, and an advance guard down the road. And get the rest of the troops mounted up again. We'll resume our advance in fifteen minutes."

"Yes, sir." Frasier turned and frowned. He knew the anti-insurgency forces Colonel Semmes had brought to Alpha-2 considered themselves an elite force compared to the colonial regulars. He also knew that was a joke. Semmes's troopers were used to gunning down mobs of protestors or breaking down civilians' doors in groups of ten or twenty. They were arrogant, and they underestimated the rebels. And that was going to be trouble.

Frasier walked down the column, snapping out orders. There was nothing wrong with the second in command doing what he was doing . . . but it *was* a problem when he was doing it because the *commanding* officer was too shaken and discombobulated to do it himself.

Frasier had no illusions. Taking casualties was one thing. Hell, from what he had gathered, it was more than acceptable—human life didn't seem to mean a whole lot to Asha Stanton. But failing to take Vincennes and the weapons stored there was quite another. And handing the rebels a victory in the first fight of the rebellion would be catastrophic. He knew the strongest force holding civilians back from supporting the rebel cause was fear. And if they came to believe the rebels could actually win . . .

No. They had to get to Vincennes. And they had to defeat whatever force was waiting there. Perhaps in spite of Major Stein.

And at whatever cost.

Sasha Nerov peered around the corner, looking out onto the empty street. Landfall was eerily quiet, the streets utterly deserted. It was early in the morning, but normally there would have been at least some people, early risers on their way to work. But between the curfew, and now the federal observer having declared a state of emergency and ordering all nonessential citizens to stay in their homes, it was a ghost town.

She still hadn't had a chance to shower, and she shuddered to think of how badly she must reek to anyone who hadn't been smell-

ing her for hours now. She sniffed, and winced. *And even people who
have been smelling me.* But at least she'd managed to find—steal—a
change of clothes. She was a little warm in the hooded cloak, but
it covered her face, and that was pretty key. That looked suspicious
itself, no doubt, especially on a day that promised to be a hot one, but
no more than being the only person on the street. And it was better
than having some camera's facial recognition algorithm pick her off
as a wanted fugitive. The feds clearly had their hands full today, and
it was possible they would ignore a strange hooded curfew violator.
That said, if they got wind of a smuggler who had attacked federal
soldiers, she was sure the response would be more aggressive.

She ducked back onto the side street, leaning against the wall
and taking a moment to rest. The night had been long and difficult one, but in the end mostly successful. *Vagabond* had a crew of
twenty-four, including herself. She and Griff had managed to warn
eighteen of them. That left four of her people unaccounted for. She
tried to tell herself they'd drunk themselves into a stupor and were
lying in some alley somewhere sleeping it off. But she couldn't help
but imagine them in federal prison cells. Or worse. Memories of
Wasp, of Sergei Brinker and his fate, flooded into her mind.

She pushed it all aside. There was nothing she could do about it.
She had sent Griff and Elisa off on their own, to the safe house she'd
long maintained on Haven. As far as she could determine, she'd left
no way to track the property back to her or to *Vagabond* and its crew.

So Griff should be safe there.

Her first officer had begged her to come, too, to lie low and hide
and wait until the worst of recent events had blown over. But Nerov
knew better. This wasn't a momentary crisis, a disturbance that
would pass in a few days or a week. This was *it*. The revolution. It
had begun, and she knew when it had finally run its course things
would never be the same again.

She took a deep breath and tried to ignore the fatigue she felt in
every centimeter of her body. She wasn't going to hide in the shadows . . . and she couldn't stay in Landfall. That didn't give her a ton
of options, but she didn't really need any.

She knew what she had to do.

She slipped out of the alley and moved swiftly down the street, heading for the outskirts of town.

She had to find John Danforth. She had to find the rebels.

"They're coming! They're coming! The federals are coming!" A young man came running out of the woods, waving his arms and shouting the warning.

John Danforth stared for a moment, uncertain what he was seeing. Then he realized he was looking at one of Killian's rangers. The man was clad from head to toe in dark green camo, and his head was covered with the beret that was the only real uniform Killian's scouts wore.

Danforth moved forward, toward the man.

Man, he thought. *More like a boy.*

The ranger moving toward him couldn't have been more than seventeen . . . and Danforth would have believed fifteen if someone had told him that was the right number. But the picture changed as the ranger got closer. His face was speckled with red, splotches Danforth knew to be blood, and the assault rifle and bandolier he carried could only have come from a federal trooper.

Danforth's eyes dropped to the ranger's waist, staring down at something dark hanging from the man's belt. He was confused for a few seconds.

That almost looks like hair . . .

Then he realized, and he had to fight back the urge to vomit. The ranger had scalps hanging from his belt, three of them. Danforth had known Killian was a hard man, driven by anger over how he'd been treated by the government. But now he realized the man was insane . . . and it seemed his mental state was contagious, that he had transferred it to his rangers.

"Mr. Danforth, is that you, sir?" The ranger's words were forced, difficult. He was panting hard, and Danforth realized he had run all the way back to Vincennes.

"It is," Danforth replied, trying to avert his eyes from the bloody hunks of hair hanging at the man's side.

"Hiram Gloster, sir . . . Killian's rangers. Sir, Captain Killian sent me to give the warning. We engaged the enemy, and Captain Killian estimates federal losses in excess of one hundred troops and fifteen vehicles. But the federals are still on the road, not ten minutes from here."

Danforth was silent for a moment, absorbing what he'd been told. He had hoped Killian's people might pick off a few federal scouts, perhaps delay the column's progress somewhat. But it was well past midday now, hours after he'd expected the federals to arrive. And now he was hearing of over a hundred casualties inflicted. Was it possible?

"Very well . . . Hiram." Danforth didn't know what to call the ranger. The Guardians didn't have ranks, at least nothing official, and neither did the rangers. Indeed, this was the first he had heard of "Captain" Killian, though he had to admit, the commander of the rangers had the right idea. The Guardians had an informal command structure, one that had been fine when they were protesting and rabble-rousing, but this was war.

That was a mistake, not formalizing ranks, one that could cost us. If we get past this fight, I'm going to have to name some officers, and some noncoms, too.

"Sir, Captain Killian reports the rest of the rangers are moving this way with all speed. He intends to harass the enemy from the rear while they are engaged with your forces."

"Very well, Hiram. Find yourself some cover, son. Things are going to get hot in a few minutes." He almost laughed at himself, telling the ranger about the heat of combat. This kid had already seen war up close, far more so than he ever had.

He turned back and looked over the open area. The Guardians were spread out in a long line, behind overturned farm equipment, rocks, piles of wood . . . anything they could find. In the center, they had dug a shallow trench, and Danforth had placed two of the heavy tripod-mounted guns there, backed up by fifty handpicked Guardians. If the federals tried to punch through the center, they'd have a fight on their hands.

Danforth stood in the open, perhaps twenty meters in front of the line, staring off into the trees, down the road that disappeared quickly into the depths of the forest. He was scared to death, but he fought it with all he could muster. He couldn't let the Guardians see that—panic was too contagious. And they all had reason to be afraid.

He heard something then, and he looked up. Transports! Coming down the road. He turned to run back to the line, but before he did gunfire erupted all along the trees. Federal soldiers, in a skirmish line at the edge of the woods. And something else . . . from above. Noise. And a shadow covering the ground. A gunship . . .

He ran back toward the trench.

Jamie sat at the controls of the transport, staring out the cockpit as he raced down the winding, forest road. He didn't know what he was doing, not really, but he wasn't about to let that stand in his way. Not when Katia's life was on the line.

He had to catch the federals before they got to Landfall. He *had* to. It was his only chance. If they got her back to the federal complex he knew he might never see her again. And his mind raced with the torments she might suffer. He knew enough about the dangers and hardships of prison, and his imagination raced with how much worse it would be for a woman—especially when federal soldiers started dying and their comrades started to take out their anger on anyone they could.

Inmates in the detention area would be easy targets.

He'd almost wiped out twice now, and he'd bounced off more than one tree, but he'd managed to keep the vehicle moving. He figured the others had a ten-minute head start, and that meant he had no time to lose.

"C'mon, you piece of shit," he muttered. "Faster . . . faster."

The transport swung around a curve. Jamie could feel the tension in his gut as the wheels on one side came off the road for an instant. *He caught his breath . . .*

And then the transport righted itself with a loud thump as the wheels slammed down. *Almost wiped out* three *times . . .*

Which is when he saw it: the other vehicle, perhaps fifty meters ahead.

It's time, he thought to himself. He'd been focused on catching the federals, but now that he had, he suddenly understood his next step: to kill everyone in that transport except Katia.

The forward vehicle was getting larger as he closed the distance. He could hear the comm unit crackling as the troopers ahead tried to contact him. He ignored it, instead shoving the throttle as far forward as he could and bracing himself as his transport slammed into the back of the truck ahead.

The vehicle shook hard, and he struggled to maintain control as it swerved wildly. He stared ahead, watching the other transport skidding across the dirt road. Its driver was clearly trying to regain control, but then the vehicle slammed hard into a clump of trees. It snapped the first one, sending it falling across the road—a few meters from Jamie's own transport. Then it came to a stop, lying on its side.

Jamie slammed on the brakes, his battered truck screeching to a halt a few meters from the other transport. He punched at the controls to open the door, grabbing the assault rifle as he slipped out of the cockpit.

He was moving quickly, acting on instinct, not thought. There was no mercy in him, no pity. The federals in that truck would die . . . or he would. He raced across the space between the two transports, leaves crunching under his pounding feet. He jumped over the fallen tree, the rifle out in front of him, ready to fire.

He could hear banging. He looked toward the transport. The side of the vehicle, now the top, was dented and pitted. The hatch was jammed, and the soldiers inside were trying to bash it open. It was a break, enough time at least to get clear of the open ground and move into position.

The hatch finally started to open, the twisted metal of the door moving slowly. He ducked down, just to the side, stepping back behind one of the large trees. His mind was screaming at him, urging him to find Katia, to see if she was all right. But his discipline held firm. He couldn't help Katia unless he took care of the feds. That was his first priority.

The hatch popped out of its frame, sliding down the side of the transport and landing with a loud clang. Jamie brought his rifle around and stared down the barrel. He took a deep breath and held it . . . and then he squeezed the trigger just as the federal's head popped out of the transport's cockpit.

Bang! He fired a single shot, and the soldier's head exploded in a cloud of red mist, his body falling back inside the truck.

That was the easy one. The others will be more careful.

More dangerous.

He leapt out of the woods, taking advantage of the time it would take the others to move their dead comrade aside and climb out. He reached the back of the truck, his eyes darting around, looking for the controls to open the hatch. He reached up and pulled on the lever. Nothing. It was stuck.

He spun around the edge of the truck, looking up toward the side door. A shot clanged off the side of the transport, maybe two centimeters from his head.

Shit!

That was quicker than I thought.

He gulped a lungful of air and leapt hard, out into the open. It was a gamble—he was playing for the instant it would take his opponent to realize he wasn't where he was expected to be. He had one shot . . . maybe.

He moved quickly, his eyes focused on the soldier on the transport. He could hear the fire, see the clouds of dirt in the air where the shots intended for him impacted.

He almost stumbled, but he regained his balance, squeezing the trigger, holding it, spraying the transport with a burst of fire. He saw the soldier pushed back as multiple shots slammed into his chest.

Jamie knew he had a chance now, before the others could free themselves and come at him. He slung the rifle over his back and raced across the few meters to the transport, grabbing on to any handhold he could get, struggling to climb toward the open hatch before the rest of the soldiers could clear their comrade's body.

He could feel his muscles burning—his arms, his back—as he powered himself up. He reached up, stretching his arm as far as he could, grabbing the edge of the hatch and pulling hard. He scram-

bled onto the top of the transport—the overturned side actually—
and he moved cautiously toward the opening. He could see the body
of the man he just killed moving, as the troopers inside pushed it
up, trying to get it out of the way. But Jamie was there already, and
he slipped the rifle off his shoulder, bringing it to bear in an instant.

You fuckers thought you were going to take Katia away from me?

He flipped the weapon to its full autosetting, and he emptied the
clip into the vehicle.

He barely heard the troopers inside shouting over the gun, at
least for a few seconds. Then nothing. He grabbed the man slumped
over the opening and pushed him over the side, staring into the vehicle's cab to make sure. There were three more soldiers inside, and it
only took one look at the hideous mess to confirm they were all dead.

He turned and climbed back down, running around toward the
back of the truck. He jumped up and braced himself, pulling with all
his strength on the jammed lever. It didn't budge . . . at first. Then he
thought he felt something, movement, no more than a millimeter.
He gritted his teeth, pouring all he had into the effort. The metal bar
moved again, a few centimeters this time . . . then the resistance was
gone and it slammed all the way to the open position.

He opened the door and looked inside. For an instant he didn't
see anything, and his stomach tensed. But then his eyes fixed on her.
She was lying on the side of the compartment, unconscious, half
covered with boxes and debris that had broken free.

Jamie climbed into the back, pushed everything aside, and
leaned over her. He put his hand to her face. Still warm. Then he
moved his fingers to her neck. He could feel her heartbeat.

His own was racing pretty hard.

He turned her over gently, and as soon as he got a good look
at her his rage returned. She was banged up from the crash of the
truck . . . but there was more. The cut on her face was covered in
crusted blood, and her clothes were in tatters. Whatever had happened to her, much of it had been well before she'd stepped into
the truck.

He reached down, picking her up as gently as he could, but not waiting to make sure he wouldn't be causing more damage. If they were found near a wrecked federal truck with five dead soldiers in it, they'd be dead for certain, so they had to move quickly.

"I've got you, Katia," he said, knowing she couldn't hear him. "I'll get you away from here . . . I promise."

Jamie felt the relief at finding her alive, but it wasn't enough to overcome the cold burn at seeing her like this.

I'm sorry, Damian, but I'm past the point of no return. I know you wanted to keep me out of the revolution . . . but there is no way now.

He'd killed nine federal soldiers.

He was ready to kill more.

CHAPTER 18

"Lieutenant Fowler, status report on jamming operations." Captain Mara Cross walked out of the elevator into the main control room. She wore the dark gray uniform of the navy of Federal America. She and her crew had replaced the colonial security forces that normally ran the station, at least in the command and key operational posts.

"All jamming operations proceeding at optimum levels, Captain. The power drain is significant, but the reactor is holding up for now."

"Very well. Maintain operations." Cross had warned Asha Stanton that planetwide jamming would strain the station's power capacity. It was unlikely the effort could be maintained indefinitely, even with the frigates *Nobellus* and *Banshee* docked and adding their reactors to the station's own. She'd had her engineering staff working under near-battle-stations conditions, watching the reactor, trying to see any issues before they truly became problems. But eventually something would slip by, and the reactor would scrag.

The federal observer had been clear, though: any revolution on Alpha-2 would be crushed, and the orbital station would be a crucial part of that. Part of Cross's mission was to keep the rebels from communicating effectively, a relatively easy thing to do with total control of the planet's satellite network. Her people had another job, too: to spot rebel positions and keep the forces on the ground supplied with up-to-date intel.

"Status of ground support operations?"

"We are providing continuous intel, Captain. The column en route to Vincennes has apparently been engaged by minor forces hidden in the woods, where our scanners cannot detect them. But we have sent Major Stein a complete map of rebel positions at Vincennes. Enemy strength is estimated at approximately 1100."

"Very well." Cross walked over toward her chair and sat down, thinking quietly for a minute. The battle on the surface would begin in earnest any minute now. She hadn't expected the rebel force to be so large, but she was confident it wouldn't matter.

It is time for those ignorant colonists to learn what it is like to face forces that have modern support.

Cross didn't have any real animosity toward the Havenites. Indeed, she tried to be as apolitical as possible, at least as far as she ever let anyone see. What she did have was a specific set of orders. And they superseded other considerations.

"All scanners on full, Lieutenant . . . and make sure we maintain our comm-lock through the jamming. Our orders are to provide all possible support to Major Stein and his forces."

"Yes . . . Captain."

Was that hesitation she heard? Or was she just imagining it?

She wasn't so naïve to think there wasn't support for the rebellion among the colonial forces on the station . . . and even some among her navy staff. Hell, if she'd allowed herself, she might have felt the same thing—she had friends who'd mustered out and retired to Alpha-2. But there was no room for such considerations. She would do her duty, and so would her people, whatever personal feelings they might have.

And God help any of them who forgot that.

Danforth had never felt anything like the panic that threatened to take him. He'd prepared for years, recruited his neighbors, drained his family fortune . . . all to get to this day. And now all he wanted was to keep running . . . deep into the woods until all he could hear were the leaves rustling in the wind.

He heard the fire from the feds along the edge of the woods. He felt as though any second one of those bullets would rip into his back, take him down short of the cover he was running toward with all the energy and adrenaline his body could produce.

The trench was just ahead, and he lunged forward, diving clumsily over the small pile of logs in front, landing hard, feeling the pain of impact vibrate through his body.

"Open fire!" He screamed as loudly as he could. "And pass the order down." For all the years he'd planned revolution, he'd never imagined his soldiers would have to fight without basic communications. Danforth knew something about the energy cost a planetwide jamming effort required, and he couldn't understand how the federals were maintaining it. Not that it mattered at the moment. The only thing that mattered was his inability to issue orders other than through the power of his voice.

He could hear the gunfire erupt all along the rebel line, and he could see the bullets tearing into the woods. The federals continued their fire, but Danforth could see they were taking losses now. Many of his people were poorly trained, inexperienced at firing weapons, especially in battle. But some of the rebels knew their way around a gun, and they were scoring hits.

So are the federals, though.

Danforth looked down the line, leaning forward in the trench. It was hard to tell, but he could see at least a dozen of his people down already. And that was just in the small area within his line of sight.

He reached around, pulling his own rifle from his back. He wasn't an especially good shot, and he didn't think one more weapon firing would make much difference.

But the rest of them seeing me on the line, alongside them firing . . . that just might mean something.

He knelt down between two of his people, bringing the rifle to bear. He paused for just a few seconds. Then he aimed and opened fire.

"Command Central, this is Jaybird One, on position over the action. Forces are heavily engaged below. Requesting permission to commence attack run."

"Jaybird One, you are authorized to attack."

Vincent Perrin gripped the gunship's controls, moving the throttle to the side, bringing the aircraft around. The Talon-class gunship was a small infantry support craft, part plane, part helicopter, with a bit of hovercraft in the mix. It was a light weapon on Earth, dwarfed by the heavy, nuclear-powered airships the powers deployed in war. But out in the colonies, it was a superweapon, and its quad chain guns were the deadliest anti-infantry weapon on Alpha-2.

"Gunners ready," he said, pushing down on the throttle, beginning the dive.

"Ready." The two men replied almost in unison.

Perrin pushed the controls harder forward, bringing the gunship down in a steep dive. He could hear the four rotors on the craft's underside, and he could feel the shaking as he pushed the gunship to the extent of its abilities. He'd been told the rebels didn't have any antiair capability, but he and his people weren't colonial security, or even anti-insurgency forces. They were from the real military, and Perrin was enough of a veteran to realize that all intel was best greeted with at least some skepticism. One surface-to-air missile could knock his bird out of the sky, and even an inexperienced operator could get lucky. That meant he was doing this by the book.

"Commence firing," he snapped, pulling back the throttle and leveling off the gunship. He'd positioned the bird perfectly, right above the rebel line.

He could hear the sound of the chain guns firing, and he almost felt sorry for the rebels on the ground. Each gun fired fifty rounds a second, spewing out death on any bodies of troops unfortunate enough to be in its target zone.

"Cease fire," he ordered. Then he pulled back on the throttle, climbing hard. The Talon was a nightmare to ground forces it attacked, but it was also extremely vulnerable to interdictive fire when it was on a low altitude run. Again, intel or no, Perrin had no intention of keeping his bird at less than three hundred meters for an instant longer than he needed.

"We're at 6 percent ammo remaining, Lieutenant," said the lead gunner.

Perrin flipped on the comm. "Command Central, this is Jaybird One. Our chain guns are almost dry. Returning to base for reload."

"Copy that, Jaybird One."

Perrin brought his craft around, angling it back toward Landfall. His turnaround time for transit, reloading, and refueling was one hundred ten minutes, less than two hours. He wondered if there'd be any rebels left when he got back.

"Jtand! Hold your positions!" John Danforth was running along the rebel line, waving a makeshift flag, really a piece of cloth torn from a blanket tied to a long stick. It was bright red, the most visible thing Danforth could find to rally the Guardians.

The two federal gunships had wreaked havoc on his forces. There were dozens and dozens dead, and the morale of the others was on the verge of collapse. The Guardians were rebels, but they weren't soldiers . . . not yet at least. They were farmers and factory workers and engineers. They had lost at least a hundred of their number to the deadly air attacks, and they were panicking.

"Hold your positions," Danforth shouted. "You're safer in your cover than running in the open. Fight these bastards! Avenge your friends. What will you think of yourselves tomorrow if you run this day? Keep fighting, and win your goddamn freedom!"

Where those words came from, Danforth wasn't sure, because God knew he was as terrified as the rest of these men and women. He'd thrown himself down in the mud when the gunships strafed the line, but somehow he'd pulled himself together. When he'd looked up, he was horrified. And he was equally disturbed when he saw how many of his forces he had lost, beyond those killed and wounded. Perhaps 20 percent of those who had gathered had trickled away, fled into the woods behind Vincennes, running like mad for home.

But as surprised as he was about those losses, he was equally surprised it wasn't worse, because the bulk of the force remained, however shaken they were.

"To your positions. The gunships are gone, but those troopers are still coming. Get ready!"

Tyler came running down from the northern end of the line. "They're holding, John. We lost some, but the line is holding."

"They're holding down here, too. Get back up there, Ty. They need to see you." Then, after a short pause: "I'm proud of you, cousin. You're doing great."

Tyler forced a smile. "Thanks, John. You, too."

John could see his cousin was scared, just as he was. But he was doing what he had to do. He was holding it together, and he was keeping his amateur soldiers in the line.

"I'll see you when it's over, John."

John nodded. Then he turned and walked back down the line. "Stay sharp, Guardians." The federal skirmish line was still firing, but after the nightmare of the gunship attack, it didn't seem like much more than a nuisance.

But he knew the main assault was coming. And he didn't know how much more his people could take.

"Hold fast, Guardians." He was waving the flag, the makeshift colors of the rebellion, and he was moving down the line. "Stand firm and fight. Fight for your freedom!"

"Lieutenant Pindry, your company will lead the attack. You are to advance quickly. Do not stop or get involved in a protracted firefight. Those are not veteran troops; they're glorified civilians, and they just endured an air attack. We need to move on them quickly, forcefully . . . force them to break. Then we can mop things up and get back to Landfall."

Frasier was focusing on his words, making sure none of his doubts came through in his tone. The highly effective strafing runs against the rebel positions had given morale a boost, but Frasier didn't kid himself. His troops were shaken, too, unnerved by the deadly ambushes they'd experienced along the road. They needed him to be like granite.

And the only way to give them that is to lie to them.

Major Stein had all but yielded command to Frasier. The CO was back in his command vehicle, halfway to the rear of the line, and he showed no signs of coming closer to armed enemies that had proven themselves to be far more dangerous than he'd imagined. He'd told Frasier to take charge of the attack, and that's exactly what the colonial officer was doing. He'd snapped out a flurry of orders, many of which he knew he should have run by Stein first. But he didn't think the force commander would care as long as he got to stay in his armored vehicle.

Pindry looked back, nodding, but far less effective than Frasier at hiding his fear. "Yes, sir," he said in a voice that was less than inspiring.

Frasier nodded. "Go, Lieutenant. And remember, you won't be alone. I'll be right behind with the reserve company." He turned and looked up to the north . . . and then down to the south. He'd sent forces in both directions to flank the rebel line . . . and if he'd timed things right, they should be engaging just as the front assault went in . . .

Pindry paused for a few seconds, as if he was going to say something. Then he just nodded again and turned around, trotting back up to his troops. He'd dismounted his infantry, leaving two soldiers in each transport, one driver and one to operate the vehicle's autocannon. The attack plan was simple. The transports would advance, the infantry formed up behind the vehicles, using them for cover as they closed the distance. The transports were lightly armored, mostly proof against small-arms fire. But anything heavier than an assault rifle could be dangerous.

Frasier moved forward—farther, he knew, than he should—and watched Pindry position himself at the front of his force. His opinion of the young officer grew. Frasier hadn't ordered him to place himself at the head of his troops—he'd done that himself.

The transports moved forward, clearing the woods one at a time, the second swinging north and the third south and so on, widening the line of advance. They moved slowly, allowing the troops behind to keep up. Pindry's company was ninety strong, with eight vehicles.

The autocannons opened up as soon as the transports moved out into the open, raking the enemy line. The rebels had dug a trench opposite the road, with a series of heavy logs deployed in front. It was a fairly strong position, one that offered heavy cover to its garrison. Which was one reason Frasier wanted Pindry's people to keep moving. Stopping out in the open and exchanging fire with the entrenched rebels was a sucker's move.

The rebels were firing at the advancing troops. When Frasier had first been briefed about the mission on the weapons dump, he had expected mostly a combination of obsolete old guns—single-shot rifles, ancient shotguns, and the like. He understood there might have been a few imported weapons, but certainly not so many.

What the hell kind of smuggling operation had been going on?

His skirmish line had suffered badly from the rebels' fire, and now he completely understood the importance of the operation. If the rebels had more ordnance like this, his people had to destroy or capture it. At all costs.

Another sound ripped through the air, louder, lower pitched. Some kind of heavy weapons. He leaned out from behind his cover, bringing his binoculars up and scanning the line. It looked like the fire was coming from two spots, and he saw one transport, bracketed by the two emplacements, stopping, and an instant later bursting into flames.

He could see the advancing forces fragmenting. Half the transports were still moving forward, but the two flanking the destroyed vehicle stopped. They were still firing, raking the rebel line, but they stayed in place, their troops huddling behind them.

Frasier watched for another few seconds. The rebels were dug in, but the guns on the transports were taking a toll. He knew if his people pushed hard enough they could break the enemy line. Then a second transport sputtered to a halt, another victim of the rebel's heavy weapons. The other vehicles slowed, and the infantry squads clumped together behind.

He pulled out his comm. "Keep going, Pindry, goddammit," he yelled into the comm, turning as he did and waving toward the column of transports lined up behind him. "I don't care what you have to do, but get those troopers moving. We've got to break through. I'm bringing up the second line now."

"Captain . . ." Pindry's voice was ragged. "Yes, Captain."

"Do it, Lieutenant." Frasier knew his officer was on the edge. And if Pindry lost it the attack would fall apart. "Just focus, Dave . . . I'll be up there in a minute."

He turned around again and shouted, "Second company . . . advance." He pulled the assault rifle from his back and flipped it to full auto. Then he ran out, in front of the second wave toward Pindry's faltering troops.

Jamie was exhausted, his legs on fire, and his back hurting like he'd never felt before. He'd carried Katia more than five kilometers, and he was coming to the last of his strength. But now he could see the house up ahead, and that gave him a needed boost.

You're almost home, Katia.

He paused for a few seconds, scanning the area, looking for more federals, but things looked clear—except for one thing: there was a transport parked in the side yard. He recognized it immediately, though, and breathed a sigh of relief.

Damian was there.

He scrambled up toward the front porch, looking around where he'd left Alexi. He was gone.

So were the bodies of the troopers he'd killed.

He climbed the small staircase, and pushed the door open, stepping inside. Alexi was lying on the sofa, half covered with a blanket. Damian and Ben Withers were standing there.

"Damian . . . my God, I'm glad to see you."

Damian ran up to Jamie, helping him with Katia, setting her down gently on the floor. He turned toward Withers. "Ben, go find some more blankets and pillows."

"Yes, sir." Withers nodded and ran out of the room, toward the staircase leading to the upstairs.

"Damian, we've got to get out of here. The feds will be back."

"I know, Jamie. Alexi told me you went after Katia. We just got Alexi bandaged up, and I was about to come after you."

"How is he?"

Damian turned back toward the sofa. "We managed to stop the bleeding. I think he'll be all right, but we need to get him a doctor. And as you said, we've got to get out of here." A pause. "How is Katia?"

"She's pretty banged up, but I think she'll be okay." He looked down for an instant, his eyes staring at the ground.

Whatever the hell "okay" means . . .

He looked back up at Damian. "Can you help them? The federals, they're after Katia. You've got to get them out of here . . . somewhere safe."

"I will . . ." Damian paused, looking at his friend with a troubled expression on his face. "What about you, Jamie?"

Jamie stared back. He couldn't go back to the farm. He couldn't go anywhere Damian hid the others either. Katia had been at an illegal protest, and Alexi had just tried to defend his daughter. But *he* had killed nine federal soldiers. And there was no doubt in his mind the surveillance devices on the transports had captured his image. The federals would hunt him relentlessly. They would never stop, and all he could bring to his friends, to Katia, was danger.

If they weren't already in danger.

Which means this won't end until it's actually finished.

"I'll find the rebels, Damian. It's the only place for me now."

Damian stood silent for a few seconds, looking back at his friend. Finally, he said, "You can stay on the farm. We'll keep you hidden somewhere." But there was no conviction in his words.

"Thank you for all you've done for me, Damian. There is no way I can ever explain what it has meant to me."

"Take care of yourself, my friend." Damian moved forward, pulling Jamie in a tight hug. He spoke softly. "Stay calm if you end up in battle. And alert. Trust your friends and trust your instincts. Never lose your focus, and you'll come through it. Believe me . . . I know."

The two men maintained the embrace for a few more seconds. Then Jamie turned and kneeled down, leaning over Katia and kissing her softly. He looked up. "Take care of her for me."

"I will, Jamie. Don't you worry about her. Worry about yourself. Stay alive . . . that's all you think about. You hear me?"

Jamie just nodded. Then he turned and walked out the door without another word.

John Danforth felt his foot slide out from under him. He reached out, dropping his rifle and grabbing on to the pile of shattered logs along the front of the trench to steady himself. He thought he'd slipped on the mud until he looked down and saw it was a pool of blood and something . . . else. There were at least a dozen of his people lying on the ground right around him. He'd picked fifty of the most reliable men and women among the Guardians to hold the central trench. As far as he could see there were perhaps fifteen left.

He bent down and grabbed his weapon. It was slick with blood, and he tried to wipe it clean with his sleeve, at least enough so his finger didn't slip around on the trigger. He was trying to get to one of the autocannons. One of them was still firing, but the other had fallen silent. Its first crew had been killed in place, and the two who were supposed to replace them had fled.

Danforth climbed over a body, and moved toward the heavy weapon. He dropped down to his knees, grabbing the gun and angling it toward the approaching federals. He had read all he could about these weapons, and so he was as familiar as he could be with this cannon. He opened fire, targeting a squad moving from around a disabled transport. They were less than ten meters away, and his fire took down three of them almost immediately. The others dove to the ground, and then opened fire on his position.

He ducked down below the lip of the trench, reaching up, trying to fire the autocannon blindly.

"Mr. Danforth . . ."

He turned toward the voice. It was one of the Guardians, a boy barely sixteen or seventeen. Danforth struggled for a name, but it just didn't come.

"What is it?" He gestured for the boy to duck down. He'd seen too many of his people killed because they were careless, and he didn't think he could take much more.

"Your cousin sent me, sir. He says there are federal troops coming down from the north, moving behind his lines."

Fuck . . .

Danforth wasn't a soldier. He'd known that before, but the day's events had pounded it home. He was dedicated, and he even fancied that he'd shown some courage. But he just didn't know what he was doing. And because of his inexperience, he'd gotten a lot of good people killed.

No more . . . not today.

The battle was lost. He'd known that already, but he'd refused to accept it. His people had gotten some of the guns out of Vincennes, but now he realized he'd have to abandon the rest. If he didn't order a retreat now, he would lose the Guardians. All of them.

"Go back. Tell Tyler to get his people out. We'll pull back to Dover and regroup."

"Yes, sir." The boy turned and headed north. He'd gotten about ten meters when a heavy round from one of the transports took off the top of his head. Danforth watched him fall, and he closed his eyes. He knelt where he was, barely hanging on, replaying the nightmare of the kid's death over and over in his mind.

No . . . you don't have time for this. These people need you . . .

He turned toward one of the Guardians standing nearby. "Go up north . . . now! Tell Tyler to retreat to Dover."

The man nodded and ran to the north. Danforth turned around and yelled, "Get to the south end of the line and pass the word. Everybody is to retreat through the woods to Dover." The two men stared back at him for a second. "Go! Now!"

He snapped his head around. There were ten of his people left in the trench. "Okay, people. Stay with me. We need to buy a few minutes so the others can pull back."

He reached back toward the autocannon, gripping it tightly. Then he took a deep breath and raised his head, looking over the edge of the trench. There were federal troops moving right toward him, at least ten in the first group, with a new wave coming up from behind.

C'mon, Danforth, this is your moment.

He opened fire.

CHAPTER 19

GREEN HILL FOREST
WEST OF THE OLD NORTH ROAD
EIGHT KILOMETERS NORTH OF VINCENNES
FEDERAL COLONY ALPHA-2 (HAVEN)
EPSILON ERIDANI II
"BLACK WEDNESDAY"

John moved through the woods, limping from a twisted ankle, but otherwise unhurt. He still couldn't understand how he'd escaped from the final federal advance . . . much less how he'd gotten away more or less uninjured.

He was surrounded by Guardians, or what was left of them, men and women moving slowly through the dense woods, many of them walking wounded, others helping their more seriously injured comrades. Danforth had no idea how many people he'd lost at Vincennes . . . or how many Guardians and other rebels had simply fled the battlefield and taken off for home. But he was amazed how many of his people had remained, even through the disastrous final stage of the battle. They were far too spread out for him to even attempt a count, but it was clear that despite the defeat and the near-envelopment of the army, he still had hundreds of men and women in arms. The revolution had suffered a terrible blow. But it wasn't over.

"Mr. Danforth, you have to come, sir." It was one of the Guardians. Harold-something . . . Danforth tried to remember the man's name.

"What is it?" His gut tensed. He'd been terrified the federals would continue after his exhausted forces, but there'd been no sign of a pursuit. At least until now.

"It's your cousin, sir."

Danforth felt as though the breath had been sucked from his body.

"Tyler?"

"Please, sir . . . come with me now."

He could see the emotion in the rebel's face. He just nodded and gestured for the man to take the lead.

He followed the man to the east. There were more Guardians there, trickling through the woods. They were exhausted, defeated, but they seemed to hold their order a little better than the shattered remnants from the center. The flanks had escaped from the federal enveloping move, and they hadn't been hit as his people in the trench had been.

They scrambled up a rough hill, and then he saw. Tyler, lying on the ground on top of a tarp, surrounded by at least a dozen Guardians. John could see their faces, and he knew them all. They were among the toughest and most dedicated adherents to the rebel cause. But now their faces were grim, and more than a few were wiping away tears.

John scrambled forward, dropping to his knees next to Tyler. His cousin was pale, sweating. His eyes were two slits, barely open, and he was groaning softly. He was covered by two large coats.

"Tyler . . . Ty?" Danforth leaned over his cousin, reaching down and taking the wounded man's hand in his. "Ty?"

"John . . ." Tyler's voice was barely a whisper.

"Yes, Ty. It's John." He was struggling, trying to hold back the grief threatening to take him. He reached down, grabbing one of the coats to pull it aside, but one of the Guardians leaned down and stilled his hands.

"Don't, sir . . ." The man spoke softly. "It's bad, Mr. Danforth."

Danforth was furious. How dare this man stop him from seeing his own cousin? But then he saw the rebel's face, the terrible sadness, the helplessness. He loosened his hand, pulled it away.

"Ty," he said again, moving his face closer.

"John . . . do . . . something . . . for . . . me . . ."

"Anything, Ty. Anything."

"Hold . . . the . . . army . . . together . . ."

Danforth closed his eyes tightly, fighting back the tears. Tyler was dying . . . and his last thoughts were of the army, of the rebellion. It tore at John, sliced open a deep wound inside. But it awakened something else, too—strength. Determination. His dedication had been shaken, his confidence shattered by the battle and the losses. But now his resolve firmed.

"Whatever . . . it . . . takes . . . John . . . never . . . give . . . up . . ." Tyler gasped for breath, and he coughed, spraying blood from his mouth. He turned his head, slowly, barely, and looked up at John. "Promise . . ."

John nodded, and then he forced out the words. "I promise, Ty. I promise."

He thought he saw a smile on Tyler's face . . . and his cousin's hand tightened, squeezing his own for a few seconds. Then Ty let out a deep breath, and his arm went limp.

Tyler Danforth was dead.

John sucked in a lungful of air, desperately trying to maintain his composure. He felt for an instant that he might lose control . . . but then he felt the coldness take over. It wasn't simply anger. It was deeper somehow. He could feel the idealism that had drawn him to the rebel cause fading away. The federals weren't the opposition anymore. They weren't his adversaries. They were the enemy, in the purest and darkest form. He hated them, and he craved vengeance. He would make them pay—for all the men and women who had died this day.

For Tyler.

"Get those explosives in place now. I want those buildings blown, and I want to get the hell out of here." Frasier knew his decision would be second-guessed, that pompous fools like Semmes would call his failure to pursue the defeated rebels an act of cowardice, of incompetence. But there was nothing he could do about that. The column had less than half the more than five hundred troops who had left Landfall still in the field, and they still had to go back down that road . . .

There were more than a hundred and fifty dead, plus as many wounded. And even those still in arms were exhausted, their morale, even in victory, near the breaking point. The force was in no condition to advance farther, let alone conduct a running pursuit across country sympathetic to the enemy. His mission was to destroy the weapons cache, and he was going to do that and get the fuck out of there.

His head snapped around as a loud crack echoed across the clearing.

Those damned snipers . . .

"Pindry . . ." His voice was sharp, tight, the anger clear in every word. "Send a squad out there and run down those damned shooters." The partisans in the woods had hurt his forces badly, both on the approach march, and later, when they reappeared just as the final assault was under way. Frasier wasn't a brutal man by nature, but even he'd taken as much as he could. He'd ordered all snipers killed on sight, no surrenders to be accepted.

Not that any of them have tried to surrender.

"Yes, sir."

Pindry was among the wounded, but it was only a minor round he'd caught in the arm. He'd had it quickly dressed, and then he'd returned to his shattered command.

Frasier hadn't known much about Pindry before the battle, but he had nothing but admiration for the officer now. The younger man had somehow held his crumbling unit together long enough for Frasier to lead up the reserves and punch through the rebel line. The final assault had reached its climax just as the flanking forces were moving against the northern and southern ends of the enemy line. The rebels, who had fiercely clung to their positions until then, collapsed in a few minutes, hundreds streaming to the rear.

His soldiers pressed the attack, gunning them down as they fled, but then the survivors reached the woods on the other side of the village. That was when Frasier knew he couldn't pursue. Sure, he had felt an urge to send his lead elements after them, to stay on their tails and prevent them from regrouping. But he remembered what the irregulars in the woods had done to the fresh column. He had visions of his troops—nearly as disordered in victory as their adversaries were in defeat—being cut off, surrounded in small groups, shot down . . . and worse.

He'd walked along the Old North Road, staring down at the bodies. He'd seen a dead man, his hair and the skin at the top of his head sliced off. No, he'd decided. He couldn't send his exhausted, battered troops plunging into the woods without any scouting reports or air cover.

Destroy the weapons, and get back home.

Not that it was going to be easy. He'd lost too many transports in the battle, and most of those still operational were packed full of wounded. That meant most of the column would be marching back on foot as it was. And he had no way of knowing what was out in the woods all around Vincennes. Were there more rebel forces on the way? How many of the irregulars were still out there? It was just too dangerous. He'd told Major Stein his concerns, and the column commander had told him to do what he thought best . . . and then he'd remained inside his armored command vehicle.

Still, there wasn't a doubt in his mind the blame for the losses suffered—and for letting the rebel survivors get away—would land on him.

Fuck . . . I really didn't need all this on my shoulders.

Pindry jogged back toward him. "The explosives are ready, sir."

Frasier looked over toward the massive barn, and the three smaller buildings where his people had found weapons. The guns were all leading edge, modern union and hegemony models. He suspected his report would stir things up back on Earth. Federal America's diplomats would scream bloody murder, lodging official complaint after official complaint about the other powers interfering in its internal matters. And the ambassadors from the union and the hegemony would throw up their hands and shout back just as loudly, denying any involvement, blaming black marketeers or accusing the Americans of setting the whole thing up to discredit them.

In the end it would all come to nothing. The last war had been over less than five years, and none of the powers were ready for a full-scale resumption of hostilities. Still, Frasier was glad at least that his involvement in the source of the rebel weapons would end with the filing of the report.

"Are all your people clear?"

"Yes, Captain."

Frasier took one last look at the building. He couldn't have imagined the effort it had taken the rebels to acquire so many weapons . . . or the cost. There was satisfaction, at least, that these hundreds of guns would do his people no further harm. That was a gain to set against the terrible losses they had suffered.

"Then let's blow these things, and get the hell out of here."

"It's true, Col. The federals took Vincennes. Solid information is hard to come by, but it sounds like the Guardians had at least three hundred killed and wounded, maybe more." Zig's normally confident cocky mien was clearly shaken now.

Jacen stared back, not responding at first. It was the third report he'd had of the battle at Vincennes, and they were all pointing to a bloody fiasco. Finally, he looked up at Welch and asked, "What are you hearing about the federals?"

"They took heavy losses, too, especially from Killian's bush-whackers." He paused. "I've heard some stories about the fighting in the woods, the ambushes—they must be exaggerations."

"Don't count on that, Zig. Killian is a strange guy. And he's gathered every half-crazy nutcase he could find."

Jacen had once considered inviting Killian into the Society. The man was certainly a rock-solid rebel, and his abilities were beyond question. But Jacen and his followers were political radicals, determined to wash away the sins of the old regime with a river of blood. Killian wanted to *bathe* in that river, to strike back endlessly at the government that had wronged him. Jacen sympathized with the ranger, and he agreed wholeheartedly he'd been terribly wronged. But he also knew Killian's experience had cost him more than his military career. It had cost him his sanity. The man was certifiably crazy, and while he appreciated the good Killian could do for the revolution in the field, he'd decided against making the ranger a true insider. Hearing this news only confirmed his feelings.

Frankly, Jacen was scared shitless of him.

"Well, crazy or not, his rangers probably saved whatever is left of the Guardians . . . and the others who rallied to Danforth's call."

Jacen nodded. "He's a powerful tool . . . but a dangerous one as well." He paused. "Nevertheless, we are at a critical stage. The rebel army, such as it is, has been battered. Morale is failing. A large portion of our cached weapons have been destroyed. And the communications blackout is stifling the spread of the rebellion." He gave Welch a significant look. "We must be able to get the word out, or we are doomed to fail."

Welch blinked. "You want to move on Cargraves. You want to break out Jonas Holcomb." The two had discussed that very plan multiple times. But it was difficult . . . maybe impossible.

And it would be costly.

But Jacen didn't see any other options at this point. The defeat at Vincennes had shown him this was not going to be an easy fight. "Yes. If anyone can find a way to cut through that damned jamming, it's Holcomb."

"But we don't even know if he'll help us."

"He's been in that hellhole for a long time now, Zig. You don't think he's going to want to get payback from the federals? We can use that."

"I guess. But it will also take almost all the cash we have left in reserve. And with Danforth on the run, his house and company confiscated, we're not likely to see more anytime soon."

Jacen nodded. "I know. You're right. But if we don't find a way to communicate, for the revolution to spread before it is extinguished, we're dead before we even get started. I don't think we have a choice."

Welch stood silently for a moment, looking unconvinced at first. But then he nodded as well. "I don't like it, Cal, but you're right. We don't have a choice."

"No, we don't. And we don't have time to waste either."

Damian sat in his library. It was his favorite place, a room he had designed himself to be his refuge, a place he could come, to read, to relax—just to be himself. He'd built a row of bookcases along one of the walls, in anticipation of the collection of old-style books he'd intended to collect in retirement, though the effort of getting a large farm in operation and the disturbances rocking his adopted world had proven to be significant distractions. As such, there were only eight volumes tucked into one corner of twenty or thirty linear meters of shelf space.

Damian had planned a lot of things when he'd shed his uniform and come to Haven, and despite the paltry number of books adorning his library, he had cause to be pleased with his efforts. But now he was hunched forward over his desk, his clothes a rumpled mess, a half-empty bottle of brandy sitting next to him.

Damian wasn't a drinker, nor was he the type of man to seek escape from his problems, preferring to confront them head-on. But for the first time in his life, he didn't know what to do, what path to follow . . . and he'd decided he needed something to quiet the voices, to dull the pain.

He'd gotten Alexi and Katia Rand out of their house before federal reinforcements arrived, and he'd left nothing traceable in his wake. He'd hesitated for a moment before he lit the fire, but he knew there was no alternative. He couldn't leave any evidence behind for the federals that might lead them to him or to the underground room where he'd hidden the Rands.

He didn't know what had driven him to build the secret refuge, but for all its utility now, he knew it wasn't hidden well enough to defeat a truly comprehensive search effort. But it was the best he could do for now. Alexi needed time to recover from his wound, and Katia . . .

He didn't know exactly what Katia had been through. She had

thanked him profusely when she'd awakened, but she hadn't said a word about her flight through the city and her escape back to her house. Still, it was clear she'd had a hard time of it, and he was damned sure he wasn't going to let anything else happen to her.

He wished he had the same conviction on everything else happening around him as he did in his loyalty to his friends. He was harboring fugitives . . . and he'd done all he could to help Jamie escape, something he knew was sufficient by itself to send him to the scaffold.

Yet he still couldn't bring himself to fully join the rebel cause. He was from the slums of Washington, a place where less than half the children born reached adulthood. The army had saved him, and his service had given him respect, prestige, even a chance to build something of value. And that service had been to Federal America. He'd followed its flag into battle; he'd fought its enemies with all he had to give. And it seemed anathema to him to raise arms against it now, however much he understood the provocations that had driven the rebels to arms.

Also, any chance of a peaceful solution was lost when the federal observer arrived. Damian had realized then and there the authorities on Earth had decided that negotiations weren't an option and that Asha Stanton's only concern was crushing the rebellion once and for all.

He suspected the government in Washington had underestimated the Havenites, and he was convinced the federals would have a much harder fight on their hands than they were expecting. Which only increased the chance his new home was facing a holocaust of daunting proportions.

But for all his keen analysis, he had no idea what to do himself. Let his neighbors, his friends, fight alone? Or take up arms, march against the flag he had served? And if he did, how many friends would face him from the other side? Alexandra Thornton was more than a just a comrade in battle. There was . . . history. Could he take the field against her? Could he target her in his sights, pull the trigger, extinguish her life, and leave her lying in the mud and filth of the battlefield? And if he did, could he live with himself?

Was he being naïve, though? Was neutrality a real possibility? His cooperation with the governor had earned him enemies among the rebels, and brought down their retribution on him. It had cost the life of one of his people.

Would the federals be any different? Would they allow him and the other veterans to go about their business, to stay out of the conflict . . . or would they demand the retired soldiers all declare for them, even call them back to the colors to fight against their neighbors?

"Fuck!"

Damian picked up his head, looking around the room. It was empty. And it was moving. Or at least it looked that way to him. Ben Withers had come in half a dozen times since he'd sat at his desk three hours before and opened the bottle. The ex-noncom was clearly worried about his old commander. But the last time Withers had asked if he was okay, Damian had sent him scurrying for the door with firm orders not to return.

He's probably peering around some corner even now, keeping an eye on me . . .

He felt guilty just thinking that, even through the alcoholic haze. Ben Withers was as loyal as a man could be.

You're a piece of shit, Ward. He was just worried about you . . .

Yeah, well—I'm worried about me, too.

Damian reached out, grabbing the bottle and looking around. He knew there'd been a glass; he remembered getting it. But now he couldn't find it. He shrugged and put the bottle to his lips, taking a large swig. He hated the taste, and it burned his throat going down. But he couldn't bear the idea of any more sober thoughts, not now. Tomorrow would come soon enough, and his problems would still be there.

For now, all he wanted was oblivion.

CHAPTER 20

John Danforth moved around, trying without success to get at least moderately comfortable on the folding chair. He looked around the makeshift table, half a dozen rough boards nailed together, stacked on top of two large crates. None of the others sitting with him looked any better off. They all had to make do with what they had—the comforts of the Danforth estate and his plush office were a vestige of the past, and a hard war lay between him and regaining any of that.

Not that any of them would complain. The Guardians had lost heavily—two hundred and two dead, he now knew, and seventy-six wounded, most of those lightly, thank God. But there were two hundred and six missing as well, and he knew many of them had been seriously injured, unable to withdraw with their comrades. A few badly wounded Guardians made it back, mostly through the herculean efforts of their fellows, but the others had been left behind.

Abandoned to the federals . . .

It ate at him, the thought of those men and women made prisoners, or dying alone, but there hadn't been anything he could do about it. If his people had stayed in Vincennes another ten minutes *none* of them would have escaped . . . and the rebellion would be over.

And those prisoners would still be prisoners, as would the rest of the Guardians.

He knew his logic had been sound, that his action had saved his force from total destruction, but he still hated himself for giving the order. For having to be the one *to* give the order. But who else was there? For good or for ill, he was their leader, and they were looking for him to do just that: lead.

So let's get started.

"We must find a way to spread the word. Even here, near Land-fall, we have supporters who do not know there is an army of rebels already in the field. And that army is not defeated. Yes, we lost a battle, but we hurt them as much as they hurt us. We *can* fight the federals! But only if we can gather more men and women and let them know what's going on."

Danforth had tried not to think about the weapons they'd lost, the fortune he'd paid to get that ordnance to Haven. It didn't seem important with so many of his followers dead or in federal captivity. At least Vincennes hadn't been the Guardians' only stash of guns. "Riley!" he shouted suddenly.

Riley James ran over to him. "Yes, Mr. Danforth." Riley was twenty-three, but her slight build and her short, spiky blond hair-cut made her look even younger. She'd been one of his assistants at Danforth Communications, until her strong rebel leanings became apparent. She'd kept her job after that, technically at least, but her work over the past year had almost entirely involved the Guardians of Liberty and Danforth's political activities. Despite her young age, she quickly became one of his inner circle.

"We need to send a party to Strickland Lake. There's another cache there . . . and we need to secure those weapons immediately. We have to get everyone rearmed and resupplied with ammo." It was the latter that gave him pause. The Guardians had expended an enormous amount of ordnance in the battle, and hundreds of them had thrown down their arms when they retreated. The astonishing amount of material it took to keep a fighting force in the field was only just dawning on him. Which made getting to Strickland Lake all the more crucial.

"And we still don't know how the federals found out about Vincennes. We can't take any chances with the other caches—if we have a spy in our midst . . ." His voice trailed off. The idea of a turncoat among his beloved Guardians was painful . . . but he hadn't been able to come up with any other explanation as to how the federals had suddenly found out about Vincennes.

"Yes, Mr. Danforth. I'll make sure it's done at once." Like every interaction he'd ever had with her, the sheer competence she exuded came through with every word she spoke. Today, however, there was also sympathy. She'd known Tyler, of course, and she had been very fond of him, as almost everyone in the rebel cause had been. And for all his efforts, John Danforth had not done a very good job hiding his pain. At least, not from those who knew him well.

She paused, as though she was going to say something else. But then she just nodded once and turned around, running down the hill to carry out his command.

Danforth sat still for a few seconds, turning his head and watching his aide. He was very fond of Riley. Indeed, in many ways she'd slipped into the role of the daughter he'd never had. Images of her passed through his mind, dark ones: her lying on the ground, covered in blood . . . the light in her eyes slipping away, as Tyler's had.

He'd involved her in his rebel activities, and now part of him regretted it. Her service, her reliability, they were crucial to him . . . but now he realized how much danger he'd put her in. He'd always known rebellion was a hazardous game, but there was a difference between theoretical dangers and the dead, broken bodies of comrades, of friends. He'd found that out the hard way at Vincennes. And just as he'd ordered the Guardians to retreat, he felt an urge to send her away, someplace where she'd be safe.

Is there even such a place on Haven now?

He shook his head. He needed her. The cause needed her. Besides, she would never leave him. He would have to break her spirit to make her go. And he knew he didn't have the strength to do that, or the endurance to look at the hurt in her eyes if he did.

He stood up abruptly. Doubts, guilt, uncertainty—there was a time and place for that. The Guardians needed a leader, and he knew that was him, no matter how much his first battle had shaken his confidence.

He turned and walked down the hill, following the path she'd taken. Things were suddenly clear to him. He had to get his people ready to carry on the fight. Equipping them was part of that . . . and *leading* them would be the rest. He knew they were scared and confused—he was, too. But he wouldn't let that become despair. For once he let them progress down that road the rebellion would truly be over.

And he was far from done. He stood up a bit straighter as he headed down the hill. He was going to be the leader they needed right now: alert, active, hopeful . . . not wallowing in his own stew of remorse and fear. He felt the determination building inside him. He would hold them together, whatever it took—whatever it cost John Danforth, the man.

And the next time the federals faced his Guardians, he swore the result would be a far different one.

Colonel Semmes scowled as he walked through the courtyard of the federal complex. The normally manicured grounds had been given over to a holding area. Rebel wounded were scattered all around, men and women, mostly those hurt too badly to escape. The hospital in Landfall was already overwhelmed dealing with the federal wounded, so Semmes had ordered the rebels to be left where they were. He hadn't had the slightest intention of providing any kind of care at all, but Governor Wells had intervened, arguing vehemently that basic decency required providing at least some level of medical attention. Semmes had argued, but Observer Stanton had sided with Wells, at least at first. Stanton had been making a significant effort to work with the governor, to make him part of the overall solution, even though she had the authority to overrule him on virtually anything.

Which pissed him off. To say he had been frustrated with Stanton would have been an understatement. For all her disdain for Alpha-2, for all her impatience to escape the provincial nature of life on the colony, she had been reluctant to allow him to take the full measures he'd requested.

It chafed. Who the hell did she think she was? His grandfather had been a senator, a titan of government. Hers, for all the war-created Stanton wealth, was a jumped-up tradesman. His authority was his birthright; hers had been purchased with family money.

For three days he'd walked through the courtyard, watched the orderlies running back and forth, bringing water to the wounded, erecting tents to protect them from the sun. And for those three days he had argued for more . . . decisive . . . measures against the captured rebels. Wounded or not, he argued, they were traitors, and they offered a real chance to make a clear point to the population. A display of the cost of treason, one the people would never forget.

Stanton had steadfastly refused the extreme proposal he had made initially, but finally he had worn her down. The lists of federal casualties had eroded her opposition, the numbers continuing to grow each day as new data was compiled. But it was the bodies, the ones she'd ordered retrieved for proper disposal, that did the trick. He could still remember the look on her face as she stared down at the half dozen corpses, five men and a woman, stabbed and slashed at least a dozen times. And the hideous wounds on their heads: the hair gone, skulls exposed and caked with dried blood.

She'd looked sick and excused herself from the room. When she came back, she gave Semmes the go-ahead he'd been seeking.

It's about fucking time, he had thought then.

He'd arranged everything (he'd had it ready even before he had Stanton's orders), even a short break in the communications jamming. This was something he wanted to broadcast for every citizen to see. So they knew as clearly as possible: this was how traitors would be treated from now on.

He looked over at the line of soldiers against the wall. There were thirty of them, and they were clad in spotless uniforms, looking like images of military perfection. They held assault rifles, and on the end of each weapon there was a shiny bit of metal. The army had long ago abandoned the bayonet as a weapon, but the anti-insurgency forces had maintained them, mostly for their utility in crowd control situations. But today they would have another use.

He turned to the left, looking up at a man standing in front of a small tower, appearing like something built from a large version of a child's erector set. There was a large camera on top, mounted on a rotating platform. The man nodded.

"All right, people . . . let's get this going . . . we don't have all day." He nodded back at the man in front of the camera tower, the signal to cut the jamming. Semmes watched as the man moved to his comm unit and called the orbital platform, relaying the command. A moment later he turned back and nodded again.

Semmes turned around and walked toward the wall, stopping in front of a smaller camera. The technician standing behind said, "Any time you are ready, Colonel."

Semmes stepped in front of the camera, standing ramrod straight. "Citizens of Alpha-2, I am Colonel Robert Semmes, commander of all colonial and anti-insurgency forces on this planet. As most of you know, rebel forces were defeated in a battle at Vincennes four days ago, and a large cache of illegal weapons was destroyed. Over one hundred rebels wounded in the fighting were subsequently captured." He paused. "You will now all see what happens to traitors, to citizens who rise up against their rightful government. These men and women took arms against their nation. They spilled the blood of federal soldiers.

"And now they will pay the price."

He turned and looked toward the lieutenant commanding the detachment. The officer saluted and spun around, shouting out commands. The soldiers moved forward, bayonet-tipped rifles pointed toward the sky. They marched forward in lockstep, and when they reached the first wounded rebels they stopped and flipped their rifles around. Then they struck, bayonetting the helpless men and women, before moving forward toward the next row.

There were cries, of pain by those who were stabbed, and of fear and horror by those next in line. But the soldiers continued. Methodical. Merciless. And in less than ten minutes it was done. Every prisoner in the courtyard was dead.

Semmes stood there smiling. Then he gestured toward the man by the camera—the signal to order the orbital platform to resume jamming. He had nothing else to say to the population. His actions had been communication enough.

He stared out over the courtyard for another minute. Then he turned and walked into the building.

"It's true, sir. The jamming has stopped, at least for now." Ben Withers stood outside the glass door leading into Damian's library. The normally tidy room was a mess, reeking of spilled brandy and days-old sweat. Withers was doing a superb job of ignoring Damian's condition. Nevertheless, even through his hangover and the fogginess clouding his brain, Damian could see immediately something was troubling his aide.

"What's wrong, Ben?" Damian asked, forcing the words from his dry, pasty mouth.

"Sir, I think you should turn on the vid . . ." He paused. "They are broadcasting it on every channel." He hesitated again. "I'm afraid something terrible is happening."

Damian reached down, tapping at the controls on his desk. A second later, the large screen at the other end of the room snapped on. A man was on the screen, speaking. He wore a uniform, and a colonel's insignia on his shoulders.

Semmes . . .

The man was talking, and Damian immediately detected the hard edge to his voice. Not anger, not exactly. Something colder, more dangerous. And then suddenly, he realized what was about to happen.

My God . . . no . . .

Damian's eyes were unmoving, locked on the screen as he watched Semmes finish his address. The camera panning over an open area—the courtyard at the federal complex, he realized. And soldiers, moving. Slowly, steadily, across a field of wounded men and women. They held assault rifles, tipped with something bright.

Bayonets . . .

"No . . ." Damian whispered as he watched the nightmare unfold.

The room was silent as he and Withers watched the prisoners murdered. All of them. He was still staring a moment later when the broadcast ended and the static of the jamming pattern returned.

Jamie stood in the clearing, looking over the shoulders of one of the Guardians. There were seven or eight of them gathered, watching the footage of the massacre of the prisoners. John Danforth had ordered data chips with the recorded footage to be distributed throughout the rebels' makeshift camp.

The clip was having the desired effect . . . or at least what Jamie suspected Danforth had intended. He didn't know John Danforth, except through Damian. He was well aware his friend respected the communications magnate—and rebel leader—but he also knew Damian had more than once refused Danforth's calls for him to join the Guardians. He couldn't help but try to imagine Damian's reaction to this latest outrage.

Damian can't possibly defend the federals, not after this . . .

But he knew the vicious Colonel Semmes wasn't the only federal on Haven, and that many of the others—even a few that were Damian's friends—were different. Governor Wells, for one, had tried to keep the peace.

But where is he now? Just because good men and women serve a cause doesn't mean it's a good one. How many millions live on Earth in poverty, misery? How many have ended up in prisons for speech crimes? For protesting the squalor they'd been born into?

Jamie was concerned about Damian . . . and he was almost frantic worrying about Katia. But this was where he belonged. He'd tasted the slightest hint of the life Damian had offered him . . . but now he realized it was an illusion, one that would have required turning his back on what he knew was wrong. Because there were certainly others like him. How many, who knew? Thousands? Millions? He couldn't do anything about the people on Earth trapped in their misery and punished when they complained. But he damned sure could give all he had to ensure that never happened on Haven.

If he could do that, if the rebels could, then they would have earned the kind of lives he'd dreamed about. Hearth and home, shared with Katia. It was all he wanted, but it wasn't something someone could give him. He was going to have to take it.

And he was ready to do just that.

Col Jacen stood in the darkness, just outside the prison's perimeter wall. Cargraves Prison wasn't like the mine. It was a maximum security installation, designed mostly to house political prisoners, men and women who had defied Federal America on Earth . . . and who were too important for one reason or another for the secret police to simply shoot in some cellar.

The mine had steady traffic in and out all day long, ore being shipped out, guards moving on and off shift. But Cargraves was different—the prison was closed up tight. Its guards lived inside, serving month-long rotations, and the facility only opened up when a new prisoner was brought in or the monthly guard and supply transport arrived. The prison was a veritable fortress, and it had been designed that way for a purpose.

For one thing, Cargraves didn't even exist, not officially—at least, not as far as anyone on Earth was concerned. It had been built on Alpha-2 to ensure that even an escaped prisoner—and none had ever managed to accomplish that feat—would be alone, far from the power centers on Earth . . . far from almost anything, in fact. Alpha-2's far hemisphere was almost entirely ocean, and the prison was on an island eight thousand kilometers from any populated land area.

Jacen looked around at the strike team. They were Society members, all of them. But they'd left their red armbands behind, disposing of anything that could identify them. There were two veterans in their ranks, and another four who had served in the colonial security forces. The rest had been criminals, smugglers, mercenaries. The key was they all had some kind of fighting experience. Just as important to Jacen, they were all radicals, dedicated to the revolution and to reordering Haven society.

And they all knew just how crucial Jonas Holcomb was to their cause.

"Okay . . ." Jacen spoke softly. "There will be a momentary lapse in the security system in—" he looked at his chronometer "—three minutes. The kill-fence will be deactivated on this sector, along with the cameras and detection devices. You'll have two minutes maximum. You've got to be inside and past the coverage area of the primary surveillance system by then."

He looked at the strike team, the closest thing he had to a group of commandoes. He'd struggled to push away the doubts, but he couldn't help but wonder if they could pull it off. It was an audacious plan to say the least. That said, so was the idea of the revolution in the first place. Without communications, they were all but doomed. And the only person on Haven with a chance to thwart the jamming was inside that prison.

"We have allies inside. They'll cut the security system, and they'll make sure Holcomb's cell is open. The guard rotations have been changed, and a virus input into the surveillance system. The cameras should ignore you, at least for twenty minutes, but we can't be sure. That's why you've all got prison guard uniforms. Still, don't look directly at any camera—you don't want the recognition software crunching on your faces—just in case some part of the system remains active."

Jacen had used one of the oldest and most reliable weapons he knew of to secure the information and cooperation he'd needed: money. He'd bribed key personnel, handing them bars of platinum equal to what any of them made in ten years from their wages. He'd been stunned how much it took to secure the cooperation he needed, but then he realized his co-conspirators were putting their lives on the line just like his people.

He stared at his chronometer for a few more seconds. Then: "Okay . . . go!"

He stayed where he was, watching the strike force move out. In twenty minutes they'd be back with Jonas Holcomb. Or without him.

Or not at all.

CHAPTER 21

"This is entirely unacceptable!" Everett Wells leapt from his seat for the third time in ten minutes, pounding his fist down on the table as he did. He'd always been a temperate man, but right now he was verging on melodramatic.

Stanton hated theatrics. Not that Wells didn't have some reason to be upset. Semmes's soldiers had been marching all over Landfall and the surrounding villages, smashing down doors, dragging civilians out of their beds. Anyone even suspected of rebel sympathies was subject to arrest . . . or worse. But that was the cost of war, and as distasteful as even she might find it, the reality was that *the rebels* had brought this upon themselves, and no amount of tantrum was going to change that.

"Governor, please sit down." She sat at the head of the table, the place Wells had occupied before her arrival. "I share your . . . mmm . . . distaste for some of the actions currently under way, but there is no question that this planet is in armed insurrection against its legitimate government. Nor is there any question that this sorry state of affairs has occurred despite the extreme efforts on your part to reach a reasonable accord with the colonists."

"But what you're—"

"Sit down, Governor," Stanton repeated, with more force than usual.

She liked Wells, and she'd gone out of her way to show him respect, especially when the decrees she carried from the senate essentially allowed her to have him shot and to take his place entirely.

In truth, she saw some of herself in the governor, though she was rather more ambitious than he was. Wells had been a fast riser in government service, and he'd been somewhat of a role model for her, having come himself from a family with limited political influence. But now she realized Wells was a true believer, that he'd been driven all those years not by an urge to advance himself but because he was doing what he believed to be right. It was a novel concept, she thought, one rare enough, certainly in government, and while she pitied him for what she considered naivety, she couldn't help but admire him, at least on a certain level.

But now he was wearing down her patience. She had resisted many of Colonel Semmes's harshest requests, but she had to admit the brutal officer had scored a success, at least a partial one, at Vincennes. The video logs taken before the caches were blown suggested that more than a thousand state-of-the-art combat weapons had been destroyed. And the Guardians of Liberty—*what a pompous name*, she thought—had been dealt a serious blow if they hadn't been destroyed outright. It was more progress than Wells had made in three years, and if it had cost a few lives, what historically significant event hadn't?

"Your Excellency." Gone was his casual familiarity with her, and she almost sighed at the childishness of it. They had been using each other's first names in most contexts, but clearly Wells was done with that.

Which almost certainly means a speech is coming.

Sure enough, Wells was saying, "Are we animals? Butchers? Is this the only way we can resolve a dispute? By kicking down doors? Arresting people on virtually no evidence of wrongdoing . . . and then holding them indefinitely in filthy, overcrowded cells?"

"Your half measures have brought us to this juncture, Gov—"

Semmes interjected, but he stopped when Stanton raised her hand, a scowl replacing the sneer he had been directing at Wells.

"Please, all of you . . . would you leave us for a few moments? I would speak privately with Governor Wells."

The others at the table leapt up almost immediately, turning and moving quickly toward the door. Semmes was slower, seeming to deliberately hesitate for a second until Stanton turned her head and stared at him. Then he got up and followed the others, his scowl deeper.

I definitely need to watch myself around him. Again, though—a problem for another time.

"Everett, I am going to speak frankly with you. I am not your enemy, and I will never be . . . unless you give me no choice. I understand your desire for a peaceful solution here, but the senate is out of patience as far as Alpha-2 is concerned. Tax receipts are down, ore shipments have come to a virtual stop. I understand what you tried to do here, and I think I comprehend why as well. I even admire you for the effort.

"But it is *over* now, do you understand me? Citizens have taken up arms against Federal America. Hundreds of our soldiers have been killed. This is not going to end well, Everett. But it *is* going to end."

"Asha, I appreciate all you have done." *Back to first names again.* She almost smiled at that even as Wells finally sat back down. He looked tired. "I know you could have dismissed me, possibly even had me arrested. I am not ungrateful. But I must beg you to consider the humanity of your actions. Please . . ."

She sighed softly. "You simply do not understand, Everett. Humanity is not a consideration in any of this. Neither is compassion or understanding. The senate wants a peaceful and compliant Alpha-2. They want economic activity and tax revenue rising again. They want the ore flowing. That is it. They aren't concerned about how that all happens. That fact is why I am amazed they allowed you to remain in your post as long as they did. But make no mistake: this planet will be pacified. If I don't do it, someone else will be sent here to sack me. The senate will send whatever forces are necessary . . . and they will consider any death toll an acceptable cost to restore order. You made a choice, one that cost you your career—" she'd never been so blunt about Wells's terrible prospects when he returned to Earth, but she was frustrated with his stubbornness and his refusal to accept the way things had to be "—but do not misunderstand my kindness to you, or the fact that I like you as a person. I will not sacrifice my future prospects as you have yours. I will not fail in this mission, and I intend to get off this bloody rock just as soon as I possibly can."

She stared at him, her eyes cold, intense.

"So either shut the hell up, or get the hell out."

Jonas Holcomb was lying in his cell, staring at the ceiling. He'd been there for days now, without interruption—and, for the last forty-eight hours, without food. He'd have been amused at the random sequences of mistreatment the federals seemed to think would break him . . . if he hadn't had to live through it all.

At least there hasn't been another drug therapy session.

That was the true torture, far more so than the physical torment. He didn't doubt enough beatings—or some of the worse abuses he knew other prisoners endured—could break him, but the federals needed more than that. They didn't want intelligence from him, a few snippets of information. If they'd wanted to force him to divulge some secret, he was certain they could have managed that the first day or two he'd been at Cargraves.

No, they wanted him back at his work, designing weapons and technology for the government. They didn't want an angry, rebellious slave, one who might sabotage his own work to strike back. It was a fine line, but they needed both a thoroughly broken man *and* one with his faculties all intact. It was like threading a needle with rope, breaking a man so thoroughly without affecting his ability to think and reason. He was pretty sure they had been close the last time to turning him into a quivering heap. It was probably only that fact that had kept him out of drug therapy for a second time.

Until they figure it out . . . or fry my brain.

He heard a sound, the door opening. *Already?* His stomach

clenched, an instinctive reaction. To the best of his ability to keep track of the clock, it was nowhere near mealtime . . . and any other time that door opened meant something unpleasant was about to happen.

He felt his body pushing back into the wall, a pointless effort to move away from whatever was coming. He felt the shakes coming on, as they often did when the guards came for him, and he struggled to control himself, to hang on to what was left of his dignity.

A man stepped inside the cell. As he'd expected, it was a guard.

Is he here to take me to the Pit?

He paused, unable to keep the shakes from returning.

Or to another drug treatment?

He knew he couldn't resist the drugs much longer, not at the dosages they were giving him. His defenses would fail sooner or later, and then they would control him completely.

Perhaps this will be the time. Or the next one . . .

"Dr. Holcomb?" It was the guard speaking, but he knew immediately something was different this time.

"Jonas Holcomb? We're here to get you out of this place, sir. Can you walk?"

Holcomb sat up and stared at the man, frozen for a few seconds in shock. "Who are you?" he said softly, sounding confused.

"We're friends, Dr. Holcomb. And if you'd like to get out of this shithole, you need to come with us now."

Holcomb stood up, wincing against the pain as he did. His jailors hadn't done any permanent damage to him, not physically at least. But they kept him in a state of constant pain and soreness, always recovering from a beating. His legs wobbled as he tried to hold himself up. They hadn't crippled him, not yet. But he could barely stay on his feet.

"Fuck—I don't think he can make it," the guard said to someone in the hall.

"No . . . just need a second." He limped across the room toward the man standing next to the door.

"I'm not sure we have a second."

"What's—"

"There's no time to explain, Doctor. Let's just say we had some inside help . . . and it's not going to last much longer, so we've got to get going."

The man leaned forward and reached for him, and he recoiled. "I'm sorry, Jonas," the man said. "I know you've had a hard time in here, but if you want to get out, you've got to let us help you."

Holcomb hesitated, trying to focus, to understand what was happening. It had to be some kind of trick, a new torment his jailors had thought up to confuse him. They'd probably convince him he was going to get out, only to rip the hope away at the last minute . . .

"You're a liar. Leave me alone. I will never do what you want me to do."

He stepped back against the wall, watching the intruder with wild eyes. He could see the man turn, once more speaking to someone in the hall. A flurry of movement and then the man had shifted to the side, allowing someone else to come in, also wearing the uniform of a guard. He had something in his hand, a cylinder, perhaps forty centimeters long, and he was moving closer.

"No!" Holcomb shouted, turning, reaching down to grab his last meal tray, pulling it up as the plate and cup on it crashed to the ground. It wasn't much of a weapon, but it was all he had.

The man lunged forward, reaching out with the cylinder, hitting the metal tray. Holcomb shrieked as he felt the electrical shock, and he dropped the tray, trying to step back, but falling instead, landing painfully on the ground.

The man was still coming, leaning forward, the cylinder out in front of him. "I'm sorry, Dr. Holcomb, but there's no other way."

Holcomb gritted his teeth. It *was* a new form of torture. Did they think they could break him that way? By varying his torments? To create the illusion they had replaced the drug therapy that he truly feared with something else?

"We've got to shut him up. He's going to bring the whole place down on us."

"I'm trying!"

He swung his arms in front of him, landing a punch on the second man, even as the cylinder neared his flesh. Something wasn't right—they'd never left him unrestrained in any previous sessions. Why were they letting him fight back, even as ineffectually as he was? It didn't make sense. Was it possible? Could these really be some kind of rescuers? He couldn't even imagine that.

Then the cylinder struck again, and his body wracked wildly. He could feel his bladder empty . . . and everything went black.

"Father, you must do something. You must stop this madness." Violetta Wells was upset. No, more than upset . . . nearly hysterical. "The brutality, the randomness. It can't go on."

"I'm sorry, Vi," he said, unsuccessfully trying to keep his own anger and frustration from his voice. "But I'm afraid it is going to go on for a good long time. The federal observer is determined to break the rebels. She won't consider any ceasefires or peace proposals. And we can't expect any restraint from Colonel Semmes."

"But you *have* to do something!"

"What the hell do you think I've been doing, Violetta?" His words were angry, far more so than he'd intended. He'd always tried to hide the harsher side of government service from her, and now he wondered if that had been a mistake. He was appalled by what Stanton and Semmes were doing, but he blamed the rebels and their intransigence as well. He'd tried to offer them a peaceful way out, and he'd put himself on the line to do it. But they had been as unwilling to negotiate as Stanton, as determined to provoke hostilities. He was disgusted with all of them.

They all deserve this nightmare they created together . . . but I'll have no more part in it.

He turned toward his daughter. "I'm sorry, Vi. I didn't mean to yell at you. But there's nothing I can do. I have no authority, and the rebels have given Asha Stanton all the provocation she needs to crush them. And she's going to do it."

"Provocation?" Violetta looked at her father with an expression of shock. "What choice did the Havenites have once that horrible woman got here?"

Wells knew Violetta had despised Stanton from the first time the two had met. He saw things differently. Stanton wasn't the same as him, but he could also appreciate that she didn't have any real choice. If she was insufficiently aggressive, he had no doubt the senate would send someone else, with another stack of decrees, reducing her to the same impotence they had him, or even ordering her home to face charges for her failures. Semmes was an evil man, a psychopath; he was sure of that. But he believed Stanton would have made a deal to keep the peace, if the rebels hadn't been so intransigent.

"Things are more complicated than that, Vi. You act like the colonists are a foreign world. How do you think this planet was colonized? Where do you think the population came from, the technology, even the basic materials before the native mines and factories were in operation? How much do you think it cost to make Alpha-2 as self-sufficient as it is today?" He emphasized the federal designation, an answer to his daughter's use of the colloquial Haven.

"That doesn't justify terminating the planetary constitution, taxing these people to death . . ."

"What about the defense of the planet? The last war was extremely costly. Alpha-2 was defended the entire time. No enemy force was able to land, no task force got through to attack the orbital platform or bombard the planet. Do you know what a federal frigate costs to operate, much less build? Should the colonists be exempted from paying their share of that?"

Wells was speaking to his daughter, but even as he did, the words were impacting him as well. He'd been angry with Stanton—and utterly disgusted with Semmes—but now he was reconnecting with what he believed. He sympathized with the rebels, but he didn't agree with them. And for all that had transpired, for Semmes's brutality and the virtual repudiation of his own powers, he realized he was still loyal to Federal America. He had served his entire life in government, and while he was ashamed of much that had been done at the behest of the senate, he wasn't ready to repudiate that allegiance.

He looked over at Violetta. Now, for the first time he suspected his daughter was. He felt a tension in his chest. Violetta had always been a headstrong young woman, but now he was suddenly afraid she would do something foolish. If she declared for the rebels, even if she simply spoke out in favor of them, she would be in great danger . . . especially with Semmes and his anti-insurgency forces rounding up anyone who gave even the slightest indication of rebel sympathies.

Suddenly, he knew what he had to do. "It doesn't matter anymore, Vi. I'm out of this. I have no authority, no way to do anything to lessen this catastrophe. And I'll be damned if I will stand around and watch helplessly while it happens." He paused. "I'm going to resign the governorship."

He looked into his daughter's eyes and took a deep breath.

"We're going home."

"Dr. Holcomb, I am John Danforth, the . . . provisional commander of the army of Haven." None of that was official, but Danforth was trying to keep things as simple as possible. He knew Holcomb was a brilliant man, but he wasn't quite sure yet how much of that brilliance had survived Cargraves. He knew this might take some time.

Cal Jacen, though, had no patience for that. "Dr. Holcomb, we broke you out of the prison so you could help us strike back at the federals—the people who put you in that place."

Danforth understood Jacen's impatience. He had risked his people and the last of his financial resources—most of which Danforth himself had provided to the lawyer and rebel leader in the first place—to arrange Holcomb's escape. He also had to give Jacen credit for breaking the scientist out of prison, for even knowing of his existence and imprisonment. And he had no idea how his ally had managed to get an aircraft to fly the escapee back so quickly. But Jacen's aggressiveness wasn't an asset here, not with a man as clearly traumatized as Holcomb.

"Cal, would you give me a few minutes alone with the doctor?"

Jacen looked like he was going to argue, but he just nodded, turned, and walked out of the tent.

"You, too." Danforth stared at the two guards standing just inside the tent flap.

The two looked at each other, then back at Danforth.

"I'm in no danger here."

The guards nodded uncomfortably, but they followed Jacen out.

Danforth turned back toward Holcomb. "Doctor, I know you were imprisoned at Cargraves for a long time—" his voice was soft, and he spoke slowly, gently "—and I can't even imagine what they did to you in there." He stopped, letting the words sink in, not wanting to push too hard, too fast.

Holcomb had been sitting still, staring down at the ground the entire time since Jacen had brought him back. Now he raised his head slightly, looking up at Danforth. "I am really out? This isn't a deception?"

"Yes." Danforth nodded. "You are really out."

"I am your prisoner now?"

Danforth shifted uncomfortably. "No, not a prisoner."

"I am free to go, then?" Holcomb's voice was shaky, but it was firming with every word.

Danforth exhaled. "Well, yes. In theory at least. But you have to understand, there is a revolution taking place. You are only safe because you are here with us. If you leave, it is almost certain the federals will recapture you . . . and send you back to Cargraves. Or worse."

Holcomb flinched.

"I won't lie to you, Doctor. We are in a precarious situation. We control these woods, and a swath of villages situated in and around them. The federals control the rest of the planet. I'm afraid if you leave this camp and go more than a few kilometers in any direction you will be in extreme jeopardy."

Holcomb sat quietly for a few seconds. Then he asked, "Why?"

"Why?" Danforth repeated. "Why did we rescue you?"

Holcomb nodded.

"It was Cal Jacen who got you out. To be honest, I didn't even know you were there . . . and I have no idea how he did. But I suspect he believes you can help us."

The man flinched again. "Help? How?"

God, what did they do to him in there?

"Even only just learning of your incarceration, your reputation precedes you—"

"I won't make you weapons!" Holcomb tried to stand, frantic to leave. "I won't! I won't—"

"Doctor, please calm down!" Danforth held his hands in front of him, staying far away from Holcomb, doing whatever he could to appear nonthreatening. And that might have worked if the guards hadn't come rushing in, alarmed at the outburst.

"I *knew* it! This is a trap!"

"It's not a trap. Get out!" Danforth yelled at the guards. He turned back to Holcomb, seeing the fear in the scientist's eyes.

"Look. Dr. Holcomb, look—the guards are gone. They were worried for me, is all. Please," he said, coming closer. "Please . . . have a seat."

"Y-you don't want me for weapons?"

"No. I promise—we won't ask you to do anything you don't feel comfortable doing. But we do need your help."

"Wh-what can I do?" He was still skittish, but he was looking at Danforth now, calmer than he had been.

"The federals are jamming all our communications planetwide, while somehow maintaining their own. We are unable to reach other supporters. There are rebel groups all over the planet, many even near enough to rally to us here. But we can't reach them or coordinate our operations. We can't communicate with anyone beyond sending messengers."

"How can I help?"

"People speak very highly of your technical and scientific abilities, Doctor."

"You think I can defeat their jamming?" Holcomb pulled himself up into his chair. "I am very grateful to be out of the prison, Mr. Danforth, and I would help you if I could. But I am not sure what I can do, especially confined to these woods with, I am assuming, no real power source or communications equipment."

"I understand the difficulties, Dr. Holcomb, and appreciate your frankness. But what if we *could* get you the resources? What would you need? Is it possible? Because I can be frank, too: I'm afraid your only escape from Federal America is our victory . . . and

Haven's independence. And unless we can find a way to penetrate this jamming, that is an extremely unlikely prospect. Help us, Doctor. Please. Try. Do anything you can. We will get you what you need if it is at all possible." He paused. "And if we prevail, you will have a home here, one where you may live free and do as you choose for the rest of your life."

Holcomb sat for a moment, quietly, taking a deep breath and exhaling hard. "Very well, Mr. Danforth. However, I must warn you, it is unlikely I will be able to achieve what you require.

"But I *will* try."

CHAPTER 22

"What are we going to do, sir?" Withers stood outside the library, holding a small tablet in his hand.

Damian had been through a rough few days. For the first time in his life he'd sought to run from a problem, to push back the difficult thoughts and wallow in oblivion. But the new transmissions left no more room for self-absorbed reflection. Or for drinking. *Damn, how do people do that all the time?* Shaking his head, he returned the greater problems on Haven. They were clear, and they demanded an immediate response.

The problem was, he still wasn't sure what that response *was*.

"I don't know, Ben, I just don't know. What are you going to do?"

Withers almost looked confused standing in the doorway. "I will do whatever you do, Lieutenant. Of course."

"We're not on the field anymore, Ben. I don't have my bars on my shoulders, and your stripes are packed away. You are not bound by what I choose to do. This is a decision you have to make for yourself."

And what a decision we're being forced to make.

Damian let his eyes drop to the screen on his desk, reading the message again, for the fifth or sixth time, driven by some irrational hope that he'd misunderstood it before. But it still said the same thing:

> Ward, Damian, Lieutenant, FA Army, reserve, is hereby re-assigned to Ward, Damian, Major, Federal Security Forces, active duty, Colony Alpha-2. The above named is to report to Colonel Semmes at the Landfall Federal Complex within twenty-four hours of receipt.
>
> By the order of Richard Semmes, Colonel, Federal Security Forces

He'd been shocked when he first read it, assuming his association with Wells had given someone the idea he was truly a federal sympathizer. But Withers had received his notice, too . . . and then Luci Morgan had called. The two had only spoken for a moment—they were using the landlines, and Damian was absolutely sure the federals would be listening—but she'd told him she and Devlin Kerr had gotten the same orders. And half a dozen noncoms who lived in the area.

"They're actually doing it. They're calling us all up. And we're going to have to decide what to do." Damian's hopes of neutrality were gone, replaced by a hard choice. If he answered the call, he'd be fighting against his friends and neighbors. He'd be firing at John Danforth and his people. At Jamie . . .

Killing them . . .

"Yes, sir. They are. The question is what *do* we do. It's easy to say it's my decision, but we all know it's not as simple as that. I've never disobeyed an order in my life, sir. You know that as well as anyone else alive. But I can't think of fighting for the federals. Or, for that matter, the rebels. I thought I was done fighting."

"So did I."

"Then why can't that be my decision?"

"What?"

"I'm thinking I might just stay right here. Besides, I'm not even sure these orders are legal. We're army, sir. Can they just reassign us to internal security forces?"

Damian sighed. "Yes, Ben . . . they can. Read your discharge docs one of these days. And they're not reassigning us, not exactly; they're transferring us to support the security units. Technically, we're still army. And *that* makes the orders legal."

"I signed up to fight enemies, Lieutenant, not my own country-men. What about Millie? I know her people support the rebels. Her brother's with John Danforth right now. What do I do, shoot him?"

Damian had known his aide had a girlfriend on a nearby farm. Millie Billings was a nice girl, but Withers wasn't kidding about her family's rebel leanings. Damian had heard her brother and Billings Senior deliver some rousing speeches . . . and he knew they both handled local recruitment for the Guardians.

"Or Jamie," Damian mused. "Or John Danforth. You're right, Ben . . . if we follow these orders, they will all be our enemies. But we can't just stay here either. You don't know this Semmes. He's crazy, bloodthirsty. If we don't obey these orders, he will send troops to arrest us . . . or worse. That's probably half the reason he sent these orders anyway—to give himself an excuse to lock up any veterans who won't join his forces."

Withers's anger was painted on his face. "So then what do we do, sir?"

Withers . . . that's a good fucking question.

"Do you understand, Major Thornton? You are the highest in rank by seniority, but on this mission you are to act as executive officer to Major Toland. This is not a sign of distrust in your abilities, but Ma-jor Toland has more experience in anti-insurgency operations of this nature."

"Yes, sir. Understood."

And by that, I mean I understand this is bullshit.

Thornton was a regular army veteran, and she had three years of service on Alpha-2 amid the growing rebellion. She knew Semmes just wanted one of his own people in charge, that he considered her too soft to lead the attack. She might have even understood . . . if the miserable bastard had even bothered to craft a believable lie.

"Major Toland, I am committing a large percentage of our available strength to this operation. It will leave us shorthanded everywhere else, but I want to ensure that you have sufficient numbers, not only to defeat the rebels, but to envelop and destroy them." He stared at Toland, his eyes on fire. "Do not let me down, Major. The rebellion ends with this battle. Is that understood?"

"Yes, sir. Understood."

Thornton looked at the other major. Anne Toland was the commander of one of the two battalions that had accompanied Semmes to Alpha-2. Thorton had taken a look at Toland's records, and there wasn't a lot that stood out. She had spent her entire career in internal security units, and appeared to be an accomplished officer—or as accomplished as one could be without the army service Thornton considered "real." She seemed competent, if a bit of a martinet. Still, she wasn't the psychopath Semmes was, and that was at least something. But Thornton didn't doubt she'd obey her orders to the letter.

"Then you may proceed."

Toland saluted, and then she turned to walk out the door. Thornton followed, but Semmes stopped them just before they left.

"And, Major . . . remember, General Order Nine is in full effect."

"Yes, sir," Toland replied, sounding as if she was trying to hide some level of discomfort.

Thornton didn't even try to hide her own. General Order Nine had been implemented by Semmes right after the battle at Vincennes. It was short and clear, just a few lines of text detailing one primary provision:

> Federal forces are henceforth prohibited from taking prisoners. All rebels or suspected rebels are to be shot on sight.

It sickened Thornton. War was awful and dirty and not at all romantic like entertainment vids might try to depict. Ideas of honor and "the rules of war" often had no place in the actual battlefield. But if an enemy was trying to surrender . . .

She still didn't know what she'd do when she came face-to-face with a rebel waving a white flag.

"The federals are coming! The federals are coming!" The boy ran into the camp, racing past the pickets who yelled for him to stop. "Mr. Danforth, the federals are coming!"

The guards chased him, catching up just as John Danforth came out of his tent. He waved them off and walked up to the boy. "What is it, son? Federals where?"

"They're almost to Vincennes. Captain Killian sent me to warn you."

Danforth stared at the kid. He couldn't have been more than twelve or thirteen. Danforth knew how essential Killian was to the rebel cause, and he'd forced himself to ignore some of the ranger's more . . . extreme . . . activities. But he had to draw the line somewhere, and recruiting boys five years from their first shave was a good place to start. He made a note to speak to Killian about it.

"Any strength estimates?"

"The captain was still sending out scouts, sir, but he said to tell you he was sure it was a larger force than the one we fought at Vincennes."

Danforth caught the "we," and his eye dropped down to the kid's arm. He had three red marks lined up just above his hand. He had heard that Killian's people were cutting lines in their arms to mark their kills. Danforth fought back a wave of nausea. The thought of this boy fighting was bad enough; the image of him killing three soldiers was more than he wanted to think about.

"Very well," Danforth said. "Why don't you go inside my tent and get some rest. You could probably use a meal."

"Sir, Captain Killian told me to return immediately with any orders you may have. He wants to know if you want us to hit the enemy along their line of march like we did at Vincennes, or if you want us back here."

Despite the massive damage the rangers had inflicted on the federals along their approach the last time, they hadn't been turned back. If this force was indeed even larger, it was unlikely Killian's forces could have a major impact. Especially since the federals would be more careful this time. Without the surprise they had enjoyed before, the rangers would suffer heavy losses. And as uncomfortable as Danforth was with Killian's methods, he knew the rangers were among the best fighters he had, and he couldn't afford to lose any for the potential to merely wound the federals.

"Advise the captain I want the rangers back here as quickly as possible. He is not to engage."

"Yes, sir." The kid stood straight. Then he turned and ran toward the woods, heading back the way he had come.

Danforth stood where he was. For a few seconds he thought about the kid, feeling as though he should go after him. But then he stopped. He didn't have time to worry about one boy turned warrior. He had his whole army to think about. The federals were coming, and he didn't know how his people could possibly defeat a force the size Killian had reported. The problem was, retreat wasn't a good option either. If his forces left the woods, the enemy satellites would track every move they made . . . and the federal airships would cut them down on their march.

Dammit, we can't run. Whatever the odds, however strong a force we face, we must fight.

He started shouting orders.

Kendrick Johnson moved through the woods, about two meters ahead of his squad. He wore sergeant's stripes now, an almost astonishingly rapid ascent from his days not long before as a private. But Vincennes had cost the federal forces a lot of experienced NCOs, and Semmes had purged the colonial units, discharging or imprisoning those his investigators flagged as having rebel sympathies, even those simply deemed insufficiently prepared to use harsh methods against the colonists.

Johnson had been all for it at first, as he had been well aware that some of his colleagues had mixed loyalties. Some of them had married local men and women, and a few, it had come out, were active members of rebel groups, double agents of a sort. Those foolish few had been summarily executed, and many of the others had been imprisoned. But most were simply dishonorably discharged and scheduled for transit back to Earth. And while Johnson wasn't a fan of some of Semmes's methods—he still had nightmares about the massacre at Landfall—he was smart enough to keep his mouth shut and do his job.

And now that job was as sergeant.

He now had ten soldiers under him, including two of his original four, the half of his team that had survived the fighting at Vincennes.

As much as it was exciting to get such rapid promotions—and the money was much better—the fact was, he wasn't sure if he wanted the responsibility.

Fuck it—I'm not even sure I want to still do this job at all.

Again, though, he kept his mouth shut. So when Lieutenant Parks said, "Johnson, get your people moving forward. We're advancing along the whole line," he simply turned to his team and signaled them to move out. Lieutenant Parks was one of the anti-insurgency troops who'd come with Colonel Semmes. Johnson had welcomed the harsh new commander and the stern forces he had brought with him, but his hatred for the colonists had waned in the past two weeks, his need for vengeance sated by the death and destruction he'd witnessed at Vincennes. He'd killed at least two rebels there, and the last one had been a shock to him. He'd fired, taking down the enemy from perhaps thirty meters. Then he'd advanced . . . and gotten his first close look. It was a young woman.

No, a girl. Sixteen, maybe . . . it was hard to tell since you blasted her face to a bloody mess.

His zeal to fight the rebels dissipated sharply after that, and the next two weeks of kicking down doors and dragging screaming colonists off to the overcrowded prisons had sapped it further. He'd seen enough crying spouses begging the soldiers to release their husbands and wives, enough children clutching to the legs of their parents as they were dragged off, to last a lifetime. His need for vengeance was sated, and now the suffering he saw made him sick to his stomach.

He still blamed the rebels for causing the whole nightmare Haven had become, but after the courage he'd seen on the battlefield at Vincennes, he couldn't *detest* them the way he had before. They might be wrong, but he had no doubt they believed in their cause, likely with more fervor than he supported the federal one.

And it was a lot easier to kill someone you hated.

A lot of that feeling came from the fact that the federals outnumbered the rebels, and their forces had moved all around the woods, surrounding Danforth and his people. His officers had assured him this fight would be nothing like Vincennes, that it would be over in a few hours, and with its conclusion, the rebellion would be crushed. But Johnson had doubts. He'd seen the way the rebels had fought . . . and he didn't expect them to be any less fierce when they were cornered, surrounded.

He was preparing himself for the worst.

He continued to move forward through the dense trees and knee-high underbrush. His head pivoted every ten seconds or so, scanning the woods on either side. He knew there were friendly units there, and scouts ahead of the main formation, but he still remembered those rebel bushwhackers. The federal force at Vincennes had suffered almost as many casualties marching to the field as they had in the main battle itself. His people had largely escaped that part of the fight, but he'd seen enough bodies to scare the hell out of him, more than one of them mutilated beyond recognition.

Johnson tried to push the thoughts aside, but it didn't really help. He was scared shitless . . . and the responsibility for ten other soldiers only made it worse. Part of him longed to shed his stripes, to slip back into the line, a private again, responsible only for himself and maybe the man next to him. But that wasn't an option. Not now.

He heard a shot, and his head snapped around, his eyes squinting, trying to see what was happening.

Another shot, and a small burst.

Then all hell broke loose.

Hundreds of rifles began firing. Then the louder, higher-pitched sound of the autocannons filled the air. It was ahead, and off to the right of his squad. But there was no question. The army had made contact.

The battle had begun.

And lots of people are about to fucking die.

The bullet whizzed by Jamie's head, so close he'd have sworn he felt it graze his cheek. He ducked down, lower, behind the large stump he was using for cover, and touched his cheek. No blood.

Be careful, Jamie boy, or the next one will take off that pretty head of yours.

Despite all the violence he'd faced growing up, all the fights he'd survived in the mine, and the nine federals he'd killed, Jamie had never actually been in a battle. For the first time, he faced the true experience of war, and it was nothing like he expected. Every other time he'd fought, it had been heat of the moment. There wasn't the long pause where you lived inside your head as you waited for the inevitable attack.

He struggled to force enough breath into his lungs, and his stomach did flips. He'd almost vomited once, and he was still nauseated. He'd never considered himself a coward, but now he was wondering. All he wanted to do was run, to get away from the death and destruction and keep going until he was safe.

But safety was an illusion, a dream that didn't exist. The only safety he'd know rested with victory. So he bore down, took in another breath, and tried to center himself. His eyes panned the woods in front of him, watching, looking for movement. He whipped his rifle around and fired. Then he ducked back down, just as a burst of fire flew over his head.

He understood now, at least better than he had, the nightmares that lived in Damian's mind. He knew the retired officer had seen many battles, watched comrades die, that he'd been wounded twice himself. He'd always respected his friend's courage, but now he had an insight he'd lacked before. And his respect only grew.

God, I wish he was here with me.

He dropped down, lying on his stomach, crawling to the edge of the stump. The fire was too heavy to expose himself again. He peered out, trying to spot any enemy soldiers. The underbrush was thirty centimeters high, though, and it blocked his view. He looked up, trying to get a look above the heavy grass and sprawling bushes.

He still couldn't see anything.

He could *hear* the fire, though, and it was only intensifying, the branches and leaves above him chewed apart by something heavier than an assault rifle.

Damn—they've got an autocannon out there.

Jamie heard a cry then, one of his comrades off to the left. He felt the urge to crawl over to the soldier's aid, but he couldn't abandon his position. If the federals got through the line here they could out-flank the rebel forces on both sides . . . and they could press on to Dover and take the headquarters and the main supply depot. That would be the end of the rebel army, Jamie knew . . . all but the mop-ping up. And he couldn't let that happen.

Not that me staying here is going to matter all that much when that autocannon comes to bear. It's going to clear out this entire sec-tion of the line and there's not much we can do to stop it.

Not for the first time today Jamie thought about how thinly they were spread here.

I know we're supposed to stay in position, but we're going to die unless somebody does something. He looked around.

Guess I'm somebody.

The fear grew in him, but he did his best to ignore it, springing into action without giving himself time to think about it. He jerked his body off to the right, out of the immediate line of fire. Then he crouched low and ran through the woods, moving as quickly as he could. He almost tripped over a root, but he managed to regain his balance after stumbling a few meters.

He heard bullets ripping by behind him, and he turned his rifle, firing off to the side as he continued to run. Then he saw it, nestled in behind a pile of branches, hastily thrown together to create some cover: the autocannon. It had been nearly invisible from his earlier spot, but Jamie was coming in from the side, flanking the gun.

His eyes fixed on the three men crewing the weapon. One was fir-ing, while another was dragging a heavy box of ammunition forward. The third was off to the side, looking through a pair of binoculars.

Searching for targets . . . for our men and women to kill.

Well, I don't have to look any farther for my own target . . .

Jamie acted on instinct. He snapped upright, standing straight. He knew he was making himself a target, but he only had one chance to take out the autocannon. He was a decent shot, better than he had any right to expect considering his lack of experience, but he'd never take out three enemies quickly enough—not crouched over and firing from an awkward position.

Exposed, he pulled the trigger and he saw the man drop the binoculars, falling back into the underbrush. He knew he should have taken out the shooter first, but something about the trooper standing there, spotting his comrades and marking them to be killed, pissed him off.

Jamie angled the rifle, staring down the sights, centering the crosshairs on the firer. *Crack*. His rifle let out one shot . . . and he watched the target fall back, the top half of his head blown off.

At this point the loader was reacting, dropping the ammo box and reaching for his own rifle. But Jamie's weapon spoke again . . . and the third man fell, first to his knees, wobbling there for a few seconds before he dropped to the ground.

Jamie was already running. He'd been stationary for too long, and he could hear the enemy fire all around him. But he wasn't heading back to his line.

No, he had zero intentions of leaving the autocannon there so the federals could move up and reman it.

He covered the ground quickly, then dropped prone, ducking below what was left of the savaged underbrush. He reached around behind his back, pulling one of the grenades hanging from his belt. It wasn't much, just a frag unit, relying on shrapnel to take out enemy infantry. But it was all he had.

And it should be enough.

He shoved it under the autocannon, and pulled the pin. Then he leapt up and ran back toward the rebel lines. With any luck, a shard of shrapnel would put a hole in the weapon's barrel. But even if it didn't, it would blow off the stand . . . and at least make it difficult to put the gun back in action anytime soon.

Jamie heard the gunfire all around him, and the deadly danger of his audacious stunt was starting to hit home. He ran as quickly as he could, pumping his legs hard. He could see his old position ahead, hear his comrades on both sides shouting for him to run faster.

But he wasn't fast enough.

It felt as though a sledgehammer slammed into his back. He stumbled forward, the blow enough to send him spinning. He tried to continue running, but the strength drained from his legs. He saw the leaves, the canopy of the woods far above him . . . and then he felt the impact.

He was lying on the ground, looking up. He was confused, disoriented. The sounds of the battle were gone, replaced by silence.

He gasped for air, but every breath was agony. He tried to move, but his limbs wouldn't respond. He saw figures moving past—federal infantry, something inside him said. But he couldn't really be sure.

And then the light began to fade . . .

Danforth stood on the edge of the village, staring out into the woods where the rebel forces were heavily engaged with the federals. He longed to move forward, to stand on the line with his people, but he couldn't.

The battle at Vincennes had been conventional at least, two lines of soldiers engaging each other. But the fight at Dover was different. For one thing, his people had outnumbered the federals at Vincennes, but now they were outgunned at least two to one. For another, the federals weren't formed up in a line. They were deployed all around, approaching the village from every direction. There were skirmishes on all sides, and fierce localized firefights. Danforth had known retreat would be death to his forces, but now he realized the option was truly gone. His army was encircled. This would certainly be its last fight if he didn't find a way to pull victory from the jaws of defeat.

I just need to figure out how the hell I'm going to do that.

Riley James ran up to him. "Mr. Danforth, the enemy is breaking through all along the perimeter. We've got multiple reports of our people falling back in disorder with heavy casualties. It looks like the Guardians are fighting well . . . but there are just too many federals. We can't hold them anywhere, sir."

Danforth sighed softly. He'd planned the rebellion for years, and in every scenario he'd imagined, the call went out across Haven. A cry for its people to rise up, to stand with the Guardians, to take back their world. As someone who had pretty much controlled communications on the planet, he'd never imagined a total blockage of the signal, an inability to spread the word. He had no doubt people had some idea of what was happening, and that they were responding. But without coordination, they would be too few, too disorganized. He tried not to think about how many had just managed to get themselves arrested—or shot—trying to find and join his forces.

So much we never really thought about. It's as if we were just playing at revolution in those basements.

"What should we do, sir?"

He turned and looked at Riley, seeing the earnest expression on her face. He wanted more than anything to come up with a stratagem, some wild plan that promised a chance of victory, and confirm to her the confidence she had in him was justified. But this was an impossible situation. He'd spent his time organizing, giving speeches . . . but he wasn't a military commander. He didn't know how to lead an army. He'd hoped Damian Ward would come around, that he would take up the field command of the rebel forces . . . but only now was he realizing how much he had depended on that.

"There is nothing to do, Riley." He had thought about ordering his forces to mass together, to attack in one or two sectors and try to break out. But that was just suicide in a different form. The federals didn't possess a lot of air power, but what they did have would cut down hundreds of his people as they fled across the plains. And while the rebels had some antiair weapons, they were hidden in a cellar in Dover. He'd never get them deployed in time.

No, all he could do was watch his people gunned down. Or surrender. He knew that meant death for him, but perhaps, amid the collapse of rebellion, some of the rebels would be spared. Governor Wells, at least, would lobby for a merciful policy.

"Order the contingent commanders to request terms of surrender, Riley. Now."

He could see the expression on her face, desperate defiance giving way to despair. "Mr. Danforth . . . no . . ."

"Do it, Riley. And then get back here. Stay in one of the houses until it's all over . . . and then surrender yourself to the first federals you see." Every word he spoke cut at him like a blade, but he knew he had no choice. He would ask his people to fight for freedom, to make the ultimate sacrifice, if necessary. But he wouldn't send them to their deaths when there was no chance of success.

Riley hesitated, and he could see the tears welling up in her eyes. Danforth knew his aide was smart . . . and that she realized a surrender was a death sentence for him, and the rest of the leadership.

"Sir . . ."

"Go, Riley," he said softly. "Do as I say. Please . . . one last time." His voice was soft, and he forced a half smile to his lips. "And thank you . . . for your service. For your friendship." He reached out and put his hand on her face. "Don't do anything foolish, please . . . save yourself."

She stared back at him for a few seconds, the tears streaming down her face. Then she said simply, "Yes, sir." She bit her lip, then with a cry said, "Goodbye, Mr. Danforth," and turned and ran toward the woods.

Danforth sighed as he watched her go. He suspected a few of his people would manage to slip away from the field . . . but to what? Unless they could hide all evidence of their involvement, they would be hunted down. Haven would be totally subjugated now; the free and prosperous world he'd dared to imagine would remain a dream. Even the remnants of liberty Havenites had enjoyed before would be stripped away. His beloved home world would be worse off for all his efforts, for the sacrifices of his followers.

Failure, defeat . . . they were bitter. But they wouldn't last long. Oddly, Danforth could at least take comfort in the fact that he wouldn't live out the day—he'd make sure of that. He tapped at his side, at the small pistol tucked under his arm. He had no intention of being taken alive, of experiencing whatever humiliation the federals had in store for the top leaders of the rebellion. No, he would die in battle.

He tapped on the pistol again. Or he would take his own life.

"Major Toland, we have rebel forces shouting out that they wish to surrender. The officers in the line are requesting instructions." A lieutenant had rushed over from the makeshift communications hut to tell Toland in her command tent.

Toland stood stone still. "They already have their instructions. There are no surrenders, Lieutenant."

"Yes, ma'am." He ran back to the communications tent.

Thornton watched as this all played out. For all of Toland's composure and lack of hesitation, once the lieutenant had left, she could see the other major slump, just slightly. Thornton knew Toland would never truly consider disregarding her orders, but she wondered—if the commander had the option—if she would accept the surrender anyway.

Would I be doing anything different in her shoes? Would I throw away my career, face court-martial and prison? Or would I do what I'd been commanded to do, and offload the guilt to the man who gave the order?

The scary thing was, she really didn't know. People found it easy to criticize others, and far more difficult to live up themselves to the standard they projected onto those around them.

So she kept her mouth shut and let Toland do her job.

As if on cue, Toland turned toward Thornton. "We are likely to face some fierce combat, Major. When the rebels realize we aren't taking prisoners—and that they are completely surrounded—many will panic. But others will gather together, and they will fight even harder, knowing it is to the death."

"I agree with your analysis, Major. The troops on the front line should move slowly, methodically . . . use their heavy weapons. Trade ammunition expenditure to cut losses."

"I concur." Toland nodded. "We will send out a—"

"Major!" It was the lieutenant, running back from the communications tent.

Toland and Thornton both turned toward the voice. The officer was clearly concerned; Thornton thought it sounded close to full-blown panic.

"What is it, Lieutenant?" Toland asked.

"We're under attack, Major. Enemy forces are hitting us in the rear at two points of impact, along both sides of the main road."

Toland glanced at Thornton, then back to the lieutenant. "Forces from *outside* our perimeter?"

"Yes, Major."

"Perhaps the rebels had a hidden force. Or maybe it's those damned rangers again." She turned back toward Thornton. "Whichever it is, our reserves should be sufficient to stabilize the situation. Major Thornton, take the Third and Fourth companies and lead them to the threatened point at once. Take command on the scene and stabilize things."

Thornton nodded and said, "Yes, Major." It still tweaked at her a little to take orders from an officer junior to her in seniority—and vastly so in experience—but she was enough of a professional not to let it show.

She turned and moved toward the two companies, snapping orders through the comm for both unit commanders to have their troops ready in one minute. She doubted it was the enemy irregulars—there had been too many reports of their style of fighting at other points along the line, inside the shrinking circle of rebel forces.

So who the hell are we facing?

A rebel detachment was a possibility, but that didn't seem right either. They had posted scouts pretty far out during the approach, and there was no sign of any enemy forces deployed within several kilometers of the road. And besides, the rebels didn't have comm.

So how could they have coordinated that kind of operation?

No . . . it's not the irregulars. It's not a detachment either—at least, not one from the main force . . . She'd had one other thought, something that she'd been worried about since they'd left Landfall. She had almost mentioned it to Toland, but something kept her from saying it out loud.

She hoped she was wrong . . . because if she wasn't, she faced a terrible choice, one she'd dreaded in one way or another since she'd arrived to take command of the colonial forces.

And if she was right, two companies of security troopers weren't going to be even close to enough to prevent a disaster.

CHAPTER 23

"Keep firing," Johnson said over his comm, "we're not taking prisoners." He was crouched behind the tree, his assault rifle out in front of him, struggling to follow his own order. It was butchery, all the worse because there was no escape for the rebels. They were completely surrounded.

The slaughter he'd envisioned earlier in the day was happening right before his eyes.

He could hear his squad's fire slacking off. The rebels' fire had almost completely ceased on his sector. What was left of the resistance had pulled back, and his people seemed reluctant to shoot down fleeing men and women who had dropped their weapons. He didn't blame them. But Major Toland wasn't an officer likely to show pity for soldiers who'd disobeyed her orders . . . and Colonel Semmes was a psychopath, one Johnson had no doubt would line his own soldiers against a wall if they failed to do as he commanded.

He hated doing it, but if it was a choice between the rebels and his own people, he'd do whatever he could to keep his team alive.

"I said keep firing," he yelled. "This battle's not going to be over until we take these rebels down. All of them."

He moved forward, slipping from one piece of cover to the next, taking care not to let his guard down. The enemy in front of him was breaking, but it would only take one rebel hiding behind a tree with a rifle to put him down.

He glanced back. His troopers were reluctantly obeying. He could hear the rate of fire increasing, if marginally.

"Forward, fifty meters." It was time to move, to chase down the rebels and end this nightmare once and for all.

And start new nightmares, I suppose.

He ran toward another large tree, pacing his troops. He caught a rebel in his line of sight. The man had thrown his rifle aside, and he was running. Johnson pulled up his rifle, training the sights on the target. He paused for an instant, fighting the urge to let the man go. Then he sighed . . . and pulled the trigger.

This has to end . . . now. And if this is the only way . . .

"Squad . . . another fifty meters . . . now."

Thornton was at the head of her soldiers, all one hundred and eighty of them. She was moving them at the double—the reports coming in suggested the situation on the flank was deteriorating rapidly.

The battle had seemed almost over, a great victory for the taking, one that would end the revolution in a single fell stroke. Though she despised the brutality Semmes had ordered, she knew an early end to the rebellion would save thousands of lives . . . and untold millions in property. But now there was this new threat, and whatever it was, she had to drive it back or there would be no victory.

And there very well might be a disaster.

I just pray it's not who I think it is . . .

She sped up, moving ahead, the two privates assigned as her escort struggling to keep up with her as she scrambled deftly over rocks and fallen trees. She could hear shooting up ahead, and as she moved farther forward, she began to see federal troops streaming back from the fighting. They were shaken, beaten. She shouted to them, tried to rally them, but they just kept fleeing.

Fucking worthless, she thought about the parade field "soldiers" streaming past her. And then something else: *no rebel rearguard did this.*

She tried to deny her fear, but the closer she moved to the fighting, the more convinced she became she was right about what they were facing.

She slipped off her assault rifle and crept farther forward, peering through the trees as she did. She could see movement now, attacking forces coming toward her position. She froze, watching them for a few seconds . . . and suddenly she knew.

She felt cold course through her . . . and a deep regret. This was her moment, the one she'd thought of as she listened to Toland relay Semmes's no-prisoners order.

It was her time to see how far she would go to obey orders.

She moved back, motioning for her guards to do the same. She had to get back to her soldiers. They would need her now, more than they ever had.

She tapped on her comm as she jogged back toward the two company columns. "All forces, deploy into line. Now! Grab some cover, and prepare to repel attackers. We're going to hold here at all costs."

And get ready for the fight of our lives.

"**Odds, covering fire.** Evens, forward fifty meters."

Damian stood and watched as Luci Morgan shouted out orders. He knew she'd been a civilian as long as he had, but at the moment she sounded incredibly sharp, as though she'd just come from the barracks.

She'd been the first one he'd gone to, in the middle of the night . . . and Devlin Kerr had been next. He'd made his choice, but he was unsure whether any of the others would join him. But Morgan and Kerr had agreed immediately . . . and Tucker Jones after them.

They'd spread the word, racing through the countryside, rousing every ex-sergeant and retired private within twenty kilometers of Landfall. By morning they'd rallied almost three hundred men and women, combat veterans all—every one of them ready to follow Damian into rebellion. Damian had known he was influential in the veteran community, but he was stunned that no one—not one—refused his call.

The veterans had fallen in just after dawn, and he'd led them on a forced march to Dover, determined to save the revolution before it was too late. Now they were attacking, and the enemy troopers were melting away before the assault.

The enemy forces had been stunned by the attack, just as Damian had planned. He knew enough about soldiers to realize there was nothing as devastating to morale as being attacked from the rear while already engaged . . . especially when it was a surprise.

Damian struggled to hold his focus on the battle, on the movements of the men and women who had followed him there. He was still conflicted, and he wished there had been any way for Haven to avoid revolution. But Semmes's order had been the last straw. Damian would have willingly obeyed the recall orders if Federal America had found itself at war again, or even if his service had been required in some natural disaster. But trying to force him to take arms against his friends and neighbors? That was too much to endure.

He still hated the idea of firing on other soldiers, men and women serving the same flag he had. If neutrality had been an option, he might very well have hunkered down on the farm and waited for the struggle to exhaust itself. But he knew Semmes wouldn't accept that. Having issued the recall orders, he would insist on them being obeyed, and he would make an example out of anyone who refused.

Fucking Semmes.

Damian sighed. Semmes was one son of a bitch he didn't mind fighting. And now that he'd made his decision, he felt a weight lifted as well. Staying out of this fight meant watching Jamie and John Danforth—and a dozen other men and women he called friends—risking their lives. Now, at least, he was here, fighting with them. It might not be enough, but at least he didn't have to watch from the sidelines as people he cared about died.

"Evens, covering fire. Odds, advance fifty meters."

Damian was impressed by the volume Luci Morgan could push out of her small frame. He'd known intellectually that his makeshift force wouldn't have any communications that could penetrate the jamming, but it had still surprised him how difficult it was to coordinate even a small force when orders and reports had to be shouted or delivered by messenger.

Luckily, some of his people had turned out to have impressive lungs.

He moved forward, following behind Morgan's people. Kerr was doing the same thing on the right, Jones on the left. Altogether, the veterans were attacking on a three-hundred-meter front, driving forward, trying to link up with the rebels trapped in and around Dover. When they did, he would send them in both directions, rolling up the federal line. His force was a small one, and it was a dangerous plan to try to outflank a force perhaps four times as large as yours. But his people would have momentum and superior discipline and training. It would be enough.

It had to be.

He held his rifle in his hands, his eyes panning the woods, looking for targets. He'd been a farmer for four years now, but he could feel his combat instincts reawakening. The memories of past battlefields floated on the edge of his consciousness.

The weapon felt oddly familiar, though it had been stored in a closet these past years. It was Federal America's regulations that had armed his hastily assembled force. Veterans returning to Earth were disarmed. The Earthside government didn't like its civilians having weapons . . . and even less trained killers returned from war. But those retiring to colonies were required to keep their arms. It was all part of the plan to leaven the colonial defense forces with a ready reserve of trained soldiers. Now that policy was backfiring.

Almost literally.

"It looks like they're breaking, sir." Withers came jogging back from the front lines. "They're running, Lieutenant . . . all along our frontage."

"Good," he said. "Good." He stared toward the front, pulling out his binoculars and looking forward. He reached out and put his hand on Withers's arm. "Go back up there, Ben. Jones and Kerr need to detach flank guards. We don't want the federals on either side moving in on us, taking the assault column in the flanks." He was sure the two officers would know that, but Damian had always been meticulous on the battlefield, and he didn't see any advantage in getting careless now.

"Yes, sir." The aide turned and trotted back, moving quickly despite crouching low as he headed forward.

Damian checked his rifle, a subconscious routine. It was loaded and ready—of course it was. But the confirmation calmed him. He'd hung back long enough to make sure the troops went in as he'd planned. But he had no intention of staying in the rear, not when his comrades were up in the line fighting.

He ran forward, right to the center of the attack, where Luci Morgan's people were already driving through the enemy lines.

He wasn't worried about being able to break through. He just hoped his people were in time, that the rebels trapped in the center were still holding out.

I'll know soon enough, he thought as he ran forward into the maelstrom.

"On me! Everyone on me!" Alexandra Thornton was in the middle of a nightmare. Dozens of federal troops were streaming by, terrified, disregarding all her attempts to stem the rout. She was able to rally perhaps one in ten—a horrible number—but at least enough to help her form a last-ditch line to block the enemy's relentless advance.

These were no rebels. Not like the others at least. These were combat veterans, and that could only mean one thing: Alpha-2's retired soldiers, at least some of them, had shed their neutrality and thrown their lots in with the rebels. And she knew the one man who had to be at the center of it all, the only one who could have rallied so many ex-soldiers so quickly. Alpha-2's most celebrated warrior.

She had scanned the advancing enemy line for any signs of Damian, but so far she'd found nothing. Still, she had no doubt he was out there.

She knew the federal army still had the numbers, but Ward's sudden appearance was a grave threat. Damian Ward was a gifted tactician. She'd even admit he was better than her. More important, though, he was vastly more capable than Toland or any of the glorified riot police Semmes had brought with him. Which meant Damian had a decided advantage. The only thing she had going for her was she had numbers . . . or did, in theory. If she could somehow figure out a way to actually get them to fight, they might be able push his forces back.

But she didn't put a lot of faith in that.

She was a soldier, though, and she had a job. So until she had new orders or was taken out of the battle, she was going to fight. "Take whatever cover you can find." She screamed to her thin line of soldiers, waving her arms and whipping her head around as she watched them slip behind rocks and fallen trees. "We've got reserves on the way, but we've got to hold them here. Stay focused, keep your eyes on the woods in front of you. Aimed shots, okay? Spend your shots one at a time."

She slipped behind a large boulder herself, just as the veterans moved up and their fire began slamming into the trees all around. She peered out of her cover, her eyes moving, looking for enemy soldiers.

These are veterans. Men and women who served on Beta-9 and Ross-154. Far better troops than your own . . .

She stared out, her eyes catching some rustling branches ahead. Her arms whipped around, almost by instinct, bringing her rifle around and firing half a dozen bursts. She couldn't tell if she'd hit anything, but there was no more movement.

"Major Toland." She held out her rifle with one hand as she gripped the comm unit in the other one. "Thornton here, Major. We've got enemy forces hitting us from behind. I have reason to suspect the attackers are retired veterans. Request immediate reinforcements."

"Toland here, Major. Are you sure it's not just a band of rebels caught outside the perimeter?"

Thornton sighed. "No, Major, I can't be sure, but my gut is telling me they're more than that. Their movements, their precision—it's all too practiced. Unless the rebels were hiding a significant reserve of highly skilled troops, this is something different.

"And they're hitting us hard."

"All right, Major. I'm sending you two more companies to strengthen your force, but that's all I have to send you. With the encircling maneuver, we're spread too thin to pull more off the line.

"Thornton, I'm counting on you to wipe out these attackers. Hold them at bay, and we'll crush the main rebel force within an hour."

"Yes, Major." Thornton disconnected the comm. She looked down the line. A good third of her people were down already, at least along the section of line she could see . . . and she could feel the second rout coming. Half her survivors were frozen in place, their rifles silent as they struggled with their fear. And she could see movement, sense the veterans moving closer, using the cover well as they pressed their attack.

If I'm right, Damian is out there. And they haven't had time to organize. If I can find him . . .

She knew what she had to do, but even as it came to her she could feel the knot in her stomach, the resistance to do what had to be done.

But Thornton was a veteran, too, and she had fought her way through hell and back. If one man dying—even Damian—could end this, she knew what her job required.

"You!" she said to a sergeant a few spots down the line.

"Me?" His eyes were wild, but at least he was still in the line. And he was the only person she could see that had any kinds of stripes or bars. *One fucking NCO to help me hold off a wave of seasoned fighters.*

But it's what she had, and so she was going to use it.

"Yes. Come here."

Swallowing, the man crawled over to her.

"You're in charge, Sergeant—"

"Alonso, Major."

"You're in charge, Alonso. You fucking hold this line, you hear me? I don't care what you have to do. I don't care if you have to shoot our own people if they run, but you're a goddamn sergeant, and I expect to find you and the rest of this line right here when I get back."

"Yes, Major." He said it with at least something resembling conviction, but she didn't expect much. Not really . . .

Which is why I have to do this . . .

Her eyes scanned the woods. Nothing. She lunged to the side, crossing a small open area before plunging into a clump of trees, leaving one bewildered sergeant to try and hold the line.

She worked slowly forward, pausing every few meters to scan the area around her. She reminded herself she wasn't a lone wolf sniper anymore; she was a major, in charge of the entire sector of the field, and second in command of the army. But she knew the battle rested on what happened now. And she could do more as a sniper in the next few minutes than she could as a major.

He has to be here somewhere.

She clutched her rifle tightly in her hands, leaning down, hiding behind the dense undergrowth of the forest. She moved forward, silent, almost undetectable, working her way toward the flank of the attacking column. Her eyes were sharp, and she saw movement in the leaves off to the side. She held her fire, though—it wasn't Damian. Shooting would give away her position, so until she saw Damian, the only weapon she could use was stealth.

She paused, waiting for the soldier off to her flank to move forward. Then she continued on, turning inward, toward the center of the enemy force.

He will be close to the front line.

She knew Damian. Probably better than anyone in his own force, she suspected. He was calm in normal conditions, but she'd seen him before on the battlefield, and he was courageous, almost stupidly brave.

He was also a deadly warrior, she knew. A crack shot, cool and calm under fire.

But this isn't a normal battle situation. Something pushed him to action, and he will still be conflicted. That's my advantage.

She moved forward, passing several other troopers. For an instant, she thought one had spotted her. She froze, not moving at all, her hands tight on the assault rifle, ready to fire if there was no other choice. But the soldier only stopped for a few seconds. Then he resumed his advance.

She turned inward, looping around, moving toward what she suspected was the center of the enemy formation. Then she saw. Four troopers. No, five. They were clustered together, discussing something. They were wary—*of course they are*—every few seconds, one of them would look around before turning his attention back to the group. But it was clear they thought they were back from the main combat area.

She stopped, crouched down behind the dense bushes under the trees, watching the five men—no, four men and a woman—talking. It took a few seconds, perhaps half a minute, to spot her target. But then one of the soldiers moved to the side, and she could see him.

She stared at Damian even as she moved her rifle up slowly, careful not to rustle any leaves or bushes. In the last war, she'd killed three dozen enemy soldiers, mostly in situations like this. She'd served as a sniper for two years before she'd gotten command of her own section. It had been almost six years since then, but it felt as natural as ever . . . save for the fact that she was targeting a friend.

More than a friend.

Alex Thornton was a creature of duty. It was all she understood, the force that had driven her life, made her what she was. But now she could feel it faltering. There was no question about what duty required now, no doubt that killing Damian was the greatest blow she could strike to secure the federal army's victory—not just in this fight, but in the rebellion as a whole. It could all end today, with the rebels crushed before they could grow their ranks and turn the uprising into a full-scale war. But for once, duty was failing her.

Despite the internal conflict, she still moved her face toward the rifle, positioning her eye in the sight. The weapon wasn't the AI-assisted sniper's rifle she used in the war, but it was good enough. It wasn't even a difficult shot. Damian was less than two hundred meters away, standing in the open. It was better than she had hoped . . . a hunter's dream.

But then she hesitated.

Her sniper's instincts were on fire, the predatory nature of the job ready to take over. Her mission had always been to seek out the highest value targets, and right now Damian was the most dangerous man on Haven. He'd cultivated the mild-mannered farmer image, but she had seen him in battle before, witnessed his tactical brilliance. If the rebel army escaped the fight she knew Damian would turn them into a powerful force. Her duty, her oath . . . they all demanded that she end that threat now.

But she saw more than the man who could lead the rebellion. More than a significant threat. The man in her sights was an old comrade, a friend. They had fought together, shed blood together. Shared battlefields . . . and bedrolls. She *knew* this man. Every scar on his skin, the way his hands felt on her body. The way his mind worked. His dreams. His fears.

Could she kill him now, this man she had loved—still loved—without warning, without mercy?

She gripped the rifle tightly, and brought Damian into the crosshairs. She *had* to do it. Duty . . . it was *her,* the driving force that made Alex Thornton the person she was. She had killed before in the service of the federal cause even when she'd had her doubts. This was no different.

It *couldn't* be different.

But she knew it was. She gritted her teeth, held herself rigidly as she tightened her finger. She had to shoot now. She'd managed to get around the enemy flank, to sneak up this close, but she knew her luck wouldn't last. She'd be spotted sooner or later, and she was deep behind the enemy line, far from any support.

Shoot . . . and use the chaos to get away before they can react. Do it now . . .

Yet she continued to stare through the scope, the crosshairs dead in the middle of Damian's head. She tried one more time to pull her finger back, to do the deed. To do her duty.

But she couldn't. She sighed softly, and her grip on the rifle loosened. She couldn't do it. She couldn't kill Damian. She still loved him . . . and for the first time in her life, duty just wasn't enough.

CHAPTER 24

"Okay, you all have your orders." Damian Ward stood in the small clearing, snapping out commands to the cluster of officers surrounding him. They didn't look like the leaders of an army. They wore civilian clothes and, save for the odd piece or two of body armor a few of them wore, looked more like a group of farmers than soldiers.

Which is exactly what we were just a few hours ago.

"Now, let's get back to the front. We've got to keep up the intensity. We have to break through before the rebels are defeated."

There was a quick chorus of "yessirs," and the group began to disperse, each of them heading off toward their makeshift commands.

Damian took a step forward and then a shot rang out, followed by another. And another. He could feel his heart pounding, the surge of adrenaline flowing through his bloodstream at the new danger.

Even as he processed what was going on, his instincts had taken over, and he was already running for the cover of the nearby trees. It only took a few seconds, but it seemed like forever. He'd made a mistake, been careless, allowed himself to underestimate the enemy. Despite his attempts to control his pride and arrogance, he was no different from most of the other veterans in viewing the federal security forces as something less than "real" soldiers.

"Sniper!" he heard coming from the woods to the west. Then more gunfire.

"Ben!" Damian crouched behind a large tree, staring over at his longtime aide as he did. "Take a squad and clear those woods." He felt a moment of guilt. Going after snipers was dangerous business, and Withers was one of his oldest friends. But the soldier's instincts were coming back to him, and on the field, need trumped friendship.

"Yes, sir!" Withers turned toward the small group of troopers standing behind him. "Let's go," he ordered.

Damian watched them move off. Then he turned and continued up toward the front. He didn't like leaving Withers and the others behind, but he needed to be at the head of his soldiers.

He hurried his pace, jogging toward the front. He could hear the gunfire behind him increasing in intensity.

C'mon, Ben . . . make it through this . . .

Alex was running now. She knew she was making noise, drawing attention to herself . . .

But I'm pretty sure they already know I'm here.

Whoever was leading the troops hunting her damned sure knew what he or she was doing. She'd picked off one of her pursuers, but the rest had moved around, almost encircling her.

Not completely, though.

She hurried her pace, her eyes darting down every second or two, trying to spot the roots and branches in her path. She'd almost tripped twice, but she'd managed to regain her balance each time. It wasn't ground for jogging, much less sprinting. But her only chance at escape now was a dead run.

She heard the gunfire. She was ahead of the enemy troopers, moving back and forth as she ran forward, denying her pursuers an easy target. She was breathing hard, from fear as much as exertion. She'd taken a crazy risk sneaking around the enemy force alone. It had paid off—or it would have if she'd pulled the trigger. She hadn't, though, and now all she could do was run for her life.

Her heart pounded, and the sweat on her neck was pouring down her back. She was putting more distance between her and the soldiers on her tail—at least, she thought so. And she was close, she knew, to reaching her own lines. To relative safety. But then she heard it, a sound just off to her right.

She spun around, perceiving the threat and bringing her rifle around.

Too late.

The man was less than thirty meters from her, with a clear line of fire even through the woods. And he shot even as she was bringing her own weapon to bear.

The first round took her in the side of her chest, almost in the shoulder. She perceived the impact, but she didn't feel the pain, not at first.

She tried to ignore it, channeling all her strength and focus into aiming her own weapon. Her only chance was taking out her attacker, but her enemy had a massive advantage now. He was only a second faster than her, but Alex Thornton had seen enough war. A second was enough. She was beaten, finished. Or she should be.

But it wasn't in her to give up.

Another round slammed into her, forcing the breath from her lungs. She definitely felt the pain this time, and she stumbled back, struggling to stay on her feet. She finally fired her own rifle, but she'd lost her aim, and her bullets flew far above her target.

Then another shot, in the chest again. She felt her breath pouring from her lungs. Her legs went numb, and she could feel herself falling, the pain as she slammed onto the cold ground.

She tried to hang on to her rifle, but her grip was weak, and it skittered away as she fell.

She gasped for air, feeling the pain, struggling to keep the fear at bay. She'd been wounded before, but this was different. She was in bad shape, every breath an agony . . . and she was behind enemy lines, far from help.

She looked up at the sky, a small patch of blue visible through a gap in the forest canopy. It was blue, as blue and perfect as any Earth day.

I've been here four years, and I never noticed how wonderful Haven really is.

Such a waste . . .

She felt an instant of panic, but then the fear subsided. She'd always known she could end up like this . . . and she was damned if she'd face it crying. She'd seen enough young men and women like that, panicking, bawling for their mothers. She'd never thought less of them; indeed, she'd tried to comfort as many as she could. But that wasn't her.

Enemy soldiers were moving on her even now. Her side might lose the battle, and she might die where she lay. But whatever happened, she would face it like a warrior. She would keep her dignity.

That was the duty she owed herself.

Crack.

Damian's rifle spat out death. Then again. And again. The federal troopers were running now, even the few who had stood firm at first were now routed, throwing down their weapons and running for their lives.

"Keep moving!"

He advanced as he shouted out the order. A sound to the right caught his attention, and he whipped his rifle around and fired, dropping another federal. He didn't like shooting at fleeing soldiers, but he'd seen too many forces rally and return to the fight. And he knew the federal army was still larger than his force and Danforth's Guardians combined.

He looked around, moving carefully from one covered position to the next, but always pressing forward. There was almost no enemy fire, but he was a veteran, and he knew carelessness got soldiers killed.

"Keep moving!" he shouted, turning his head and screaming in the other direction.

He stopped suddenly, listening. He could hear shooting up ahead, a soft rumble through the dense woods.

It's time . . . either we roll up the federal army and send them fleeing back to Landfall . . .

Or we get caught in the center, surrounded alongside the Guardians . . . and end up just another three hundred dead, extinguished along with the spark of revolution . . .

"Let's go!" He held his rifle in the air as he shouted the command. "To victory."

Then he plunged forward, rushing to the final fight.

The overturned trailer was good cover, large, heavy enough to stop at least a normal round. Danforth crouched behind, pulling cartridges from the ammunition box and handing them to his fighters. He was proud of his Guardians, of the courage these ordinary farmers and workers had shown. They had no real training, just the few exercises Danforth had managed to arrange. Few of them had ever been shot at, at least before Vincennes, but they were holding their own against the federal forces that surrounded them.

For what that was worth.

Because the battle was all but lost. Worse, it had become a fight to the death. He'd ordered the Guardians to surrender, to throw themselves on the mercy of the victorious federals . . . but the enemy had refused them quarter.

The fact was, he was scared to death. He was also ashamed, especially when he admitted to himself he was handing out ammo partly because it let him stay behind the trailer, back at least a few meters from the front line.

He considered himself an honest man, and the work he had done to prepare the Guardians, to push Haven toward taking a stand against federal tyranny . . . it had all been sincere. He truly believed his home world would be better without the tight controls Federal America imposed, that its people would flourish if they were allowed freedom to do as they chose. It was a dream, one full of optimism and high-minded ideals.

But now he had seen men and women die—people he had essentially *ordered* to their deaths. He had watched his own cousin slip away, bleeding to death from his wounds. He still believed in liberty, but his idealism had all but faded, replaced by a grim cynicism. The cost of liberty was just too much blood.

If it was even possible anymore.

I understand Damian better now, I think. He's seen war, watched men and women die in the hundreds. Would I still have pushed for re-

bellion if I had truly comprehended what it was like? It is one thing to speak of war, of heroic death on the field, quite another to see . . . this.

He grabbed the last few cartridges, handing them to the next trooper. She was young, perhaps eighteen . . . and perhaps not. She had her brown hair pulled back tightly, and her face was twisted into an angry scowl. There was no youth left there, no optimism. Only the cold-blooded eyes of a killer.

A killer I created.

Is this what you wanted? To unleash such fury on this world?

But intentions mattered little now. What mattered was that he *had* opened Pandora's box, and he was responsible for the monsters that now stalked Haven.

Danforth shoved the empty crate aside, waving to a pair of his people carrying another over. He turned and looked out at the thinning line of his people. They were behind trees, barricades, piles of shattered brick and stone. There were bodies everywhere, some of them clearly dead, others wounded, moaning in pain, crying to their comrades for help. Those who could move were staggering toward the rear.

Rear. Ha! What rear? There's just the center of a shrinking circle . . . and soon we won't even have that.

He watched as a pair of Guardians turned and ran back from the line. One of them dropped his rifle, the other held on to his. But both had abandoned their position. Danforth wanted to be angry, to call them cowards, even to shoot them down as they fled. But then he saw the bodies. They were the last two of at least a dozen, the others all cut down by a federal autocannon. These were no cowards; they were brave fighters who had reached their limit.

He could feel the line starting to collapse. There were just too many of his people down, too little ammunition. They were all exhausted, their throats parched with burning thirst. It was as if they could all taste the end of the rebellion. The cause of liberty was dead, stillborn. Destroyed before it even had the chance to spread.

He grabbed his rifle and turned toward the two troopers carrying the ammunition crate. "Hand that ammo out." He knew he was going to die, either here, rifle in hand, or on the gallows. And if that was his choice, it was one easily made. He moved forward, yelling out, "Hold firm, Guardians! Hold your positions!"

There was gunfire all around. The federals were pushing hard against his perimeter, shrinking it steadily, forcing his survivors together in a tight cluster around the village. *Keep pushing, then. Let's see if you're willing to pay the price our deaths will cost you.*

"Keep firing. Make them pay for every millimeter."

He crouched down behind a pile of wood, the shattered remains of a large fence. He aimed his weapon. He was a middling shot at best, but he took his time, resisting the urge to hurry the shot. If he was going to die, he was going to take as many of these bastards with him as he could, and that meant not wasting any of his precious ammo. He squeezed the trigger, and saw as his target fell to the ground. He fired again, missing this time.

Then the federal fire slammed into his shaky cover, sending shards of wood in every direction. He flinched, felt the urge to crouch lower, to lie on the ground and wait for the end. But if he was destined to die, he resolved he would do it well. He aimed again, and moved to pull the trigger. But his target dropped before he could shoot.

For an instant, he thought one of his people had shot the federal. But then he saw another federal fall—*forward*. His first thought was that Killian and his rangers had managed to get behind the federals attacking the village. But then the entire enemy force started to break up, troopers fleeing to the left and the right, trying to escape from . . . something.

What the hell?

"Watch your fire!" Danforth leapt up to his feet and shouted to his troopers. "There are friendlies out there somewhere."

He didn't know who it was, but someone was definitely attacking the federals from behind. He watched for perhaps half a minute, staring in wonder as the soldiers who had been about to destroy his army lost all cohesion, their retreat turning quickly into a panicked rout.

Maybe . . .

Hope coursed through him. "Attack!" Danforth ran out onto the ground that had moments before been a deadly no-man's-land.

"Guardians . . . charge!" He was screaming as loudly as he could, waving his rifle over his head. "Charge!"

He had no idea if this was tactically sound—he was almost certain it wasn't—but he knew, in his mind, in his gut, that this was the moment for action.

The moment his battered forces could snatch victory from the jaws of defeat.

"Let's go!" He ran across the frontage of the rebel line, gesturing wildly, calling to the exhausted men and women of the army. For a few seconds, no one moved forward. Dozens of rebels, hundreds, clung to their fortified positions, watching in wonder as their leader stood out in the open, where a moment before the fire would have cut him down in half a second. But the federals were on the run now, and the rumble of their gunfire had ceased, replaced by the more distant shooting of whatever force had slammed into the federal flank.

"Victory is there, my soldiers. It is there for the taking. It is time, time to avenge our dead, time to strike a blow for freedom!" Danforth's voice was raw, but he shouted again and again, each time louder than the last. And his efforts began to show their effect.

One by one, the Guardians began to respond. Soon, groups of men and women were leaping from their cover, rushing toward their leader. They were silent at first, but it wasn't long before they were shouting a wild battle cry.

Danforth held his arm out, his rifle pointing the way. "Let's go! You all, with me to the left. The rest to the right. Roll up the federal line . . . and don't stop until you meet your comrades on the other side!"

He spun around and ran across the battered plain at the outskirts of the village, plunging into the woods in pursuit of the broken federals, his ragged army crashing behind.

He had no idea what was happening, but he knew it was a chance . . . a chance that had seemed impossible just moments before.

"Victory!" he shouted.

"Victory!" they screamed.

Please, God . . . victory.

CHAPTER 25

"Luci, take your people and Tucker's. Stay on their heels. Don't let them rally. They've still got enough force to come back at us if they reorganize." Damian stood on the edge of the village, passing out orders to his officers.

"Don't worry. We won't give them time to stop and take a piss." She quickly turned and trotted to the perimeter of the village, shouting out commands to a group of her soldiers and leading them off into the woods. Damian watched for a few seconds, taking a tiny moment for himself. He was exhausted and covered in sweat. His arm throbbed. It wasn't much of a wound—the bullet had just grazed him—but it still hurt.

"I guess I did a better job of persuading you than I thought."

Damian turned around, holding out his good arm toward his friend to shake hands. "I don't know, John, maybe. But I think you really have Colonel Semmes to thank for our aid."

"Semmes?" Danforth sounded like he'd tasted something bad, even as he reached out and took Damian's outstretched hand. "What did that son of a bitch do?"

"He activated the reserve clauses in the veterans' discharges. He ordered us to report for duty with the federal forces." Damian paused. "I still don't feel good about fighting against the flag I served under, but I couldn't take the field against my neighbors, my friends.

Perhaps more important, I could never serve under a man like Semmes. And that's the choice he put to us."

"Well, as soon as we find a bottle, we can toast that piece of shit. Because I don't mind telling you—you saved our asses. Hell—you saved the revolution."

"For today, maybe," Damian said.

"What do you mean?"

Damian looked around Dover. The buildings were mostly wrecked, torn apart by hundreds of autocannon rounds and grenades. More than a few had burned to the ground, the smoke still rising over the blackened wreckage. People had lived here, called it home. But now the village was gone, little remaining of the vibrant community save smoldering shards and broken chunks of masonry.

Another cost of war.

One of the few barns still standing had been turned into a field hospital, but it was proving to be woefully inadequate. There were wounded men and women all around, holding blood-soaked shirts and jackets as they waited—either to get treatment, or to die. They completely filled the structure, and most were still lying on the ground outside. The moans filled the air, and the smell of smoke and blood was a nauseating mixture. He was initially disgusted at the apparent neglect the Guardians had for their wounded, but it quickly subsided, and turned to pity. He knew Danforth's people were doing their best with what little they had. The rebels had stockpiled weapons, but not medicines. Not blankets and bedrolls, not food to sustain the hundreds—thousands—it would take to win freedom. The few doctors they had were ill-equipped to treat grievously wounded soldiers, and he suspected the injured rebels were dying where they lay, when even a few more triage units might save their lives.

"The battlefield is never a pretty site, my friend." Damian looked at Danforth. "And this is far from the last one this rebellion will see if we are to achieve your goal of independence. You have planned this for years, John, but now you are only beginning to see the true face of what you craved. How ill-prepared your people truly are, despite your efforts."

Danforth took a deep breath, but he didn't respond.

"I know you are a good man, John, that you were driven by what you thought was best for Haven. But now perhaps you see the well-spring of my doubts, my hesitation. What I mean is that you may call me the savior of the revolution, but how many more will die before it is through? If I am a savior, I am a devil, too. Our intervention offers no promises of victory, no independence . . . only the certainty that hundreds more will die. Thousands. I will always bear the guilt for what I have done today, for it was partly motivated by selfishness. I could have remained on the farm, refused the summons to report to Semmes . . . and dared him to move against me . . . against all the veterans. You, at least, did what you have done purely, you risked all for what you believed. I wouldn't even be here if I hadn't been personally threatened."

Danforth stood silently for a moment. Then his eyes locked on Damian's. "You take too much blame, my friend. We all have our motivations, the thing that drives us to action. And you assign your-self too much responsibility for the sacrifices rebellion demands. More will die perhaps; indeed, they almost certainly will. But we *do* understand the cost. These men and women all volunteered to fight, to put their lives on the line for a chance at freedom."

"And the children, John? The ones who will die when a shell lands on their house? The ones who will cry through the night when they are starving? When their parents never come home? The civil-ians, the elderly, caught in a war zone? The widows and widowers? The orphans?" He gestured toward the remains of Dover. "What about those who lived here? Did they all volunteer as well? And what of those who remain loyal to Federal America? You must know not every Havenite craves independence. Indeed, many of my old comrades are deeply conflicted. We fought for that flag, and now we wage war against it. What of the others, those who refuse to accept rebellion? Will they become enemies, traitors? Will we fight them as well, shoot them down if they stand against us? If they, too, take up arms for what they believe, even as you have?"

He sighed deeply.

"I don't mean to pour this all on you, John. But I tried to stay out of it. I tried to do my part to ensure peace. And now we're all caught up in this, and it's as if we're all adrift without any plan other than 'beat the federals.' We did that once. I don't think they'll underestimate us anymore. And if we don't figure out a way to fix this rebellion, then we've lost anyway. All these brave men and women are then dead for no reason."

Danforth nodded. "I'm sorry, Damian. I know you wanted to stay neutral. But I won't apologize for being glad you're here. As you said, there's so much we don't know. And this victory *has* to mean something."

"Damian!"

He turned toward the voice. It was Withers, but he couldn't remember the last time his aide had called him by his first name.

Which meant something was wrong.

"What is it, Ben?"

Withers ran the rest of the way toward Damian before speaking. "You have to come with me, sir." He was out of breath, struggling to get the words out. "Now."

Damian looked over at Danforth. "I have to go, John." He turned and began to follow Withers. "What is it, Ben? What's wrong?"

"It's Alex Thornton, sir. We have to hurry . . ."

Vincent Perrin moved his hand slowly, easing the throttle forward, sending the gunship into a sharp dive. He could see the federal forces now, streaming out of the woods in complete disarray. There were transports in the lead, the soldiers lucky enough to be mounted racing ahead of their less fortunate comrades who followed behind in a panicked rout.

Perrin shook his head. He'd never imagined he'd see a federal force so badly defeated by the rebels. For an instant he felt the urge to leave them to their fate, a fleeting thought that the cowards deserved it. But he knew his duty, and he intended to see it done.

He could see the rebels coming out of the woods now, too, moving into the plain in pursuit of their fleeing enemies. They might have broken the federal army, but now they had gone too far. They'd had cover in the woods, but out here they belonged to Perrin and his crew.

He pushed the throttle harder, steepening the descent. He had to make this count. The army needed a chance to regroup, and he was in the best position to give them time.

"Raven Two, this is Raven One. Follow us in—we need to keep those rebels pinned in the woods and buy the army time to get away."

"Raven One, this is Raven Two. Copy . . . we're right behind you."

Perrin knew that a pair of Talons was a weak force to provide air support to ground troops, but the rebels had nothing at all, and that was definitely a force amplifier.

The rebels continued to run from the cover of the trees, following the federals, gunning down the fleeing soldiers.

That's about to stop.

"All right, boys, stay sharp. It's time to show these rebels what air support can do."

His two gunners snapped back their "yessirs." He could hear the feral tone in their voices.

His eyes darted to the altitude readout. Less than a kilometer, and diving at almost a hundred meters a second.

"Ready . . ."

Five hundred meters.

He took a deep breath.

Three hundred meters.

"Fire!"

He heard the distinctive sound of the quad chain guns unloading, sending hundreds of rounds blasting down at the rebels. He held the throttle firm for another second . . . two. Then he pulled back hard, hearing the gunship's engines blasting at full. He'd waited a long time, almost too long, and the ship skimmed along eighty meters from the ground before it began to climb again.

His focus was forward, on piloting the ship, but he could hear the gunners cheering behind him.

He twisted his arm, bringing the ship around, flying back over the strafing zone, five hundred meters up this time, just in time to see Raven Two finish its deadly run. His eyes darted toward the ground, and he felt a wave of satisfaction. The rebels had stopped their pursuit, and they were fleeing now, racing back to the cover of the forest . . . and leaving at least thirty of their number behind.

"Ammunition status?"

"About 50 percent, sir. Enough for another run."

Perrin nodded to himself. He *was* tempted to bring the airship around for another attack. But the rebels were already back under cover, and that would be a waste of his ammo. His orders were clear: do whatever was necessary to ensure the defeated army was able to disengage and rally. Wasting half a bird's ammo hoping to pick off one or two rebels in the woods wasn't going to get that done.

"No. The rebels are back in cover. We'll hold our ammo in case they come out again and stay in position as long as fuel allows." He repeated his plan to Raven Two, who confirmed, and then angled the ship around, slowing down, hovering above the tattered remnants of the federal army.

"We're going to follow the army back to Landfall. That said, if any rebels poke out their noses, we're going to send them straight to hell."

"I came to find you . . ." Alex's voice was weak, strained. "I saw you, across the field . . . in my sights . . ." She was looking up, but her stare was vacant, as if she was seeing images in her own mind and not the darkening sky above. "But I couldn't . . ." She paused again, gasping a raspy breath. "Couldn't . . . not you . . ."

Damian knelt down, leaning over her, his hand reaching down, taking hers. He fought for words, overcome with confusion. He imagined her, the stone-cold sniper he remembered from the war, holding her rifle, having him dead to rights . . . and not firing. She'd let him live, she'd held her fire, even though he was leading soldiers in an attack against her own.

And one of my people shot her.

He looked down at her, at the terrible wound he knew was mortal.

One of my people killed her . . .

"Alex . . ." It was all he could force from his mouth.

"Damian . . . I am so sorry . . ." Her voice was soft, weak. "I never thought I would be on the other side . . . in battle . . . facing you. I am so sorry . . ."

Damian could feel the sorrow in her voice, the regret. He knew that no politics of hers had led her to this field, only her sense of duty. If she'd been an officer like him, she might have mustered out with a farm of her own; indeed, she'd have likely been at his side, joining the rebels as he had, as most of the other veteran-farmers had. But she'd been a noncom, and among her more modest prospects, a commission in the security forces had seemed the most attractive. Damian knew he might have made the same choice in her shoes.

"There is no cause for sorrow, Alex, and no reason for you to apologize." Softly he said, "Alex, you are one of the best people I know. I am grateful to have served at your side . . . and for all we shared together."

He felt a twinge of guilt, for more than the gunshot that had mortally wounded her. The two had been close when they'd both been noncoms—more than close. They had been young, passionate, facing the prospect of death in battle at any time. That had been the extent of things for him, at least beyond friendship and camaraderie. But he knew now that Alex's feelings had been different, deeper. She had loved him. And he had broken her heart.

The regs he'd used to justify ending their relationship, the prohibition on sexual relations between officers and noncommissioned personnel, were valid, but they were also widely ignored in the service. He had believed he was just following the rules, or at least he had convinced himself of that, but now he realized he'd used his promotion as an excuse to end the relationship.

She spared my life . . . but would I have done the same? Or would I have seen the enemy commander, understood the effect her loss would have on her soldiers?

Would I have killed her, this woman who was once so close, this loyal friend . . . and old lover?

"Alex, I am so sorry," he said again, knowing it didn't come close to conveying what he was feeling. "The medic is coming." It was a lame thing to say, he knew, but it was all he could manage.

"I don't need a medic, Damian. We both know that." There was sadness in her words, but mostly quiet resignation.

He looked down at her, squeezed her hand. His mind was reeling, his emotions swirling. Affection, at least, for her, if not love. Guilt. Sorrow.

She turned her head slowly, looking up at him.

"Do not cry for me, Damian . . . do not grieve. We are soldiers, you and I—warriors. It is what we were born for. We may crave peace, imagine quiet sunsets and lives filled with joy and love, but that stuff isn't for us. We're good at *fighting* for them, not living them. We hear the horn of war blowing. It calls to us and we can't ignore its summons. It's why I joined the colonial forces, when I might have followed a civilian path. It led you to this field today. We are not destined to die in soft beds, surrounded by children and grandchildren, Damian, as much as we might want that. It is here, in the red-tinged mud of the battlefield, amid the cries of the wounded that we will meet our ends, me today . . . and you, my friend, my old love . . . I would have it be many years from now for you."

He'd lost friends before, watched comrades die on the battlefield, but this was the worst, the hardest to endure.

It gutted him.

"I was a fool, Alex. Please forgive me. We should have been together. I . . .

"I love you."

She looked up at him, but the focus was gone again from her eyes. Her lips curled into a tiny smile. "You were never a good liar, my love."

Then she laid her head down, took a deep breath . . . and fell silent.

Alexandra Thornton was dead.

CHAPTER 26

"You can't allow this! We can still salvage the situation. We don't have to behave like animals."

Everett Wells stood in front of his old desk—technically still his, on loan, more or less, to the federal observer. His face was red, and there was sweat beading along his hairline. He flashed a glare at Semmes before returning his gaze to Stanton.

"Please . . . reconsider this. It is just this kind of heavy-handed action that drove the veterans into the rebel camp . . . and cost you the victory at Dover. And now you want to escalate further?"

Stanton sat silently for a few seconds. She felt tired—not surprising since she'd been up two nights straight. "I'm sorry, Everett, but things have gone too far. I was sent here to restore order on Alpha-2, and I intend to do just that. I would have preferred to see it done with a minimum of bloodshed, but it is clear that is not going to be the case." She stared right at Wells.

My God, he looks more exhausted than I am . . .

"And I have no intention of being stuck here for years as you have been, nor of letting this place destroy my career."

Stanton didn't relish approving the measures Semmes had brought to her. They were brutal, the plan of a man who had been born a sadist. But she didn't share Wells's optimism that the rebels could be contained by negotiation, and she knew damned well the senate would never agree to pardon colonists who had risen in armed revolt and killed federal soldiers. Especially not after the losses at Dover. The rebels had set the agenda; they had left her no choice. She had to see it through, however . . . uncomfortable . . . that would be.

"Asha . . ."

"I'm sorry, Everett, I really am. But this has gone too far. My God, Major Thornton was among the dead at Dover. She served under you during your entire term here. Are you content to allow those responsible for her death to walk away unpunished?" She held up her hand. "Don't answer—it doesn't matter. The die has been cast. What comes next is out of my hands."

She looked down at the tablet in front of her, and then up at Semmes. She pressed her thumb against the screen, and then she handed it to her military commander. "Your requests are approved, Colonel." She stood up, moving slowly toward the door. Instead of opening it, however, she looked back at Semmes. "I've given you the tools and political cover to do what you must. But I expect to see this rebellion crushed as quickly as possible."

"Yes, Your Excellency."

"And Governor Wells is correct about one thing. Your issuance of recall notices to the veterans was a foolish mistake, one that cost us a chance to end this destructive conflict at Dover. No more mistakes, Colonel. Do you understand me?"

"Yes, Your Excellency. I understand."

His scowl on his face told a different story.

Pout all you want, Semmes. You might have the family pedigree, but I have command. And I'm not going to sit here and let you sabotage it. I need you—your decisiveness, even your brutality. But you're just a weapon in my arsenal like any other. And we're going to break this rebellion.

"One more cheer—for our friends, our neighbors, who came to our aid, who allowed us to win the victory!" John Danforth stood on top of a tractor, shouting out to the crowd clustered around him. There were Guardians there, and the others who had rallied to their cause . . .

and there were veterans, too, the men and women Damian Ward had led to save the rebellion from destruction.

The sound was loud, though, almost deafening. Hundreds of rebels raised their hands above their heads, and shouts of "Victory!" filled the air. The veterans were scattered throughout the multitudes, and all around, the Guardians reached out to them, offering hands and hugs, and speaking personal words of thanks.

Victory. What victory? More like survival . . .

Danforth continued. "And now, the commander who led these veteran warriors to our aid, one of our own all Havenites know, a war hero and a man I am proud to call my friend: Damian Ward." Danforth looked down from his perch, gesturing for Damian to join him.

Damian took a deep breath. His thoughts were elsewhere: with Alex, with the reawakened beast inside him. He was imagining what Semmes was doing, what response the psychopath would devise to avenge his humiliation.

"Damian . . ."

He wanted more than anything to be left alone, to brood on what had happened, and on what was likely to come. But Danforth knew how to handle a crowd, and the rebels were chanting Damian's name, urging him to address them.

He climbed up the tractor, moving next to Danforth. The crowd's volume rose, hundreds of men and women shouting his name again and again. He raised his hands, gesturing for the crowd to be silent, but they just continued screaming his name, cheering wildly.

"Please . . . please . . ." He waved his arms as he spoke, and slowly, gradually, the shouting died down.

"Thank you, thank you all. I—we—are honored by all this. As you know, many of us have been reluctant to join the rebellion. But we're here now, ready to fight alongside you. And that means we must all move forward. Reluctant or not, we are all rebels now. There is no other way to secure freedom for Haven, no path that leads to anything but destruction and tyranny." Damian glanced at Danforth. "I applaud the efforts of my friend John Danforth—and I urge all of you to remember always those who have sacrificed all they had to our cause. Tyler Danforth . . . and the hundreds who died in battle here at Dover and at Vincennes."

And Alex Thornton, who was nothing but a loyal soldier and a woman who deserved better than to love me . . .

"I also thank all the men and women who followed me into the fire today," he said, addressing the veterans. "My gratitude for your help today, for your skill and courage—I have no words. But please know: you are under no obligation. You have sworn no oath to join the rebellion. You each risked your life in battle, but if you wish to leave, know you go with all our thanks. If you stay here, I know the Guardians will gladly welcome you and your expertise, and the chances for a free Haven will be that much greater because of your presence.

"And I swear this now—I will be right here with you! I am with you, *all of you*, and I shall fight until Haven is free!"

He looked back at Danforth and turned to climb back down, but he felt a hand grabbing his arm, holding him in place. John Danforth stood there, smiling, waving. The crowd was cheering loudly, but Danforth wasn't done.

"Damian Ward!" he said, and the cheering escalated. He looked at Damian, then back out over the mob.

Damian caught a look in Danforth's eye, and he felt a rush of discomfort.

What is he doing now?

Danforth spoke. "I have done all I could to enable this rebellion, to provide it what it needs to succeed. And I am forever a patriot—forever a Guardian of Liberty—of Haven! But . . . but I am no military leader."

No . . .

"I don't have the skills, the *strength*, to lead our army to victory."

Please, no.

"There is one here, though, who has those skills. Who has that strength. Who has shown, today, that he is a natural leader."

John . . .

"I hereby propose that we appoint him the commander of all

rebel forces, the general in chief of the army of Haven! By acclamation, I ask you to approve our new commander, Damian Ward!"

The crowd roared its assent. Damian just stood there, numb. He
wanted to refuse, to slip back into the crowd, to serve as a soldier,
even an officer. Anything but commander. But then he saw his own
people, the veterans . . . and they were cheering even louder than
the others.

He stood still, silent, trying to decide how to refuse . . . but then
he realized he was trapped. But there was no refusing. There was no
scenario he could envision where he didn't take command. There
was no way out, none that wouldn't threaten the future of the army,
of the rebellion.

So finally, he just raised an arm into the air, nodding his assent . . . and he stood atop the tractor looking out at the soldiers of the
rebellion—*his* soldiers now. He felt the turmoil inside, the hopeless
need to escape. But he knew what he had to do.

"To victory!"

Johnson felt sick. He'd left most of his lunch on the tray, eating only a
dry piece of bread, but now even that threatened to come back up.

Kendrick Johnson was a federal soldier, loyal to his oath and to
his comrades. Until a few days before, he'd boiled with rage, anger
at the citizens of Alpha-2 for the friends he'd lost in the mine, and at
the governor for attempting to deny the fallen soldiers justice. He'd
craved vengeance against the rebels, and he'd longed to make them
pay in blood for all they had done.

Now he'd seen enough of blood. Too much. He was choking on
it. He'd fought at Vincennes, and at Dover, too. He'd lost more comrades in both those bloody fights . . . but he'd seen the rebels paying
the same price, watched as his enemies showed their courage, their
own devotion to their cause and comrades. He still felt anger at them
for causing the war, but there was something else there now, too.
Respect, or at least the beginnings of it. He disagreed with their politics, opposed the "right" they claimed to cast aside their nation and
government. But he knew now they would fight, that many of them
would die, before they would surrender their ideals.

War was bad enough—and he had to admit to himself he'd never been so scared to death as he had been at Vincennes and Dover—but this duty was a nightmare.

"This is it." He looked at the house, glancing down at the tablet in his hand. He hesitated for a few seconds before he nodded at one of his troopers.

The soldier moved forward, holding a thick metal cylinder. He stopped at the door, gesturing with his head to the trooper standing behind him. The two men gripped the ram and swung it against the door of the farmhouse.

The cylinder slammed against the wood with a loud crash, breaking through in one section and sending a large crack running down the length. They pulled it back and swung again, this time sending the shattered door back, shards of splintered wood flying everywhere, leaving a small remnant hanging from the upper hinge.

Johnson stood where he was, listening to the sound of a woman screaming inside. "Go!" He waved to the line of armed soldiers, standing with their rifles ready.

The corporal at the head of the detachment nodded. "Yes, Sergeant!" His rifle snapped down, held out in front of him. "Detachment, forward."

His detachment of the soldiers ran into the house, and he stood and listened to the screams, a woman inside shouting and also the cries of children. He closed his eyes, and just for a moment he was somewhere else . . . anywhere. But orders were orders.

His soldiers came out of the house, pushing the woman forward. She was bleeding from her mouth, her face covered with a bruise almost certainly caused by the impact of a rifle stock. She'd been screaming before—and most likely fighting with his soldiers—but now the will to resist was gone, and she just whimpered as the troopers pushed two children through the wreckage of the door.

"Please . . ." The woman turned toward Johnson, tears flowing down her face as she spoke. "We haven't done anything . . . we're just farmers. Please . . ."

Johnson wanted to let her go; he wanted to tell her to take her children and find someplace to hide.

God do I want that.

"Where is Henry Rivers?" he said again, trying to sound as emotionless as possible. It would do no one any good—not him, and not this woman—if he gave the impression he could be swayed from carrying out his orders.

He wondered if he was even close to hiding his emotions.

"He's . . . working in the fields . . ."

Johnson winced. It wasn't even a good lie.

"Really? Working in the fields? The fields we passed on our way here? The deserted ones, that look like they haven't been tended to in weeks?" He paused. "You mean he's not with the rebel army? He did not take up arms against his rightful government? He didn't shed the blood of federal soldiers? He is not guilty of high treason?"

Johnson stared at the woman. He wasn't waiting for answers. He knew all he needed to know.

"Take them." His voice was cold, but it was more from the emptiness he felt inside than from any hatred for these colonists. His orders left him no latitude. He'd been provided with suspects, lists of residences of men and women suspected of fighting with the rebel forces . . . but he'd also been directed to arrest any members of a household with people missing. The absence of any documented adult member of a household was to be considered proof of rebel activity. It was one of Colonel Semmes's directives—the families of all men and women in armed rebellion were to be arrested at once. And any who resisted were to be shot.

"No, please . . . my children . . . we haven't done anything . . ."

"Take them to the transport." He gestured toward the large truck his people were using as a mobile jail. There were a dozen people in there already, mostly elderly and children.

He turned and walked back toward his own transport, trying as hard as he could to ignore the woman's continued cries.

"Jamie!" Damian ran to his friend, his gloom momentarily fading.

"Damian!" Jamie leapt to his feet, wincing as he turned too quickly. Damian could see why: he had bandages in three different places.

"I'm glad to see you, you crazy fool." Damian embraced his friend, loosening his grip when Jamie winced once more. "Sorry . . ."

"It's nothing. Just a few scratches." Jamie paused. "I was surprised when I heard it was your people attacking the federals. I didn't think you'd change your mind."

"I won't lie to you, Jamie: I would have stayed out of it if I could have. But in the end I had no choice. None of us did."

"Damian—Katia . . ."

"She's fine, Jamie. She's safe at least. And her father. He's still in rough shape, but he's going to make it."

Jamie sighed hard. "Thank you so much, Damian. I don't know what to say."

"You don't have to say anything."

"Damian . . ." It was Danforth, running up from the half-standing building they'd chosen as the army HQ.

"What is it, John?"

"We're getting reports . . . it's terrible."

Damian looked around. There was clearly a disturbance in the camp, rebel troops moving around, gathering in groups.

"General Ward . . ." A small cluster of troopers moved toward Damian, the woman at their head calling out to their new commander.

"What is it?" he asked, not sure if he would get used to being called "general."

"We got word from home, sir. It's the federals. They came to my house. They took my mother, my father, my little brother . . ."

"And my wife . . . and my children . . ."

"They came to the village where I live, too, sir . . . and they hauled everyone away. My son here—" a man pointed to a boy of perhaps twelve standing at his side "—he was out in the woods. He managed to escape, but he saw everything . . ."

Damian stood and listened to the accounts, almost a dozen of them. The weight pressed on him with each telling. It was as he'd told Danforth: the war was starting to suck in the innocent.

He turned toward Danforth. "We've got to get out the word, send out parties, warn the people. We have to get to the rest of the towns and villages around Landfall before the federals. We'll bring the civilians here. They must grab what they can quickly and come at once."

He didn't even begin to know how he was going to feed thousands of civilian refugees, but there was no choice. He couldn't allow a butcher like Semmes to get his hands on all those people. It was unthinkable . . . but brilliant, too. Better than attacking him outright, the colonel's plan would destroy his army if he did nothing. It was one thing to ask of soldiers to fight, to risk injury and death in battle. If their courage and success on the field would condemn their families, though . . .

"I'll see to it, Damian." Danforth ran back toward the HQ building, shouting out commands as he did.

Damian looked out at the cluster of soldiers, the men and women who had spoken of their families, already captured, beyond aid. He wanted to say something, but no words came. Finally, he managed, "We will do all we can to secure the release of your loved ones." He knew the words were empty even as he spoke them. But they were all he had.

Jamie walked over toward Damian, limping as he did. "I have to go get Katia, Damian. Once they realize you've joined the rebellion, you know they'll come to the farm."

"Katia and her father are well hidden, Jamie."

"Damian . . ." Jamie said, incredulous.

"Yes, Jamie—you're right. We've got to get them out of there. But not you."

Jamie opened his mouth to argue, but Damian held up his hand to silence his friend.

"Be reasonable, Jamie—you can barely walk. Let me send Ben with some men. They can move quickly, and if they run into a federal patrol, at least they'll have a chance."

Jamie frowned, but he nodded. It must be killing his friend to stay behind, but there was nothing he could do about that. If Ben Withers couldn't rescue Katia and Alexi Rand, no one could.

CHAPTER 27

Everett walked along the line of heavy metal fencing, looking in at the hundreds—no, over a thousand now—of civilians confined in the camp.

Camp Liberty.

Semmes is a son of a bitch, but he's got a sense of humor. A sick one.

The people in the camp had committed no crime. They had seen no court. Had no due process. They were simply the relatives of suspected rebels—the fathers and mothers, sisters and brothers, spouses and children of men and women who had taken to the field to fight for the rebellion.

It was a brutal tactic, one Wells had never even envisioned. He'd been sure that Asha Stanton would put a stop to it, but she'd simply nodded her assent. Stanton wasn't a monster like Semmes . . . but she knew a failure to crush the rebellion would destroy her, even as Wells knew it had done the same to him.

He looked through the chain-link perimeter, and he felt sick to his stomach. The men and women in the camp were crowded together. They were outside, with no shelter, no place to sleep save on the ground where they lay. They were soaking wet now, from the morning's rain, and they sat in the mud, looking at each other with vacant stares.

They were on minimal rations. They hadn't been there long enough yet for malnutrition and starvation to take a toll, but Wells knew it was only a matter of time.

"My God, you have to do something about this!"

Wells turned abruptly. He'd been lost in dark thoughts, and Violetta had crept up on him.

He turned toward his daughter, saw the horror in her eyes. "There's nothing I can do, Vi. I argued with the observer, but she won't budge."

"You can't let this happen!"

"I don't have the power to stop it."

Violetta turned and looked over at the miserable prisoners clumped together, staring off at nothing with glassy eyes.

"There must be something you can do . . ."

Wells turned and looked again at the prisoners. "I don't know what, Vi . . . but one thing is certain. I can't be a part of this anymore." He turned toward his daughter. "I told you before. I'm going to resign the governorship." He paused. "Get ready to leave, because we're going back to Earth."

Ben Withers crept slowly forward, holding his hand out behind him, signaling his troopers to wait. Damian's farm was mostly open country, but the eastern edge stretched into the meandering section of forest north of Landfall. Withers knew every centimeter of the farm, better even than Damian himself, and this was the best way to sneak close to the house and the cluster of buildings surrounding it.

He looked out over the open, slightly rolling countryside. He could see the house, off in the distance. At first he thought everything was calm, with no signs of enemy occupation. But then he realized there was no activity anywhere. No hands in the fields, no tractors or plows operating. Nothing.

His senses went on alert. It could be nothing. Perhaps everyone was hiding, waiting for word from Damian. But that's not what his gut told him.

"All right, we're going to move on the storage shed to the left of the main house. They're in there." He paused, looking out again, still seeing nothing untoward. "We stay away from the main house, you understand? If there are federals on the farm, they will be in there for sure."

He turned, looking at the ten troopers he'd brought with him. They all nodded and offered a ragged chorus of "yessirs."

"Okay, let's go. Stay behind me." He lunged out of the woods, swinging hard to the right, moving through one of the cultivated fields. He crouched down, staying under the cover of the shoulder-high crops. It was better than running out in the open . . . but he knew anyone with combat experience would pick off the movement.

He raced forward, reaching the end of the field. There was a stretch of grassland between his position and the building. He stopped for an instant . . . and then he moved out, running as quickly as he could. There was no way to sneak up on the main compound—Damian had seen to that when it had been built, his military instincts kicking in, driving him to have a two-hundred-meter swath of land cleared all around the house.

He reached one of the barns, throwing himself against the wall and watching as his troopers did the same thing. He took a quick glance at his small force. They were good soldiers, he knew, all of them. He'd served with three of them during the war, and he'd heard of the others, men and women who had fought on other fronts. They were all decorated veterans, handpicked by Damian for the operation.

Withers swung around the edge of the barn, his rifle down. His eyes darted back and forth, looking for threats. For targets. But there was still nothing.

He waved for the troopers to follow him, and he raced across the open courtyard between the main house and several of the outbuildings. He reached the door to the storage shed . . . and he froze.

His eyes caught the edge of the vehicle, barely visible from his angle. But he knew what it was. A federal military transport.

Shit.

He turned again, flashing a warning to his people. Then he poked at the small pad next to the door, entering the access code. He held his breath. If the federals had disabled the farm's AI system, his codes wouldn't work . . . and he'd have no chance of opening the secure door to the safe room. Not without blowing it to bits.

Crack. The door popped open.

Withers exhaled hard. Then he slipped inside, waving for the others to follow. The sooner they were all out of sight, the better. He ran across the poured concrete floor, over to a stack of crates.

"Let's go." He leaned down, pushing a crate to the side. It looked heavy, but he knew it wasn't. It was full of straw, just like the others covering the hidden entrance.

He knelt down as his troopers pushed the rest of the boxes away, and he felt around for the loose chunk of concrete. He knew it was there, but for a few seconds he couldn't find it.

Damn, we hid this well . . .

He felt a rush of hope—if the federals had found the room, they'd never had taken such care to replace it the concrete . . . or the crates.

Then his fingers felt the slight give in the floor. He reached around, finding the edge and pushing down. A small chunk of concrete popped up, revealing a pad similar to the one at the door. Withers punched in a code, and there was a loud click as a section of the floor rose slightly and moved to the side, revealing a dark tunnel below.

"Stay here." Withers climbed into the hole, his feet feeling around for the ladder he knew was there. He stepped down to the bottom and turned around. There was a door, with another pad next to it. He punched in the code again, and it opened.

He stepped inside . . . and saw someone lunging toward him, swinging a chair . . .

He jumped back, evading the blow as the chair broke into shards on the side of the door. He brought his rifle around, ready to fire. But he held. Katia Rand was standing in front of him with a jagged piece of wood still in her hands.

"Katia . . . it's Ben Withers. We're here to get you out."

She froze, looking at him with shock on her face. Then she dropped the remnant of the chair. "I'm so sorry, Ben . . ." She paused an instant, and then she ran up to him, throwing her arms around him.

He returned the embrace, his eyes scanning the room. There were two knives on a small table behind Katia, and a few tools that looked like makeshift weapons.

She stepped back from the embrace, seeing his expression and then turning toward the table.

"I saw them on the surveillance system . . ." She pointed to a small screen set into the wall on the far side of the room. "I wasn't going to let them take me again . . ." Withers could see her stare, angry, the hatred in her glazed-over eyes. "Never."

"Okay, Katia . . . we've got to get out of here now." He moved toward a small doorway in the back of the room. "How is your father? Can he travel?"

He burst through the opening before she could answer. Alexi Rand was lying on a makeshift bed. His shirt was off, and his midsection was covered in bandages.

"Alexi, it's Ben Withers. I'm sorry, but we've got to go."

Rand turned his head and stared at Withers with a hazy look in his eyes. "Ben . . ." His voice was soft, weak. "No . . . take Katia . . . get away."

Withers shook his head. "That's not how we operate here. We don't leave friends behind."

"I will slow you down . . . go . . ."

Withers ignored Rand's words. "Can you stand?" He reached around, sliding his arm under Rand's shoulder. "Come on, I'll help you."

Rand grunted as he struggled to his feet, clearly in pain.

"I'm sorry, Alexi, but there's no other way."

Withers slid under Rand's shoulder, slipping the wounded man's arm around his neck.

"Lean on me, Alexi. One step at a time."

The two moved slowly into the other room, toward the ladder.

How the hell am I going to get him out of here?

He looked up to the main floor of the shed. "I need a rope . . . there should be some up—"

He heard a muffled crack, a sound he'd have recognized anywhere. Then another . . . and a dozen more in rapid succession.

Gunfire.

Semmes was standing by himself, watching the roughly three hundred men and women lined up in the courtyard of the federal complex. They stood holding weapons, though most of them looked out of place with the military grade assault rifles. They were farmers, office workers, professionals of various kinds. And they were also loyalists, citizens of Alpha-2 who remained faithful to Federal America.

His troopers had been scouring the countryside around Landfall for a week now, rounding up anybody even suspected of affiliation with the rebels. But they'd also been spreading the word, recruiting volunteers to fight alongside the federal soldiers, men and women who wanted their world to remain as it was.

Asha Stanton walked up next to him. "Are you sure this is a good idea, Colonel? I appreciate the additional forces, but they are completely untrained. How much use will they be?"

Semmes turned toward Stanton. "It will take a while, at least militarily. But they will have other uses. Who knows the rebels better than their neighbors? Who is more motivated to have peace restored to their lives? Whatever their motivations, they're here, and I'm going to take advantage of that."

"I am concerned you're stretching the limits of my orders, though. I understand the need at times for harsh measures, even brutality. But the prison camp, the attempt to pit the colonists against their neighbors—that is not what you proposed to me the other day. Besides overstepping your bounds, I'm worried that some of your measures will simply breed greater resistance."

"We have discussed this idea multiple times, Your Excellency. This constant second-guessing is extremely counterproductive. You give the colonists too much credit. They may have managed to gain a minor victory in the field—with the help of a pack of traitors—but if we inflict enough pain on them, they will crumble . . . and the revolution will die with a whimper."

Stanton felt a surge of anger. She knew Semmes was a pompous ass, but he wasn't even trying to show her the respect her station commanded. She'd have fired him long before . . . if his father hadn't been such a powerful man. She knew she had little chance to prevail in a political struggle with the Semmes family.

And now that Alex Thornton is gone, who else could I put in charge? The rebels have proven to be a more difficult adversary than I'd expected . . . but I don't have a better option than this fool . . .

"You will remember, Colonel, that I have the final say on any operations conducted on this planet. I will decide what we do and when we do it. If I issue a new order, it is not a 'second guess'—it is the order based on my observation of the situation. Is that clear?"

She was provoking Semmes, and that was dangerous, especially when the situation of Alpha-2 was in such flux. She was also savvy enough to know who Earth would support if things went south here . . . and it wasn't her. Hell, the next supply ship could arrive with a representative carrying orders relieving her and putting Semmes in her place.

But that hadn't happened yet, and so until it did, *she* ruled here.

"Yes, Your Excellency. It is *clear.*"

"Very good, Colonel. You may continue organizing and training your loyalist units, but you are not to deploy them to combat operations without my approval."

"Yes, Your Excellency."

Stanton nodded. Then she turned and walked toward the main building.

"What the hell is going on?" Withers climbed out of the underground room, his head snapping around as he did. Most of his troopers were up against the door they'd come through, weapons drawn, returning the fire coming from outside.

"Federals, sir. I don't think more than four . . . at least, not engaged."

"Fuck . . ." Withers moved toward the doorway. Two of his people flanked the narrow opening. They were crouched behind the cover, shooting back at the federals. "We don't have time for this shit; even if they're the only ones here, they'll call for help. If they haven't already." He peered around the corner, his eyes darting around, locating the enemy positions. "I've got two—one by the corner of the main house and one near the north barn."

"The other two are by the house, too, sir. They pulled back. I think we might have hit one. The other is probably on the comm calling for backup."

Withers paused for a few seconds. Then he turned and snapped an order to a pair of troopers in the middle of the room. "Get Alexi and Katia up here. Now!" He spun around. "The rest of you, on me. We don't have time for a firefight. We have to take these fuckers out now and get out of here."

He turned and peered around the edge of the doorway again. "All right, Hepps, Krill, Gantz . . . I want you guys to stay here and lay down some heavy covering fire. Just keep their heads down . . . and make sure you don't hit any of us. Lloyd, Wring . . . you guys charge the guy over by the barn. Nothing fancy, just get closer . . . and if he shows his head, blow it off."

The two troopers nodded. "Yes, sir."

"Sawyer, Vilmont, Jarrit . . . you three are with me. On my mark, we bolt out of here—right for the house. Same deal, keep your eyes open . . . and shoot anything that moves."

He turned and looked at the three troopers. They all nodded.

"Okay, everybody . . . covering fire on three . . . two . . . one . . . now!"

Three of the soldiers opened fire, their weapons set on full auto. They sprayed the areas around the house and the barn, and Withers could see one of the federals dive deeper into cover.

"Charge!" He lunged out, running across the mostly level ground at a dead sprint. His rifle was out in front of him, and he was firing in bursts, his eyes staring, looking for any target.

He could hear the other troopers right behind them, their own fire adding to his own. He pushed himself, putting every scrap of strength he had into his legs. He knew half a second could be the difference between life and death.

He came up to the corner of the house, slamming against it with his back, his eyes locked on the corner of the building. He moved slowly, steadily . . . and then he spun around, firing on full auto as he did.

He saw one of the federals go down, at least three of his shots finding their mark. The man dropped, and Withers knew he was dead. His eyes caught another enemy soldier, the one his troopers had thought was hit earlier. He was lying on the ground, still alive, reaching for a pistol on the ground nearby. Withers snapped up his rifle and fired, hitting his target in the chest. The soldier dropped back, and he lay unmoving.

"That's two!" He looked around, trying to find the third soldier. The other troopers fanned out behind him, rifles at the ready. Up ahead, there was a staircase leading to the house's main level, and beyond, the wall turned at a ninety-degree angle. He hugged the wall, working his way around to the corner, waving for the others to hold back, to be careful. He stepped forward slowly, easing around, staring ahead.

Something hit him, on the back of the shoulder. He fell forward, stumbling twice before he fell to the ground. He heard his rifle skittering away, out of reach, just as he saw the soldier, standing at the bottom of the stairs, a large crowbar in one hand . . . and a pistol in the other.

Withers reached around behind him, going for his own pistol. But even as he did it, he knew it would be too late. The federal had him dead to rights. It was over.

Crack!

Withers closed his eyes instinctively, knowing he'd been shot. But there was no pain, nothing at all. He looked down, ran his hands across his chest and midsection. No blood . . . nothing. Then he saw the federal double over and fall down at the base of the stairs.

He whipped his head around, looking behind him. Sawyer was standing there, his assault rifle still aimed at the spot where the federal had stood.

"Are you okay, sir?"

Withers sat up, rubbing the back of his neck with his hand. "Yeah, Sawyer. I'm okay." He stood up slowly, groaning as he did. "Thanks to you."

The soldier smiled and nodded. Then the two turned and walked back to the storage shed.

"And, Sawyer . . . I'm no 'sir.' I'm a sergeant just like you."

CHAPTER 28

"Well, Dr. Holcomb . . . what can you tell us about this jamming?"

Damian struggled to keep the worry from his voice. None of them needed to hear that from the commander in chief, even if he was at his wit's end about how he was going to supply his army, recruit the reinforcements he needed—hell, even how he was going to move them more than a few kilometers from where they were. He needed communications, and right now the escaped prisoner, haggard and badly shaken though he might be, was his best chance to get it.

Holcomb did look terrible, but given what Damian had heard about his treatment and Jacen's impressive rescue, he wasn't surprised. He wished he could let the man rest—hell, he wished he could let them all rest—but they had no time. The doctor stepped forward.

"Well, it appears they are employing a selective interference wave, one that blocks all communications except specific frequencies they designate—in this case, the channels used by their own forces. They would have to change those frequently, though, or we would be able to find and use them, which means they are utilizing a sophisticated AI routine to manage it all. It is actually a very ingenious operation. I am impressed that they have managed to implement it so effectively."

"I'm glad you find it interesting, Doctor, but men and women are dying because of it. How do we stop it?"

"Yes . . . sorry . . . I understand. Stopping it *is* crucial. But I'm afraid it will be very difficult. I believe I *can* cripple the system . . . but there is one problem."

"Yes?"

"Well, General, the federals are undoubtedly using the orbital platform and its array of satellites to broadcast the wave—though even with the station's resources they must be getting extra power from somewhere—"

"Which *means* . . ."

"Yes. Sorry. I'm afraid it means that there isn't a way to cut the jamming from the planet's surface. I would have to be on the platform itself."

The hope fled.

"So much for regaining communications. As you can see, Doctor, we're pinned down in these woods. We might be able to sneak you into Landfall, but there's no way to get you onto that platform."

And that means no communication. They can call me general all they want, but without comm I can only lead them to destruction and defeat.

"I can get the doctor up to the station."

Damian heard the voice, but it took a second for it to sink in. He turned toward a woman standing on the far side of the table.

"Excuse me?"

"I said I can get the doctor to the station, General." The woman was tall, her long hair tied tightly behind her head. She was about his own age, perhaps five years older. Her clothes were filthy and worn—it was clear from her look she'd had a rough few days.

I guess I could say that about most of us.

Danforth had introduced her to him the day before. Her name had seemed vaguely familiar, but he couldn't remember why.

"And how can you do that, Captain Ner—"

"I can do it with my ship, *Vagabond*. But there's just one problem. The feds have seized it. We would have to go to the spaceport and . . . persuade . . . them to give it back."

"**Medic! We need** a medic . . . now!"

Jamie had been carving staves for the palisades, not really in a condition to patrol or dig trenches. But he had to do something.

When he heard that cry, though, he put down the pole and looked up to see Withers coming out of the woods, shouting as he raced toward the middle of the camp. His troopers were just behind him, and they looked like they'd been through hell.

Katia!

He looked around frantically, trying to see her face, but the group was quickly surrounded by men from the field hospital. They looked exhausted, having worked around the clock since the battle.

Jamie couldn't care less about them. He moved as quickly as he could, making his way to the group.

His heart caught in his throat when Withers ordered two of his men to lower a body to the ground: it was Alexi. Once more, his eyes darted through the group, trying to find the only face that mattered to him.

And then he saw her.

Katia was just behind the two men carrying her father, and she now dropped down to her knees next to him, putting her hand on his face. Tears streaked down her face.

Just as they were doing down his. *She's alive.*

"Katia!"

"Jamie!" She leapt up and ran into his embrace. Burying her face into his chest, she said, "I'm so glad to see you."

He didn't even notice when Damian ran up and stopped at the edge of the circle that had formed around Alexi.

"I think we can save him, sir, but it will take a lot of blood substitute."

Jamie saw not only his friend, but Danforth, Jacen, and a number of the other leaders of the rebellion. He knew Damian and the doctors had been making harsh decisions over the past few days, rationing dwindling medical supplies. And Alexi wasn't even part of the army . . .

"Do it. Do whatever you have to, but save him."

Jamie heard Damian's voice. His friend spoke firmly, but he

could hear the discomfort there, too. Was the army's commander consigning some other soldier to death to save his friend?

"Yes, sir. We have to get him to the hospital . . . now." The medic pointed out to Withers's men who had carried Rand. "You two, help us move him."

The soldiers reached down, taking hold of Rand's unmoving form, lifting him up. They followed the medics across the open area to the field hospital and disappeared inside.

Katia pushed off Jamie and ran up to Damian, throwing her arms around him. "Thank you, Damian. Thank you."

Jamie just stood where he was, though, looking over at Damian. Their eyes met, and he knew he had communicated his gratitude to his friend.

Damian put his head down into his hands. The pain in his skull felt like a runaway train had bored its way through his brain, but he wasn't about to requisition so much as an aspirin from the army's overtaxed medical supplies, not when there were wounded men and women in *real* pain being denied sparse drugs. He'd done that once already, for Alexi Rand. The blood he'd ordered the medic give Alexi was a precious resource, and he'd let his emotions trump the needs of his army.

Never again.

He was glad Withers had made it back with the Rands, and he was grateful Alexi would live. But he'd been stupid, and he couldn't afford to be stupid. The rebels couldn't afford him to be stupid.

Especially now.

The meeting was smaller than the earlier one, and he decided that was something to be thankful for. The plan Sasha Nerov was proposing wasn't just risky; it was downright insane. Worse, it was really the only option, a wild gamble that he knew was their only chance. That was better discussed in front of as few people as possible.

He looked up, staring right at Nerov. "Captain Nerov, I appreciate your proposal, but I'm still not sure how we can do it. Let's assume for a moment we can get a strike force to the spaceport and take possession of your ship long enough for you to blast off. How are you planning to get close to the station? That thing's got enough firepower to blast a federal task force to atoms. With all due respect to your vessel, you won't last more than a few seconds once you enter weapons range."

"We won't have to deal with the weapons at all, General."

"And how is that, Captain? Do you think they will just let you approach?"

"I wouldn't say 'let,' General, but yes—if we come in at the right angle I believe we can reach the station without exposing ourselves to hostile fire."

"Go on."

"The station was built to defend the planet, General, not to fire on it. Its energy weapons are all positioned *outward* . . . to fight off an attacking fleet. Even the fire arcs of the secondary batteries can only target vessels in orbit."

"But wouldn't your ship be in orbit? I would think the secondaries would be more than enough—"

"No, General—*Vagabond* will *not* enter orbit. We will launch directly at the station, coming up from below. We will stay in its fire shadow, and we will dock on the underside."

"How would you do that? There are no ports on that side."

Nerov smiled this time. "*Vagabond* is a special ship, General. My people hauled cargo. *Controversial* cargo."

"You're a smuggler."

"I'm an entrepreneur. Regardless what you call me, trust me when I say my ship can do the job. During the last war she had some special enhancements. Including a forced boarding portal."

"You were a privateer during the war?"

Nerov didn't answer. She just stared back, a noncommittal look on her face.

Damian just nodded. Federal America had issued letters of marque to any ship owners who were willing to arm their vessels and prey on union or hegemony shipping. Now he remembered the name, why it had been familiar when Danforth had introduced him to the smuggler. Nerov had been the terror of the outer colonies, capturing over a dozen enemy freighters. Until something happened . . . some kind of scandal that had ended her career as a privateer. He'd never known what it was, but he found himself feeling more confidence in Nerov's abilities. Damian nodded at Nerov. "I am not a spacer, Captain, but if I am not mistaken, what you are proposing would require some extremely difficult and dangerous maneuvering."

"It is a . . . complex . . . liftoff, General. But if your people can get us to *Vagabond*, my people can manage it."

Damian nodded, not sure whether he was reading confidence or bravado in her voice. Then he looked out at the others. "Okay, so let's assume Captain Nerov can get Dr. Holcomb to the station. We need a strike team strong enough to defeat any security at the spaceport . . . and also to board and take the station if . . . when . . . Captain Nerov is successful in docking."

"I will lead it. My people will take the spaceport."

Damian knew the voice instantly, and he felt his stomach tighten. Patrick Killian was a veteran, a warrior of unquestioned ability. But he was also crazy, driven to the edge of insanity by some kind of injustice he'd suffered. Damian didn't know the details, only that Killian had been dishonorably discharged, which had been a shock for such a decorated and experienced veteran.

Damian held back a sigh. "Thanks for volunteering, Captain Killian, but I don't believe your rangers will be sufficient." He turned and looked down the table. "Colonel Morgan, you will go as well. Put together a force of fifty of the veterans to bolster Captain Killian and his people . . . and another fifty to take the station. You will have overall command of the operation." He'd hastily conferred field promotions on several of the veterans, and Luci Morgan had been the first to gain the kind of massive increase in rank he'd experienced. Damian knew he had to take a more comprehensive look at the forces under his command, to make more thoughtful and informed decisions, but for now he just needed a few people he could trust in key positions.

"Yes, General."

He looked at Morgan . . . and then at Killian. "I don't have to remind both of you how crucial this mission is . . . and how dangerous. You may carry the success or failure of the rebellion with you."

"Yes, sir." Morgan's response was sharp, disciplined.

"Understood, General." Killian answered crisply, too, but his eagerness gave Damian a chill.

"Very well . . . go now and prepare. You will leave for the spaceport tomorrow just after dark. Dismissed."

Damian watched the others file slowly from the room. He stayed in his chair until everyone had gone, and then he put his face back in his hands and sighed.

Is this crazy plan really our best chance?

CHAPTER 29

"All right, I'm only going to say this once. When I give the word, we move out. And we don't stop until we control the entire place." Killian stood behind a wall on the outskirts of Landfall Spaceport. It was just after midnight, and the area was almost deserted. Landing and liftoff of spaceships was a daylight affair, at least on a colony like Haven.

At least until tonight . . .

"Yes, Captain." Ash Tull nodded as he replied, his voice preceding the others by half a second. Tull was one of Killian's closest friends, and he was generally considered to be the only one among the rangers who was as certifiably insane as their commander.

Not that he considered himself insane. Just really, really angry.

"I can't overstate how important this mission is to the rebellion. If we do not get *Vagabond* off the ground, the cause is dead. Not today, maybe, but soon . . . and any hope for freedom will die with it. There is no failure, do you understand me?" Killian paused as his people responded with a series of nods.

"And that means there is no room for half measures, no weakness. No pity. You see any federal troopers, spaceport security—any armed personnel—you scrag them. If you shoot, you shoot to kill. Any spaceport staff, unarmed civilians, you . . . take prisoner." He had argued they shouldn't leave anyone alive, that even a nonmilitary staff member could be dangerous, but Danforth had insisted . . . and Damian Ward had ended the debate in no uncertain terms. He liked Danforth, but he still might have shrugged him off. Damian Ward, though—there was no question about following his orders. So unarmed civilians who surrendered were to be spared.

But if one of them pulls out so much as a pocket knife . . .

"Anyone else—if they have a weapon and they don't surrender immediately, you take them out." Killian was pushing General Ward's authorization to the limit, and perhaps beyond, but he'd be damned if he was going to let some federal functionary in the airport delay an operation that depended on speed for success.

"Colonel Morgan's people will be right behind us with Captain Nerov and Dr. Holcomb, so there's no stopping. They're counting on us, so we go in, take over the control center, and secure the area around *Vagabond*. No stopping, no matter what. If you get wounded, you're on your own."

Killian looked down at his rifle, double-checking it, making sure the cartridge was firmly in place. He dropped one hand to his side, confirming his other weapons—two pistols and four blades—were there.

"Everybody ready?"

The rangers had been checking their own equipment, and they looked up, nodding to their commander as they did.

"All right, then . . . let's go!"

Damian sat in the chair, staring at the battered wall of the field hospital as the vial attached to his arm filled slowly. The blood donations had been Holcomb's idea, something he'd remembered his parents talking about when he was a child. The antigovernment forces had been desperate in the closing stages of the civil war, and they'd resorted to using actual blood to treat wounded fighters. It was archaic, an almost ancient custom that predated mass-produced blood substitutes, one that seemed almost barbaric to Damian. The old practice required careful blood-typing and was rife with danger for spreading communicable diseases, but his army was almost out of blood substitute, and they had no way to get more, not while they were trapped in the woods around Dover. And using real blood was a hell of a lot better option than watching his soldiers die when they might be saved. He'd ordered everyone in the army to donate a half liter . . . and now he was giving a second one himself.

It was late, well past midnight, but he wasn't going to be sleeping tonight, not while his people were moving on the spaceport. He'd wanted to go with the strike team, to lead it himself. His days as a lieutenant at the head of a platoon were over, though. Being responsible for every man and woman under arms meant he had to be here, even though he suspected the rebellion's very survival rested on the success of the op.

"That should be good, General." The medic reached out to Damian's arm, slowly pulling out the long needle. "You've donated a whole liter in less than twenty-four hours, sir. You need to wait at least four or five days before you give any more."

Damian just nodded.

And will that kill one of my soldiers, that four-day delay and half a liter of blood?

He stood up, but he paused, grabbing the armrest of the chair to steady himself.

"Are you dizzy, sir? Perhaps you should sit for a few more minutes."

"I'm fine." Damian found himself annoyed, not really with the medic, though he suspected it had sounded that way. He was tense, worried about the men and women he'd sent to get *Vagabond*. Beating himself up over sending his people on a near-suicide mission was bad enough . . . but he'd be damned if he was going to sit in the hospital nursing a little dizzy spell.

He walked across the large main room. It had been a barn, built for grain storage and not for treating wounded men and women. The conversion had been a hasty one, and there were large cables on the ground, crisscrossing their way around the room, bringing power from the village's generator to keep the lighting on and the few pieces of advanced medical equipment running.

Everything is so goddamn piecemeal.

That pretty much summed up the rebellion itself. He knew there was widespread unrest across Haven, that thousands would rally to the rebels if only he could reach them, organize them.

And that meant Sasha Nerov and Killian and the others had to make their crazy plan work.

He walked up to one of the makeshift beds, stopping and looking down at its occupant. Alexi Rand was pale, gaunt, his black-and-gray hair hanging around his face in greasy hanks. But he was alive.

"You look like hell." He forced a smile. His friend was still in bad shape, but the doctors said he was going to make it.

"I hear you're in charge of all this now. I'd like to complain about the accommodations." Rand's voice was weak, but he managed to return Damian's grin. "Damian . . . thank you. For all you did . . . for me, and for Katia . . ."

"What's a friend if not someone who will hide you when half the federal army is out looking for you?"

Rand's smile faded. "Is that why you are here, Damian? Because of us? Because we got you in trouble with the federals?"

"No, Alexi . . . it wasn't your fault. Colonel Semmes activated the recall provisions in the veterans' discharges. Let's just say we refused."

"I'm sorry, my friend. I know this must be difficult for you."

Damian nodded, but he didn't reply immediately. Rand moved to sit up, but he only got a few centimeters before he gave up and let his head fall back. "Where is Katia?"

Damian paused. "She's with Jamie, Alexi. She's been back here half a dozen times, but you were asleep. The doctors finally said you were going to make it. I think she kissed them both when they told her."

"I bet Jamie took that well."

"I'm surprised you care." Damian didn't think Alexi actually disliked Jamie, but the engineer had been adamantly against his daughter's relationship with someone who faced so many challenges.

"Are you kidding? The kid saved both our lives. Seriously, though,

Katia loves him. It's time for me to accept that. And with the way the world is falling apart, let them have what happiness they can steal." Rand paused. "We're all dead anyway, Damian, aren't we?"

Damian sighed softly. He wasn't a man who liked lying to his friends. But he wasn't quite ready to give up all hope either, not even if the spaceport raid failed. So it wasn't *really* lying.

"Things don't look good, Alexi, but I wouldn't say they're hopeless. We've got a plan to get the word out, rally the entire planet. Until then, though, we're pinned down here—if we go too far out of the woods, their air power will cut us to ribbons.

"Listen—I've got to go, Alexi . . . and you should get some rest. I have a feeling we're going to need your skills soon." He leaned forward and put his hand on Rand's. "I'll check in on you later."

Rand smiled again and nodded.

Damian walked toward the door. He had people out there, probably in a desperate fight even now. If he couldn't be with them, he felt he should be in his headquarters. It wouldn't do anything—he had no communications—but he knew that's where he had to be.

"I'm sorry, Asha, but I've made up my mind. I may have failed here, but I have no intention of being a part of what is going to happen now." Everett sat in their shared office. It was quiet, only the humming of the HVAC system breaking the background silence. It was an odd time to be discussing business, but Stanton had called him an hour before, asking him to meet with her one more time. He had no intention of allowing her to change his mind, but he'd agreed to come anyway.

"Everett, don't be a fool. This business may be extremely distasteful—I don't relish it any more than you—but it is necessary. The rebels who rebuffed all your attempts at reconciliation are at least as responsible for current events as any actions by Federal America. Your resignation doesn't change anything about the current situation, except possibly making it worse. At least with you here, you can act as a voice of reason. And when this is over, you can help restore the planet. You know the people here and you know what needs to be done to make this place work. I can't guarantee you won't be dismissed anyway, but the fact that the senate didn't send me with orders to do so immediately has to mean they see value in you being here. As do I.

"Or, if you want, once the rebellion is over you can go back to Earth with me. I assure you I will be leaving as soon as things are pacified. I will do all I can to help you salvage your career, to share the credit for putting things in order here. We can both advance our positions."

Wells shook his head. "You think this is about my career? Asha, this is about what's *right*. I'm sorry, I just can't."

"What's *right*? Is rebellion right? Do these colonists think about the enormous cost of maintaining the transports routes here? The ships that ferried them so far from Earth. The navy that protected them when the hegemony and the union would have conquered their pathetic little world? God, Everett, you are a fool."

Wells looked across the desk at her. He had a passing urge to argue with her, to try to make her understand. But he just shook his head. They were products of the same corrupt system, and he understood how she had become what she had. And he knew the same thing could have happened to him.

There but for the grace of God go I . . .

Finally, he just said, "Goodbye, Asha. Be careful. Keep an eye on Semmes. You think the rebellion is all but crushed, but I know these colonists better than you. They are strong . . . and they won't give up easily."

"You needn't worry about me, Everett. Semmes is . . . controllable. And I don't underestimate the colonists. I respect their will, and I'll admit Damian Ward is a twist I had not anticipated. But he's just one man, and while he's brought with him a group of veterans, they're still isolated and contained. They are unable to communicate in any effective manner, and that means they can't recruit help. We know where they are, and once we have a plan of attack, we'll rout them. Or they'll simply run out of food. And ammunition. Their position is untenable. This will all be over in a matter of weeks. And crushing the Guardians and their allies will be a lesson to all the other potential rebel groups on this planet—not to mention the other colonies—one they will not soon forget."

Kill all the Guardians, and a new group will rise up in their place. Make your martyrs, though—just leave me out of it.

"I wish you the best, Asha . . . I truly do. Now if you will excuse me, my ship leaves tomorrow, and I have—"

The comm unit buzzed. Stanton looked down at it, startled. It was late for anyone to be calling her.

She reached down, tapped the button on top of the unit. "Stanton here."

"This is Captain Polk, Your Excellency. There is some kind of disturbance at the spaceport. We've lost contact with all units on duty at the facility and in the surrounding area."

Wells sat still, listening. He didn't know what was going on, but he had a pretty good idea things had already become more complicated than Stanton had expected.

"I /urrend—" Killian's gun spat death, and the federal soldier fell back, leaving a spray of blood from half a dozen wounds. The captain had his orders, but he also had his experience. He'd seen phony surrenders used as deceptions, as ways to kill. It was a tactic favored by the hegemony special forces, and he'd seen comrades die as a result. Taking fighters prisoner in the middle of an operation this desperate jeopardized its success . . . and along with it the very survival of the rebellion. Besides, he'd seen the man he'd just killed shoot down two of his own people a few minutes before. He'd have roasted the bastard on a spit if he'd had the time.

"We've got the communications center, sir." Ash Tull came running up, emerging from a dense cloud of smoke in the center of the main concourse. "We disabled everything. The federal observer's people were trying to get through, but we just shut the channel down."

"That should give them something to think about." Killian looked down and shook his head. "It also means we're going to have soldiers here . . . and soon. We've got to get Captain Nerov to her ship. Now."

"Yes, sir. Her people are already on the way. Colonel Morgan's troops are with her." Tull paused. "I sent a squad of rangers with them, sir. It was all we could spare at the time."

Killian smiled, amused at Ash's thought that eight or ten of his rangers could somehow save the day if fifty veterans couldn't. It was a trait of military formations, to match themselves in a hierarchy, to imagine themselves better than their enemies . . . or even their friends. He knew his rangers were capable . . . but he'd served in the war with some of the people following Morgan to *Vagabond*, and he knew they were damned good, too.

"All right, Ash. I want you to take command here. You need to secure the rest of the spaceport . . . and hold off any attempts to retake it before *Vagabond* lifts. Then you get the hell out. You understand me? We're here to get that ship in the air, and that's all. Once that's done, I don't want one more ranger dying to hold this place. Just get the hell out. Understand?"

"Yes, sir." He stared back at Killian. "What about you, sir?"

Killian looked out into the concourse. His vision was mostly blocked by the smoke, but he knew what lay beyond. The docking area. *Vagabond*.

"I'm going to the station, Ash. I'm going to make sure nothing up there gets in the way of this mission succeeding."

CHAPTER 30

"The engines and the reactor are stone cold, Captain. We need at least thirty minutes to warm up the systems." Griff Daniels slid into his chair, his hands flying over the controls. He knew *Vagabond* as well as the ship's captain.

Almost as well at least.

"No chance, Griff. We'll have to do a cold start. The reactor first . . . and then two minutes later the engines. I want *Vagabond* in the air in five minutes, max."

"Captain, that's crazy."

"No argument there. But that's what we're going to do anyway. It's what we have to do." She stared at her first mate. "Griff, people died to get us here. They're still dying. We got lucky, scored a surprise victory here . . . but do you think we really have thirty minutes? You think our escort can hold this place for half an hour? No—they can't. So we get this ship ready, and we get the fuck out of here so they can do the same."

Nerov leaned back in her seat. She hadn't intended to unload on her first officer, but she wasn't someone who was comfortable with others making sacrifices for her. She'd seen the fighting in the spaceport, and it had been fierce. Killian's people had taken the facility, but they'd paid for it in blood. And they were going to pay more until *Vagabond* was airborne.

Daniels was silent, staring across the ship's tiny bridge toward her. "I'm sorry, Griff. I know you're right, but we just don't have time."

Daniels nodded. "I understand, Captain. But if we blow up trying to launch, the rebellion is doomed . . . and everybody lost here died for nothing."

Sasha didn't answer. There was nothing to say. Daniels was right. But there was still no choice.

Griff turned back toward his controls. "Give me ten minutes, Captain. We can do a controlled reactor start in that time and get the engines warmed up a little."

Ten minutes . . .

Every minute would cost lives. But the extra time would increase the chances of success, too.

"Do it . . . but not a second more. We launch in ten minutes no matter what."

"Yes, Captain."

Nerov jumped out of her chair, moving swiftly through the hatch and back toward *Vagabond*'s cargo hold. The corridor was small, and in several places conduits and pipes ran low, forcing her to duck. But she knew every nook and cranny of her ship, and she dodged every obstacle effortlessly.

She opened the hatch to the cargo area and stepped inside. It was full of armed men and women, rebels, combat veterans all. The force that would take the orbital station . . . or be wiped out trying.

They were all here, a few of them gripping small handholds, but most just standing in the center of the hold.

Nerov saw Luci Morgan. The colonel was speaking with Captain Killian. Nerov couldn't hear what they were saying, but it was obvious neither of them was happy.

"Colonel . . ." She glanced over at Killian. "And, Captain . . . we're executing an expedited launch procedure, so we need to get your people as secure as possible. I'm afraid *Vagabond* doesn't have nearly enough berths, so we're going to have to improvise." She reached to the side, opening a small compartment. "These cables are for EVAs, in case we ever need to repair anything on the ship's hull." She pulled out two large loops. "We'll have to string these across the hold . . . and your people will just have to hold on the best they can. It's far from ideal, but I can't think of any other way."

"Thank you, Captain." Morgan's tone changed, the anger Nerov had seen virtually gone, replaced by at least some level of respect. "We will manage." She turned and looked out over the mass of her troopers. "Sully, Hastenbeck . . . get over here and take these cables. We've got to string them around the bay so you grunts have something to hold on to."

Nerov watched for a few seconds. Then she went back toward the bridge. She glanced at her chronometer. Six minutes to launch.

She stepped through the corridor, reaching out, touching the cool metal of the wall to the side. *Vagabond.* Her ship . . . almost her child. She knew she was taking a crazy risk . . . and even if it worked, the federals would retake the spaceport. Win or lose, she knew she wouldn't be landing anytime soon.

C'mon, old girl, we've been through a lot, you and me. But this is the tightest spot we've seen . . . don't let me down now . . .

She stepped through the hatch and headed back toward the bridge. She looked down at her chronometer.

Five minutes . . .

"What the hell is the problem up here? The order is forward. Are you going to let yourselves get bogged down by a bunch of rebel scum?"

Johnson looked up at the officer. He didn't know Captain Crandall all that well, and what he knew he didn't like.

"Sir, they've got two heavy autocannons . . . situated there . . . and there." He pointed out toward the spaceport as he spoke. "We need to move around, approach from a different—"

"Your orders are to attack, Sergeant, not to second-guess strategy. Those people are nothing but criminals, traitors. They won't stand against a concerted assault."

Johnson caught himself before he said what first popped into his mind. He was sick and tired of these officers from the anti-insurgency forces. They considered themselves elite soldiers, but they were nothing more than bullies, used to crushing unarmed mobs. But Johnson had seen the revolutionaries in combat. Up close. And he had no doubt the forces in the spaceport were the best the rebels had.

"Yes, sir."

"Take your troopers in, Sergeant. The entire platoon is to move forward at once."

"Yes, Captain." He turned, looking down the line at his troopers, most of them prone behind a small berm. "Prepare to assault!"

He could see the soldiers looking back at him; he could feel their fear. He wasn't sure they would even follow him forward . . . but he was certain none of them would get to those guns.

He grabbed his rifle and he waved it over his head. "Platoon . . . advance." He jumped up over the small lip of ground, and he ran forward. There was no enemy fire, at least not for the first few seconds. He suspected the rebels had limited ammunition, precious rounds they wouldn't waste firing at his soldiers in cover.

He glanced back, getting a glimpse of his people surging forward. He didn't know if they were all moving, but at least some of them were. He pushed harder, realizing there still wasn't any fire.

Maybe we caught them sleeping! Maybe they're out of ammo . . .

He felt a surge of excitement. They were a good third of the way to the enemy now. Perhaps his people would take the position after all . . .

Then he heard it. A loud crack, ripping through the air. And all hell broke loose.

The rebel autocannons roared, and all across the frontage of his platoon they spread death. His troopers began to fall, one at a time at first and then in clumps.

The soldiers hesitated, frozen in the middle of the field for a few seconds. It was the worst thing they could have done.

The autocannons ripped into their ragged line, and Johnson saw them going down. A quarter of his people were hit . . . then a third.

The fear speared him in the gut, a terror like nothing he'd experienced before. His people weren't going to make it to the rebel guns. *He* wasn't going to make it. And if he didn't get them out of there he wouldn't have any soldiers left.

"Retreat!" His voice was ragged, his panic clear. "Run! All of you . . . run!"

Even as he yelled to his soldiers, Johnson was fleeing himself. Not sure that it even mattered. There was nothing in his mind, no thought save the need to escape . . . and the choking fear.

"They're running!" The ranger turned from the autocannon as he spoke, the weapon falling silent as his finger slipped from the trigger.

"Maintain fire." Ash Tull was crouched behind the position. He'd handpicked the two spots for the autocannons—an educated guess on where the federals would attack. His people had given them a bloody nose, but he knew they would come again . . . and they would move around, find a less protected spot to assault. He didn't have enough people to defend the spaceport, not for long. With the casualties they'd suffered and the people Killian had taken on *Vagabond*, Tull had less than thirty rangers left. And they had to cover kilometers of spaceport perimeter.

The ranger at the autocannon hesitated, just for a second.

"I said fire!" Tull's voice was harsh, loud. The federals were running and ammunition was low. He understood the trooper's thought process. But every minute counted now . . . and the more he could shake up the federals, the more time he would have.

Tull looked out as the autocannon opened up again, watching as another federal fell almost at once, and perhaps two or three more in total before they got back in cover. He stared at the field.

They won't come back this way—they'll move around the perimeter . . .

His mind whirled about what to do. The other side of the spaceport, the periphery farthest from Landfall, was the weakest held, with just a few pickets in place. But it would take time for the feds to redeploy. They'd have to go around the circumference, at least fifteen kilometers.

They won't want to wait that long. They'll move in both directions, just far enough to be out of range of the autocannons.

"Ranger, get that gun ready to move. I want you half a klick south of here. Grab the best spot you can, a good field of fire and as much cover as you can find."

"Yes, sir." The man turned and flashed a glance at his partner. Then the two of them began pulling the weapon off its stand.

Tull turned and walked twenty meters north toward the second emplacement. "You men get that weapon moved. Now. One-half kilometer north. Dig in and get ready. The federals will be back."

"Yes, sir."

Tull turned and walked back, taking a deep breath as he did. He looked at the four rangers he'd positioned along this section of line, all that would remain once the autocannons moved. The four men were twenty-five meters apart, far too much ground to cover with an assault rifle.

I hope I'm right moving these guns . . . because if they come back this way, they're going to slice through like a knife through butter.

He looked out over the ground, no-man's-land, at least for a few moments more.

Hopefully long enough.

"I've only got seven troopers left, sir." Johnson stood in front of Colonel Semmes, trying to hold himself as erect and steady as possible. He'd managed to avoid taking a bullet—somehow—but he was exhausted and sore. He'd fallen twice, and a shard of rock had ripped a nasty cut in his arm. His people had charged three times . . . but the rebel commander's intuition was uncanny. The bastard had managed to move his heavy weapons around, placing them in exactly the right spots to repel each assault.

"I understand that, Sergeant, but we cannot take the pressure off. I have brought up reinforcements. You are to take a fresh platoon and attack again . . . at once." There wasn't a trace of understanding or sympathy in the officer's voice.

Johnson stood in front of the army commander, trying to hold back the shakes. He'd almost lost it when the first attack was crushed, and he'd routed himself, for a moment. But he pulled it together, just barely. He'd never felt fear like that before, the almost overwhelming need to run away, to escape the field, whatever the consequences. He'd managed to get control of himself, and even to lead two more attacks, both of them repulsed almost as severely as the first. But now he honestly wasn't sure he could do it again . . . even though he knew Semmes was likely to have him hanged—or to shoot him where he stood—if he refused.

"Sir, with all due respect, we should move around the perimeter of the spaceport. The enemy is much weaker—"

"There is no time for that, Sergeant."

Semmes's tone was clearly intended to discourage further commentary, but Johnson held his ground. *What the hell do I have to lose?* "Colonel, sir, I request that you commit more than a single platoon to the attack." He stood nervously, struggling to hold Semmes's gaze. The colonel had quickly established a reputation for arrogance and for disciplining subordinates harshly. But the thought of sending another platoon into a useless slaughter was even harder to take.

Semmes glared back for a few seconds. "Very well, Sergeant. We have three platoons ready to go . . . and I will commit them all." He paused for an instant. "And you will lead them. Prove to me you are correct. Retake the spaceport, and you will have your lieutenant's bars as a reward."

Johnson stared back in shock. He'd expected to escape the burden of commanding the assault, but it was still there . . . and heavier than ever. Semmes had offered him a great reward for success.

And he didn't doubt for a second the penalty for failure would be severe.

"Yes, Colonel. I will see it done, sir."

There was nothing else he could say.

"The reactor is at 40 percent, Captain. I've initiated emergency warm-up procedures for the engines."

"All right, Griff. Keep going. We need that reactor at 90 percent for liftoff . . . and we're going in two minutes no matter what." Nerov sat in her chair, restless, fidgety. She was about to put her beloved ship through its greatest test. The minimal warm-up time allowed a much better chance of success than the desperate dead cold start she'd originally planned, but it still wasn't ideal. Moreover, she hated that those extra minutes weren't free. Without communications, she didn't know exactly what was going on along the spaceport's perimeter, but *Vagabond*'s external microphones were picking up the sounds of gunfire . . . and that meant men and women were dying to buy her that time.

She put her hand down on the communications panel, flipping the switch to the intercom. "Colonel Morgan . . . is everybody in place and hanging on back there?"

"Yes, Captain." Morgan's reply sounded confident, but Nerov had her concerns. She doubted the retired officer had been through a liftoff with no more restraint than hanging on to an EVA cable. The whole mission would be pointless if *Vagabond* managed to dock with the station with a hold full of injured soldiers, too battered to take out the security forces.

"Reactor at 60 percent, Captain."

Wow . . . 60 percent already. He's pushing it to the edge.

"Good, Griff . . . keep it up."

Her eyes dropped to the small screen in front of her. She'd plotted the ascent three times . . . and checked it another half dozen. It was spot-on, there wasn't a doubt in her mind. But she checked again anyway.

It was a tight route, with little room for error. If *Vagabond* lifted too quickly, she'd enter orbit . . . and the station's secondary batteries would be able to target her. Nerov knew her ship was tough, but that kind of firepower at point-blank range would melt her to plasma in seconds.

If the ship ascended too slowly, it would miss the insertion angle needed to come in precisely in the station's blind spot . . . which would leave her the choice of entering orbit beyond the platform — and getting blasted to atoms — or landing back at the spaceport — and getting blasted to atoms by the federals on the ground.

No, she had to hit the target dead-on. If her piloting skills failed, by even the smallest margin, she would end up dead . . . along with everyone else on the ship.

"Reactor at eighty, Cap." Daniels looked over at her, his expression anxious.

"Let's get the engines going, Griff."

"Feeding power into the drive systems. Engine temp is climbing. Two hundred degrees. Three hundred . . ."

Nerov leaned forward, her hands gripping the ship's controls. She was *Vagabond*'s pilot as well as its captain, and if Griff and the two crew members in the ship's engine room managed to quick-start the engines, the success of the mission rested with her flying skills.

"Six hundred degrees, Captain. Reactor at 90 percent."

She nodded, her eyes focused on the control panel. Ninety on the reactor was fine, but six hundred degrees was still cold for the engine core.

She paused for a few seconds, the only sound on the bridge the gunfire transmitted from the ship's hull sensors. It was getting louder . . . and closer. There was no time.

She flipped a series of levers, feeding power into the engines. Then she switched on the intercom. "Prepare for launch. Everybody in the hold, hang on to those cables!"

She gripped the ship's throttle, and she looked down for a few seconds at the engine firing control. Then she pulled the throttle hard . . . and flipped the launch switch.

Ash Tull was running. The federals had been fools for a long while, arrogant and disorganized, sending platoon-strength forces against his prepared positions. He'd known, perhaps longer than anyone on the rebel side save Captain Killian, that one of their greatest weapons was the sense of superiority many of the federal officers felt, the contempt they had for their opponents. It had been on display again . . . and it had allowed Tull and his people to buy the time for *Vagabond* to lift off.

They'd finally learned from their mistake, and sent a force his rangers couldn't possibly handle.

He paused and glanced up for a second, looking at the still-visible glow of the ship's engines as they moved higher, bound for the orbital platform. Tull didn't know much about spaceflight, but he was well aware Captain Nerov had her plate full executing the hairsbreadth maneuver. He was also aware he couldn't do anything about that. His people had accomplished their mission. It had cost them half their number . . . and the survivors were running for their lives. Yet he felt good about his role.

Gunfire echoed behind him. The federals were as disorganized in victory as they'd been in defeat, and the pursuit was a confused affair. He could only imagine what the federal commanders were thinking, watching as *Vagabond* rose into the sky. Would they figure out the plan? Or would they just assume a smuggler was trying to escape, to get off-world and run the federal blockade?

He moved forward, slipping around the edge of a large storage structure. He was alone—all his people were. That was always the plan. The instant they heard *Vagabond*'s engines roar to life, they were to scatter, disappearing into the spaceport, giving the federals no single target to pursue.

He snuck around the edge of the large concrete building, peering around the corner before he continued on. The sounds of the gunfire were receding, the main federal force far behind him now. But that didn't mean he couldn't run into a guard or a scout somewhere out here.

He could see the woods ahead, his immediate destination. All his people were heading there, by whatever route they could manage. The forest wasn't exactly a safe refuge, but he knew any of his troopers who made it there had a good chance of getting back to Dover.

But how many will get to the woods?

He didn't know . . . and he realized there was no point in making wild guesses. He'd see soon enough how many of his rangers escaped . . . and he'd have the final count of the cost of taking the spaceport and holding it long enough for Nerov and the strike team to take off.

It's going to be steep. I fucking hope it's worth it.

He glanced back up, but *Vagabond* was gone now, the fiery trail of her engines too far up to see, even in the darkness of the night sky.

Vagabond would reach the station in less than twenty minutes . . . and then the fighters in her cargo hold would carry the future of the rebellion with them into battle, as his own people had when they held the spaceport.

And then we'll find out if we're the heroes who saved the rebellion.

CHAPTER 31

"A smuggler's vessel?" Asha Stanton stood in the situation room, watching the footage from the spaceport. "They launched an attack to steal a smuggler's ship? That doesn't make any sense. They have to know the blockading ships will be on alert. They'll never get out of the system."

"Yes, Your Excellency . . . but nevertheless, that is what they have done. My people have retaken the spaceport. We attempted to take prisoners for, ah, interrogation . . . but unfortunately, they all fought to the death."

Wells was sitting silently at the table, watching this all unfold. Semmes was full of shit on one thing at least. His words suggested the rebel force had been wiped out . . . but Wells had seen other footage from the spaceport's security cameras, scenes of men and women moving back toward the woods, escaping. Semmes had retaken the spaceport, but he'd lost ten soldiers to every rebel casualty . . . and he'd been too late to stop the smuggler's ship from lifting off.

And I very much doubt the rebels risked that just to help a smuggler escape.

"That is far from an adequate report, Colonel."

Semmes stood still, not responding. He was confused, still trying to figure out what had happened. It just didn't make any sense. If the orbital platform didn't blast the ship to atoms, the blockading squadron would. If it was an attempt to escape, to get back to Earth, say, and seek help from one of the other superpowers, it seemed insanely desperate. Their chances of getting out of the system were nil . . . and none of the other nations would come openly to the aid of a rebellion that was on the verge of defeat.

The rebels' options were limited, but he'd have expected an all-out assault on the federal complex before something like this.

What can they gain by getting a single ship off the ground?

"I want information, Colonel, and I want it now. Get me a prisoner, review every second of security cam footage—whatever it takes. But I need to know what is going on."

She's scared.

Wells watched Stanton as she paced back and forth across the room. She had publicly discounted the possibility that the rebel attack was any real threat . . . but he suspected she was far less confident than her public performance suggested. And he was, too. He didn't know what was going on, but he had warned her not to underestimate the rebels. He certainly wasn't.

An aide called out, "Your Excellency, I have Captain Cross on the line."

"Put her on, Lieutenant."

"Your Excellency, we are tracking the vessel the rebels seized. It should enter weapons range in five minutes, thirty seconds. What do you want us to do?"

Wells watched, knowing Stanton had no real choice. He was sure she'd love to have the crew in her hands, to question them and find out what desperate plan was behind the attack. But she'd never take the chance of trying to capture the rebel vessel and failing. She couldn't.

"Destroy it."

Wells sat silently, wondering what the rebels were up to. He had no idea, but he was damned sure they didn't pull the stunt they had to run a ship up to orbit only to get blasted to dust.

Vagabond shook hard. Nerov was taking her ship up at a sharp angle, a far more vertical ascent than it was designed to handle. In her mind she saw the hull glowing, the heat coming right to the verge of melt-ing even the iridium-alloy armor her smuggling profits had provided. But it was the only way this was going to work. If she missed the right angle—and hitting the orbital station was like shooting a tossed coin with a bullet from ten kilometers—the station's batteries would open up, blasting *Vagabond* to atoms.

Just hold together, girl.

She wondered how the troopers in the hold were keeping it to-gether. She could only imagine how rough a ride they had back there. She was a hardened spacer, and even her stomach was rebel-ling against the wild turns and the rapid ascent.

And she was strapped in. She couldn't imagine it was pleasant in that rear compartment right now.

"All right, Griff. We're coming up on final approach. I'm going to need all the power I can get . . . and you need to be ready with the boarding portal."

It had been more than five years since *Vagabond* had boarded another vessel, and even then, it had been a freighter, not a giant orbital fortress. The dynamics of the approach were far simpler in space than coming up out of a planet's gravity well . . . and there weren't many cargo ships that could have blasted *Vagabond* to scrap if her captain misjudged the approach angle by a fraction of a degree.

"The reactor's at one zero five, Captain. The portal's ready."

She could hear the tension in Daniels's voice. She had tremen-dous confidence in her first officer, but she knew he'd never been at the controls during a hostile boarding action. He'd been on board *Vagabond* during the war, but he'd been one of the crew, waiting next to the portal, weapons in hand, while Sergei Brinker sat in his current place.

That's all right. You've never boarded an orbital fort from below either, so if you can do it, so can Griff.

She tapped the intercom. "Colonel Morgan, are your people okay back there?"

"Ah, yes, Captain Nerov. We're ready." She sounded anything but; however, what else was she going to say?

Nerov suspected the boarding party was more than ready to get off *Vagabond* . . . at least until the federals on the station started shooting.

"Okay, Colonel, we're going in. We'll be docking in . . . one hundred thirty seconds."

"We're ready," Morgan said with more conviction this time.

"Roger that. One hundred thirty seconds."

Nerov had gone over *Vagabond*'s layout with Morgan, at least in the minute she'd been able to spare before launch. The boarding portal was close to the cargo hold, but Morgan would have to get her bruised and nauseated troops down the main corridor and up one ladder to the upper deck. In two minutes.

"Griff, I'm bringing us in on final approach." She paused. "Double the breaching charges."

Daniels turned back and looked at her. "Double . . . Captain, that could blow the portal."

"There's no choice, Griff. The armor on that thing is lighter on the planetary side, but it's still a hell of a lot tougher than any freighter's hull. And if we don't penetrate in the first twenty seconds, we're going to snap the portal off clean anyway. That will be the end of the mission . . . and mostly likely the end of us."

Daniels turned back to his workstation, moving his hands over the controls. "Charges doubled, Captain."

Nerov sighed softly.

One more big risk.

She angled the throttle, cutting *Vagabond*'s thrust slightly. The station wasn't visible yet, but her scanners gave her a perfect image. She tapped the controls again. And again. She had AI data programmed into the nav system, but she knew this was going to take her own experience, so she was flying by instinct as much as anything.

"Sixty kilometers." Daniels's voice was edgy.

Nerov stared at the scanner, ignoring everything, tapping the reverse thrust, slowing *Vagabond* as it closed with its target. She angled the throttle, adjusting to the greatly reduced gravity and air pressure at this altitude. The ship was close to the edge of the station's blind spot. Too close. She pulled harder on the throttle, bringing *Vagabond* up right under the station.

"Thirty kilometers."

She could see the station now . . . barely. The scanning plot showed the five-kilometer behemoth, and *Vagabond*'s location as well. But the fire arcs of the platform's batteries were as much guess-work as anything more substantive. When Nerov had proposed the plan, she did so with a greater degree of certainty than she'd actually possessed. The brutal truth was, there simply wasn't another option. So it was just as easy to let Damian Ward believe she knew the specs of the station with more assurance than she did.

"Ten kilometers."

It was time for the final approach.

She took a deep breath and gripped the throttle tightly.

"Forty seconds, Colonel!"

You can do this . . .

"The rebel ship is still in our blind spot, Captain."

Mara Cross sat in her chair in the center of the station's main control room. She'd been watching the vessel approach, waiting for it to enter into the range of her guns. Her orders were clear—no warnings, no negotiations . . . she was to destroy the ship.

But the enemy hadn't moved into her fire arc. The platform's main guns faced outward, positioned to defend against any vessels approaching the planet. Even the secondaries could only hit targets in orbit . . . or a bit below that if she used the positioning thrusters to reorient the station.

What the hell are they doing? They can't stay down there . . . and as soon as they show themselves we'll blow them to bits . . .

"Lieutenant, get me Commodore Quintel." Cross had consid-ered every option—every one she could think of—and she didn't see how the rebels were going to get past her. But there was no sense taking chances.

"Commodore Quintel on your line, Captain."

"What is it, Mara?" Quintel and Cross went way back, to the pre-war navy, and she knew the commander of the blockading squadron was a true professional.

"Commodore, we have an unauthorized vessel approaching the

station. The federal observer has issued orders for its destruction. I suggest you put your squadron on alert in case it gets past us."

"Why haven't you destroyed it already, Mara?"

"The ship's been coming at us from our blind spot, sir. All the way from liftoff." She paused. She couldn't see how the ship could get by her . . . but she knew whoever was flying that thing was good. Really good.

Quintel was silent for a few seconds. Then he said, "Very well, Mara. I will go to yellow alert." He paused. "Just in case."

"Thank . . ." Her words stopped dead. Suddenly, she understood. "Commodore, I have to go. I request you go to general quarters and await further word." She cut the connection, hardly proper protocol when dealing with a superior officer, especially one you just asked to bring his force to red alert. But she knew what the rebel was going to do. And she was almost out of time.

"Lieutenant, bring the station to red alert. All security forces are to report to the lower levels, armed for battle."

The bridge officer hesitated, staring back with a surprised look on his face.

"Now, Lieutenant!" Cross's tone was harsh, urgent. "We're about to be boarded!"

"As soon as the portal opens we go in . . . and we go hard. No hesitation to fire, no prisoners . . . not until we secure the station." She hated how much she sounded like Killian. The ranger was standing off to the side, with about ten of his people. He had the best poker face Morgan had ever seen, but she could see that he was surprised at the brutality of her orders.

The difference between us, you psychopath, is that I do what I have to do and you enjoy it.

"You all have the public data on the station's configuration, but the control and defensive systems are all guesswork. We've got two goals and only two. We take control of the station . . . and we get Dr. Holcomb safely to the bridge or the main data center."

She turned toward Holcomb. "Doctor, I need you to stay back." She gestured toward four men standing, two on either side of him.

"These men are here to protect you, Doctor. They're all decorated veterans, so please do whatever they say—and remember, if you get killed, we're all dead, us here and the rest of the rebel forces on the ground. We must succeed, and you're the only one who can do it. Every one of us is expendable. You are not."

Holcomb nodded. "Yes, Colonel." The scientist had never been a soldier, but he didn't look too happy about hiding behind his new allies when the shooting started. She didn't know much about Holcomb, no more than most soldiers knew about the man who had designed half their weapons systems. But her respect for him was growing.

She looked at her soldiers. They were veterans, every one of them, but most of them were pale now, or one shade or another of sickly green. The cargo hold was a nightmare, clumps of vomit floating everywhere in the zero-g environment. She'd been thrilled when the order came to ready her people to board the station. But gut-sick soldiers weren't at their best for combat.

Vagabond shook hard . . . then a few seconds later even harder. Morgan didn't know Captain Nerov, at least not beyond a brief introduction at the planning sessions for the mission. She knew the smuggler had never been in the military, but Nerov carried herself with a quiet discipline that reminded Morgan of some of the better naval officers she'd known. She'd ended up as confident in Nerov as she could be in anyone executing such a wild and reckless scheme.

"All forces . . . prepare to board . . ." Nerov's voice blasted out of every speaker in *Vagabond*.

Morgan's eyes were locked on the hatch in front of her. She knew she should be farther back—she was the expedition's commander, and if she went down in the first seconds of combat it would imperil the entire mission. But some things defied logic . . . and she was where she knew she had to be.

A series of loud booms echoed through the corridor, and the ship shook hard again. The boarding charges. They had either blown a hole in the station's hull . . . or the mission was over, a failure, with nothing left for her people to do but die . . .

The hatch swung open. She hesitated, for just an instant, staring through the meter and a half diameter tube. Then her eyes focused . . . the shattered section of hull, and the interior of the station beyond.

"Let's go! Forward." She leapt into the portal, bending down and moving as quickly as she could. She could feel her soldiers behind her, but she was alone in front.

She saw movement, and she fired, almost by instinct. She wasn't sure if she hit anything, but she lunged forward, leaping down from the portal to the deck half a meter below, feeling the impact as her boots hit the hard metal. *Vagabond*'s lower levels were close to zero g's, but the station's stabilization jets provided a reasonable level of artificial gravity.

She moved to the side, her eyes darting around, looking for enemies. She almost stumbled, her body reacting sluggishly to the change in gravity, but she caught herself, just as she saw the federal. She didn't know if he was armed security—or just naval crew here cleaning up or fixing a burnt-out system—but she didn't wait to find out. Her finger tightened on the trigger, and the federal went down.

She heard a blast of fire next to her, the trooper behind her firing at the same target. She glanced back quickly—three of her people were through now—and then she looked across the compartment again. It looked like some kind of storage area, with a row of metal canisters lined up along one of the walls.

"Check those cases, Corporal. Make sure there's nobody hiding over there." She pointed as she snapped out the command, and then she raced forward toward a large hatch on the far side of the room. "The rest of you, with me."

She stopped at the hatch, her fingers moving across the small control panel on the wall next to it. She tried to open it three times, but it wasn't working. She knew what that meant. Whoever was in command of the station, he or she had put the defensive systems on alert.

She reached into a pouch hanging from her belt, pulling out a small lump of a gray putty-like substance. She pushed the plastic explosive against the edge of the door.

"Back!" She waved for her troopers to move away. Then she followed, ducking behind a small crate and pushing the button on the detonator in her hand.

The blast was loud, the sound echoing throughout the compartment. She ran forward, waving for all her people to follow as she raced through the now-open doorway.

"You all know what to do. Move out, find the control room. And keep your eyes open—nobody gets scragged because they're not paying attention."

Her troopers were all veterans, but they'd been retired for years now . . . and a sluggish return of battle reflexes was a shitty reason for any of her people to die.

She held her rifle in front as she ran through the hatch, her head whipping back and forth, scanning the hall, looking for threats, even any hints of movement.

Carelessness was a shitty reason for her to die, too.

CHAPTER 32

"Team Alpha, move toward Yellow Section. Team Delta, to Blue Section." Mara Cross was staring at her display, watching the action as her people fought to repel the boarders. She was too experienced a spacer not to take the threat seriously, but she hadn't really thought a group of rebels could take control of the station. But these weren't shopkeepers and farmers, that much was obvious. They were trained soldiers . . . and they were outfighting her people.

"Captain, we've lost contact with Team Epsilon. The AI reports enemy incursions in White Section . . . moving toward Red."

Fuck.

The control center was in Red Section, along with everything else the invaders needed to capture if they were to gain control over the station.

She leaned down over the comm unit. "Belay my prior orders. All forces, pull back toward Red Section. Hold at all costs at every entry point."

She looked around the control center. Cross was a veteran of the war; indeed, most of her people were. But she hadn't considered the rebels to be a real enemy, not really . . . and certainly not capable of taking the station. But the casualty reports told a different story. She was losing three troopers to every rebel her forces took down. And she didn't outnumber them enough to sustain that ratio.

She reached down to her comm unit, punching at the small keypad. "Commodore?"

A few seconds passed as the signal traveled to the ships on station in the system.

"Yes, Captain?"

"Commodore, we've been boarded and there is a possibility the enemy could gain control of the station. Requesting immediate assistance."

She waited again, her stomach twisted into knots as the seconds passed. This would hurt her career, if not end it permanently. No board of inquiry would rate a bunch of rebel raiders the equivalent of her people. She would take the blame, almost certainly. But right now she was just worried about making sure the enemy didn't gain full control of the fortress . . . and surviving.

"We're on our way, Captain. Estimated arrival in two hours, ten minutes."

"Thank you, sir."

Two hours and ten minutes . . .

She'd known the amount of time it would take for the squadron to intervene, of course, at least roughly. But now it truly hit her. Quintel and his ships could retake the station, but they would be far too late to save her and her people. If they were going to hold out, they'd have to do it themselves.

"Lieutenant, you have the con." She stood up, reaching down to her side, pulling her pistol from its holster. "I'm going to command the defense directly. You are to keep me informed of the rebels movements—you're my eyes and ears."

"Yes, Captain." The officer didn't sound pleased about the responsibility, but Cross didn't care. The control of the station would be decided in the corridors and compartments leading to the critical areas, not sitting on the bridge looking at screens and shouting out orders that were already too late as she spoke them.

If they want my station, they'll have to take it over my dead body . . .

"**All ships, attack** pattern Sigma-5." Simon Quintel stared straight ahead, his eyes on *Emmerich*'s main screen. The squadron's commander was a hero of the last war, and his performance in the final battle of that conflict had won him his commodore's star. Like most federals, he didn't think much of the rebels on Alpha-2, but he knew Mara Cross. He'd seen her in action. And the fear he'd heard in her voice had driven home just how serious the situation was on the station.

"All ships confirm, sir. Attack pattern Sigma-5."

Quintel nodded and sighed to himself. He thought about Cross and her people, about the fight he knew was going on inside the station, and his frustration grew. *Emmerich* was more than two hours out, and some of the squadron's vessels were farther still, much too distant to intervene in the fight now under way. But he swore one thing: if he wasn't there in time to save Cross and her crew, he'd damned sure avenge them. Quintel wasn't a brutal man by nature, but he was intensely loyal . . . and he had no pity for any rebel bastards who killed his fellow spacers.

"All ships increase thrust to 110 percent."

"Yes, sir."

Quintel was pushing hard—perhaps harder than his ships could handle. It might even cost him a ship or two from the eight frigates under his command, their reactors scragged. But damage could be repaired, and he wouldn't need the whole squadron anyway. The fortress was heavily armed, but the AI would disable the weapons systems if an enemy gained control. And the rebels wouldn't be able to reactivate them, not in a couple hours. That would take a miracle.

So even if just one ship gets there, we should be able to finish these rebels off.

"All ships report 110 percent thrust, sir."

Quintel nodded. "Very well, Lieutenant. Steady as she goes."

Hold on, Mara.

We're coming.

"**What the hell** is going on up there?" Asha Stanton stood at the end of the table, looking utterly spent. "They're trying to take the orbital platform? Why? Even if they seize it, they'll never hold it. The squadron will retake it before they can make any use of it. Unless . . ." She turned toward Semmes. "Colonel, they can't turn the station's weapons on the planet, can they?"

"No, Your Excellency. That's part of the reason they were able to board . . . because none of the weapons are positioned to fire on Alpha-2." Semmes paused. "They might be able to retask some of the missiles, but that would take days, and a lot of expertise they don't have."

Wells had been sitting quietly in the corner, trying to decide if he wanted to intervene or just wait things out. Alone among those in the room, he grasped that the federal position was in deadly peril. He'd almost decided to remain silent, but then he saw Stanton standing there, looking lost for the first time since he'd met her. As much as he hated what the federals had been doing since she arrived, he was still a part of the Federal America government himself—at least until his resignation reached Earth—and he couldn't let her lose this fight, not without trying to help.

"They're not going to launch missiles at the planet. They don't want to destroy this world; they want it for themselves."

Semmes glared at Wells. "Then what is the purpose behind this attack? What could they possibly gain?" The officer seemed surprised Everett had even spoken, but that didn't keep the dismissive tone from his voice.

Wells rolled his eyes at the man's bluster. "I tried to tell you, Colonel. I tried to explain the true nature of the unrest here, Asha. But you wouldn't listen. You both looked at these people as simple malcontents, as protestors who were only as bold as they were because I allowed them to become that way. But you misread the people, just as those on Earth who read my reports did the same."

Semmes shot out of his chair. "You piece of—"

"Sit down, Colonel!" Stanton shouted. The force was enough for him to slow, and the look in her eyes was enough to stop him completely. "We don't have time for egos. If Governor Wells has insights into this situation, we *will* hear them.

"Everett—what are we missing?"

He turned his attention fully on Stanton. "They don't want weapons of mass destruction to use on this world. They want to cut your jamming. They want to get the word out. What we're missing is that the Guardians in Dover aren't the only rebels on Alpha-2. There are thousands of citizens who will rise up and join the rebellion. But only if those leading it can reach them, coordinate with them. Your greatest weapon—in fact, the one move that's been the most effective since you arrived—is the jamming. It's crippled the rebellion—and yet they've still fought you to a draw. Imagine if they had their full numbers? The lack of communication has saved your forces from being overwhelmed, from being penned in and hunted down by a force that outnumbered them ten to one. Twenty to one."

Semmes stood in place, his expression leaving no doubt he thought that Wells was insane as well as incompetent. But Stanton had a different look on her face, one of dawning realization.

"It's a lovely fantasy you spin," Semmes said, "but you're forgetting the station's AI will shut down all functionality. They'll have to destroy the equipment, if they can even find it. They only have two hours, then the squadron will move in and take the station back."

"No, Colonel, *you're* forgetting the recent breakout from Cargraves Prison. Who do you think facilitated Dr. Holcomb's escape? And where do you think the doctor is now?" He shook his head. "You're underestimating them again."

Stanton stared at Wells, her expression morphing into one of shock, of near-panic. "Holcomb is a weapons and communications expert, Everett. Could he cut the jamming system in two hours? Or could he reactivate the self-destruct protocols or overload the reactor?"

"I don't know, Asha. But if I was you, I'd start thinking about how I'm going to deal with massive uprisings planetwide."

He wanted to feel satisfaction, knowing those who'd been sent to replace him now found themselves in a world of shit. But this was as much his fault as theirs, and despite the fact that he faced the almost certain end of his career, he was still loyal to Federal America. Sure, he understood the rebels, more at least than Stanton and Semmes and others like them, but he did not believe they had a right to revolt.

They were citizens of Federal America, and he condemned them for attacking their own government. And he knew there were thousands of inhabitants of Alpha-2, perhaps close to half to population, that remained loyal to the Earth government. The road to independence for Alpha-2 was a terrible one. He'd tried every way he could think of to avoid it, but to no avail. And he realized the worst still lay ahead. For both sides.

Morgan pressed herself against the bulkhead, standing back from the corridor. Her people had done well, but they weren't finished yet. Holcomb had made it clear he needed access to the control room to have any chance of disabling the jamming system. And the bridge was the last place the station's guards were holding out.

"Colonel . . ." Sasha Nerov's voice crackled through on the comm. The jamming was directed at the surface, but it was still affecting *Vagabond*'s comm, if less than completely.

"Yes, Captain?" She regretted the impatience in her tone the moment she uttered her reply. She knew if Nerov was calling her in the middle of the battle it had to be important, and most likely downright critical.

"We've got federal warships inbound, Colonel. Looks like eight ships, the entire blockading squadron." She left unspoken the one thing both of them knew. Each of those vessels had a full platoon of shock troops, more than enough to board and retake the station.

"Fuck." Morgan muttered the curse under her breath. "How long?"

"One hour, fifty minutes, at least for the first three ships. The others are strung out, coming in from their patrol stations. But they'll all be in range in less than eight hours."

"Three ships will be more than enough. There's no way my remaining troops can repel over a hundred fresh federals."

"Then you've got less than two hours, Colonel. Or all this was for nothing."

"Understood. Morgan out." She looked down the corridor. She had fourteen of her people here. Another dozen, at least, were down, and the others were scattered around the station, spread too thin as it was. She needed to rush the bridge, and damn the consequences. But she had to have more strength . . . and there was only one place to get it.

She tapped her comm unit. "Captain Killian . . ." She paused, almost changing her mind. But it was the only way. "I need your help. Can you get up here immediately with your people?"

"On my way, Colonel." The connection was staticky, but she could hear it in his voice, the thing she feared.

Eagerness.

"In place, now . . . all of you. We have to hold the bridge until the squadron arrives." Cross knew that wasn't going to happen, but no thread of her experience as a leader told her she should be honest with her people, not now. They needed to believe they had a chance, and she had to feed that delusion any way she could. The fighting on the station had been brutal, with neither side offering or expecting quarter. And if her people were marked to die, she'd resolved it would be weapons in hand, fighting to the end.

She'd watched the battle out in the corridor, everyone on the bridge had. She'd been on her way to direct the battle personally, but she'd only gotten a few meters down the hall before she heard the sounds of fighting just ahead and scrambled back.

The guards outside had been in a strong position, with a deadly field of fire down the only approach available to the invaders. The rebels had been pinned down, but then something had lit a fire under them. They'd launched an all-out attack. They paid dearly for it, but they'd also reached the outer door to the bridge . . . and killed every federal soldier they found there.

Now the glow of a plasma torch cutting through the armored bulkhead was visible. In a minute, perhaps less, the rebels would be through . . . and the final battle for the station would begin. Cross only had half a dozen of her people with her—two security troopers and the rest bridge officers.

The final battle wouldn't last long.

She walked behind a large console, ducking down and pulling her pistol from the holster. She stared at the door, aiming, ready, watching as the sparks from the torch moved up . . . then to the side.

The bridge was silent, save for the sounds of her people breathing and the crackling sound of the torch cutting through the bulkhead. Each passing second was slow, excruciating, but she held firm, waiting.

Waiting . . .

"Let me be perfectly clear, Captain. Anyone who surrenders in there is to be taken prisoner. Not gunned down, not slit across their throats. Not *scalped*." She had heard the rumors and she had no intention of tolerating barbarism from anyone under her command.

She wasn't sure Killian realized he was actually under her command, but if he pressed her too hard, he would find out.

"Understood, Colonel." The ranger's voice was matter-of-fact, with no trace of defiance or resentment. And that made her even more nervous.

Morgan looked down the corridor. The two troopers with the torch were almost done; in a few seconds her people would swarm inside the station's control room. The fortress would be theirs. For an hour and a half. Then the federal ships would be there . . . and her battered and exhausted forces would try to hold out against the fresh federal shock troops, an effort she knew would be futile.

"Prepare to assault!" Her people were exhausted. The fight to take the station had been a hard one, and they'd lost heavily. But she knew they could do this. So could Killian and his people. Whatever she thought of the rangers and their ways of battle, they were effective fighters. For all they unnerved her, she was glad to have the bushwhackers with her.

She watched as the torch reached the end of the door. The two soldiers pushed forward, and the heavy metal hatch crashed to the floor inside the control room.

Her people poured through, firing as they did. The enemy was shooting as well, and she saw one of her people fall. Then another.

Two of the enemy had been hit as well, and they were lying over the consoles they'd used as partial cover.

Morgan dove for her own cover, snapping up to firing position behind a large structural support. She saw one of the federals behind a workstation, turned away from her, moving to target one of her people.

Her pistol snapped up. It cracked. Once, twice. The federal fell back, his hands moving to his neck as blood poured from a clearly mortal wound.

She was already slipping around the edge of the girder, moving along the periphery of the bridge. The assault had bogged down into a firefight, her people and the surviving federals exchanging fire from whatever cover they could find.

She'd been surprised how easy it was to shoot the federal soldiers, how deeply the call of battle had taken her. She might feel differently later, that the emotions conflicting within her could break out of the place she'd penned them in. Probably would. The troopers on the station weren't colonial security forces or anti-insurgency forces from Earth, forces she regarded as little more than bullies in uniform. These were Federal America regulars, and if the personnel assigned to station security weren't quite the veteran soldiers who'd fought at her side in the war, they weren't different enough to prevent her from feeling something about the fact that she'd just shot them down.

She crept forward, looking out across the bridge. She caught a glimpse of an officer—the station commander, she realized immediately. The federal was staring toward the door, exchanging shots with two rebels.

Shoot her . . . shoot her now and this is over . . .

She moved slowly, silently, bringing the pistol to bear. She aimed carefully, methodically . . . but she didn't shoot. She couldn't.

She lunged forward before her mind had time to react. When it did, it was screaming at her to stop, but it was too late. The impulse had taken her. She raced across the cold metal floor of the bridge, right toward the federal commander.

The officer heard her, turned to face the onrushing threat. She brought her weapon around, a pistol not very different from Morgan's own. But the rebel commander was on her before she could fire. Morgan slammed into the federal, and the two fell back, struggling, grappling.

The federal's pistol fell from her grip and skittered along the floor. Morgan's was still in her hand, but her adversary was reaching up, gripping her arm.

The federal fought well, but she had to use both hands to hold back Morgan's pistol . . . and that was all the advantage the rebel needed. She slammed her fist down—a solid punch in the face, then another.

And another.

The federal still struggled, but her strength began to wane. She looked up, her face a mask of blood, staring with shock at her assailant.

"Surrender." Morgan twisted her pistol arm free, and she pointed the gun down at the federal's face. "It's over. Don't make us kill the rest of your people."

The federal commander looked back at her, blinking, trying to keep the blood from running in her eyes. Then she turned her head, getting the best view she could of the bridge. She hesitated, clearly struggling with the choice. Finally, she exhaled hard and looked back at Morgan.

"I surrender." She moved her head again, looking out across the bridge. "All of you . . . . surrender. The fight is over. There is nothing to be gained by throwing your lives away."

Morgan felt a wave of relief, tempered by the controlled paranoia of a veteran. It would only take one rogue federal to put a bullet in her head. But she knew in her gut her people had won. They had taken the station.

The fight was over. At least for a little over an hour . . .

CHAPTER 33

"Access denied. Command-level passcode required."

The voice of the station's AI lacked personality. Morgan wasn't sure why the federal armed forces gave their electronics such fake-sounding voices. It would be just as easy to program natural, human-sounding tones.

She was frustrated, too, angry at her inability to access anything on the command system. Her people controlled the station, but she knew there were enough federal troopers on the way to kill all her soldiers three times over. The station's defenses were strong, powerful enough to hold off all the federal ships. But she couldn't access the defense programs . . . and the automated system wouldn't attack vessels with federal transponder codes, not without manual override.

She punched another series of keys, staring anxiously at the screen as she finished.

"Access denied. Command-level passcode required."

"Damn!" She slammed her fist down on the console.

"Let me have a look at that, Colonel."

Morgan turned around. Jonas Holcomb was standing there, flanked by two of the soldiers she'd assigned to follow him wherever he went.

"Dr. Holcomb, I thought you were working on the communications system?"

"I believe I can deactivate it, Colonel, but I'm afraid it will take considerably longer than an hour. I have also checked the safeguards on the reactor and vital systems. They are all equipped with my own protocols, which means it will take a considerable amount of time to gain sufficient access to destroy the station. I'm afraid holding against the federal fleet is a prerequisite to completing our primary mission."

Morgan looked up at Holcomb, surprised at the animated tone in his voice. She'd expected him to be in a near state of shock, as civilians often were when they got their first taste of real battle. But Holcomb was energized, and his eyes had a sparkle they had lacked when Cal Jacen had first brought the scientist to Dover.

What must it be like for a mind like his to sit idle? No outlet for his brilliance, no stimulation. It must have been a nightmare.

"Whatever you can do, do it now."

"We can attempt to breach the reactor core manually, though without the right equipment, that won't be easy either. But perhaps we can hold the station." He glanced down at the workstation, then back at her. "With your permission, may I give it a try?"

Morgan leapt up from the chair. "Do you think you can regain control of the defensive systems?"

"I don't know. I mean, yes, I almost certainly can. The real question is, can I do it in time?" He sat down, staring at the workstation for a few seconds. Then he put his hands on the keyboard, his fingers moving so quickly Morgan could barely follow them.

"Can I help you in any way, Doctor?"

"I'm afraid not, Colonel. Nothing beyond seeing I am not disturbed . . . and hoping for the best. Good thoughts may not accomplish anything, but we've got nothing to lose."

Morgan just nodded. Then she turned toward the two guards. "No one is to disturb Dr. Holcomb." She glanced back at Holcomb. The scientist was already deep in concentration, his eyes fixed on the screen as his fingers flew over the keyboard. "He is to have anything he requests . . . and if anyone gives you a problem, call me at once. Understood?"

"Yes, Colonel." The two soldiers replied in unison.

Morgan took one last look at Holcomb.

A few weeks ago he was a political prisoner, held captive in the deepest, darkest hole in all of Federal America. And today he is our last hope.

She turned and walked away. The next hour was going to be the longest one of her life.

"All ʃhock troopʃ to the ready rooms." Quintel sat in *Emmerich*'s command chair. In wartime, a commodore like Quintel would serve in a pure fleet command role. But on blockade duty, he filled two roster slots, one as the squadron's overall commander and another as *Emmerich*'s captain.

The three ships closest to the station had enough shock troops to retake the facility, he was sure of that. His caution urged him to wait until some of the other vessels arrived, but he rejected that outright. He didn't know why the rebels had gone to so much trouble to take the station, but he suspected time was more precious a resource now than having a larger edge in numbers. He knew his casualties might be a bit higher this way . . . but then again perhaps not. If the rebels had enough time to prepare, maybe even to gain control over some of the fortress's systems, things could get bloody fast.

"Laser batteries on standby." Quintel didn't intend to bombard the station. There would be minor damage, no doubt, from the boarding actions and the ensuing battles, but if his ships opened up, the destruction would be widespread—and he didn't want to do that unless it was a last resort.

"Laser batteries report ready to fire on command, sir."

"Standby targeting on designated systems." Quintel's people had detailed schematics of the station. If the boarding force ran into unexpected trouble, he could support them with targeted bombardments. That would cause significant damage to the station, but much less than an indiscriminate barrage.

"All batteries report ready. Targeting confirmed on designated station systems. Entering weapons range in six minutes, Commodore. Projected docking in eighteen minutes."

Eighteen minutes. And then his shock troops would retake the station.

"We hold here, do you understand? I don't care what comes down these corridors, we don't fall back. We fight it out right here. Here!" Morgan had put each of her people in place, handpicking the locations. Her troopers had dragged crates and furniture into the hallway, building barricades and setting up makeshift cover. The soldiers who were coming outnumbered her people five to one, and they were fresh. She had twenty-three troopers left. They were exhausted and low on ammo. Their only advantage was knowing where the enemy would come. The station was large, but the docking bays were all on one side . . . and a pair of corridors led to them all. The federals might defeat her forces—they almost certainly would—but they'd have a fight on their hands, she'd make sure of that.

She glanced down at her chronometer. Less than twenty minutes before the federals would attack. And if her people were going to make their last stand here, she was going to be with them. But she had enough time to get back to the bridge and check on things one last time. Holcomb had been working feverishly, trying to regain control of the station's AI. She had no doubt the scientist could do it—the man was clearly brilliant. The problem was doing it in time. That was a resource that was rapidly dwindling.

"Everybody stay sharp. I'll be back before the federals get here." She turned and moved toward the elevator, jumping in the car and hitting the button for the bridge.

As the elevator raced up, so her mind raced about the upcoming fight. She'd already played it out in her head, but a new thought emerged: she could at least get Holcomb off the station, as well as Nerov and her crew. They had all done their part, and she owed them a chance at escape. She knew the federals would have control of the spaceport again, but with the blockading forces converging to attack the station, perhaps Nerov could get past them and make a run for it. There was nothing waiting for any of them on Haven now but defeat and persecution, and for all they had done for the cause, none of them were natives. They didn't deserve to die in someone else's war.

For some reason, knowing she could try to save them made her feel better.

The elevator doors opened, and she walked down the hall, slipping through the open bridge entry. "Get me Captain Nerov." She looked over at the trooper manning the comm station as she sat in the command chair.

"On your line, Colonel."

"Sasha . . ."

"Yes, Colonel."

"We're going to be boarded in less than fifteen minutes. You and your people should make a run for it. The federals are all converging on the station. If you whip around the planet and head off into deep space, you might just make it."

"Colonel . . . my people are ready to fight alongside yours. We—"

"No, Sasha. It's pointless. I'd accept if you could make a difference, but . . ."

She didn't want to say "we'll all die anyway."

"Then get your people back on *Vagabond*. Maybe we can all escape."

"I can't do it, Sasha. We're Havenites, all of us. We joined the rebellion with ours eyes open. We can't run now, not while our comrades are down there, hiding in the woods, praying for our success."

The line was silent.

"Go, Sasha. Your people dying won't accomplish anything; it will only add to the tragedy." She paused, glancing over at Holcomb. "And I want you to take Dr. Holcomb with you."

The scientist had been engrossed in his work, but now he looked up. "No, Colonel. I'm not going anywhere. I'm close. I designed half these systems, and I know I can get past this security—"

"There's no time, Doctor. You've got to go. Now."

"No, Colonel. I'm not leaving."

Morgan was about to argue when Sasha's voice blared through the com. "We're not leaving either, Colonel. We took a vote: all of my people want to stay and fight alongside yours. We'll win together . . . or we'll all die together."

Morgan felt a wave of frustration, but also something else. A deep respect, an admiration, for the people at her side in this fight. If her troops were fated to die, they couldn't ask for better company.

"Very well, Sasha. I can't think of anybody I'd rather have at my side in the last battle." She turned toward Holcomb. "Are you sure, Doctor?"

"Yes, I'm sure. Now I need quiet." Holcomb's face snapped back to the workstation, his fingers moving wildly over the keys. He looked up again and waved toward the door. "Go, all of you. I'll be better in here alone."

Morgan paused. Then she turned toward the two troopers she'd left on the bridge. "Let's go . . . get your rifles. It's time to hold this rust bucket."

She took one last look at Holcomb . . . and then she turned and led the two troopers out into the hall.

"All boarding parties report ready, Commodore. Estimated time until docking: four minutes, thirty seconds."

Quintel sat quietly, listening to the comm officer's words. He was sure his people could take the station, but he was fighting back doubts about his decision to move forward with just three ships. By all accounts, there were combat veterans among the defenders . . . and the layout of the station was tightly constricted around the docking bays.

If the commander over there is worth anything, they'll be dug in at the choke points. The troopers will get through, but they'll have to push through a nasty killing zone.

It was too late to change his mind . . . and all the original criteria remained valid. It was just too dangerous to leave the rebels in possession of the station. The losses would be harsh, but there was no way around that.

"Three minutes to docking, sir."

"Prepare system overrides. We want to take control of the station's systems as soon as we dock." He looked down at his own screen, punching his personal passcode into the keypad.

"Override passcode authorized. Quintel, Simon, Commodore."

Everything was ready. As soon as *Emmerich* docked and connected with the station's information net, his ship's AI would link with the station's and the access code would give him total control. He'd shut down the elevators, freeze the hatches. The rebel troopers would be trapped in place. They'd blood his people coming down the corridor, but then it would be all but over. They'd be cornered, their escape cut off . . . and their dug-in position would become a death trap.

"Two minutes to docking . . ."

CHAPTER 34

"Come on . . . come on . . ." Holcomb entered the code again. He'd designed much of the station's defense system, but the government had added a ton of frontline security over it. He wondered if that had happened before or after his arrest.

He was sure he could control the AI if he could penetrate the system, but it was fighting him like crazy. He'd been locked up for a long time, and it had been years since he'd truly used his mind. He was rusty, and it was showing in the time it was taking him to finish his task.

He had tried to ignore all other data, to focus on his work. But he couldn't help but notice that the federal ships were about to dock. He was out of time.

Almost . . .

He tried to calm himself, to focus his entire mind on the problem. There had to be a way . . .

And suddenly he saw it. The pattern. The federals had added external security, but now he realized they'd used the same patterns as his base system. It wasn't a solution, not quite, but it knocked the possible permutations to the thousands. That might not seem like much, but it was much better than the several quintillion before.

His hands moved quickly, writing a short program, one that

would analyze each possible code, and run through the possibles a million times more quickly than he could.

His eyes darted up to the display. The system cameras were feeding in images of the federal ships, so close to the station now they almost completely filled the screen.

One minute . . .

He typed the last line, and then he ran the routine. The screen went blank, and then numbers flashed by, too fast to read, no more than a blur on the screen.

The scrolling seemed to go on forever, and the mesmerizing image was enough for him to lose track of time. Then, suddenly, it stopped. The screen went to the main display.

I'm in!

He paused for a few seconds, stunned. Then his eyes caught the chronometer. Forty-five seconds.

"System, respond."

"Station control unit 3097C."

"System . . . this is an A1 priority message. The vessels approaching the station are broadcasting Federal America protocols, but they are not friendly. Repeat, they are not friendly. This is an enemy deception. Activate defense systems and prepare to repel the hostile spacecraft."

Holcomb held his breath, waiting for the response. He'd know in half a second if he truly controlled the system.

"Affirmative. Approaching vessels tagged as enemy craft. Activating weapons systems."

The lights dimmed, and Holcomb could hear a low-pitched hum in the background. He'd have known the sound of his guns charging anywhere. His eyes darted to the timer. Twenty seconds.

The hundred-megawatt lasers would be charged in ten seconds.

Now that is cutting it close.

"**Sir, we're picking** up energy readings from the station . . . almost off the charts."

Gregory Jacobs sat at *Condor*'s command station, his eyes locked straight forward at the looming bulk of the fortress less than five hundred meters from his ship. His shock troops were ready, and he'd switched over to his positioning thrusters.

But if that is the station's weapons grid . . .

He saw a flash on the screen off to *Condor*'s port side. He knew what it was, even before the reports came streaming in.

"The station is firing, sir." A pause. "Those are primaries!" Lieutenant Merrill was hunched over his display, his hands gripping the scope.

"*Emmerich* was hit, sir." A short pause. "Captain, I've got Commodore Quintel for you."

"Put it through!"

"Captain," Quintel's voice came over the comm, "the rebels are in control of the station's defense grid. Open fire immediately and pull back. Get that ship out of there . . ."

"Yes, sir." He cut the line and turned toward Merrill. "Full thrust away from the station. Reactor to 110 percent. Main batteries open fire!"

He stared at his display, watching as *Condor*'s lasers ripped into the side of the station. His ship was at point-blank range. It was impossible to miss . . . and the blasts hit with full power, melting the outer armor and penetrating deep into the station's hull. But the fortress outmassed his ship a hundred to one, and he knew it could take a lot of hits to seriously hurt it.

He leaned back into his chair, feeling the thrust as the engines engaged. The g-force dampeners reduced some of the pressure, but the engines were blasting at more than six g's, and some of that came through. But thrust was crucial now. Returning fire was all well and good, but if the rebels controlled the station's entire defense grid, three frigates didn't have a chance against that kind of firepower. If he didn't get *Condor* out of there, she'd be a cloud of glowing debris in a few minutes.

The ship shook hard, and the bridge lights dimmed for a few seconds. "Damage report!" Jacobs was staring down at his own display even as he shouted to Merrill.

"Hull breach in section 6A. We've lost pressurization in six compartments. Two confirmed dead, at least seven wounded." Merrill paused. "We lost one of the reactor coolant valves, too, Captain. We've got to cut output by at least 30 percent or we're going to lose the core."

Fuck.

Jacobs hesitated. He needed all the power he could get . . . but Merrill was right. If they didn't cut back they'd lose the entire reactor, and that meant the ship, too.

"Batteries cease fire. Move the reactor down to 70 percent. All power to the engines . . . maintain full thrust."

"Engines maintaining full thrust, Captain. Reactor steady at 70 percent."

Jacobs's eyes dropped to his display once more. It looked like *Roanoke* was going to get clear. She was moving at full thrust, and the station seemed to be ignoring her. But *Emmerich* was a different story. The flagship had been hit three times, and she took another blast amidships as Jacobs watched.

Condor shook again, but the impact was weaker than the last one, a grazing blow. He looked down at his readout. Light damage, some sensor arrays, a couple exterior compartments breached. And two more of his people dead.

"Time to exit firing range?"

"One minute, twenty seconds, Captain. Assuming the reactor holds."

Jacobs just nodded. He knew a minute was an eternity, easily long enough for the station's laser blasts to cripple or destroy his ship. But there was nothing he could do but wait . . . and count off the seconds as they slowly passed.

"Captain . . . *Emmerich!*"

Jacobs's eyes darted up to the main screen. There was a long-range image of the flagship on the left side . . . and a stream of data moving down the right, distress calls and damage reports.

Emmerich was leaving a trail of frozen fluids and debris behind her. The ship's stern was a wreck, nothing but twisted remnants of metal where her engines had been. She was moving at sixty kilometers per second, but it was clear she had no thrust capacity, no way to speed up . . . or to decelerate.

"Get me Commodore . . ."

Jacobs's words trailed off, his eyes fixed on the screen. Another of the station's powerful main lasers slammed into the ship, invisible over most of its eight-thousand-kilometer journey but electric blue as it passed through the debris field around the dying vessel.

Emmerich hung there, floating in space, seeming still despite its velocity. Then there was a flash, a glimpse of fire inside, extinguished almost immediately by the vacuum as the hull ripped open, exposing the shattered innards of the flagship to space. Then another flash, a different section of hull torn apart, a hundred-meter gash looking like a knife wound in the vessel's midsection.

Come on, Commodore . . . abandon ship . . .

Emmerich was done. All that was left now was for the crew to escape.

If they escape.

He was still thinking that when another deadly lance of blue light hit the vessel, blasting right through one of the shattered hull sections into *Emmerich*'s innards. For an instant, perhaps a second, nothing happened. Then the image on the screen was replaced by a blinding white light.

Jacobs knew immediately what had happened. *Emmerich* had lost reactor containment. Commodore Quintel was dead. His entire crew was dead, and for an instant, their ship had become a miniature sun.

Then a few seconds later it was gone. Just gone.

Luci Morgan stepped through the bridge doors, her people following behind her, cheering. They'd been waiting for the federals to board the station . . . and they'd watched as the fortress's massive laser batteries opened up, driving back the attacking ships. It was clear almost immediately that the threat of a boarding action was gone. The federal ships had fired a few shots, but they'd only done minor damage . . . and none of Morgan's people had been killed or wounded.

"You did it, Doctor!"

Holcomb was still at his workstation. He looked up, turning toward Morgan. "Yes, Colonel. I was able to engage the defense system just in time. I'm afraid, though, the jamming algorithm is protected by a second level of security. But don't worry—I should be through it shortly. If all goes well, we can restore planetary communications within the hour."

Morgan nodded. "The defense systems . . . are they still under your control?"

"Yes, of course. I reprogrammed the AI to take orders only from me. But I can add anyone else to the authorized list."

"We've got what? Thirty-seven of us?" Morgan stared intently at Holcomb. "Can we run this whole station with so few?"

"I'd say that depends on what you want to do, Colonel. You've got prisoners to guard, right? How many? Fifty? Eighty?"

"About seventy."

"How many people do you need to handle that? To watch them? Feed them?"

"More than the one I've got on them now. So maybe three or four."

"So that's twelve, at least, to cover them around the clock?"

Morgan nodded.

"It's none if we throw them out of the airlock." It was Killian, standing against the far wall. He'd been listening quietly up until then, but now Morgan wasn't sure if the grim ranger was serious or kidding. She didn't really want to know.

"That will be all of that, Captain." She turned back toward Holcomb, looking expectantly at the scientist.

"Twenty-five to run the station, maybe eight per shift?" He paused, thinking. "We could probably keep basic functions going, Colonel . . . and the defense systems are AI-controlled, so if the federals decide to attack again, we'd be able to fight." He frowned. "The big question is, how long will we be up here? The station's got repair bots, and we can control those . . . but sooner or later things are going to start to break down. I can figure out most of these systems, but I can't keep this place running forever, not by myself. Eventually, we're going to need engineers, technicians, specialists. And sooner rather than later if we have to fight again, and the station takes more battle damage—don't forget, there are still seven ships out there. We got lucky this time . . . but next time they might hit a vital system."

Morgan nodded. "But you believe we can manage things, for a while at least?"

Holcomb nodded. "I don't see why not. Do you think it is that useful, though? Our mission was to destroy the jamming equipment. Not that we can go back anyway. The federals must have retaken the spaceport by now."

"We'll worry about that later. As for our mission, things have changed. First, we don't *destroy* the jamming setup. Can you modify it, control it?"

"Control it? I suppose so. For what purpose?"

"Can you rig it so our forces can communicate . . . and the *federals* can't?"

Holcomb paused, a smile slipping onto his face as he grasped her intentions. But it quickly faded. "I don't think so, Colonel. As you have noticed, there were two frigates docked with the station. They have been providing supplemental power. One managed to escape during the battle, and the other took damage when the federals fired at us. She had a skeleton crew, no more than a few maintenance personnel, but they surrendered as soon as they realized they couldn't get away.

"Besides, we don't have nearly enough crew to maintain such a jury-rigged setup . . . and without the extra power, there is no way we can jam communications planetwide." He paused. "Though we should be able to easily cover Landfall and the surrounding area . . . where most of the federal forces are located. That should give General Ward an edge at least."

"More than an edge, Doctor. The federals are in a precarious position now. As long as we maintain our hold on the station—and keep its weapons systems functional—we've cut them off. We can stop any vessel from approaching Haven. Every supply ship, every courier, every troopship. The federals don't know it yet, but they're under siege now . . . and they'll stay that way until the navy can assemble a fleet strong enough to take on this station. That should take months. They'll be throwing rocks down there by then . . . and if General Ward can keep them penned in at Landfall, they'll be eating sawdust, too."

Holcomb nodded. "I see. I'm afraid for all the weapons I designed I'm not much of a soldier. But what you say makes sense. And if General Ward's people can retake the spaceport, *Vagabond* can return and bring back more troops . . . and engineers and other experts, too. Then we can hold out here indefinitely, even against a federal task force."

"I can't overstate what you have done for the cause, Doctor. The federals will rue the day they sent you to prison."

Holcomb didn't respond. He just looked back at her . . . and an unmistakable smile slipped onto his lips.

CHAPTER 35

"Colonel Morgan calling General Ward. Do you read?"

Damian rushed into the building, moving toward the comm unit, not entirely sure he wasn't hallucinating.

"Colonel Morgan calling General Ward. Do you read?"

"This is Ward." He grabbed the headset, putting it on as he spoke. "I can't tell you how it feels to hear your voice, Colonel."

"Your comm should be clear, General. The mission has been a complete success. We have secured the station, sir, and disengaged the jamming setup. The federal squadron attempted to land shock troops, but Dr. Holcomb was able to gain control over the station AI and activate the defense system. One frigate was destroyed, and the others withdrew."

Damian was stunned. He'd considered the whole thing the craziest of desperate maneuvers, a near-suicide mission to gain control of the station for just long enough to destroy the jamming setup. But what Morgan had described went far beyond that.

"Colonel, I'm speechless. Well done!"

"Thank you, sir. And when you're ready to address the planet, we can transmit from here. You'll be loud and clear on every frequency."

"Congratulations, Colonel . . . to you and all your people. I can't even express what your great victory means for all of us, and for the rebellion itself."

"Thank you, General. I will pass your words on to the men and women. But Dr. Holcomb is the true hero. He got the defense systems online and drove away the federal squadron. If he hadn't managed that, we'd all be dead now."

"Please relay my heartfelt thanks to the doctor."

"General . . ."

"Yes, Colonel?"

"I am reluctant to say too much over an open channel, but it will be some time before we can develop an encryption routine."

"What is it, Colonel? Speak freely."

"General, Dr. Holcomb has revised the jamming system, and we may be able to make use of it ourselves. We don't have adequate power for planetwide coverage, but we believe we can jam all federal communications in and around Landfall."

"Are you saying we can do this now, Colonel?"

"Yes, sir. Dr. Holcomb is just finishing the final setup."

"That is extraordinary, Luci . . . just extraordinary. You can start jamming them as soon as . . ." He hesitated. "No, wait. Not yet. Wait until I make my broadcast—let them hear what I have to say. And then cut them off as soon as I'm done."

"Yes, sir. And, Damian . . . with the weapons system active and the satellites hooked into the defense network, we can intercept any ship approaching Haven. The federals don't know it yet, but they're under siege. My people will hold the station at all costs . . . and we won't let anything through, not a delivery of food, not a load of ammo. Nothing."

"You do that, Luci. Hold the line up there . . . and we just might score a massive victory."

"Yes, sir."

Damian cut the line. Morgan's report was still sinking in, its staggering implications difficult to comprehend.

It was time.

Time to steal a march on the federals.

Time to rouse the planet.

Time to drive the enemy off Haven.

"I don't care what you have to do. I want communications with the station restored." Stanton's voice was angry, raw. Semmes's troops had taken back the spaceport . . . but then the orbital platform had gone silent. She'd put the troops in Landfall on full alert, but the rebels hadn't budged from the woods around Dover. Then she got the report. The jamming net was down.

"We have tried, Your Excellency." The aide spoke nervously. "We have attempted contact on all frequencies. They do not respond."

"Then try again." Stanton glared at the junior officer. "Now."

She turned toward Wells. "Everett, what is going on? Do you have any guesses?"

Wells took a breath and exhaled. "It seems clear to me that the rebels used the smuggler's vessel to dock with the station . . . and that they somehow managed to gain control and destroy the jamming equipment."

"That's just not possible . . ."

"Asha, I've tried to get you to listen to me since you got here. Again and again you have underestimated the colonists. They are not like citizens on Earth, cowed, accustomed to doing as they are told. They don't live their lives under constant surveillance. You know Federal America's policies, the people they send out to the colonies. Criminals, political agitators, men and women who resist authority. Troublemakers. Everyone they want off Earth. Yet you expect them to behave like a mob in Washington. You imagined rebellion could be defeated with no more effort than calling in a flight of gunships to break up a food riot."

"But the station was defended by regular military as well as colonial forces. How could the colonists possibly have taken control?"

"Colonists? What do you think that means? These people have tamed a world, built cities, farms, factories where there was nothing before. And Colonel Semmes's clumsy, heavy-handed attempt to bully the veterans drove almost all of them into the rebel camp, Damian Ward among them." He stared at Stanton. "Before you arrived, I had Lieutenant Ward helping me *discourage* rebellion. Now he is General Ward, the commander of the rebel army. And they *are* an army. Capable of much, much more than you give them credit for, obviously."

"What do we do?" And for the first time since he'd met her, there was no confidence in her words.

Unfortunately, Wells didn't know what to say. He was about to try to answer when the doors opened and Semmes came running in. Wells had never seen the officer without an arrogant smirk on his face. Until now.

"We just received a communiqué from Captain Jacobs, the commander of the frigate *Condor*. He confirms the rebels have control of the orbital platform. The blockading squadron attempted to land shock troops to retake the facility . . ." Semmes paused.

"What is it, Colonel?" Stanton took a step toward Semmes. "What happened?"

"The rebels have apparently accessed the station's defensive grid. They fired upon the frigates as they approached." Semmes looked around the room, every trace of his former arrogance gone. "*Emmerich* was destroyed. Commodore Quintel is dead. Captain Jacobs has provisionally assumed command of the squadron. He advises that he does not have sufficient firepower to engage the station. The ships have withdrawn beyond weapons range."

Stanton stared at Semmes for a few seconds. Then she turned toward Wells. "That means they control access to the planet . . ."

Wells nodded, a somber expression on his face. "It means we're trapped, cut off. No reinforcements, no ammunition resupply." He shook his head. "No food. We'd better put together a plan to forage in the countryside, because if we dig in here in Landfall, we're going to starve sooner or later."

"No." Stanton was almost in a state of shock. "No . . . it's not possible. Federal America will send naval forces, they will retake the station."

"That will take months, Your Excellency." Semmes stood, looking frozen in place. "Far longer than our supplies will last."

The room fell silent for perhaps half a minute. Then the display on the wall lit up, the speakers crackling to life.

"What the hell—"

"Attention citizens of Haven . . . this is General Damian Ward, commander in chief of the army of Haven. For weeks now, you have been unable to send or receive any transmissions, but we have now restored communications to the entire planet. For those of you un- aware of what has happened around Landfall during this time, know that your neighbors and fellow Havenites have risen up in righteous rebellion, that they have fought two battles against the federal forces and taken control of the orbital platform. We have dealt them a pow- erful blow, and now it's time for all of you to join us, to strike an even greater blow for Haven's freedom!"

Wells listened to the transmission, knowing he was hearing about the defeat of the federal forces on Haven even before it happened.

The rebels have won the first round. The senate will now have to respond by sending more forces, by cracking down even harder. But that would take months, perhaps a year.

And we'll all be dead long before then . . .

". . . rise up, gather together, take control of your homes, your cities. Follow your neighbors with military experience, and benefit from their knowledge. Secure the future . . . for your children. And for their children. Today is Haven's Independence Day . . . and if you are willing to fight for your future, the victory is ours."

Damian Ward turned and walked away from the camera. "So, what did you think?"

John Danforth nodded, a hint of a smile on his face. "You were perfect, my friend. For a man who has come late to rebellion, you have become a true fire breather."

"I should have supported you much sooner. I was held up by the past, though. I remembered battles I fought, soldiers who served at my side. I thought of a flag, and of the men and women who struggled—who died—fighting under it. But a flag is just cloth, and outstanding men and women have fought for poor causes through- out history. Federal America is—was—my nation . . . but it is un- just, controlled by men and women who see themselves superior to those they rule. Haven is different. The people that have come to this place have made it something special. And Federal America is looking to destroy that. They seek to turn our home into another version of Earth. And we can't let that happen. No matter what it takes."

Danforth reached out and put his hand on Damian's shoulder. "We'll have that future, Damian. And you can't beat yourself up. You *did* join us. And not only did you join us, you *saved* us. You pulled our revolution from the brink of defeat. You gave—no, *give*—us hope."

Damian shook his head. "We won a victory, my friend, and we won it together, all of us. But real independence remains a dream. No matter what happens in the coming weeks, we have a long way to go. And a lot of suffering still to come."

"I'm well aware of that. But allow yourself a moment of satisfaction, Damian. You have done well, far better than we could have hoped. Savor it. There will be time to face tomorrow's trials tomorrow. For today, at least, we're free."

Damian just nodded, offering his friend a smile. But his thoughts were darker. They dwelt on the realities that lay ahead, on the crushing burdens of command.—

But there was no point in giving too much time to those thoughts. Whatever his doubts, the rebellion was his life now, his sacred responsibility. And Damian Ward wasn't a man who ran from his duties.

"Well, John, before we start worrying about how big a victory we've won, we have a lot of work to do."

"Just tell me what to do, Damian. You're in charge now."

"First, we should be hearing from some of the rebel groups anytime now . . . and we've got to get them organized. And we need the ones close to Landfall to march here, join us. We had a good day, but the federals could still strike; indeed, that's what I would do if I was them. They can put together a timeline as easily as I, and it's only a matter of time before they start feeling the pinch on their supply chain. Once they figure that out, they'll come after ours. So while we wait for our reinforcements, the second thing we need to do is double all patrols."

"I'll see to the patrols, Damian . . . I mean, General." Danforth smiled at his friend. "Then I'll come back . . . and we can start rallying more support. I've got a list of groups, other chapters of the Guardians of Liberty to begin with. It's time to build a real army."

Damian watched his friend walk out the door. Then he turned toward the two officers sitting at the comm units. He could hear the queries already coming in—resistance groups, even individual colonists, calling, seeking to join the rebellion.

It had begun.

CHAPTER 36

"Are you sure about this, Damian? They wouldn't have dealt with us so mercifully." Luci Morgan had been a reluctant rebel who'd only joined the fight when Damian himself had called on her. But she'd become a firebrand in recent weeks, one of the most aggressive hawks among his officers. "What about the wounded they massacred? The innocent people they arrested and imprisoned?"

"Vengeance will serve no purpose, Luci. And for every federal atrocity, I could counter you with one of ours. I'll remind you of the rumors of what the rangers did in the woods near Vincennes."

Damian used the word *rumors*, but he knew exactly how Killian's people had behaved. He'd spoken with the commander of the rangers about it . . . and told Killian in no uncertain terms that if it ever happened again, he would hang for it. It had been a tense meeting, but Killian was a veteran, however extreme and brutal he'd become, and he accepted Damian's position as army commander. The two had managed to work together since then. More or less.

"If you think the federals will take your mercy into consideration . . . or honor any agreement they make here, you're mistaken, Damian. You know that, right?"

"Colonel, I have made a decision, one driven by my own sense of decency, not an idea of what the federals or anyone else will do. But if you need more than that, consider what happens next. You and I both know the federals will send an expeditionary force, larger and far more powerful than the glorified security guards we've faced until this point. Do you think it is wise to give them a rallying cry? How would we have reacted if we were sent someplace that had murdered hundreds of captive soldiers? What would have been in your mind as we landed?"

He paused, staring back at Morgan, who had fallen silent.

"Also, consider an honest assessment of the losses we would take assaulting Landfall, not to mention the civilian casualties and the damage to the city. We outnumber them five to one; there is no doubt in my mind we could prevail. But most of our forces are untrained, unblooded. How many would blunder into enemy fire? How many would panic and run at the first shot, spreading disorder among the ranks? Our victory here would be neither quick nor bloodless, I'm afraid." He paused. "No, if there is an opportunity to gain time— time to train these enthusiastic but disorganized recruits—we have to take it.

"I hate what they did to our people, Luci. But whatever savagery lies ahead, whatever atrocities or barbarism, it will not start with us. Is that understood?"

"Yes, sir."

A trooper stuck his head in the tent. The man had two stripes on his sleeves, the insignia a makeshift affair, clearly cut from another garment, but the meaning was clear enough. "Sorry to disturb you, General, but Governor Wells and Observer Stanton are here."

"I will be right there, Corporal." He turned toward Morgan. "You see, Colonel? They were both willing to come here under flag of truce, accepting my word that would be respected and they would not be harmed. That is something, is it not? I do not expect the senate back in Washington to act honorably, but such dealings do have their place, even if we cannot expect reciprocity. Our actions define us, Luci. You know that. Besides, what do we do? Assault and trigger a holocaust? How many babies do you want to starve to death to compel the federals to surrender? And what of the prisoners, the civilians, in the detention camps? Would you let them die, too?"

"You're right, Damian. I'm sorry." Morgan's voice was soft, apologetic. "It's just hard to accept so much loss and not want to strike back. I guess I had too much time up there with nothing to do but think." Morgan had spent the past two months on the orbital platform her people had taken. She'd just returned the past week, after rebel forces retook the spaceport. Since then, *Vagabond* had made half a dozen trips back and forth, returning the strike teams and ferrying reinforcements to the platform, as well as engineers, technicians, communications specialists. The fortress was now strongly held, its batteries active and barring the way of any supply vessel seeking to reach the federal garrison.

"I understand, Luci. Don't think I don't have the same thoughts. But we must be who we are, who we choose to be—not a poor copy of our enemies." He turned and walked out of the tent, Morgan following behind.

They walked across the camp. He turned and looked at Landfall. The city was less than two kilometers away, and there were works as far as the eye could see, the fortified positions of the rebel army besieging Haven's capital.

No, a mob. Not an army. Not yet.

Volunteers had poured into the rebel camp since Damian's broadcast, and groups had risen in every other city on the planet, sweeping away the token federal garrisons and taking control. The main rebel army around Landfall was now ten thousand strong, though many of them were still barely organized groups serving under local commanders. The process of organizing the entire mass into a true army was an ongoing project, one that had taken his every waking hour and then some.

Damian was grateful for the response to his call, but concerned as well. Organizing the army was only one problem. Another was that there was no real government on most of Haven now, and more than a dozen revolutionary tribunals had sprung up in the vacuum. Some of them were reasonable enough, just local citizens seeking to fill the void and keep basic services running. But others were more radical, more aggressive. Many answered to something called the Society of the Red Flag. As Damian learned more about them, he'd become suspicious of their motives. And their still-secretive nature. He'd heard accounts of federal officials being shot, even of loyalist Havenites harassed, killed.

That was another reason to end the standoff at the capital.

Landfall was the only place on the planet still held by federal forces. If Damian could end the hostilities, even temporarily, he and Danforth could begin to address some of these issues, start the process of creating a real government for Haven.

One thing at a time.

Damian walked over to the two federal officials. "Governor Wells . . . it has been some time, hasn't it? When we last met, I was assisting you, trying to prevent hostilities. I am truly sorry our efforts were not more successful."

"As am I." Wells paused, his eyes darting uncomfortably from Stanton back to Damian. "I want to thank you for granting this parley."

"And I thank you for coming. We must be willing to talk if we are to resolve this matter without further tragedy."

"Mr. Ward," Stanton said, "we are prepared to agree to a limited ceasefire on the condition that your forces withdraw back to Dover and that the orbital fortress allows shipments of basic necessities to land." Her voice was firm, but Damian knew it was a charade. The federals were in dire straits, in no position to dictate terms. And he found her refusal to address him by rank amusing, a bit of misplaced arrogance.

He looked at her silently for a few seconds, pushing aside the irritation he felt at her demeanor.

"I'm sorry if my invitation to attend this meeting created any misconceptions. So let me clear that up right now. We are not here to negotiate. We are here to discuss a specific proposal, one I am prepared to offer to you.

"All federal forces will agree to withdraw from Landfall immediately. All political prisoners currently held in prisons and in detention camps will be released—unharmed—at once, and control of the prisons handed over to us. Your soldiers, and all civilians wishing to join you, will be allowed to leave the planet. The federal frigates in the system, as well as three supply vessels currently holding position out of range of the fortress, will be allowed to land—one ship at a time—to board your people."

"That is preposterous. I won't—"

"Madame Observer, I really don't care what you feel is reasonable. I could recite you a litany of atrocities committed under your rule, but that would serve no purpose, and could only serve to further erode the productive nature of this meeting. What I will recite is the current state of your situation: you are surrounded, trapped in Landfall; you are low on food and other supplies; and you have little hope of resupply in the immediate future."

Damian looked at Wells. He could see agreement in the governor's face. But he wasn't the one he had to convince.

"I can assure you my decision to offer you these terms is not popular with many of my officers. Left to their own devices, they would storm Landfall and take the city by force. I'm sure you can imagine what would happen in that event. My army would take thousands of casualties, and the cries for 'justice,' for harsh terms toward you and your forces, would become irresistible. You would certainly be tried for war crimes, alongside many of your officers. And I cannot even imagine how the soldiers would react toward your people, especially if their illegally imprisoned families in Landfall were injured or killed in the fighting. Or through any act perpetrated by your people."

Stanton's face was twisted in a combination of anger and fear. "You are *threatening* me? That is why you brought us here?"

"Yes, that is correct. You may consider my proposal a threat; indeed, it most certainly is. But that's the wrong way for you to view it. Because you can also view it as a chance to save your people. And quite possibly to escape the gallows yourself. But I demand a decision now. If you leave this camp without agreeing to these terms, they will be immediately revoked, and my army will assault the city. If you would like a moment to discuss this privately, though, I am happy to accommodate."

Damian turned and took a step.

"Damian, wait." It was Wells.

"Asha," the governor said, "we need to accept these terms. There is no other solution. Our position is hopeless. I know this will be a setback for your career, Asha, but don't throw your life away. Please."

Damian watched, waiting to see what Stanton would decide. He didn't doubt he could take Landfall, but he knew the cost would be staggering. He'd seen the terrible cost of assaulting a city before, as part of a force of veteran, professional soldiers. And his army, such as it was, consisted mostly of armed civilians.

Stanton looked at Wells. She hesitated, as if she was struggling with herself to say the words. Finally, she spoke. "Very well. I . . . we . . . accept your terms. All political prisoners will be released. And all federal forces will withdraw from Alpha-2 as soon as transport can be provided." Her tone was bitter.

"Very well. You may return now and make whatever preparations are required." He turned and looked at Luci Morgan. She'd been standing behind him the entire time, silently watching.

"Colonel Morgan, please prepare a detachment to go with Governor Wells and Observer Stanton to coordinate the release of the prisoners. I'd like to begin bringing them here today." He glanced over at Stanton. She nodded.

"Yes, General." Morgan snapped off a textbook salute, more for the benefit of the federals, Damian suspected, than any other reason. The rebel army didn't even have a set of protocols for such things. Not yet.

"Ben . . ." He turned the other way, looking toward Withers. "We don't know what condition the prisoners will be in when they arrive. Put the medical staff on alert, and make sure adequate food supplies are available. I suspect they will be hungry, at the very least."

"Yes, sir."

"Damian . . ." It was Wells.

"Yes, Governor?" Damian kept his address formal. He knew Wells wasn't a brutal man, but for all his evenhanded pronouncements and his truce offer, Damian wasn't feeling too kindly toward any federals at the moment.

"Thank you. For your reason, for your humanity. I know many of your people will be angry about your letting the federal forces leave. You have saved many lives today, Damian. On both sides."

"My troops' personal feelings on this are irrelevant. They will follow their orders." He paused. "But I appreciate your words, Everett." Another hesitation, longer this time. "I—I wish you the best. We find ourselves on different sides of this conflict, but you are a good man. If there were more like you in federal service, we wouldn't be here." He turned, looking at Stanton for a moment, but he didn't say anything else. Then he turned and walked away, glancing over at one of his officers on the way.

"Lieutenant, please escort the governor and the observer back to their lines and see that they arrive safely." Then he made his way across the dirt road of the camp and disappeared into the command tent.

"No, you can't do this, General." Killian came barging into the tent, his face twisted into an angry scowl. "You can't let them go, not after all they have done."

"Major Killian, that will be enough." Damian's voice was hard, cold. It brooked no disagreement. But Killian wasn't about to be silenced.

"You can't, General . . . at least, not Colonel Semmes. Let the others go if you must, but Semmes is a monster. How many deaths is he responsible for? He must pay for all he has done."

Damian stood up and faced Killian. "Patrick, I understand your anger. But I can't exclude Colonel Semmes from the agreement. It is too late. If we try to add conditions now, we jeopardize the entire ceasefire. Is keeping Semmes worth that? Worth losing thousands of troops if we have to assault Landfall? Worth risking the deaths of the civilians in the camps? How many people should die to bring one man to justice?"

Killian exhaled hard, his hands clenched into fists. He didn't respond, but Damian could see how agitated he was.

"What is it, Patrick? I understand the desire to bring Semmes to justice, but after all—"

"It was him."

Damian looked back, a confused expression on his face. "What was 'him'?"

"Semmes. He was the officer. The one who cost me my career. It was on Shinjen-3, when we were facing the hegemony's counteroffensive. We were outnumbered . . . but we had a good position. And reinforcements were on the way."

Damian looked at the ranger, a man he'd come to consider cold, hard, ruthless. But now all he could see was vulnerability.

"All we had to do was hold. But Semmes lost his nerve. He ordered us to fall back . . . out of the heavy cover and into the open. I argued with him, pleaded, tried to explain. But he wouldn't listen."

Killian stared at Damian, his eyes moist, sucking in a deep breath. "They died, sir . . . all of them. Figgie, Harry, Pug. We'd fought together for four years, served on half a dozen planets. They were the best, that crew . . . comrades, friends. *Brothers and sisters*. And I watched them die, all of them. Fifty-one of Federal America's best men and women. All because Semmes lost his guts and ordered them out into the open. And I was the only one who made it back.

"Semmes had bugged out ahead of the unit. He spouted some bullshit about getting to headquarters to report, but he was just a coward. He ordered his soldiers into a death trap . . . and he ran, abandoned them to their fate."

Damian had never seen the ranger so unnerved. If he'd known, he would have demanded Semmes be turned over as part of the truce.

Would you? Would you have jeopardized the ceasefire, condemned thousands to death in a needless battle, just to punish one man? Whatever he'd done?

No, he answered himself. *No. You took this responsibility, and you have to consider all factors in your decisions.*

He would have refused Killian's request, even if the ranger had come before the deal was made. He just couldn't allow thousands of colonists to die in the ruins of Landfall when he could save them . . . not so one man could have his revenge. However well-deserved it was.

"Patrick, I'm sorry . . . I truly am. I can't imagine what you went through. But I have to consider—"

"I reported him when I got back. Semmes. I went to the battalion commander. He knew me, he knew my service . . . and he assured me he would investigate. But Semmes's family is powerful. His father is a senator. There was no investigation. None at all." Killian paused. "And then I was arrested, charged with gross negligence, with leading the unit into a slaughter. It wasn't enough to let him off; they blamed it on me. A guilty enlisted man no one cared about . . . and an insurance policy against any dirt sticking to Semmes."

Killian stared right at Damian. "I sat there, Damian. I sat there and listened to the charges, to every name. My comrades, my dead friends. They said I ran, that I left them. That they were out in the open on my orders, that I lost it in the heat of battle and abandoned them all." The coldness was back. "Then they offered me a deal. Accept a dishonorable discharge, and never speak of it again. Or face prosecution and a firing squad. I refused, I said no. But they were bluffing. Couldn't risk a trial, the chance that the truth would come out. So they went forward without my consent; they forged my confession . . . and they cast me out. They knew no one would listen to a disgraced sergeant, a man everyone believed had left his soldiers to die. And they were right, Damian."

Damian walked up to Killian, putting his hand on the man's shoulder, hating himself for what he was about to say. "Patrick, I understand. But I can't risk the ceasefire, not even for something like this. You know those volunteers out there will be massacred if we have to fight now. I need time to train them, to make them an army that can face what's coming." The torment in Killian's face was almost too much, but he pressed on. "I can't do what you ask, Patrick. I have to base my decisions on what is best for the army, for the rebellion." He paused. "I'm sorry."

Killian stood in the tent, silent, staring back at Damian.

"I understand that you want to see Semmes held accountable, Patrick." Damian suspected Killian's intent went well beyond "accountability," but he kept that to himself. He didn't imagine he'd feel much different in the ranger's shoes. "But I need your help now, to train this army, to use the time we have and not waste a moment. You know as well as I do, the federals will be back. And if we're not ready, this world will be reconquered . . . and all of us will end up on the gallows. We can't let that happen. I know this is painful for you, but you have to let it go."

Killian stared back. His expression was a mix of emotions: anger, frustration, confusion. He didn't argue, but he didn't say anything. He just stood there looking back at Damian, silent. Then, finally, subtly, he nodded.

"I'm not going with you." Violetta Wells stood in the doorway, glaring at her father as he packed the last of the items from his desk.

Wells turned toward his daughter. "Don't be foolish, Vi. We don't have time for this now. The ship launches in less than six hours."

"You're not listening to me. I am not leaving."

Wells stopped what he was doing and took a step toward Violetta. "Look, Vi, I know all this has been upsetting, but—"

"Upsetting? Watching men and women rounded up and penned in cages like animals? Did you see those camps? Did you *smell* them?" Her voice was emotional, angry. "Did you watch those soldiers—murderers—kill the wounded men and women in the courtyard? Have you tried to imagine the screams of the victims? The last thoughts that went through their minds as they lay there, wounded and in pain, realizing there were soldiers moving toward them . . . to kill them?"

"Violetta, you don't understand. Those were terrible acts, without question. You know I don't support those kinds of tactics, that I fought and argued against them."

"To no avail, though." She sighed. "I know you are a good man . . . but you serve something evil. And I can't be a part of that anymore."

"You're being naïve, Violetta. The rebels have committed atrocities, too. That is war. It's why I tried so hard to prevent it."

"And what did that get you? They sent *that woman* to replace you . . . and that monster Semmes. How could you go back there, continue your allegiance to them . . . even as they strip you of your posts?"

"Federal America is our nation, Violetta. Its government is

flawed, but we must labor to change that, not fight against it. The civil war was a humanitarian disaster. A quarter of the population perished. Would you have that happen again? Would you have those who seek to overthrow the government plunge the nation back into chaos and despair?"

"Yes." Her voice was cold, her tone one of absolute certainty. "You cannot reach good by serving evil, Father, no matter how commendable your intentions. The Havenites are right. They can only protect their rights by fighting for their freedom. The wrong side won the civil war back on Earth. I pray that doesn't happen here . . . and I am prepared to do anything I can to see that doesn't. I intend to volunteer for the army, Father. I will fight alongside these people. I will become one of them."

"Violetta! You cannot say such things." Her comments about the civil war were enough to get her sent to a reeducation camp back on Earth. The great conflict that had resulted in the birth of Federal America was a heavily proscribed topic on Earth, and the histories and accounts of the war were tightly edited.

"No, Father. *You* cannot say such things. You remain a slave of those who would rule your life. But I renounce my allegiance to Federal America. I am a Havenite . . . now and forever. This is my home."

Wells was upset. He moved across the room, reaching out to his daughter. "Violetta, please. I have to go back. You can't stay here."

She looked up at her father, her expression softening as she did. "I am sorry, Father. I love you . . . I always will, however much we disagree. But I am staying here. There is no place for me back on Earth. Not now."

"There will be war here, Violetta. You know the senate will never accept the terms Damian is sending to them." Wells was carrying a proposal from Damian and the rebels, one proposing a long-term ceasefire while the two sides discussed a permanent agreement. He doubted the powers on Earth would even consider it . . . and he suspected Damian knew the same.

He tried to imagine his daughter, his only child, alone on Haven, in the middle of the firestorm he knew was coming.

He felt hollow inside. For all that had happened, and for the un-

certain future that awaited him back on Earth, he'd never imagined
having to say goodbye to Violetta. He wanted to scream, to break
down and beg her to come with him. But he just stood there, staring
helplessly.

He felt an urge to remain himself, to stay with her . . . but he
knew it was impossible. He'd tried to prevent the rebellion; he'd softened federal policy and put his own future on the line. But he knew
most people viewed him simply as a tool of federal oppression. There
were loyalists on the planet, he knew that. But the rebels were firmly
in charge. And they would never accept him, even if he'd been able
to stay. Which he knew he couldn't do.

His sense of duty was a strong one, and it compelled him to return, to do whatever meager amount he could to moderate federal
policy. He didn't suspect he'd have much influence when he got
back to Earth, but he had to try.

"Are you sure about this?" Wells knew his daughter well enough
to realize that once she'd made up her mind, no force in the galaxy
could change it.

"I am. I'm sorry, Father. I know you have to go. But I have to stay."
The firmness and anger in her voice was gone, and he could see the
tears welling up in her eyes. "I will miss you." She lunged forward
and put her arms around him, squeezing hard and sobbing.

"I will miss you, too." He had to gasp for breath to squeeze out the
words. He was just realizing the true extent of what was happening,
and it took everything he had to maintain his composure. "Promise
me you will be careful . . . and take care of yourself."

"I promise." Her arms tightened, pulling him closer.

The two stood there, hugging, for a long time. Finally, Violetta
pulled away slowly. She paused for a few seconds, wiping the tears
from her eyes. Then she turned and walked out the door.

It was a few days later when Damian stood in the control center of the
spaceport, watching as the last of the troops boarded the transport.
When the vessel lifted off, there wouldn't be a federal soldier or political official left on Haven.

He felt a rush, a hint of the joy of victory, but he quickly pushed it aside. His people had scored a tactical triumph; there was no doubt about that. But he knew the rebellion wasn't over. The senate back on Earth would surely be enraged. They would take out some of their anger on Wells and Stanton; he had no doubt the two federal appointees faced a difficult immediate future. But then the federals would turn their attention to Haven. It would take time to assemble forces. Federal America's peacetime footing and the postwar force drawdowns meant they would have to divert forces from the various garrisons and bases, and transit times between planets slowed mobilization. And they would have to assemble a fleet strong enough to overwhelm the orbital fortress.

But it was coming.

A year. At most. That's how long we have.

They would be back with thousands of troops. And this time it wouldn't be just security forces and colonial units. The federals would send regular army units, frontline soldiers with battle experience from the war, supported by aircraft and complemented by a navy that would have total control of local space around the planet. Apart from his core of retired veterans, none of the rebels had ever faced an enemy like that.

And I will have to look across the field at federal regulars, men and women I served alongside, and do everything I can to kill them.

Not everyone shared his grim thoughts. There were celebrations all across Haven, parades and gatherings. And he knew they served a purpose as well, however premature they might be. He would allow them to continue—he would even encourage them . . . for a while. But he would focus on the business at hand, so when the celebrations ended, the work could begin. He had to turn these thousands of recruits— farmers, office workers, tradesmen—into an army. A real army. One that could stand and face the federal forces when they returned.

One that could fight and win the final victory . . . and secure Haven's independence forever.

He didn't know if he could do it, if he could lead Haven to true independence . . . but he was resolved to try, and if he failed he knew one thing: he would not survive the war to see the defeat.

EPILOGUE

"The vote is unanimous, forty yea and zero nay. The motion passes."
John Danforth stood at the front of the room and raised his hands in
the air. "We have done it, my friends. My fellow Havenites. May the
free world of Haven prosper for a thousand years!"

The assembled delegates leapt to their feet and roared their approval. Then they began to chant. "Haven . . . Haven . . . Haven . . ."

"Let us go, fellow delegates. Let us go out and tell the people."

Danforth walked across the room, to the large double doors leading out to the street, Damian and the others following behind.

The building had originally been built as a theater for a company
of actors doing live-action plays. They had folded years ago, before
Damian had even arrived on Haven, and the building had sat idle
ever since. Until John Danforth chose it as the first meeting place
of the Haven Provisional Congress. Damian couldn't remember the
original name—Starlight, Moonlight, something like that—but he
would never forget its new one. Freedom Hall.

He followed Danforth onto the landing outside, a large flat area
with stairs going down on two sides. There were hundreds gathered—no, thousands—the streets packed in every direction as far as
he could see.

Damian stood on the platform and looked out over the crowds, the men and women who had assembled outside Freedom Hall for the momentous proclamation.

Danforth stood next to him, holding a small tablet in his hand. He'd offered Damian the chance to read the words to the crowd, but the general had demurred. He knew Danforth had been the father of the rebellion more than any other single man or woman.

Besides, he thought what his fellow Havenites had done was foolish.

He had turned down a seat in the congress, stating that he didn't believe the military commander should also hold a civilian office. But that was mostly bullshit. The truth was, he had great reservations about what had been done, and enormous concerns the Havenites had just foreclosed even the remotest chance of a negotiated settlement.

He didn't object to the idea of independence, but he felt declaring it *now* was foolish. It changed nothing. It didn't put another soldier in the field, nor did it replenish the dwindling supplies of weapons and ammunition. And he knew how Federal America would respond.

He'd hoped the senate might agree to some kind of compromise, even after all that had happened . . . especially if he managed to win a victory or two when the war resumed. The cost of diverting ships and soldiers to Haven in sufficient numbers to fight the rebellion would be crippling, and he'd had a spark of optimism the federals might eventually accept an arrangement reaffirming the terms of the planet's original constitution, perhaps even adding a few new guarantees. In return, Federal America would keep its colony, officially at least, and the flows of ore and other precious goods would resume and grow. But Damian knew Federal America would never accept Haven's independence. It couldn't. It set a precedent to every other disaffected colony world, one the government back on Earth could never allow. What happened on Haven would send a message, one way or another. That independence was attainable . . . or that any attempt to achieve it would be treated as the gravest treason and drowned in a sea of blood.

The vote just concluded set the future in stone. Total victory . . . or abject subjugation.

"It is done, Havenites! The vote has passed unanimously!" Danforth's voice pulled Damian from his thoughts. The revolutionary leader turned back, passing his eyes over Damian, and the other representatives even now pouring out of the hall. Then he looked out over the crowd again.

"As it is the responsibility of free men and women to take whatever steps are necessary to preserve the basic liberties that are natural to all mankind . . ."

His voice was strong, powerful, as he read the document. Damian watched, realizing that John Danforth had worked for years for this moment. He'd spent most of his family fortune . . . and he'd lost his cousin, killed in the first battle. Damian was happy for Danforth, that his effort and sacrifices had been successful. Whether he agreed or disagreed with the proclamation, he knew Danforth was a good man. A man of integrity.

"And, as there are forces and powers extant that would strip away those freedoms, and impose upon the people burdens and arbitrary and capricious obligations, it is incumbent upon said men and women, being threatened with the yoke of servitude, to take whatever actions they deem necessary to break the shackles of grim and brutal rule and to secure for themselves, and generations to follow, the bright light of freedom, now and for all time."

Damian held back a sigh. He wondered if Danforth and the other politicians understood how similar they sometimes sounded to their Earth counterparts, so easily reciting lofty words that served their purposes. They spoke proudly of liberty and freedom, yet there were multiple factions in the new congress, each with its own agenda, and many hating their rivals nearly as much as the federals. Their definitions of freedom rarely extended to those who disagreed with their own points of view.

Damian was glad he was a soldier. Politics left him cold. It seemed to invariably bring out the worst in those caught in its web, turning even honest and admirable men and women into conniving things, maneuvering constantly for power. He didn't know if Danforth would go down that path, but he'd seen nothing in his life to make him feel optimistic. He would do all he could to win the war . . . but what his fellow Havenites would do with that victory, if somehow his soldiers were able to attain it, he had no idea.

"As such, we, the first congress of the planet Haven, speaking for the free men and women of our great world, do here solemnly pronounce as follows. All ties and bonds connecting the planet Haven to the nation of Federal America are hereby immediately and forever severed. Henceforth, the free world of Haven shall be independent, and part of no external polity, wherever said entity may be located."

Danforth looked up from the tablet. There was more. As with politicians since the dawn of time, the members of the congress had droned on at great length, paragraph after paragraph of soaring language that said virtually nothing of substance. But he had read the important part.

The part that will bring the true wrath of Federal America down on Haven.

Damian looked out at the crowd. They were screaming, waving banners in the air. And Danforth was urging them on. "Join me now in a cheer for the free world of Haven!"

The mob erupted, the sound even louder now, almost deafening.

Damian cheered, too. But inside he could only see two possible futures. One dimly lit, for he knew even in victory the cost would be great . . . and the people, the politicians, all who would struggle for control, could easily usher in a dark age for Haven, one with less freedom and not more. The other was the road to defeat, one that was as dark as the blackest, moonless night and offered nothing but death and servitude.

He took a deep breath. He knew what was coming, the forces his people would have to face. He had been a part of that army, and he'd fought with it to victory over two other superpowers. And now he had to find a way to defeat it.

But he just didn't know if that was possible.

Alistair Semmes stood behind the desk, staring out the massive window at the Washington cityscape below. The office was colossal, and

richly appointed, one that befitted his station. Semmes was a powerful man, a senator with three decades of service in Federal America's governing body, and the current patriarch of one of the nation's
strongest political dynasties.

He was trim, looking younger than his sixty years, his hair still
mostly brown, closely cropped in a style that looked almost military.
His suit was simple but clearly expensive, the tailoring perfect.

He had a reputation as dedicated lawmaker, one devoted to protecting and serving his constituents. But that was a charade, the prod-
uct of a carefully executed and well-funded public relations effort.
In truth, Semmes owed none of his terms to the vagaries of anything
so quaint as an actual election, at least not an honest one. He rarely
gave a second thought to those who voted for him, either the actual
constituents of his district, or the thousands of dead voters who remained on the rolls, their votes automatically tallied for him whenever the polls opened.

"This is the second time I have been forced to use my influence
to save you from the damage caused by your own failure. The inci-
dent during the war was bad enough, though that was resolved easily
enough by shifting the blame. That is not possible here. This disaster
is so colossal, it requires blunter methods. There is no unfortunate
NCO to frame this time. I must expend hard-earned political capital
on this, favors I could have used to great gain . . . but must now waste
on you."

Alistair Semmes stared at his son, making no effort to hide his
anger and shame. Robert sat quietly, enduring his father's rage and
abuse. He wanted to argue, to say that he hadn't been in charge on
Haven, that his efforts had been held back by Stanton and Wells. But
he knew his father well enough to realize that silently enduring was
the better strategy.

The elder Semmes walked over to his desk, leaning down and
grabbing a small box. "You are fortunate, boy, that you were born
into this family. By any reasonable assessment, I should cut my losses
and allow you to sink. But no Semmes is going to fade into disgrace
and oblivion. I owe that to my father and grandfather more than to
you. It was they who built the foundations of this family's power and

influence. And no son of mine will damage that legacy." He paused, glaring at Robert. "Not even one who is a blundering imbecile."

He threw the box at Robert, who bobbled it and dropped it. Alistair watched his son with renewed disgust. "Pick it up."

Robert knelt down, scooping up the box. Then he stood up and looked back at his father.

"Open it! By God, if you didn't have the Semmes eyes, I'd suspect you weren't even mine, that your mother had managed a dalliance with a security guard or some other weak-minded fool."

Robert felt a rush of anger, but he suppressed it. He was a cold man, but he'd loved his mother, and he'd seen how the senator had tired of her . . . and how she'd been left with nothing after the divorce. She'd ended up performing some type of menial labor to support herself. Robert never knew much about it. He'd only been allowed to see her twice a year, and that under guard. Then she died a few years later, under circumstances he'd never truly understood.

He opened the box . . . and his eyes froze. There were two single silver stars inside.

He looked up at his father. "A general's stars?" He tried to hide his surprise, but he realized immediately that had been a complete failure.

"Yes, a general's stars. I can assure you it was not easy to attain those . . . and the orders that accompany them."

"Orders?"

"Yes, orders. You are fortunate indeed. You will have a chance to redress your failure, to emerge from this business strong and powerful . . . instead of weak and disgraced."

Robert just stared at his father, a confused look on his face.

"You are going back to Haven." Alistair made no effort to hide his frustration and impatience. "I have secured for you the top command of the expeditionary force being sent to crush the rebellion. You will have no one in your way now. You will be the supreme commander, in charge of all federal forces and personnel in the system."

He glared at his son. "Your orders are simple. You are to crush the rebellion. We cannot allow this kind of thing to spread to other colonies . . . or to Earth itself. You will destroy the rebel armies, execute their leaders. You will drown this revolution in blood, and before you return, Haven will be prostrate and obedient . . . and it will be a century before anyone in Federal America dares even think the word *rebellion*."

Robert nodded, a smile creeping onto his face. He had scores to settle on Haven. "Thank you, Father."

Alistair nodded. "Use this opportunity, my son, and use it well, for it was not cheaply bought."

"I will, Father."

"And, Robert . . . do not fail me again. There will not be a third intervention. So, if you cannot defeat the rebels, do us both a favor. Get yourself killed in battle and save the family the disgrace."

The smile slipped off Semmes's face, replaced by a cold, hard stare. He felt the usual struggling emotions, hatred for the man who'd sired him, battling with the old craving for his father's love and approval. When he finally spoke, his voice was frozen. He stared at his father, and spoke just three words before he turned and walked out the door.

"I won't fail."

ABOUT THE AUTHOR

Jay Allan currently lives in New York City, and has been reading science fiction and fantasy for just about as long as he's been reading. His tastes are fairly varied and eclectic, but favorites include military and dystopian science fiction, space opera, and epic fantasy—all usually a little bit gritty.

He writes a lot of science fiction with military themes, but also other SF and some fantasy as well. He likes complex characters and lots of backstory and action, but in the end believes world-building is the heart of science fiction and fantasy.

Before becoming a professional writer, Jay has been an investor and real estate developer. When not writing, he enjoys traveling, running, hiking, and—of course—reading. He also loves hearing from readers and always answers emails. You can reach him at jay@jayallanbooks.com, and join his mailing list at http://www.crimsonworlds.com for updates on new releases.

Among other things, he is the author of the bestselling Crimson Worlds series.